B. & May
Christmas B.
2005

# WALLS
# OF
# SILENCE

# WALLS OF SILENCE

## PHILIP JOLOWICZ

ATRIA BOOKS
New York London Toronto Sydney Singapore

ATRIA BOOKS, a division of Simon & Schuster, Inc.
1230 Avenue of the Americas, New York, NY 10020

Copyright © 2002 by Philip Jolowicz

Published simultaneously in Great Britain in 2002 by Transworld

Library of Congress Cataloging-in-Publication Data
Jolowicz, Philip.
Walls of silence / Philip Jolowicz.
p. cm.
ISBN: 0-7434-2844-7 (alk. paper)
1. Consolidation and merger of corporations—Fiction. 2. New York (N.Y.)—Fiction.
I. Title.
PS3610.O46 W35 2002
813'.6—dc21
2001058832

First Atria Books hardcover printing June 2002

10   9   8   7   6   5   4   3   2   1

ATRIA BOOKS is a trademark
of Simon & Schuster, Inc.

For information regarding special discounts for bulk purchases,
please contact Simon & Schuster Special Sales at 1-800-456-6798
or business@simonandschuster.com

Printed in the U.S.A.

To my wonderful wife, Corinna

# PART I

## Summer 2001

# ONE

I was a morning person.

So when JJ Carlson rang me at 6:00 A.M. that Monday, he caught me on my second cup of black coffee and the last page of the *Wall Street Journal.*

He had something to show me, he said. Something neat. No clues. I was just to get myself to the corner of East 80th and First. I knew it was going to be special, worth the journey. It wouldn't be JJ's vacation snapshots.

I was with him in no time. I stood and stared.

My God, it was a beautiful car.

I ran my hand along the silver paneling. The headlights glared from the foot of a massive hood that reared up into a subtly tinted sweep of windshield. A thousand car magazine clichés ran through my mind as I fought to find a single word that might do justice to this piece of machinery.

"A McLaren F1," I murmured.

"Yup," said JJ Carlson. His tanned and manicured finger tapped lightly on the bodywork. "Only one in Manhattan, least that's what the guy said."

He was probably right. In my five years in New York, I'd never seen an F1 weaving through the clutter of yellow cabs and buses or stuck in a line headed for the Lincoln Tunnel. But JJ would've wanted it in writing. He never left anything to chance.

He towered over me, sleek as the car. He opened the gull-wing door and signaled for me to get inside. I wanted to look casual, cool. But it wasn't easy as I squatted down low and eased a leg over the sill. I was then confounded by the sight of the steering wheel on a console sticking out from the center of the dash. Where the hell was I supposed to go?

Then I noticed that there were three seats. The driver's was in the middle.

I eased myself back into the rock-firm leather. The seatbelt was like a parachute harness. JJ slid behind the wheel and turned to buckle me up.

I scanned the dash—utilitarian, serious; portholes of precise data.

"Two hundred and forty miles per hour," JJ said, reading my mind. "And before you ask, a million and change."

A million dollars for a car.

I whistled appreciatively and JJ seemed pleased. He turned on the engine. To my surprise the noise wasn't anything special, neither a purr nor a growl. JJ put the car into first gear, brought up the clutch, and gently pressed on the accelerator. The light caught pricks of sweat on his temples as he tilted his head back a fraction.

He rammed his foot down.

I was thrust back into my seat. We headed down East 80th, hitting one hundred miles an hour in too few seconds to count.

JJ's arms stretched out, locked on the stubby steering wheel at an unyielding three o'clock. Eyes glossed by a film of adrenaline.

The world outside was a blur. Before I could begin to assess the likelihood of bowling over a pedestrian or atomizing another car coming out of a parking space, JJ slammed on the brakes and came to a dead stop at the junction of East 80th and East End Avenue.

I felt the steel grip of his hand on my shoulder.

"What do you think?" he asked.

I thought of those gut-wrenching roller-coaster rides I'd never completely enjoyed as a kid. "Awesome," I managed.

"It's only a car," he said, then started to listen intently to the rumble of the idling engine. "I heard a noise."

He toed the throttle a little.

"Sounds okay to me," I ventured.

"Maybe you're right," JJ said after a moment. He pressed something and my door opened. "But I just want to give it another run." He turned to me with a grin. "No distractions this time."

As I got out, JJ leaned over and gave me a helpful shove. His eyes were cold blue now.

"Chill out, Fin," he said. "When I get back I'm going to let you have a go behind the wheel. You like?"

"Oh, yes, I like." I smiled.

"Cross over East End Avenue and wait for me at the end of East 80th. I'll be with you in two minutes."

JJ waited for the light to turn green before easing the car from a standstill and turning right to head around the block.

"What the hell was that?" a dog walker asked, rocking back on his heels and yanking at about ten leashes like he was auditioning for the chariot race in *Ben-Hur*.

"A McLaren F1," I said.

"Never heard of it," he said. "But I guess it goes pretty fast."

"About two-forty miles an hour."

The dog walker thought for a moment. "What's the point of a car like that in Manhattan?" he said.

"I'll get back to you on that," I replied.

I looked up East 80th and could make out headlights flashing about two blocks up. I ran to the other side of East End Avenue.


East 80th at this point was a dead end. A sign made that quite clear. And to emphasize the fact, there was a stoplight showing a permanent red. The street ran about twenty yards before terminating at a steel barrier. Beyond the barrier there was a sheer drop into a deep gully, about thirty feet across. Beyond the gully lay the FDR Drive. I could hear the hum of early-morning traffic nose-to-tailing it down the southbound lane. Beyond the FDR lay the East River.

I headed toward the barrier so that I could stand facing up East 80th and get a full frontal view of the McLaren as it approached. I noticed that there was some old burlap and a few strips of lumber lying on the sidewalk. Unusual in this part of town; the residents would not be pleased. Two pieces of lumber were laid up against the barrier.

I heard the shriek of an engine at full throttle. JJ was about a hundred feet from the junction. He covered the distance between us in a blink and I realized he wasn't going to stop. I threw myself to the side and looked up in time to see the front wheels mount the lumber. The wood snapped, but the car had cleared the barrier and spun out over the gully.

There was silence.

I watched the sun flash against bodywork as the McLaren rolled and revealed its dark underbelly. For a second, the car held still at the top of its arc, as if it had a decision to make.

Then it dropped.

There was an ear-splitting crash as it landed in the midst of the traffic on the FDR. I could hear the helpless thuds of vehicle after vehicle piling into one another.

Then, again, silence.

I got up and looked over the parapet. The nucleus of the impact was an insoluble puzzle of twisted metal, shimmering in a haze of gas vapor and boiling coolant. Farther back, the zigzag of wreckage was more intelligible, somehow retaining more familiar shapes, badly bent but still recognizable.

For a moment, there was nobody to be seen. It was as if dozens of vehicles had decided to stage a mass suicide and just gone out and done it, leaving their owners at home.

Then I heard the screaming. Cars don't scream. People do that; hurt, trapped people. And then those who weren't trapped—or dead—started to emerge, stooped, bloodied, like blitzkrieg survivors venturing from their bunkers.

Drivers and passengers from the cars in front of where JJ had landed were running toward the center of the conflagration that had missed them by less than the jolt of a second hand. Those in their wake had been doomed by an extra spoonful of cereal, the clean bra they couldn't find, the lazy gas pump attendant.

"What the fuck happened?"

It was the dog walker again.

"I don't know," I said weakly.

I stared at the carnage, trying to make sense of it.

Then the sirens came.

The noise rose, the cranking up of the emergency service's cacophony. Time dissolved into shouts and the scrape of cordons being dragged into place. The rattle of helicopters vied with the drone of generators powering lifting and cutting equipment. A news reporter, one hand cupped over his ear, yelled real-time commentary at a camera set up next to a van gored by a transmitter mast as tall as a tree.

I didn't bother to check my wristwatch. Time was now the allotted slice of satellite uplink.

I wanted to go back to my apartment and hear the seconds lazily clack by on the simple kitchen clock.

# TWO

**B**ut I didn't go back to the apartment. I went to the office instead. There I was, in the unremarkable lobby of the Credence Building, checking in with security and heading for the bank of elevators that would take to me to the twenty-fifth floor and Clay & Westminster's New York headquarters.

Clay & Westminster. English attorneys. A leader in London. Europe and the Far East too. But here in New York, something smaller, something clinging halfway up a modest tower facing the East River, a stone's throw from Wall Street. Yet for the past ten years it had survived here; more than survived, it had prospered to a degree: attracted clients, made money. It didn't generate waves, but its ripples were regular and well defined.

People were staring at me. I checked myself up and down: charcoal suit, black laced shoes. I fingered the knot of my burgundy Ferragamo tie, returning it to geometrical precision across its bed of crisp white cotton.

I tried to review the day's schedule in my head. A blank. Meetings.

Something tedious droned from a recess of my mind, but wouldn't identify itself. The social calendar? That wouldn't be up to much. No, wait. Ernie. Drinks with Ernie Monks. Ernie visiting from London; another fish out of water. Was it today or tomorrow?

"Are you okay?" someone asked.

A little light-headed, maybe.

I stepped into the elevator and checked my watch. Nine-thirty. Late. Just a few more, lingering minutes. That's all I needed, a short linger. Then I'd be fine; then things would start swimming back into focus.

In reception, clients and visiting attorneys sat in black leather arm-chairs or perched awkwardly on the edge of matching overdeep couches. They were reading newspapers or studying files, ignoring me, uninterested. A lone woman stood with her back to the floor-to-ceiling window. She would have a choice of views: to her left, the Brooklyn Bridge, to her right, Governor's Island. Ahead, the quaint sailing ships of South Street Seaport, and below, the FDR. I could hear the sirens; nothing unusual about that, though. Glancing at me, she frowned and turned away.

The receptionist stirred and slid her headset onto her shoulders. Was I okay? she asked.

Smiling, I ran my hand along the mahogany curve of her desk before heading down the hallway leading to the attorneys' offices.

Paula, my secretary, was coming the other way, as if she had been hanging around for my arrival.

"Fin, where the hell have you been?"

With my buddy, JJ Carlson, where else?

"Sorry I'm late." I carried on walking toward my office, letting her trot beside me.

She tugged crossly at my sleeve. "What happened to you?"

To me? Nothing really. To JJ, to those poor bastards on the FDR—they should have ignored the alarm clock.

We reached my office and I satisfied myself it hadn't changed since eleven-thirty the night before. The dark-stained wood shelves still held the same books and journals, the spinach-green leather-topped desk still supported a PC and brimming in-trays. The phone still winked its unchecked messages.

The newness of the day was heralded only by the presence of a faxed copy of *The Times of London* crossword puzzle, my affected genuflection in the direction of the Mother Country. At the top of the single sheet: "To Fin Border—your Red Cross parcel. Regards, Jessica."

I didn't know Jessica. Secretaries for attorneys at my link in the food chain put little distance between joining Clay & Westminster and leaving it. But she knew me, it seemed; the temporary keeper of the lighted candle in the window back home.

I fired up the PC while Paula planted herself in front of me and pointed at my forehead. Paula had been with me five years, the whole of my expatriate life in New York. My interpreter, my streetfinder.

"You seen your face?" she said.

"What do you mean?"

"You got a cut. It's difficult to tell where it is, there's a mess of blood all over."

I put my hand to my forehead and could feel the crusty ridges of clotted blood from behind the hairline down to my eyebrows. How could I have missed it? Suddenly it felt itchy. A splinter from one of JJ's snapping launch ramps, perhaps.

"I better get cleaned up," I said.

I started to lever myself out of the seat, but Paula splayed her hand across my chest and pushed me back.

"I'll take a look at it," she said. "Then either you're going to the emergency room or you go to your meeting. You're already late." She sighed theatrically. "Look at your screen, boss, while I get something to clean you up."

I logged into my calendar. There it was: nine-thirty, Schuster Mannheim. Our office, Conference Room B. Coffee and cookies to be provided.

Fin the Quartz. That was the pet name Sheldon Keenes, our resident partner, had christened me with. Never late, dependable.

Paula returned with the office first-aid kit and sidesaddled on the edge of the desk before tipping gauzes, creams, and bandages over it. Dunking a ball of cotton in a plastic cup filled with warm pink liquid, she started to sponge me down. I didn't say anything; I just looked up into her beautiful black face and those dark, dark eyes, slightly scrunched up in concentration. She would make a great nurse.

After a while and about five wads of cotton, she arched her back to assess her work.

"You'll live," she said. "Like most head cuts, it looks worse than it really is. You don't even need a stitch." She took a small bandage and stuck it near the center of my forehead.

"So *now* tell me what happened," she said.

I tried to piece it together in my head, an autopilot rehearsal: telephone call, car, speed, road. Crash. I hadn't been in the car, had I? No, no. It was JJ. JJ Carlson, Jefferson Trust's star banker. I didn't know where to begin. I smiled wanly and massaged my temples with both hands. I had a headache.

Paula gave me a curious look. "Anyway," she said. "While you've been bumping your head, things have been happening on the FDR up in the eighties. Big car wreck, shut the whole thing off. Ten people dead, they reckon, and a whole lot more injured. It sounds bad."

"How do you know?" I murmured, not that it mattered how she knew.

"Clara looks at the news every ten minutes on the net; she says it makes her feel part of the real world. I know what she means. Sometimes the inside of this place feels like all there is."

Paula would have no reason to suppose that I would have been that far up the FDR. I lived in Battery Park; just ten minutes' walk to the downstairs lobby.

"Did they say who was killed?" I asked. Among the twisted metal were names and the names belonged to people.

"Don't be stupid," Paula scolded, "it only just happened. They're not even sure how many. They haven't started interviewing the relatives yet. That'll be on tonight's news." She tapped the screen on the desktop computer.

"Thanks, Paula," I said. "I know what a TV is and how to use one."

"That knock to the head must have shaken you loose. Look where I'm pointing, you turkey."

She had a long red fingernail leveled against my meeting with

Schuster Mannheim. "What do you want to do about the meeting? I think you should let me get the doctor, you don't look so good."

I shook myself like a wet dog. "No, I'm fine."

"If you say so," she allowed reluctantly. "Sheldon was mad that you didn't show for the start and he said he'd go on without you. What papers do you need? Which deal file? You haven't told me, and the schedule didn't say."

Ninety-nine percent of my world was Clay & Westminster, and ninety-nine percent of that world was known to Paula: the files, the clients, the details. All the screwups. She had a better handle on my workload than I did.

But she didn't know much about this deal, maybe no more than the rumor-mongers knew. And the rumor-mongers usually got this one wrong. The twists and turns had provided a natural smokescreen. The deal was on, it was off, it had changed in some key respect. But, as of eleven-thirty last night, the deal was on, it was hot. And I was now missing a crucial meeting.

"I don't need anything, thanks. Just my brain," I said.

"Then we're in big trouble." Paula slid herself off my desk and put what was left of the first-aid kit back in its box. She gave me a look that told me she knew I wasn't leveling with her.

Sheldon Keenes came into the room. I heard Paula mutter good luck to me under her breath. She gave me a conspiratorial wink.

"Would you excuse us for a moment, Paula," Sheldon said.

Paula blurted a quick "I'm outta here" and almost ran from the room.

"Where the hell have you been?" Sheldon's voice was usually smooth, quiet, upper-crust English, but it wasn't now. He looked flustered and his normally bouffant blond hair was in disarray. He glanced at the wastebasket, saw the wads of bloodied cotton, and looked perplexed. He came up and peered at the bandage on my forehead.

"What silly buggers have you been playing at?" There was something in his tone that told me the answer to the question might be important to him.

I told him what had happened.

"You were there," he said in a horrified whisper.

"So you know about it already?"

"Of course I bloody know about it. The whole of New York knows about it. But they don't yet know that our primary contact at one of our main clients was the star turn. And they don't know that one of our attorneys was guest of bloody honor."

What else did Sheldon know, I wondered, as he pushed past me and snatched at my phone? He punched in a four-figure number and waited long enough to deliver five or six impatient thumps to my desk with his fist. "At last," he said. "Get me Mendip on the line and have it put through to my office. I'll be along in a moment. And answer the phone a bit quicker in future." He slammed down the receiver.

"You go to the meeting now," he said. "Tell them something came up and I'll be back soon. Say sorry." He made as if to leave the room.

"What if they ask me about what's happened?"

Sheldon didn't stop. "You've got amnesia," he said. Then suddenly he pulled up and pursed his lips. "On second thought, they may find out you were there." He paused. "Tell them that it may involve a client and we can't say anything at the moment. Try not to piss them off."

# THREE

Conference Room B was at the core of our half floor of accommodation. There was no Conference Room A—Sheldon Keenes didn't want outsiders to know how small we really were. A windowless, airless room, walls white to relieve the potential claustrophobia, while the white was itself relieved by a few prints of Victorian London, no doubt chosen by Sheldon to remind visitors that they were in the offices of an English law firm.

Four sour-faced people, three men and a woman, returned my gaze. They formed a squad along one side of the saffron sweep of a yew boardroom table, a tray of coffee and cookies untouched in front of them.

Who were these people? All I could see were zombies walking through wreckage. I could smell the gasoline, the coolant.

One of the faces smiled.

The smile dragged me back into the room. Lawyers from Schuster Mannheim. I needed to hold on to that.

I sat down.

From my lone position opposite the Schuster tribunal, I apologized for my tardiness and tried to make light of things, how we were at the mercy of clients, how life would be easier without them. But nobody was smiling now.

"Sheldon said you were caught in traffic." Ellis Walsh: forties, hotshot, no time for human frailty. Like JJ Carlson in some ways; but there'd been a depth to JJ, a piercing comprehension of the defects in the human condition.

My eyes glazed over the hillocks of paperwork arranged neatly on the table. In the corner of the room there were four storage boxes, still lidded, filled with more of the same.

"So where were we?" I asked.

Walsh gaveled his Mont Blanc. "Didn't Sheldon fill you in?"

"No," I said. Sheldon would be speaking to Charles Mendip, our senior partner, and wouldn't be worried that I was up to my neck here. Sheldon would tell me that landing me in it was the act of a good teacher honing his pupil's ability to perform under fire.

"We were nearly finished on our respective banking platinum accounts," Walsh said.

I groaned inwardly. Thirty hours already spent sifting through records of all our banking clients, highlighting those we billed for more than a million dollars a year. These were the platinum accounts, the ones where the schmooze was laid on extra thick. These clients could ask for discounts and be given them. We had to entertain and patronize them till we dropped. Identifying them wasn't difficult—my blue highlighter fingered them easily enough from the lineup. More difficult was the subjective work, the quizzing of the relationship partner, the associates, even the trainees, getting their assessment of the clients and whether they would be good for another million next year. Then we had to divine what kind of business they'd do: cross border mergers and acquisitions, share issues, litigation, office relocation, staff reduction. It didn't matter that such crystal-ball-gazing exercise was meaningless: Clients didn't behave predictably or, at times, even rationally.

The people from Schuster Mannheim were trying to read the same tea leaves. This was the fifth such meeting and they had alternated between brain-numbing boredom and almost hysterical controversy.

But the meetings were essential: Schuster Mannheim and Clay & Westminster had agreed in principle to merge and each had to know in molecular detail what the other was bringing to the party.

Party, party . . . It suddenly occurred to me that my friend, JJ Carlson, had never invited me to a party, to *any* gathering of his friends. I knew he had parties. He told me about them, unembarrassed about my uninvited status. He'd boast of the cream of Manhattan society he could pipe onto his birthday cake, year after year. And, man-oh-man, the fireworks, he'd declare, sparking the sky like a Baghdad blitz.

Then I had an insight. One for the news-crews, if I were called upon to give my eyewitness account of the crash on TV.

"There was no fire."

I must have said it out loud because the Schuster tribunal looked at me as if I were crazy.

*There was no fire*: All those vehicles had piled into each other, JJ's car among them. In the movies, the whole thing would have gone up in an effervescent ball of orange flame, cauterizing the mayhem. But there had been no fire. Would that have disappointed JJ? No fireworks. Man-oh-man.

Walsh cleared his throat.

"Sorry," I said. They'd have to figure out the spaghetti in my head. I couldn't.

Walsh ran his finger down a list of clients, his Harvard ring glinting as it crossed the harsh beam of one of the ceiling spotlights. "Saracen Securities," he said flatly. "One of yours—we've never done work for them. You sure you billed them more than a million?"

Saracen Securities was a good client. One of Ernie Monks's.

Saracen Securities fired deals in salvoes at a whole slew of our offices: London, Paris, Frankfurt, and Istanbul. Complex deals, some of them somewhat shady, perhaps. One to watch, but not lose. Ernie certainly wouldn't want to lose them.

"The statement says we billed them nearly two million last year," I said.

"But do they *pay* their bills," Walsh said.

I didn't bother answering.

Fragile shoots of familiarity started to bud as I speed-read a mess of papers Sheldon had left on my side of the table.

"Saracen Securities: a Turkish setup," I said. "Acting mainly out of London," I added. "It has no US operations or ambitions, that's why you've never heard of it."

"Any potential conflicts?" Walsh asked. That was always the real question. Was a client of Schuster suing a client of Clay & Westminster? Big problem if it was. The combined firm might lose both clients. But Clay & Westminster didn't do much litigation, so it hadn't been an issue so far.

"Unlikely," I replied.

One of Walsh's acolytes pushed a piece of paper in front of him. Walsh frowned and pushed it back.

"Delicate," said Walsh. I tried to glimpse the document, but the table was too wide. The acolyte shoved it triumphantly under a sheaf of others.

"What's so delicate, may I ask?"

Walsh hesitated. "There is a potential conflict."

I asked what kind of conflict. He said he wasn't sure that he should say.

"There's an ethical wall around us," I said, irritated now. "Just tell me. You know I can't say anything to anyone but the advisers." We were all sworn to secrecy and the most trivial of breaches would stop the deal in its tracks. The advisers to the merger: the merchant banks, the management consultants, the accountants, had all displayed a neurotic aversion to the attorneys discussing their respective client bases and had only agreed to it when those few involved in the process had signed in blood that they wouldn't leak. My blood was on the agreement and Walsh wasn't supposed to hold out on me.

"Is Sheldon going to be back soon?" he asked.

That was his way of saying that he would rather talk turkey to a partner than an associate. "I don't know," I said coldly, "but you know perfectly well that I'm mandated to discuss anything in these meetings."

Walsh sighed. "Our client is Reno Holdings," he said. "Million-plus

biller. Reno ran its slide rule over Saracen about a year ago. Didn't come
to anything then, but a file was opened and they said they might look at
it again when the emerging markets settled some more."

"So it's not an active conflict." It didn't sound too serious, a
bridge to fall off when we came to it. Did Ernie know that Reno fancied Saracen? Ernie didn't like clients being taken over; he took that
kind of thing personally.

*Tonight at six. Not tomorrow. The Lubber's Club. Drinks with
Ernie.* I was glad. Ernie would be a tonic. Soused with plenty of gin.

"It's not that simple," Walsh said.

What wasn't? I'd lost the thread.

Walsh stood and admired one of the wall prints. He ran his finger
along the top of the frame, as if he was checking for Victorian dust.

"Reno is a platinum client," he continued.

I found the thread. So Reno was platinum. So what? We were
only discussing platinum clients anyway.

Walsh wasn't finished. "It's a platinum client with big potential;
worldwide aspirations and the backing to achieve them. We wouldn't
want them alienated."

He was playing the my-client's-more-important-than-your-client
game and he wasn't supposed to.

"Rather than argue about it here," I said, "why don't we just
write a piece for our respective bosses and let them slug it out on the
conflicts committee." Walsh would hate that—he wasn't the sort that
liked to admit that he had a boss.

"If you feel unable to progress the issue on your own, then of
course we must do as you suggest." Walsh smiled openly at the
acolytes. He looked at the list again, and before I had any chance to
backtrack and maybe debate the potential Reno Saracen conflict, he
had already barked out the name of the next client.

Sheldon Keenes appeared. Maybe he'd had a shower: His hair was
back in place and the anxiety was washed from his face. He was a
scrubbed cherub in a suit.

"Sold the family silver, Fin?" he said cheerily. He sat next to me and
took the client schedule. "Ah, Saracen Securities. Platinum-plus client,
one of Ernie's favorite cash cows. Bit murky, but bloody lucrative."

Ernie Monks, our own office Oscar Wilde. The senior partner's right hand, his perimeter fence; there to protect Charles Mendip from the squalor of real human beings and their petty problems and aspirations, leaving him free to conduct affairs of state.

I turned to Sheldon. "Ellis was just pointing out that their client Reno Something or Other had taken a look at it as a potential target."

Sheldon frowned. "Bit hairy-chested of them." He rotated the signet ring on his little finger, as if Walsh's Harvard ring, which stuck out like a scarab, had made him self-conscious about the size of his own.

"What do you mean: hairy-chested?" Walsh asked.

"Even if the owners agreed to sell," Sheldon explained, "your clients would be buying a mystery wrapped in an enigma. Hell of a gamble. Ernie knows a bit about them, but even he would admit he doesn't know much."

"You're telling me you don't know a whole lot about a client that pays two million in fees?" Walsh said pompously.

Sheldon slanted a bushy blond eyebrow. "We can't toss a client just because we don't know his inside leg measurement."

My father had once told me to toss anyone I couldn't get the measure of. He didn't use the word *toss,* or *measure,* but his meaning was clear. And as he'd been sucking at a whiskey tumbler like a pacifier at the time, I knew that *not* tossing someone or something had just cost him more than he could afford.

"One for the conflicts committee, I guess," Walsh said.

Sheldon looked at his watch. "Listen; there's been a slight change of plan. Charles Mendip is flying over from London tomorrow morning. I know he wants to see Jim and so I'd better get on with the arrangements. I suggest we adjourn this meeting and look at getting together tomorrow sometime, maybe after lunch."

Jim McIntyre was the senior partner of Schuster Mannheim. He and Charles Mendip had been pictured together in the press a lot lately. This was the biggest transatlantic law firm merger to date, and it was making a splash. The PR shots were clever, they had to be: Charles was six-foot-three and McIntyre was five-foot-four and this was supposed to be a merger of equals. And yet, McIntyre looked the bigger man; at ease with his place in the spotlight, unfazed. While, with Mendip, there was a sense of stoop and surprise, as if the shoot was unscheduled, as if he had been caught by his wife with another woman. He looked frightened of the camera, of McIntyre too. It was the first time I'd seen him frightened of anything.

"Shall we say two o'clock tomorrow at our offices," Walsh said. "It's my turn to play host."

At least that meant I'd get out of the office for a while. Schuster Mannheim occupied a respectable slice of the GE Building in Rockefeller Center, loftily proud of their chunky brass doors, deco elevators, and marble floors, ever watchful for potential lebensraum in the levels as yet unannexed by them, although willing to concede that the Rainbow Room restaurant and the ice rink twenty floors down, sunk below street level, would remain the domain of tourists forever. Walsh had told me that, after the merger, the New York contingent of Clay & Westminster would be moving in, taking a corner of the fifty-third floor currently undergoing refurbishment for something more important: additional filing space or was it a library? Whatever. He made it sound like we would be refugees, with barely legal right of entry and even less right of welcome.

The acolytes took the boxes and disappeared down the hallway toward the reception area. Anyone looking at them would have known we were working on something big and more than once we had been criticized by Schuster Mannheim and their advisers for our lack of security. It was okay for them; as prestigious tenants of Rockfeller Center, they had hideaways and secret elevators for their sensitive assignments.

As Walsh made his way to the door, his cell phone rang. He seemed of two minds about whether he was going to answer it, then flipped it open. "Walsh." He listened. His eyes narrowed and he gave both Sheldon and me a meaningful glance. He hung up after about a minute without having said anything. "Apparently an investment banker from Jefferson Trust has driven his car onto the FDR Drive and killed himself and some fifteen others," Walsh announced as if he was telling us the time of the next Hoboken Ferry. He sat down again at the table.

Sheldon followed suit and motioned me to do the same. I thought I was going to be sick. The body count had gone from ten to fifteen in the space of half an hour. "Dreadful business," said Sheldon. "We have only just heard about it ourselves."

Walsh looked worried. "Jefferson Trust is one of your most important clients, isn't it?" He seemed to be looking for something; maybe the client schedule. "I don't know how much you billed them, but it was a lot."

Sheldon nodded. "About six million. Not too bad for a British law firm. They have been very active in Europe and the Far East, where we pick up most of the business. Naturally, we don't do any domestic US work for them. But neither do you. It's rather a glaring gap on your client list."

"Did you know the banker who died?" There was some emotion in Walsh's voice, but I sensed this stemmed from the billing implications of the tragedy, not its human dimension.

"We knew him," said Sheldon. "We know lots of bankers at Jefferson Trust."

But JJ Carlson was one of a kind.

"So the guy gave you work?" Walsh asked.

Sheldon stood up. "I'm not sure I understand where this is leading, Ellis. But wherever it is, it's a little premature and rather inappropriate, don't you think? There's been a terrible accident and people have been killed and hurt. Perhaps we should focus on that. Charles Mendip will be in New York tomorrow and, to the extent it has any bearing on things, I'm sure he will discuss this tragic turn of events with Jim McIntyre. You and I can then take our cue from them."

Sheldon extended his hand toward Walsh to indicate that he should shake it and then get the fuck out.

"I've got a few more calls to make," Sheldon said when Walsh had left the room. He went over to a phone on a small table in the corner. "Go back to your office. I'll speak to you in a moment or two and then you can go home. You must be pretty shaken up."

I realized I was still sitting and staring at a print of St. Paul's and feeling, for the first time in five years, something bordering on nostalgia for London.

"Don't worry, Fin." Sheldon cupped his hand over the mouthpiece. "They're not all like that little turd. Schuster Mannheim is a
great firm, and we'll make it even greater. You're part of history in the
making."

Sheldon had misread me. I wasn't *worried* about anything. I was
consumed. The image of the FDR consumed me, an image with all the
hallmarks of history in the making.

# FOUR

Paula was sitting on my desk when I returned to my office.

"You were there, weren't you?" she said, handing me a scorching cup. I smiled gratefully and took a suck at its contents through the little hole in the lid. Coffee, hot and sweet.

I felt guilty. Not about leaving Paula's question unanswered. It didn't need an answer, she just knew, as she always seemed to. This was guilt on a less easily definable, but grander scale.

I'd been there. I'd sat in the murder weapon, like it was a carnival ride. Then just watched what followed. I'd been flattered by an invite into JJ's gilded world; finally I'd been asked to one of his parties.

Bodies would be pulled from the wreckage now, broken, dripping, and distorted. And I was safe on the twenty-fifth floor of a tower block. Drinking coffee.

There was a world around me, a world that might have an attitude about my role in all this. My clients, Charles Mendip, my mother. The police . . .

Fucking hell. The police. I hadn't spoken to the fucking police.

I hurled my coffee into the wastebasket and reached for the phone.

"I haven't spoken to the police," I whispered.

"You're kidding me," Paula said.

I shook my head. It hadn't occurred to me.

I was the witness to a major wreck, one planned and executed by a senior banker at Jefferson Trust, a major Wall Street investment bank. The police might be interested in these facts. The victims might be interested too. I was a lawyer and should know this.

The telephone hovered near my ear. "Who on earth do I call? 911?" I was a securities attorney; I didn't have a hotline to the cops.

"I'll get them for you," Paula said.


At first, the officer who took the call was incredulous. Could I seriously be suggesting that I'd overlooked contacting the police in the immediate aftermath of such a huge incident? I managed to move him from emphatic disbelief to utter contempt for my stupidity. After that I gained a foothold on his sympathy. The cop wanted to know the gist of what had happened and then asked me to come to the precinct house if I was up to it. Alternatively they could come to the office. Sheldon would love *that*. I'd come to them, I said. Did I need a ride? They could send a car. No, I would make it under my own steam.

The call lasted about ten minutes and Paula must have been watching the indicator light, because she was in my room almost as soon as I had hung up.

"Safe to come in? You're not a fugitive from justice?"

"Yes and no," I said. "I've got to go down to the precinct and make a statement."

"I've already called for a car. Do you want me to come with you?"

"No. You'd better stay here in case Sheldon needs to know what I'm up to. And while I remember, can you reschedule any meetings I'm missing and call Jocelyn in Frankfurt to say his subscription agreement will be late? I'll have my cell phone on."

# FIVE

The precinct building was hotter than hell, an old brownstone mausoleum that managed to be even smaller on the inside than it looked from the outside. If there was air conditioning, it was well hidden. Organizational behaviorists would have pigeonholed the place as a hostile work environment. I checked in at the front desk and was escorted out back through the flotsam of villainy and victims locked in fierce altercation with hard-pressed cops. There was a derelict having an argument with himself, as if he wasn't prepared to wait in line for someone to shout at.

I was taken to the end of a dark and airless hallway and shown into a small room. The walls had once been white and there was an air conditioning unit centered in an old sash window. A garbage truck had contrived to squeeze itself into the narrow alleyway outside and was now revving its engine.

A man with Mediterranean features, dressed in plain clothes, was already in the room. He came up to me and shook hands.

"Sorry about the noise," he shouted. "We were supposed to go into a new building about three years ago. So, of course, they haven't spent a cent on this place since then: No soundproofing, wacky air conditioning, and I wouldn't recommend you use the bathroom unless you really have to."

He motioned me to sit on one of two schoolroom chairs that were set against a plain formica table.

"I'm Detective Manelli. You spoke to one of my colleagues."

Through the din of the garbage truck and the rattle of AC, Sicilian boyhood fought with New York manhood in Manelli's voice. He was young and relatively fresh-faced, although the job had given him premature shopping bags under his eyes.

"We have some witnesses," Manelli continued. "But you seem to know this Carlson guy and, if I've got it right, he actually asked you up there to see his new car."

"That's right," I said.

"So tell me about what happened."

I told him. I guessed I would be repeating the story a few times in the next forty-eight hours.

"So, what was he like?"

What *was* he like? A master of the universe. One of the top ten dealmakers on Wall Street. A legend. Or maybe, I was starting to think, a myth.

"He was a client," I began. "A senior investment banker with Jefferson Trust. You know Jefferson Trust?"

"Sure, I know it. Who doesn't?"

"I'm an attorney with a British law firm called Clay & Westminster. We have an office in New York, a small one: a resident partner, four associates, and some admin staff. You won't have heard of us."

Manelli didn't disagree.

"We work for Jefferson when they do deals in Europe or Asia. They're good clients and JJ was one of our main contacts."

"Was he a friend as well?" asked Manelli.

If he had asked me twenty-four hours earlier, I'd have said one of the few I had in New York. I had hardly spread my wings in the last five years; socially, I was more mollusk than butterfly. There was JJ, there was Carol Amen, the senior in-house banking attorney for

Jefferson Trust. Marty Smith of Callaghans, but now he was in the Netherlands Antilles, so evenings out with him were a thing of the past. Work-related appointments filled my diary and, even where these involved lunches and dinners, professional transactions—not intimacy—were the main menu items.

"A friend of sorts," I said, "though, I realize now, not a close one. I never even went to his house or met his wife. He took me to a few ball games and we used to go for a drink after work now and then." Monthly Jack Daniels evenings in a dingy midtown bar where we'd get drunk and talk crap and then stagger out to the limos that JJ had called for us. His to take him to his Central Park West aerie, and mine to my serviceable but rather pedestrian apartment in Battery Park.

"How long have you been living in New York?" Manelli asked me.

Five short years. People could be tedious when they spoke of how quickly time passed, but this five years *had* shot by. Five years of deals, schmoozing clients, and playing office politics—the politics of partnership not yet bestowed.

"When are you going back to England?"

"Hopefully never," I said.

"You like it here, Mr. Border?"

I did—I loved it.

But why? The Empire State Building? I'd never been up it. Bloomingdales? I'd never shopped there. The shows? Two in five years, and both British. The friends I'd made? Yeah, like JJ.

"Okay." Manelli got up from his chair. "I'm going to have someone take a full statement from you and then you can go."

"Will you need to see me again?"

"Sure. Maybe a couple of times when the picture gets clearer and we know what we're dealing with. But with your input we can start asking around to see why he did this thing. You've been very helpful."

"I'm sorry I didn't come in earlier."

Manelli waved his hand. "You've had a big shock. We'll send over a trauma counselor, maybe tomorrow, to help you out."

"I don't think I need one." Jesus, a trauma counselor.

"They're good," he said. "Speak to them. They know what they're doing—they've got plenty of traumas to practice on in this city."

# SIX

It was lunchtime when I stepped out of the precinct building and into the wall of people skittering around in their search for food or shopping. They needed a good reason to be outside—it must have been ninety degrees.

Doing my civic duty hadn't been too bad. Society, in the shape of Detective Manelli, seemed grateful enough. It didn't look like it was blaming me for what had happened on the FDR. I was, after all, merely a bystander.

But still I felt guilty. Should I have seen it coming? How, for Christ's sake? I hadn't even been inside his apartment, let alone his head.

The meager information I had on JJ couldn't begin to explain why he had invited me to his suicide.

At six that morning I thought I'd been humoring a kid with a new toy, not a homicidal maniac with a death wish.

I decided to go back to the office. There was plenty to do on the merger and, anyway, Frankfurt would be hoarse from screaming over the subscription agreement. I'd call Carol Amen at Jefferson Trust and get her take on things. We could talk freely. She'd understand. There was a time when I thought we might get to talk without the impediment of clothing. But . . .

Anyway, there was gin with Ernie at six to look forward to.


"I see you got promoted in my absence," I said on entering my office and finding Paula in my seat.

She smiled, but only very slightly.

I glanced at the in-tray to check for new arrivals. "Don't tell me, I should be at home with my feet up. I just want to keep active, that's all."

"You're over twenty-one. If you don't want to chill, then don't," she said tersely.

"What's the matter?"

Paula got up and mimed cleaning my chair with her hand. "You better ask Sheldon Keenes." She started to leave the room.

"Wait a minute, Paula. I'm asking you. Come on, tell me."

"Sheldon's mad at you for calling the police and then going there without telling him."

"So? He's cross with me. Why should that upset you? Like you say, I'm over twenty-one and can look after myself."

"He got pretty mad at me too."

"Shot the messenger?"

"Kind of." She picked up a handful of files from my meeting table. "Anyway, I'd better get on with these and you better go see Sheldon. He tried to call you on your cell phone and was going to get you to come back to the office. Lucky you showed."

"I had my cell phone with me." I felt for and found the solid lump in my jacket pocket.

"Was it switched on, genius?"

I took the phone out of my pocket. The little screen was dead. I looked up to share my exasperation with "off" buttons that could press themselves. Paula didn't look like she wanted to share anything with me.

"You're still pissed with me," I said. "Is there something else, Paula?"

She hesitated. "You've had a bad enough day. It'll keep."

"No," I said. "Spit it out now. It'll make me feel worse if I know there is something bugging you and you won't tell me."

"Your meeting, this morning," she said. "Was that about the merger?"

*Of course it was, Paula. You know it was, but you're not supposed to ask.*

I returned the cell phone to my pocket.

"Fin, is it going to happen?" she asked. "Mergers affect people; this one affects me. Is it going to happen?"

"If it does, you'll be safe," I said. Mendip was my protector, family almost. And in turn I'd be Paula's protector, her knight.

"How do you know?" she hissed. "You know nothing about me."

She didn't shut the door as she left my room; maybe she couldn't trust herself not to slam it.

She was right. I knew nothing about her—apart from the death of her husband and the daily drama of her commute from Brooklyn. She had loyally listened to all my daily woes and grumbles; she had managed my minimal domestic requirements: the cleaning lady, the cable guy, and the landlord's agents. She knew as much about the fabric of my rather flimsy life as I did.

When I'd arrived in New York, she was already with the firm. I had just assumed she always would be there, that she would continue to ride in my exhilarating slipstream.

I realized how little I'd really known about those around me.

I left my office to go and see Sheldon Keenes.


Sheldon was on the phone, but his flapping hand briskly drew me in. I flopped onto his leather couch. I scanned the dark cherry-wood fittings of his office and noticed the cut-glass tumbler of Perrier on his desk. Ice lolled around between the slice of lime and the still vigorous bubbles. Partners got couches, Perrier, lime, and refrigerators. My father once had all the accessories of partnership at this firm. Would I ever lay claim to them?

Sheldon had made a home of his quarters: family photos, the pictures of famous fairways to remind him of his triumphs on the golf course, the crayon birthday card from his four-year-old daughter. Then there were the clear Lucite blocks that encased summaries of the transactions he'd done—tombstones, dead deals.

He put down the phone.

"As my nanny used to say: You're a caution," he said. "I told you to wait for me. The next thing I find, you're down at the police station blurting everything out to the boys in blue."

The lecture failed to display the conviction of a pro. Ernie could carry it off, but Sheldon couldn't.

"I'd left it too long," I said. "I had to go."

He nodded gravely. At thirty-five, six years older than me, the cherubic face was at odds with the young fogey's affectation of age and wisdom. "I understand," he said, "but I would have preferred it if you had been accompanied by one of us. After all, you were in shock."

"I just told them what happened, nothing more or less," I insisted. "I obeyed the rule of interviews and didn't speculate or meander."

"I'm sure you handled it perfectly, Fin. But this tragedy involved one of our most important clients and we don't want to take unnecessary risks."

"Risk of what?" I could feel myself getting irritated. "Is the client going to sack us because one of its bankers has some kind of brainstorm and invites me to his suicide? I don't think so."

"I don't think so either. But everyone's edgy. Charles especially so, and he is still three thousand miles away. You must understand that there are sensitivities. Or is it sensibilities? Whatever. People are edgy, that's all."

"Is that why you chewed out Paula when she was just doing her job?"

"She should have known better," Sheldon said, taking the tiniest of sips of his Perrier as if to show how little sweat my observation had generated.

"For God's sake," I said, "she just did as she was told. There was no need to shout at her."

"I didn't shout at her." He paused. "I don't shout; you know that."

Point to Sheldon. His self-perception was accurate: He didn't shout. Paula hadn't even said that he had shouted.

Sheldon smiled patronizingly. "Look. You're upset and that's understandable. Of course you should have spoken to the police, but you should have spoken to me first and I would have arranged support."

I nodded wordlessly—I certainly wasn't going to apologize.

Sheldon opened his desk drawer and took out a single clean sheet of paper. "What are you working on at the moment?"

Staying sane in the aftermath of JJ's suicide, mainly.

"Plenty," I said. Sheldon was the resident partner and was supposed to know everything that went on in the office. He required schedules of progress on all clients, no punches to be pulled on the glitches, and no preening over the successes. He required two meetings a week with me and the three other associates where he tackled everything from late-paying clients to the brand of mineral water to be kept in the kitchen refrigerator. On the surface he was a democrat, but in reality he was a control freak who liked to know the opinion of everybody before he ignored it.

Therefore the clean sheet of paper was entirely redundant; he simply needed to look at my latest progress report on the system. But Sheldon was a man of ceremony, a lacquer fountain pen flecked with firey shards of silver, the swish of black ink across thick cartridge paper, the zen of calligraphy. It obviously gave him pleasure and in the scheme of things it was harmless enough, I supposed.

But why a list? Why now? At this particular moment. Fear started to skitter among the guilt, even though pride should have been my dominant emotion. I had more than my fair share of large deals, ones that mattered for billing and profile, ones that counted for the league tables, ones that earned fat tombstones.

Sheldon looked up expectantly, pen poised.

"There's Hudson Food Retail," I began, "and their proposed

acquisition of the UK network of Bellamy Stores. Straightforward enough, except for a few antitrust issues. More complex are the two Eastern European GSM cell phone licenses up for grabs with US members of the consortiums."

"Consortia," Sheldon corrected.

"Next would be the Romanian brewery that Busch wants—can't imagine why, Romanian beer is gnat's piss."

"Spare me the tabloid commentary," Sheldon said.

"What's this for, Sheldon?"

"What's what for?" He laid down his pen and stared at me over his steepled fingers. I wanted to twist his cherub nose.

I waved my hand over the sheet of paper that was filling up with immaculate copperplate. "This. This bloody list. What's it for? You could look at the computer and find it out and I could be recovering from the wobble you seem determined to diagnose for me."

"I'm the resident partner," Sheldon said quietly. "I want to know what one of my staff is doing—exactly what he is doing. A computer wouldn't give me the nuances."

"Nuances?" I sneered. "These are deals we're talking about, bits of paper, piles of money. They don't have fucking nuances."

He closed his eyes. "Calm down, Fin."

Lists were dangerous. Lists were inventory, something to help keep track of valuables in transit. Were my deals about to be in transit?

"Are you firing me?"

Sheldon groaned. "Don't be bloody absurd."

"Then why this? Is it because of JJ?"

"You've had a terrible shock."

"And this isn't helping."

Sheldon picked up his pen and his pink lips puckered, like caterpillars in a clinch. "One step at a time," he said. "Finish the list and then we'll talk."

My immediate boss wanted his list. Edited highlights, he could have edited highlights. "Three private placements," I said, "BAM, Cypher, and Rubbex. No Securities Act registration; they're all 144A issues. Fairly straightforward, except for Rubbex—that's the condom manufacturer—where the roadshow is proving a little controversial, for obvious reasons. Pitstop B2B listing on NASDAQ. And, of course, our very own merger with Schuster Mannheim."

I uncrossed my legs and dug myself deep into the couch.

"Those are the important matters," I said, daring Sheldon to challenge me on what was important and what wasn't.

"And the small items?" he asked.

The crumbs from around the deal table. The speculative research, the confidentiality letters to review, the engagement letters to draft, the company investigations to perform.

He put the cap back on his pen when I'd listed them all. "Impressive," he said. "Quite a portfolio."

"And now you want to sell it off, don't you?"

Sheldon finished his Perrier, letting an ice cube slide into his mouth.

Crunch.

"Just lighten your load for a while."

"Why?"

Sheldon sighed. "Do I really have to spell it out?"

"JJ," I said. "I was in the wrong place. You're worried about my mental equilibrium—or lack of it. I might frighten the fee-paying horses. What else, Sheldon? Or have I grasped the essential point?"

"In broad terms, yes, although I wouldn't have expressed it that way."

"I see." It had been so quick. This morning I had a client list and now . . .

"So you don't think I can hack it, that I can't judge for myself if I'm well enough to do my job?"

"It's not like that." There was a slight stammer over the *l* in *like*. "Charles thinks that . . ."

I slapped my hand on the arm of the couch. "And who gets the list, Sheldon?"

"Paul, Alf, and Terry."

Lamberhurst, Silverman, and Wardman. Who else? The three dysfunctional musketeers: each for himself and not one for the others. Sheldon was credited with much that was good about the New York office, but establishing an esprit de corps wasn't part of it.

Christ, no. I moaned out loud. "They'll trample all over my files."

Sheldon bridled. "They're good lawyers. And they aren't *your* files, they belong to Clay & Westminster." He paused. "Anyway, they will be terrific stewards until—"

"Until, until. Until when?"

"Until you're better."

"I was overlooking the FDR, Sheldon, not crashing into it. I was only a bystander, for Christ's sake."

"Please, Fin. Fifteen people—"

"This isn't about the smash, though, is it? This is an opportunity you've been waiting for."

Sheldon froze. "I think you ought to stop right there."

"Charles foisted me on you and you've wanted to shake me off ever since."

"I'm warning you, Fin—"

"For five years I've delivered the goods, swelled your profit share. But your lip still curls, doesn't it? Not cut from quite the right cloth, am I?" No nanny, no Oxbridge degree.

"This isn't about the chip on your shoulder," Sheldon said.

"When will Charles be here?" I asked. Charles Mendip liked me, was almost family, had made a speech at my parents' wedding. He was my godfather, for Christ's sake. My protector, my mother's too, *in loco parentis* to us both. Sheldon had beguiled him for a moment, but Mendip would protect me again. That was the godfather's role when the father wasn't around anymore.

"He'll be here tomorrow." Sheldon leaned forward. "The hand-over of files was *his* decision, Fin."

No. Mendip wouldn't do that. Sheldon was using the big man as his shield. Anyway, it would offend Mendip's dictum about finishing what you begin, something he used to lecture my father about. What had my father said? Don't take half-eaten files and don't give them—heartburn will follow. Maybe the musketeers would choke on the damn things. But I didn't want that, I just wanted what was mine, what I'd built.

Sheldon looked exhausted. "It's settled, Fin. Go home."

"No," I said. "There's still work to be done on the platinum clients for tomorrow's meeting with Walsh." *Mendip will be here tomorrow. Hang in there.*

Sheldon shook his head. "You're off the merger as well." He slipped his pen into a little leather holster and glanced furtively at his computer screen.

"You can't," I murmured.

But they could. They had. It was a done deal. The molten Lucite was bubbling in the saucepan ready to pour into the mould for the tombstone.

"One more thing," Sheldon said. "We'll need some handover notes." He waved at his own notes. "These won't be sufficient. They need fleshing out."

I nodded absently.

"I suggest you do them at home and e-mail them in." He stood up. He was blushing. "Then think of somewhere to go. A holiday. England, maybe. Or wherever takes your fancy. Sun or snow. On the house, as it were. Within reason, of course."


Outside Sheldon's office I had another flash of memory. A woman, standing in the midst of the wreckage on the FDR. I realized now what was odd about her: not the blood, nor the summer dress stuck to her like something out of a grotesque wet T-shirt competition. Nor the eyeglasses bent and twisted but still on her face.

She was holding a dog leash. The remains of her dog hung from the end of it. She hadn't buckled him up properly.

The woman just stood there, as if she was waiting for Pooch to take a pee and then trot off alongside her.

# SEVEN

Ernie was already settled in the ersatz salty sea dog atmosphere of the Lubber's Club at South Street Seaport when I arrived just before six. A gaunt dome seated alone at a table for six with a prime view overlooking the dockside, he was watching the tourists peer in through the netting, lanterns, and wax fish, as one massive hand tilted a tumbler of gin and the other toyed with a cigarette smoldering illegally in a saucer alongside him.

"Unreal City," he said as I sat down. T. S. Eliot, *The Waste Land*. Eliot had been describing London, but the line suited New York better. Ernie summoned a waiter with a regal wave.

"You poor thing." He squeezed my hand. Inclining his head slightly, he brought his face up close to mine. Sad, rheumy spaniel eyes. "Silly bankers getting sulky and offing themselves in front of one of my lavender-scented innocents. The world is a darkish domain, much in need of compassion and sound ministry."

He glanced up at the waiter, now standing at attention next to him looking like a crossbreed of butler and Captain Ahab. "A Barracuda's Colon with a twist of fennel, if you please," he said solemnly.

"Excuse me, sir?" the waiter said impassively.

"Large Gordon's and tonic." He turned and grinned at me. "Home of the cocktail and they don't even know of the Barracuda's Colon. Bloody disgrace."

He studied my face again. "Hmm," he said, mopping his massive forehead with the crisp linen napkin before tossing it onto an empty table nearby.

"Seen Mendip yet?" he asked.

I shook my head.

"Just come off the phone with him," Ernie said, patting his vest. I could make out a cell phone peeking from the folds of his enormous midriff. "He rang me on this thing. They issued me with one so they could keep tabs on me—they assume I will never find the off button. Bloody right, the bastards."

Ernie took a mouthful of gin. I guessed it wasn't his first; he had that lubricated look.

"Haven't the foggiest notion where he is. Didn't ask—he could be on the ninth fairway at Wentworth for all I know. But he's pretty cross with you, I'm afraid."

"Why? I haven't done anything wrong."

My drink arrived and Ernie allowed me to consume about half of it before elaborating. "You were *there*," he said. "Wrong place, wrong time. Rotten luck, of course. Not your fault that you got caught up in the Jefferson Trust laundry basket, but Mendip finds himself in a delicate position. While he's busy negotiating the merger that will get him his knighthood and fill our pockets with loot, our biggest client has one of its uberwankers slaughter fifteen good citizens—with you looking on with your opera glasses and popcorn."

But was it necessary to strip me of my client base?

"Vicious and totally unnecessary." Ernie took hold of my hand again, rolling it on the generous mattress of his palm. "I remonstrated with Charles about that, but he responded with an agonized more-in-sorrow-than-in-anger speech about how the partnership constrained him." Pain boiled in his eyes. "It breaks my heart. More likely one partner, rather than the whole letterhead: Apparently the Hitler Youth is spitting bullets and insisting upon it."

Sheldon Keenes—the Hitler Youth—kept the office dagger well whetted for Ernie's back. Sheldon saw Ernie as the hulking obstacle in his path to the pinnacle of the Clay & Westminster mountain.

Ernie was one of the old guard, though, and Mendip had always made sure that Sheldon's cutlery did no real harm. But now it seemed that Sheldon had Mendip's ear and was whispering poison into it. Had I lost my protector?

*"Nil desperandum,* Eyelash," Ernie whispered, pushing my glass of gin toward me. "Remember: you're still a favorite. Just like your Dad, the silly plonker. If he were here, I'm sure he would say: Keep your head down, let Mendip give you a bit of a spanking, sing the Firm song, and boldly march forth toward your allotted pedestal in the great pantheon of Clay & Westminster."

My father wouldn't have said anything of the sort and, anyway, he wasn't a role model that I was remotely tempted to follow. I needed a living, breathing intercessor. Ernie was as close as I was going to get until Charles arrived.

"They've taken me off the merger as well," I said. "Surely you can do something, get through to Charles. He'll listen to you."

Ernie sighed. I noticed an olive flush staining his face, aging it. He'd grown old since we'd last met. "I'm an irrelevance now," he said. "Or irreverence, as Charles dubbed me the other day. My station on the letterhead is a fig leaf, Fin. Of course, I have too much capital and too many friends for them to ignore me entirely. But I don't bill very much anymore and my rather colorful behavior excludes me from drumming up new clients. They want me to help see them through the merger with the Shyster Guggenheims and then bugger off into the sunset. And I'm inclined to go along with their spastic little plan."

He dipped his finger in his gin, sucking on it sensuously. He looked out at the ships and hummed.

"No room for an old poof like me in the new regime," he mused. My father once said that Ernie's camp exterior was mere chintz, veiling something complex and delicate: a web surprisingly un-English and tragic. Ernie sighed. "But I can't quibble that it's the right thing to do. Anyway, even if it wasn't, arguing with ten thousand management consultants would bring me out in spots." Suddenly he brightened.

"Still, I shall have my pretty friends to visit me and pay homage. I expect you to sit at my feet and receive counseling—after all, you are an orphan and need a father figure."

"My mother's still alive," I observed.

"She's a woman. Doesn't count."

"You must've had a mother, Ernie."

"Perhaps," he said, but didn't seem to want to pursue his normal line of misogynist banter.

"We were talking about Saracen Securities at the merger client committee today." I knew I shouldn't be telling Ernie this.

He didn't seem very interested anyway. "Metals, dull or shiny, although predictably gold's their favorite. Turks, you know. But they smoke a lot and have a healthy regard for sodomy, so we mustn't be too harsh. Who was at the meeting?"

"Ellis Walsh."

"Walsh is a cunt."

I raised my glass. "I'll drink to that."

"What else were you working on?" Ernie said. "Before the Hitler Youth raided your client base, that is."

I told him.

He looked troubled. "That's quite a net-full, Fin. Did Sheldon say he would handle them himself?"

"He's going to divvy them out between Lamberhurst, Silverman, and Terry Wardman. That's my fear, Ernie. I may get my clients back soon enough, but what shape will they be in after the trio have hacked them up?"

"Hmm. Terry will tend the plants well enough," Ernie said. I knew that he and Terry went back a long way, but to the rest of us Terry was a mystery: a quiet, fastidious man who dealt with regulatory matters with a ruthlessness and success that was totally at odds with his shy, gentle grayness. I always felt that I had even less rapport with Terry than the others—he was always polite but there seemed to be an edge of animosity directed toward me that I couldn't fathom.

"As for Silverman and Lamberhurst," continued Ernie, "you're right to be concerned. Competition lawyers: buried in Brussels and Hart Scott Rodino, counting out washing machines and hatchbacks.

That's not law, it's kindergarten arithmetic. They shouldn't be let loose on grown-up deals. I'll have another word with Charles, if you like. Not that I think it will do any good."

It wasn't much, but it was something.

"I don't know why he did it," I said.

Ernie lit a cigarette. "Carlson, you mean?"

"He had everything. Only three weeks ago he was on the front cover of *Mergers and Acquisitions Monthly*." They'd taken an air-brush to his teeth and hair, but it was a pretty accurate likeness. "A wife and two kids as well."

Ernie smiled grimly.

"Okay, Ernie," I said. "We all know your views on family life."

JJ hardly ever mentioned his family; in fact, I may have learned that he had children from someone else. But, even when drunk, his eyes didn't trace the trajectory of a cute ass or return the twinkle of a dolled-up loner along the bar top.

"Probably teed off at his bonus," Ernie said. "Twenty million hardly goes anywhere these days."

No, not that. He loved money, sure. But he used to say he would swap it all for freedom. He felt constricted by Wall Street. No space and silence, he'd say. Give it up, I'd reply, you can afford to. Buy your own island and lie on it. No, he'd say, there's a guard at the door. Then he'd order another drink.

"And why me? Why ask me along to watch?"

Ernie shrugged. "Perhaps he loved you, Eyelash. Did you brush his hand away from your crotch one evening? Hell hath no fury like a banker scorned."

Ernie was smashed; he was getting stupid.

"I think he was lonely," I said. But why? People would have paid to spend an evening with him. And why hang out with me? I had kid-ded myself that it was the chemistry of respect, the alchemy of turning fine legal work into friendship. But it hadn't been real friendship, had it? He talked; I listened. I prattled and he got drunker and drunker, his vigorous, clean-shaven features melting, his stolid head sinking onto the backs of his perfect hands, his dark, swollen eyes roving, from their glass-level vantage point, along the ranks of bottles. Perhaps he was looking into the mirror behind the bottles. Seeing something that I couldn't see for myself.

"And angry," I said. You had to be angry to kill fifteen people. It had been a deliberate act with near certain consequences.

To whom would the police turn to get a foothold on JJ's loneliness and anger? Miranda, his wife. Fellow bankers. Carol Amen, chief investment banking counsel for Jefferson Trust, JJ's favorite legal architect for his deals. Cofavorite, with me, the outside counsel.

The rest of his family? What family? I didn't know if his parents were dead or alive, if he had brothers or sisters. Was there a cousin in Baltimore? I knew nothing about him.

Ernie shifted himself in his seat and called the waiter over.

"Same again." There was no energy in the voice, his multiple chins spreading over his upper chest like a glutinous slick, partially obscuring the knot of his tie.

He picked up the pepper shaker and absently sprinkled some of the gray powder over the end of his lighted cigarette. A few fizzes and sparks, then a return to the lazy blue column of smoke.

"You have to know where to look," he said. "Follow the fear. It gathers in the unseen crevices, like dust."

"What do you mean?"

"I will show you fear in a handful of dust." He carried on tipping pepper on the cigarette until it was asphyxiated.

He straightened himself, lifting his chins off his chest. "T. S. Eliot."

Who else?

Ernie liked to drift in and out of poetry, out of the garrulous and into the morbid.

Fear. What did fear have to do with anything? "You've lost me, I'm afraid."

Ernie scowled. "The climate of fear. Your fear for your career. Sheldon Keenes and his fear of me. Mr. Charles Mendip and his fear for the merger, his knighthood. Jefferson Trust and their fear of the fallout from Mr. Carlson's auto aerobatics. Schuster Mannheim will feel it too. It gets into everything. Maybe Mr. Carlson was afraid."

He lit another cigarette and laughed, his face reanimated, the chins inflated. "But bugger fear, a pox on it. The important issue is *your* anger. Keep it in check, Fin. Lie low. Don't panic. Your Papa panicked, God rest him. Don't get stuck in the same crevice as him."

He tousled my hair. "And what about your loneliness? Isn't some siren stroking the gorgeous cock that undoubtedly slinks beneath your rather indifferent suit?"

It was some time since anyone had stroked any part of me, let alone my cock. In the office by eight, out at eleven, often later. Sleep in between. The exhausting road to partnership was narrow and featureless. True, there was the odd movie with Silverman or Lamberhurst or the frantic whistle-stop around Manhattan for the periodic wide-eyed visitor from London. Most of them knew New York, though, and didn't need a guide. Work and get sloshed. Then more work.

Relationships, I realized now, didn't feature. A few stolen lunches, guilt over my truancy making it hard to swallow the food. Six fumbling, heavily condommed fucks in six different apartments, seen for dinner but never for breakfast. I doubted if my trysts would fill a single commercial break in an episode of *Sex and the City*.

Only Carol Amen came close. So close. If the gap had only narrowed more, allowing my hand to run through the swathe of caramel-colored hair, letting me feel the heat from her blazing chestnut eyes. Such a paltry distance, less than the length of her powerful forearm. Near, nearer, like a wave on the beach foaming whipped cream over my feet, but no farther.

Ernie heaved himself out of his seat and flung a hundred-dollar bill on the table.

"Find yourself a stroker, Fin. Blow off the dust and douse yourself and your chosen belle with almond oil and stroke yourselves into oblivion." He closed his eyes. "Ah, me," he murmured.

"You're incorrigible."

He took a last puff from his cigarette and stubbed it out in the saucer, letting the smoke jet from his nose, like twin exhausts. I noticed he didn't have any nasal hair.

"There's been enough sensation for one day," he announced. "It's time for you to rest your eyelashes and I will safeguard the firm's interests over a large T-bone and a prodigious intake of Stag's Leap Cabernet."

As we left the Club, he put his arm around my shoulder. "Dante's *Inferno*," he said. "I always find that when I've witnessed someone kill fifteen people and my client base has been torn from my teats, reading the *Inferno* helps put things in their proper perspective. That and a bottle of 1980 cask-strength Dailuaine malt whiskey. Now piss off back to your little box in your horrid tower block." He patted my behind and gave me a push in the direction of my Battery Park apartment while he peeled off in the direction of our office.

# EIGHT

The images in the papers the next morning were pretty much freeze frames of the previous night's footage on TV, footage that had stalked me into an exhausted sleep; shots from the steel barrier, shots from the air, pendulous film taken from a boat on the East River, grainy telephoto intrusions into the gory nucleus of JJ's finale.

When I arrived at the office, it seemed quiet, subdued. As I walked through reception, I sensed that my connection with JJ was a poisonous vapor trail, paralyzing anyone who caught a whiff of it.

Lamberhurst muttered something about how his commute took twice as long that morning.

They knew I was there. But, as yet, the media didn't. For the moment, I had a breathing space, a welcome and probably short-lived refuge from the clamor.

Paula was kneeling on the floor by my desk, surrounded by blue files. Keenes must have gotten in early, told her to start sorting things for the handover to the musketeers. Christ, he'd been quick off the mark.

She looked up, surprised. "Keenes said you wouldn't be in. You should be at home resting."

I toed one of the files. Bellamy Stores. Three billion dollars; there would be a fat tombstone at the end of that one.

"I didn't like the homework Keenes set for me."

Paula stared guiltily at my desk. "I wouldn't have left the newspapers lying around if I'd known you were coming in."

A tablecloth of the *Daily News, Wall Street Journal,* and the *New York Times.*

"You've seen them already, I guess," Paula said.

"Some of them." I traced a finger along the picture of a poignant hand dangling from a dense tangle of twisted metal. I sniffed at the printer's ink smearing my fingertip. Sweet, dusty.

Paula stood up, splaying both hands across the small of her back and thrusting forward her pelvis.

"Getting old," she said.

"You're only forty," I replied.

"What do you know, you baby?"

About her? Precious little. About as much as I knew of JJ.

I noticed a plastic thermos on the table; blue, opaque, the kind used for picnics.

"What's that?" I asked.

"Soup. I was going to bring it over to you later."

"That was sweet of you. What are you doing, as if I didn't know already?"

"Spring cleaning, was how Keenes put it," Paula said.

Rearranging the dust, recalibrating the fear.

"How very Keenes," I said. "Charles Mendip showed up yet?"

"I heard Keenes talking to his secretary—later today sometime, I think. I also heard him say that JJ Carlson's funeral was this afternoon."

I picked up the *Daily News.* "Star Banker in FDR Carnage."

"That's quick," I said. "I'm surprised the police would allow the body to be released so soon. Not that there would be much to release."

The relatives would want him under the turf pronto, I guessed, less chance of being mobbed by the families of the other victims at the graveside. Still, it was hardly twenty-four hours since the smash. A burial so soon must have taken some string-pulling. Some Jefferson Trust string-pulling, and a postmortem performed with the speed of a Japanese chef preparing sashimi.

And thus far, Jefferson Trust had, understandably, kept a low profile—a lone statement from an anonymous communications guy, expressing condolences to the bereaved and injured, and that was it. No comments from colleagues, fellow bankers. Jefferson Trust had comprehensively zipped up their staff and it was left to the journalists to piece together JJ's career from already published sources: Most were accolades, bolstered by catalogs of breathtaking deals done in countries a geography teacher wouldn't know. No talk of his family, though. Nothing of his upbringing. His life started at Harvard Business School, it seemed. He was born in a lecture hall.

What had gone wrong? The newspapers asked: What had unhinged him? The Wall Street hotshot life, the twenty-four-hour days, the travel, the computer screens, the meetings, the unrelenting pressure to make money, the scrap heap if you didn't? Why didn't the banks, the law firms, the accountants, have clinical psychologists and organizational behaviorists dogging the employee's every step? We do, protested the institutions. Well, you don't have enough of them, blustered the editorials.

Then they turned their attention to the protection afforded to drivers on the FDR: Were the parapet walls high enough, sturdy enough? Weren't the traveling public manifestly at risk from aerial bombardment? Hadn't anyone noticed? Someone was to blame. There had to be somebody to take the heat.

I had a terrible feeling I knew who that somebody would be. They would paint a target on my forehead and start shooting.

"Myers Myerling," I whispered.

"What you say?" Paula asked.

"Clay & Westminster's PR people for the merger. I wonder if Keenes has told them that I was with JJ . . . They should be briefed. When it gets out, we'll need them. I'll need them."

"Do you want me to get them on the phone?"

"I'd better speak to Keenes first. The way he is, he might fire me for not consulting him."

I called his office. His secretary said he was busy. I couldn't leave a voicemail—Sheldon didn't believe in voicemail, as if it was a moral issue. So I relayed my respectful suggestion that Myers Myerling should be contacted, adding that I was sure that Sheldon had thought of it already.

"I'm sure he has," his secretary oiled. If he had, she should know, I thought.

I spent the next couple of hours typing up my notes as Paula knelt on the floor, making sure that the files were sorted properly between correspondence, drafts, and final documentation. I looked at her from time to time, back hunched over the piles of paperwork, her elegant hands sifting and selecting pieces of paper as if they were priceless papyrus just unearthed from the darkest corner of a pharaoh's tomb. I found the scene strangely calming, and felt myself relax.

Paula must've sensed that I had stopped typing. "I got eyes in the back of my head. Get on with your work," she said without turning around.

"Do you think I should go to JJ's funeral?" I asked.

"Hell do I know?"

"I mean he *was* a friend and a client."

"Funny kind of friend that asks you to a killing."

At that moment I decided to go. I realized I wanted to. Perhaps I couldn't fully accept what had happened without witnessing something tangible of its aftermath. I didn't want to see JJ's body in a glass-top casket and weep over it asking why, why, why? But maybe seeing his wife, Miranda, and the other relatives would give the whole thing a much-needed human dimension.

"I'll go," I said. "What time is it?"

"Two o'clock," Paula said. "You'll be quicker if you grab a cab outside rather than order a car."

The cab was a sullen knot in the rope of traffic that slithered slowly across Long Island, finally making good its escape from the misnamed

Expressway at Exit 40, thereupon losing itself in the roads threading through the seemingly endless acreage of cemetery that dominated this part of the Island. It was like a national park for the dead.

The driver had professed to know the precise location of Pinelawn Memorial Park. He didn't. And by the time he dropped me at the estate offices just beyond the entrance, I was well and truly late.

A clerk in the office directed me to the Garden of Freedom and handed over a map. I should have kept the cab: The place was huge, a city of the dead with its own stop on the Long Island Railroad, which ran alongside.

I started the jog through the thin drizzle to the Garden of Freedom, down Lillian M. Locke Drive, past Fountain Garden, the Garden of Remembrance, to a T-junction into Holly Drive, past angels, headstones, mausolea, modest squares and circles of slate and stone, like manhole covers in the immaculate lawn.

Onto Vista Road, a curve right into Adams Drive, and then a left into Freedom Drive, clogged by a parked convoy of ubiquitous funeral cars abutting a rampart leading up to the raised central area of the Garden of Freedom.

Ahead of me, beyond the cars and on the slope, a dreary clump of blackness stained the gray green, forlorn under a gazebo on wheels, protected from the elements by white canvas.

A sad gathering appeared like a rain cloud over the brow of the central knoll. JJ's party, it had to be. I'd have missed the interment itself, but I could pay my respects anyway.

A small woman shuffled, the walk of old age performed by a youthful body. She was supported by a man in his mid-fifties. His brittle gray hair was tied back in a small ponytail, face a wrinkled wreck, but familiar, bearing recognizable traces of Carlson. Father? It didn't feel right. Brother, perhaps. His expression displayed no emotion, but his step seemed to harbor an impious energy that didn't respect funerals.

Behind the pair strolled a dysfunctional group; singletons in close proximity rather than a unified body welded by shared grief. Carol Amen and Sheldon Keenes. Three others, all men. And a fourth, already yards away from the train, a cop maybe, assigned to scout for clues among the mourners.

The man with the ponytail kept turning back to survey the group, appearing to keep his gaze on Carol longer than the others.

I approached. The small woman looked up at me. Her eyes were masked by a pair of enormous sunglasses.

"Who are you?" she said.

Miranda Carlson didn't look anything like I'd expected. She wasn't unattractive and had a firm intelligent mouth, but she was mousy: mousy face, mousy hair. And the baby mice weren't in tow.

I told her who I was.

"You saw it happen," she said flatly. How did she know? The police must have told her. She took a small handkerchief from her sleeve, but it wasn't to deal with tears. She wiped the front of her glasses, which were covered in a thin film of rain. The man with the ponytail took the glasses from her, finished the job, and handed them back. He never moved his eyes off me.

"Yes, I saw it happen. JJ asked me to come and see his new car," I said.

"Now why would he do that?" she asked. There was a twang in the voice that came from someplace a long way south of New York.

"I don't know," I said. Didn't *she* have the answer? My job had been to accompany JJ to meetings and draft his documents or share a few Jack Daniels with him in a bar or sit next to him at a ball game. She lived with the guy. She ought to have *some* idea of why he killed himself.

"You were his friend," she said, traces of emotion beginning to show through the funereal veneer.

"I didn't know him that well, Mrs. Carlson," I said gently. "He was a great person and I admired him enormously, but he didn't confide in me. I'm sorry."

"No one knows him anymore." She sounded scornful. "Two days ago he was a hero, people loved him, they all told me what a great guy he was, how they had a ball when he was around. How he gave to good causes, the scholarships he endowed, hospital bills he paid for strangers. Now no one knows him, no one will say they were his friend, and no one knows why he killed himself and fifteen others, leaving me and two kids wondering what in Christ's name went wrong."

"I'm very sorry," I mumbled.

She moved toward me and took off her glasses again. Her eyes were as dark as berries and their rims puffy with weeping. "You were an adviser, weren't you? His attorney? Well, Mr. Attorney, advise me, tell me what happened. I expect you pocketed enough dollars during his lifetime. Said you were his friend. Now you don't know a single goddamned thing and you crawl back to the sewer saying sorry."

She turned around and addressed the gathering. "The friends of the great JJ Carlson," she screamed. "Three attorneys and some deadbeat bankers. Did you come to help me and support me? You're no help or support unless you can tell me what happened." She buried her head in her hands and the ponytailed man closed around her. Was there the ghost of a smile on his face?

Suddenly she lifted her head and freed herself from the embrace, surveying us all with undisguised contempt. "None of you can tell me. I don't know what you're doing here." Her voice was quiet, featureless.

She turned to her chaperon and took his hand. "Let's go. I don't know any of these people."

The two of them walked away from us, and no one seemed willing to follow in their angry wake.

Sheldon emerged out of the following phalanx. "I wasn't expecting you," he said. He looked irritated, as if Miranda's outburst was my fault. "Have you finished getting your files straight for a handover?" he asked. I nodded, disgusted but unsurprised that he'd raised the question in this particular setting. "Good," he said. "Charles has arrived and he'll want to know it's been done." He paused. "By the way, we had already contacted Myers Myerling. Don't call them yourself. I'll let you know when we have the script, and *when* it comes, stick to it. Extempore efforts on your part will be unwelcome."

There was a rumble of thunder in the distance and Sheldon patted the small folding umbrella that stuck out of his jacket pocket. "Graveyards and thunder. How bloody fitting." He eyed Miranda Carlson disappearing into the mist. He seemed lost in thought. "Think about where you want to go on holiday," he said at last, and wandered off in the direction of the line of cars. The bastard hadn't even offered me a ride back.

The three bankers were talking with Carol and I heard one of them ask her if she wanted to share their car back to Wall Street. She told them that she'd be with them in a moment. She walked over to me.

"It was nice of you come," she said. She looked as emotionally wrecked as Miranda, but the small round dark glasses and the damp silken mass of hair made her exotic and mysterious. She wore a bracelet, an Eastern filigree of dull silver. A black skirt and blouse completed the effect, as if she was ready to film a rock video among the gravestones.

"JJ would have given you hell for being late," she said. I took this to be a funereal joke, but Carol didn't betray any signs of humor, her rich lips fixed in a sad droop. "You know how he was with people turning up late for meetings." JJ had been a hypocrite on that score; often he hadn't turned up for meetings at all.

"You got hurt," she said, looking up at Paula's bandage. I had forgotten my injury. The bandage would be looking like a flattened piece of gum by now.

"A splinter. It's okay."

Carol nodded. I didn't get the impression that she wanted any more details of my injury, such as it was.

"I'm sorry you got caught up in this," she said and started walking.

"I'm not sure what I'm caught up in, if anything. Do you have any idea why he did it?"

As she walked, Carol stared ahead of her. "I'm glad the kids aren't here," she said.

I muttered my agreement. The last funeral I'd attended had been my father's. But the memory was dim: I was on tranquilizers, my mother was on tranquilizers, and it was a bedraggled little band that had watched him lowered into the next world.

"He often said you were a very good attorney," Carol said.

The words my father never said to me.

Carol stepped off the turf and onto the road. She scraped damp shards of grass from her plain black flat shoes against the brick edge.

"He was a good banker," I said.

She just whispered, "Yes," and carried on walking, looking up at the soupy sky as a wave of thunder burbled over the cemetery.

"You want a ride?" she offered.

With Carol on her own, it was a no-brainer. Along with three Jefferson bankers . . .

I said no thanks.

"I think we're in for some heavy rain. You'll get soaked." Her concern touched me, surprised me even.

"I've got my cell phone and can call for an office account car," I said. "Thanks all the same." I didn't actually know if a car could be arranged to pick me up from this far out, but I would figure something out—I needed to test my resourcefulness, even in the smallest matters.

We reached the line of cars. A black stretch was waiting with its engine running and one of the bankers standing beside it, holding a door open. He asked whether Carol was coming or not, as they had to get back for a meeting and needed to leave right away.

The rain started to get heavy. "You sure you don't want a ride?" Carol asked. Inside I was hesitating, but my body language had already declined.

She looked up again at the gray sky. "Shitty weather. Maybe I'll go somewhere hot and dry." She turned to me. "The next deal may be in India. India's hot, isn't it?"

"But not necessarily dry," I said.

"You been there?" she asked.

I didn't answer. If I were looking for somewhere hot, it wouldn't be India. It wasn't on my map anymore.

She seemed uncertain about her next move. "See you soon," she said finally, and turned away.

As I dialed the car company, my shoes scuffed the asphalt in annoyance at my decision. A lazy voice on the end of the phone told me that the car would be with me in an impressive fifteen minutes.

I walked back into the Garden of Freedom. JJ had found his freedom, I supposed. What of the others buried here? I looked at the stone crosses, angels, and the intermittently grandiose memorabilia of death scattered across the vast expanse of cemetery. The inscriptions on the headstones could stay unread: much missed, much loved, blah, blah. The attraction for me was to experience the utter peace of thousands of corpses lying in their discrete plots quietly working on being dead. Not like the man screaming for help as he tried vainly to pull the door pillar of a Lincoln Towncar away from the neck of a woman who had already qualified for her slice of cemetery.

I trudged back toward the estate office—taking another route: around the Garden of Psalms, along Greenlawn Avenue. A train rattled slowly a few hundred yards away from me. From the parking area at the end of William H. Locke Drive, I made my way to the canopy at the entrance of the estate office.

Carol Amen stood in the porch. When she saw me she didn't move. Her lips just curved into a gentle smile.

"I hope you figured out how to get picked up," she said. "It's a long walk back to Tribeca."

# NINE

Carol's loft apartment wasn't new to me. But this time it was different. The studio set hadn't changed—old furniture, mostly American and thoughtfully coordinated with rugs and throws and plants. No chrome, no steel—just woods and bright materials and savvy knickknacks dotted around for the curious eye. A room at ease with its inhabitant. And very, very comfortable, everything designed to enfold you, draw you in. A giant cocoon of a room, just enough of the noise of a summer's evening in Tribeca filtering in, to confirm how hip the place was, but not so much as to interfere with its internal harmony. It was as if someone knew precisely where the volume control should be set.

But the script had changed. I felt that I was supposed to be here, not just a visitor like all the times before. No agenda and preset departure time. Maybe it was just the after effect of a rather quaffable Beringer Pinot Noir. Second glass, ready for a third. I reached over and filled up, replacing the bottle in the teak coaster on a huge coffee table made from an ancient door.

Carol came back into the room, carrying her glass, empty now.

She'd discarded her mourning wear and settled for blue drawstring shorts and a T-shirt. Shapeless and shapely all at once. And bare feet, no makeup on her anywhere, jewelry gone: no rings, no bangles, no wristwatch. Just her. Carol, soft and alluring.

She filled her glass and sat next to me. Near me. She slid her legs up onto the cushions of the ample couch and looked at me through a curtain of hair that had fallen across one side of her face. She swept the curtain aside and took a sip of wine. I noticed the blond down on her forearms, hairs as fine as spiderweb.

"Nice," she said.

I nodded. What was she thinking? Not about wine.

"You hungry?" She asked.

Not about food either. But the question came out so easily, naturally.

"Not really," I said.

"Me neither." She was watching me, slow blinks alternating with slow sips of wine. Blink, sip, blink, sip.

"I expect we don't want to talk about JJ or the funeral," I said.

"Damn right."

A pause. Blink, sip. The hum of the street. Carol leaned over to the table and picked up a remote control, pressed a button, and the sound of Stan Getz came over some speakers I couldn't see. I laughed.

"What's so funny?" She was laughing too.

"Well," I said, "and don't take this the wrong way. We come here, you slip into something more comfortable, pour out the wine, and put on the background music. It just made me think. I mean . . ." I paused. "I found it funny, that's all."

Carol replaced the remote on the table. "Do you like apple pie?"

I shook my head. "But don't let me stop you."

She clicked her tongue impatiently. "I didn't ask if you wanted any. I just asked if you liked it."

"Sure I like it."

"Apple pie's a cliché," she said. "You know: As American as apple pie. But it doesn't mean it isn't good, worth cooking, worth eating."

"Fair enough," I said. I had no idea where she was going with this.

"You like what I'm wearing, you like the wine, you like Stan Getz?" She gave me a look of mock terror. "Well, don't you?"

"Umm," I said slowly. "Yes. But what if I hadn't liked apple pie?"

"I'd have had to throw you out."

"I like it, I really like it." I smiled and touched her arm. It felt as good as it looked.

"When people need help they should send unambiguous signals. I learned that someplace."

I wanted to know where. I wanted to know everything. But supplemental questions were for lawyers and we weren't being lawyers right then.

"There's a line that sticks in my head," she said. "Something about not waving but drowning."

Another favorite of Ernie's. Jesus, I'd had more poetry in the last twenty-four hours than in the previous five years. I realized how little poetry there had been in my life.

"Stevie Smith," I said. I could recite the line; it had become a tad worn with use, but it was still good. "I was much further out than you thought and not waving but drowning."

Carol's face lit up and she tapped my nose with a finger. A light tap, but it felt like a magic wand. "That's the one," she said. "Ambiguous signal, you see. Look what happened. The guy drowned."

"And do you need rescuing?" I asked.

She looked deep into her wine, nursing the glass with both hands. "Maybe not rescuing," she said at last. "Maybe just . . . whatever it is, I looked at you today and I figured you could use the same kind of thing. We've known each other a long time and, well, I just. . . . Tell me if I'm wrong. You standing in the rain, with a widow screaming at you. I knew you would understand what I was talking about."

She was right.

"When Miranda Carlson let me have it," I said, pausing to think, "I knew it wasn't her fault, but she put me in the searchlight and it hurt."

Both our wineglasses were on the table, so there was no need for awkward movements, no minutely rehearsed choreography, no complex hand/eye coordination. I just leaned over and kissed her on the lips. I sensed a sigh, a release from the pressure of waiting, the devil of a day fading in the rhythm of a heartbeat. We held each other tightly, unmoving.

I still had my suit on. I hadn't even taken my jacket off. I sat up and Carol removed it, folding it neatly, smoothing out the lapels, aligning the sleeves. She seemed as if she were going to lay it carefully over the back of the couch, but then she threw it across the room.

She had the rest of my clothes off me in moments and I lay back naked with her sitting on top of me, still dressed.

She shed her T-shirt and bent her head over my face and Eskimo-kissed me. "Maybe it's time for outside counsel to become inside counsel." She smiled.

"I haven't washed," I said. "There's the rain and heat, you know . . . I could take a shower, for the greater comfort of my client."

She nuzzled herself into my chest, nibbling my meager hairs and encircling a nipple with her teeth. "No need. You're fine."

I drew her to me and our mouths met like old friends while the rest of our bodies writhed with a burning need to get on with it.

She sat up. And then stood up. Over me. With swift and perfectly poised movements she removed her shorts, revealing nothing further to unpeel. She slowly began to lower herself on me. I wanted to watch all of her at once: her face, her breasts, her hands, the divine sand-colored delta, the curve of her hips. And the eyes: pupils wide, the chestnut brown interior, a concert of darkness and light. I raised my arms and held Carol's head, combed her hair with my fingers, explored her face. Traced the lines of her ribcage. Her breasts. There would be no ambiguity here.

I awoke from a deep sleep. I was in a bed. Carol's bed, I remembered. It seemed to be moving ever so slightly. I turned my head. Carol was sitting upright against her pillow, knees drawn up, the sheet held tightly against her neck. Hugging her knees, she was rocking gently and from the streetlight sneaking through a gap in the curtains, I could see her face, raw and wet with tears. She was staring ahead.

I hoisted myself onto an elbow. "What's the matter?"

She didn't look at me. "I didn't want to wake you."

I sat up and took her in my arms, burying my face in her thick cushion of hair, feeling her softness, the tremble of her body.

She sobbed.

"The TV. Horrible."

JJ, she was talking about JJ. Had she, like me, foolishly kept the light off as she'd watched the horror played out over and over on every channel the previous night?

"I know. I know," I said. The images had been so graphic. In the end, I'd switched off, ashamed to have witnessed it live, in the light of day.

"It was so . . ." She couldn't find the word and broke down again.

Suddenly she pulled away from me and wiped her face with the sheet, letting it drop, leaving her top half naked, exposed. Her vulnerability was both tragic and erotic.

"There was graffiti," she said.

I hadn't noticed. "Where?"

"On the wall along the FDR. It was on the news. It said 'shit happens.' "

I didn't know what to say.

She eased herself back into my arms. "It was written in those fat dumpy letters, you know: graffiti letters. The *e* in *happens* had been made into a smiley face, a little tongue hanging out of it. Disgusting."

I held her tight.

"I'd been in a meeting with him just the day before. He was chewing me out, chewing everyone out. He wanted to get some documents to a client. It was all he seemed to care about. That and a visit to . . ."

She tensed. "I was somewhere once. A good place, but it was a bad place too, if you know what I mean."

I had no idea what she meant.

"Was that where you learned how to give unambiguous signals?" I asked.

It was as if she hadn't heard me.

"I don't want to go back."

"Then don't," I said.

Her legs unbent, I heard them slide against the sheet.

I felt her teeth on my neck, then biting into my shoulder. Her fingers were gripping me; nails like talons. She pulled me on top of her, grinding her pelvis against mine, legs scissoring me. The nails again, this time digging deep into my buttocks.

Her eyes were wild.

"Make love to me." Her voice was breathless. She moaned. "Fuck me. Fuck the carnage out of my head. I want to feel you in me, fucking me. That's all I want to feel."

# TEN

It was 6:00 A.M. I was back in my apartment. My body was un-showered but I felt cleansed. An hour before, Carol's warm body had bathed me, anointed me for the day ahead.

On returning, I'd been ready to find that twenty-four hours had conjured a makeover on my home: white sheets drawn over the furniture, spiderwebs hanging from the light fixtures and curtains. I expected my footsteps to disturb a layer of dust.

Wandering into my compact kitchen, I pulled an iced tea from the refrigerator. I stripped off and wrapped myself in a towel that had been left hanging damply over the back of a kitchen chair. I padded across the living/dining room and slumped into a big overstuffed chair, a chair I'd picked up in my first days in New York and to which I had become thoroughly attached.

I liked my apartment. It wasn't impressive or even homey, but the walls were solid and neighbors could play Eminem at top volume or screw with bacchanalian abandon and I'd never hear them. And there was plenty of space, more than enough for my few possessions: the computer, the random furniture, the stacks of books, a few framed photos, CDs and videos, and a rather tired yucca plant. Visitors would have had difficulty deducing my personality from my living quarters. Not like Carol's place: Her fixtures and fittings spoke of someone who cared about her surroundings, who matched and selected things rather than simply stuffing a credit card in her bag and sauntering around midtown until she'd assembled an ill-matched ensemble of household items.

Grand Central Station hung over me. A huge photograph, sepia, grainy. Great shafts of light aimed down from high windows to form discrete pools on the floor of the main hall. It was like a cathedral, where the worshipers were constantly on the move rather than nailed to their pews. Some were caught in the spotlight, while others lurked in the shadows, waiting to be exposed.

Carol, naked, walked across the marbled floor. Beneath her luxuriant crown of hair, her eyes danced and she was laughing. She was coming toward me.

In her hand she held a dog leash, nothing attached to it, dangling, redundant.

Carol opened her mouth slowly. Would she say something? Would she scream? But she uttered a buzz, electric and insistent, inhuman.

The buzzing filled my head. But my eyes were open now.

Alongside the buzzing from my front door I could hear the rain beating hard against the windows.

If I had been more awake, I'd have noticed that the bell to the apartment itself had buzzed and not the intercom. It was the concierge who usually announced guests. But I was still fuzzy, still gripped by sleep. I loped along the hall, didn't bother to look through the spy hole, and was able to open the door wide as I had forgotten to attach the chain.

It was the detective I'd spoken to in the precinct the day before. He was accompanied by a uniformed officer and neither looked very friendly. They were also soaking wet.

"Detective Minelli," I said, trying to sound welcoming.

"Manelli," he said crossly.

He asked me if he could come in as he and his partner barged past. I overlooked their presumptuousness and led them into the living/dining room, switching on lights as I went.

"Do sit down," I said.

They sat down together on the overstuffed couch that in a prestained age had matched my overstuffed chair.

"What can I do for you?" I asked. "It's a little early for trauma counseling." I looked at my watch. It was, in fact, just after ten.

"Yeah, right." Manelli toyed with his attaché case. I offered them a cold drink. They ignored me.

"You and Mr. Carlson both shared an interest in cars," Manelli said.

I laughed.

"What's so funny?"

Lawyer's instinct told me not to laugh; the same instinct acted like smelling salts under my nose. I was awake. Alert. At work.

"Well, it's true that we talked a bit about cars. But he had a passion he could indulge: Ferraris, Porsches, you know the kind of thing." Manelli looked disdainful. Rich kid toys. "I don't own a car in New York," I continued, "and the cars I've driven in England wouldn't have excited JJ very much. That's why I laughed."

"What did you think of the car he wrecked?"

JJ had committed an act of sacrilege. There was the story of the English judge who'd added an extra year on to the sentence of an armed robber because he had sawn off the barrels from a set of Purdey shotguns. I was certain that a New York judge who knew anything about cars would have done the same to JJ.

"The McLaren F1," I said. "Everyone has their own opinion about cars, as with wine or paintings, but in my view it is the ultimate. It will be a long time before someone comes up with something better."

"Why don't you tell us about the car, sir."

"I've told you. A great car. I'm not an expert; in fact I'd never seen one up close before. JJ had just bought it and he called me to show it off. At least that's what I thought. Obviously he had another objective. That's it, that's all I know."

Both of them shuffled and exchanged a knowing look. "Cut the bullshit," said the uniformed cop.

"What do you mean? Everything I've told you is true," I insisted. "I have nothing to hide. I let you into my apartment voluntarily and you turn aggressive. Why? And I don't like to be told to cut the bullshit when there isn't any to cut. Ask your questions, say your piece, then leave me alone."

"You left it a long time before coming to speak with us," said Manelli.

"I've explained why. You seemed to understand when I came down to the precinct."

"Is that your injury?" asked Manelli, pointing at the small scab on my forehead. I nodded. Manelli leaned over and peered at it. "Don't look too serious to me," he said.

I told him I agreed, but it was the shock that had delayed me, not the splinter in my forehead. Manelli's partner sniggered.

They'd come with an agenda, but they wanted to toy with me first. Why?

"What about narcotics, Mr. Border?" said Manelli. "Was that another interest you shared with JJ Carlson?"

Apart from four or five joints at college, I was on safe ground. "I don't know what you're talking about."

"Come on." He zapped the wavelength of the confidante, the crony. Go on, you can tell us, a few joints, a snort in the bathroom, we understand, it isn't a big deal, we know all about Wall Street.

My receiver wasn't set to that frequency. "No. Never."

"Carlson used cocaine," he continued, no longer the confidante, now the interrogator. "A great deal, spent more on it in a week than I earn in a year. At least that's what the pathologist reckons. He reckons he was stoned out of his skull when he died. What do you reckon, Mr. Border?"

Maybe JJ *had* been a little trippy. I remembered the mad grin, the eyes. But I'd just put all that down to the thrill of speed and scaring the shit out of me. Anyway, he was always rushing around, from place to place, idea to idea. Coke? Quite possible. On our Jack evenings he'd go to the bathroom a few times, but so did I. It was possible he was going for a refill while all I was doing was having a piss or, on one or two embarrassing occasions, a rib-splitting vomit.

"I can't say whether he used the stuff," I said. "I never saw him, but I couldn't rule it out."

Manelli gave me a sideways glance and slight smile to show that he didn't believe me.

"So, nothing to say about Mr. Carlson's drug use, nothing to say about the car. And yet you were his friend. I just don't know what to think." He gave me a helpless look.

"I've told you what I know," I said.

Manelli opened the attaché case and took out some papers. "Take a look at these." He handed me half an inch of paperwork.

Their agenda on the table at last.

They were vehicle registration documents for a McLaren F1. They were very recent and, more important, they had my name on them. According to these papers I was the owner of a million-dollar car.

"What the fuck," I said involuntarily.

"Like to tell us more?" said Manelli's partner.

"It isn't true," I said. "I didn't own that car. I've never owned a car in New York. I've already told you. I don't understand it."

"Where would you get the kind of money to buy a car like that?"

"I couldn't, I mean I didn't. The question's academic. I didn't own the car so I didn't need the money."

"That paper says you did."

"The paper's wrong. It's a mistake."

"Pretty big mistake, I'd say."

"JJ must've arranged it, something like that."

"You're kidding me, right? Your buddy buys a fancy car, registers it in your name, and takes a dive onto the FDR."

"I told you, I simply don't have that kind of money. I would never be able to buy that car."

"These guys think you have the money," said Manelli.

I found my hand accepting another piece of paper. It was a letter from a company called Delaware Loan. It looked like a very respectable company, apparently established in 1978 and specializing in prestige car finance. The letter was addressed to me at the apartment and it went on to congratulate me on becoming a valued customer of the company and confirmed that they had wired nine hundred and fifty thousand dollars to the account of a car dealer in Boston.

My thoughts ground to a halt. "This is addressed to me," I managed.

Manelli sighed like a weary teacher. "You're quick."

"I've never seen it. It isn't real. Where did you get it?"

"The tooth fairy."

I looked at the letter again. It referred to a schedule attached, which outlined the repayment timetable. Apparently I had signed a loan agreement two days earlier.

The schedule was missing. A part of me was intrigued to know what a nine-hundred-and-fifty-thousand-dollar unsecured loan would cost to service every month. I felt as if I was tied to the tracks, trying to make out the insignia on the front of an oncoming train.

"This has nothing to do with me," I said indignantly. "I have never signed a loan agreement. I've never even heard of Delaware Loan and I doubt that they would ever lend me such a large sum of money. This is all a breathtaking fabrication." I threw the letter back at them.

"You had the fifty-thousand-dollars down payment."

I had about sixty thousand dollars in my Chase Manhattan savings account and my stomach crawled as I was handed another piece of paper. It was the statement from a bank account. My bank account. Giving it a reluctant, sideways glance, I caught the solitary occupant of the debits column. Fifty thousand dollars. In the margin it said the entry related to a wire transfer.

I had been robbed. Somebody had made a down payment on my destruction—with my money.

"It must have been JJ," I whispered.

"Now why would he do that to his good buddy, do you suppose?" sneered Manelli. "You had a fight, maybe. You were screwing his wife, maybe. You'd spilt beer on one of his suits. You'd called him a faggot. You forgot his birthday."

"I don't know." I wished they would stop using the word *buddy*. It had lost all meaning and its consonants drilled into my head.

"You don't know because it's fucking horseshit. It was your car and your loan. It was him driving, we know that, and he took aim at the FDR quite deliberately. We don't know why, but we reckon you do. You could be looking at a charge sheet that runs into several pages."

A charge sheet saying what? Owning a car, borrowing money? But I didn't own the car, hadn't borrowed the money.

"Did you take out insurance on the car?" Manelli asked.

"Why would I insure a car that I don't own?"

"Wiseguy. There's fifteen dead and a lot more injured. There's going to be plenty of people fishing for plenty of money."

"My money's gone, Manelli," I said. "And I don't think that fifty thousand would have done much good, anyway. The fishhooks will be dangling over Lake Carlson, not my wretched pond."

"You're the attorney, Border." Manelli said. "But I reckon before long there'll be a hundred of your kind taking a long, hard look at this pool of shit."

He was right; the rods would be primed for a legal fishing frenzy.

"Am I under arrest?" I asked.

"No, but I wouldn't bet on that state of affairs lasting, and anyway, we have a few more questions for you."

"I have to get to work now," I said, standing up. "Please leave. You know where I am if you need me. I won't be running anywhere."

"So you still maintain that the car wasn't yours?" He affected incredulity at my brazen denial in the face of his bits of paper.

"I will say it again, in case I wasn't clear the first time around. That wasn't, isn't, my car." I indicated that I wanted them off my couch and out of my apartment.

"We will find out what happened, with or without your help, and then we'll nail you," said Manelli.

"I hope you do find out what happened," I said. "Because I've already been nailed. I've been robbed of fifty thousand dollars. That fact seems to have become obscured in this conversation."

"Sure, Mr. Border," said Manelli. "We'll get a twenty-man team on it right away." He and his companion walked to the door. I watched them stride down the hallway toward the elevator. I could hear the uniformed cop's handcuffs, holster, and club squeak and clack as he went.

I realized that more than just my client list was hanging by a thread now. Everything was at stake.

Shuffling back into the living room, I pulled up the window blinds. The rain swept past in gusts. Four floors below, I could see a police car, presumably Manelli's, parked a little ways down along the sidewalk. Fifty yards the other way was another car, an anonymous sedan. A man leaned against it, seemingly oblivious to the rain swirling around him. He was bald, the rain battering his smooth wet pate. If he was a cop, he was plainclothes: A gray sodden suit hung loosely from his stick-insect body.

Was it my imagination? He seemed to look up at me.

Suddenly, he pushed himself out of his slouch against the car, opened the door, and drove off at high speed. A moment later, Manelli and his partner came out and got in their car and cruised away in the other direction.

# ELEVEN

**T**hink. I needed to think. Space for thinking: my apartment. Silence for thinking? No. A sounding board. Carol? Not yet. Ernie Monks? Nobody from the office; there'd be enough buzzing from them soon enough. Who then?

The message light winked on the phone. My finger hovered over the "play" button.

"I've called three times now and you haven't given me the courtesy of a . . ." Mother. Talk about timing.

I was her joy, I was her sorrow. I was her lifeboat when the ship that was my father went down. I was her despair when I deserted her for New York. I was the empty chair at the dining table of her Cotswold cottage. I was the treacherous gap. I'd be back, I'd told her. Later. A traitor's later.

I hit "delete" and stroked the bump that would speed dial me to the center of the Cotswolds. It would be 4:00 P.M. there: teatime, in the garden if it was fine, our dog Chuff standing sentinel over a Victoria Sponge cake, certain of the wedge that would be his reward.

The familiar English tone rang about ten times and I was near to giving up—of course she didn't have an answering machine—when there was a click and the sound of someone out of breath.

"Mrs. Elaine Border speaking."

"Hi, it's me," I said.

There were a few more wheezy breaths.

"Findlay? I'm sorry I took so long to come to the phone, but I was in the garden and one of those infernal jets whizzed overhead as the telephone rang. They should come up with silencers for those things."

"What time is it there?" she asked.

"Eleven," I said.

"Morning or evening?" She could never work it out.

"Elevenses eleven."

She laughed.

"There's something I want to talk to you about," I said.

"You're coming home. A New England lass in tow. A summer wedding. How marvelous." Her laughter was brittle, suggesting she already knew there was bad news on the way. She'd had more than her fair share of bad news, my mother.

"A friend of mine killed himself, and fifteen others, in a car that the police now say I owned."

Silence.

"Are you there?" I asked.

"Yes, Findlay." Her voice was empty; she was listening to the impact of a rocket launched into her otherwise tranquil rural idyll.

"There was something in the *Telegraph* about an accident in New York," she managed.

"If it looked serious then that would be the one," I said. "It was in all the papers and all over the TV here." A small window on the carnage would have opened into her Cotswold retreat, as unreal as famine in Africa or a plane crash in central China.

"My God. I don't know what to say."

"Nor do I. And Charles Mendip will be in the office by now, expecting me to say something."

"Surely Charles won't believe it was your car. He'll see them off." Gallant Charles, champion of the mop-up and cover-up, smoothing over the barbed and dangerous bones of my father. Wrapping his capacious arms around the sorry remnants of the Borders.

"Yesterday," I said, "Charles sanctioned the rape of my client base. He pulled me off the merger too." My mother didn't really understand the merger, but I knew that she had been indiscreet enough to boast of my pivotal role in it.

"*Charles did that?*" The voice of outrage that my mother was so practiced at. That's why I'd called her. It was good to hear unfeigned, unalloyed indignation at my predicament.

"His mouthpiece was Sheldon Keenes," I said. I could hear the audience hiss at the villain.

She was playing her role to perfection.

"You don't believe that Charles would really do that?" she asked at last.

"I don't want to believe it, Mum."

"Have you been charged with anything?" she asked.

"No." But that wasn't the point—wind the tape forward and the position would be different. Failing to have insurance? Allowing a cokehead in the cockpit? Leaving the scene? Could any of that be extrapolated into manslaughter, murder even? My knowledge of US law was pretty much confined to the securities industries.

"I will be charged with something," I said. "I can count on it. I need a good attorney right away."

"Can I send you some money?" Bless her. She'd have in mind the sort of sum to draft a basic will. She never believed my father when he told her his hourly rate. She'd throw her head back, waves of brown hair shaking with her laughter. Her naïveté was enchanting, and my father rarely disabused even the most improbable of her assumptions.

But she wasn't stupid or weak. She had merely wanted to believe the best of everyone. Five years earlier her worldview had undergone the severest of tests, and her neck was now unbending, the hair no longer brown. Nevertheless an ember of optimism still glowed feebly, deep inside her.

"Clay & Westminster will have to pay." The certainty in my voice was counterfeit. "I'll choose the firm. They'll pay."

"Are you sure?" She'd detected the bravura; she was testing it.

"No." But that had to be the objective: Get bankrolled, keep control—normally mutually exclusive aims.

"Why do they think you own the car?"

"Registration documents in my name. A loan too. Good forgeries by the looks of it. Christ knows how he did it."

"But . . ." She was struggling with the monstrous injustice done to her child; there had to be a mistake. "They have tests, don't they? Chemicals, people who can detect forgeries, that kind of thing. I've read about it. Surely, in America . . ."

"Time, Mother," I interrupted. "My career could be reduced to rubble before they unravel what JJ has done. I could be up to my neck in litigation, bankrupted, unemployable."

"That's rather gloomy, isn't it?"

That's right, Mum. Optimism. Fan those flames. However unrealistic, fan them. Just like you did before. It kept us going until the truth was an undeniable rash that covered our whole bodies, but by then I'd hardened myself. Against my father, against the world. And now the intervening five years had made me complacent, blunted my edge. I needed to reclaim that edge.

"You could come home," my mother said.

"I don't think so, Mum." For the second time in as many days the thought of going back to England wasn't repugnant to me. Pubs, the BBC, Wimbledon. Rose-tinted stuff. But the smell would cross the Atlantic with me, cling to my clothes. The Law Society would smell it and strike me off.

"I think the only place to sort this out is in New York," I said. "If I came back I would be damaged goods."

"Do you have any friends there?" she asked. "In New York, I mean. The sort of person you could confide in and depend on? I know so little of your life, your circle, your interests outside work."

What could I say? I had just slept with a friend, her fragrance still clung to me—but I didn't know what it really meant, its significance or otherwise hadn't had time to form a meaningful shape.

The rest of my friends were just points of acquaintance; they hardly formed a circle. In my quest for partnership I had foregone a life and now it looked like the partnership was shot to hell too.

"I have a few friends," I said. "It remains to be seen how fair-weather they turn out to be."

"I think you're very alone, and I think you should come home."

"I need to stay here." Here was the only place I could be innocent; everywhere else I was guilty, condemned by my flight.

My mother was quiet for a while. "You could tell me, you know," she said gently.

"Tell you what?"

"Tell me that you *did* buy that car. In a fit of madness or something. You could tell me and I would bite my tongue. It would have been an act of supreme folly and even sillier to let your friend have a go at the wheel. But I wouldn't say so. Well, not in so many words."

"I didn't buy the car, still less let JJ drive it. I was in the wrong place at the wrong time."

"And you're still in the wrong place." Beside her in the garden, turning compost or deadheading rose bushes, would be the only right place as far as she was concerned.

"Mum, please."

"I'm sorry," she whispered. "I should be glad, I suppose, that you rang me and told me."

"Of course I'd tell you. I may take my time, but I tell you everything." Except for one thing. If she knew *that* about my father, it would kill her.

"Do you want me to speak to Charles Mendip?" she said. "Your father always said he respected me."

"No Mum," I said gently. "I just wanted you to know what was happening, not hear it from another source. I won't say don't worry, that would be dumb, but I don't want you to get in a state." Like before, Mum. Don't visit that place again.

"I haven't taken those little pills for three years now," she said. I sensed the swell of pride, tinged by a fear of relapse.

"Don't start again, for Christ's sake." Those little pills were cannon balls; artillery that didn't discriminate which brain cells were obliterated.

"Fin." Cracks were showing in the voice. "I won't be a passive onlooker at another catastrophe in our much reduced family. I *need* to help if I can."

"You weren't passive last time, Mum."

"I wasn't in my right mind then."

Sometimes one needed to be in the wrong mind to do the right thing. Another of Ernie's epigrams.

"We don't have to sit back and take this, you know," she said, it was her umbrella-wielding voice, the one she used for obdurate official-dom. "We don't deserve this. I'm sure it will be all right."

That's why I called you, Mum. To hear just that: emphatic, heart-felt, but utterly irrational optimism.

## TWELVE

No e-mails to speak of," Paula declared, as I bounced into my office at around noon. The bounce was a manifestation of the irrational optimism that I would need to get through the day.

It was a dead cat bounce.

"Keenes took most of the mail," Paula continued. "He left a few flyers for seminars and courses, said you might like to choose a few, highlighted the ones he was speaking at. Keep your hand in, he said. That some Brit expression? Anyway, I didn't tell him to stick them up his ass, but I think he got the message. A new messenger came by and took your files. His name's Kevin, a real dweeb. You got no meetings, no conference calls. Charles Mendip's in town. His secretary told me he would be seeing you later, but didn't give a time. His *London* secretary, for Christ's sake. The nerve. A guy called Myers from Myers Myerling called to say that he *didn't* need to speak to you and that he'd be sending draft statements direct to Keenes and Mendip. So, I guess that means that you can join me for solitaire on the PC for the rest of the day. Peachy. I hope you're not feeling sorry for yourself, counselor. You know how I feel about that kind of thing."

"And a good morning to you, Paula."

She covered her eyes with one hand and handed me a FedEx package with the other. "And this just came for you. It must be your citation for a Congressional Medal."

I studied the shipping docket. The sender was a firm of attorneys, large and Washington-based.

Inside the plastic sheath was a paper envelope with my name and office address on it. And inside that was a single-page letter. It didn't take me long to catch its drift. Sandy Richter, partner of Marshall, Forrester, Kellerman, and Hirsch, said he acted for an insurance company that had written an umbrella insurance policy for JJ. To the extent that victims of JJ tried to claim against the policy, they would deny liability, but should they ever be ordered to pay anything, they would look to me for reimbursement. I was on notice. As far as they were concerned, I should never have allowed JJ behind the wheel of my McLaren F1, and I was liable for the whole damn thing.

He also said that he had received a call from my insurer.

My insurer? I didn't have insurance, except a few thousands' worth for the contents of the apartment and some incomprehensible health policy.

But apparently I was insured, according to Sandy Richter; a policy underwritten at Lloyds of London through a company called Clerkenwell Associates. Richter left me with the strong impression that I'd better pray my insurance was significant, and copper-bottomed. I'd be needing it.

He wanted a response within seven days outlining my view on life at a granular level.

"Not good?" Paula ventured.

I shook my head.

She perched on my desk. "I'm sorry if I seemed flip about this stuff, but my mom always said that you had to show adversity your teeth, with the corners of your mouth turned up."

"Can you get me the number for a Clerkenwell Associates in London, please," I said, trying to take her mom's advice.

"Sure. I'll bring you a coffee too."

I scanned my desk. "Where's my crossword?"

Paula toyed with the silver crucifix that hung in the shadows of her cleavage. "Jessica said she didn't have time to send it anymore."

One lousy page with my name scribbled on it. My Red Cross parcel. It wasn't the betrayal of Jessica; a dozen different people had sent me the crossword over the years. It was Clay & Westminster—the institution as a whole—that was closing me down. The tubes were sliding out, the respirator was being turned off.

I put in a call to Carol, conjuring the image of her, airbrushing out the dog leash.

Voicemail. Some routines didn't change. I left a message for her to get back to me.

I called Chase Manhattan.

"It's Fin Border here. May I speak with Karen Bardak, please?" My account relationship manager. Sixty thousand dollars hadn't rated much of a relationship. Ten thousand probably wouldn't even qualify me for a Chase Christmas card.

"Mr. Border, and how are we today?"

I didn't tell her.

Instead, I explained how fifty thousand had disappeared from my account and it wasn't me that had taken it. I tried to remain succinct and even-toned. I'd give Ms. Bardak a chance to tell me it was all a terrible mistake; the fifty thousand was still there, tucked up safe.

Then maybe I'd scream.

There was no mistake. The money was gone and Manelli had already spoken with her. She'd said nothing, preserved my confidentiality, but they'd looked into the background paperwork in the meantime. It checked out. I had come into the bank in person and signed an instruction. The signature looked good.

"It wasn't me that signed the form," I insisted. "What's the date on it?"

"The twelfth."

Wednesday. I did go to the bank on Wednesday. Some bills to pay. Forms? One or two. But not a transfer instruction for fifty thousand fucking dollars.

"I want that money back in my account pronto," I said. "Or else it's with the police, the regulators, and my attorneys."

Calm flowed down the line; Ms. Bardak wasn't easily spooked. "Sir, like I said, it's already with the police. As for the regulators, our compliance people will handle that—we'll write to you today outlining your rights. Maybe it would help if you gave me the name of your attorneys so I can pass it on to legal for you."

I didn't have an attorney. So little had happened outside work for five years, there'd been no call for one. No divorce, no house, nobody had sued me.

It looked as if I was about to make up for lost time.

"I'll get back to you with a name."

"Sure," Ms. Bardak said amiably. "I don't think I can help you further right now on the withdrawal; it's kind of out of my hands. But is there anything else we can do for you today?"

Paula poked her head around the door and crooked her index finger in a signal for me to end the call.

"No thanks," I said to the phone. "You've done quite enough."

"Mendip wants you," Paula said. "Now."

Charles Mendip sat behind a small desk in a cubicle near reception. He always said that he didn't want his New York visits to disrupt the smooth routine of the office by commandeering something more in keeping with his status of senior partner. As long as there was a phone and the coffee was good, he'd be fine.

He looked like he always did: creased, off-the-rack suit, grubby shirt sleeves, indifferent shoes, neither shiny nor dirty. But the face was alert, like a whippet. It was the face of someone accustomed to being in charge, unless he happened to be standing next to Jim McIntyre.

Mendip had a habit of flicking his index finger across his cheek and I could hear it rasp as he said good morning to me.

I squeezed myself onto the only other chair in the room. If I'd been Ernie, my stomach and chins would have smothered the desk.

There were no windows, no pictures. So my only view was of Mendip's face. It seemed to ripple with anxiety.

"Good flight?" I asked.

"They ran out of cornflakes." He toyed with a thin brown folder on the desk. A dossier on me and JJ? If it had been compiled by Keenes, the spin would be so severe Mendip would have to hold it down.

Mendip's piercing gray eyes narrowed. "It doesn't make very happy reading."

"I've also received this." I handed him the letter from Marshall, Forrester.

Charles glanced at it for a second and slowly handed it back. "Seen it," he said wearily. "Mr. Richter sent us a blind copy, no doubt to raise the chilling prospect of their claiming at some point that you were in the course of your employment with Clay & Westminster when you let Mr. Carlson spread himself across the FDR Drive— thereby rendering this firm liable for your stupidity. Bad law in all probability, but a good tactic nonetheless."

Charles riffled through the pages of the folder as if he was looking for a hint of good news among the bad.

"Have you completed the list of your work in progress for Sheldon?"

I wondered if Ernie had managed to speak to Charles and to plead on my behalf for getting some of my clients back. "Pretty much," I said.

"Well done," Charles said. If Ernie *had* spoken to him, it had obviously made no difference.

"Do I have to come off the merger as well?"

Charles seemed to be studying the blank cover of the folder and then lifted a single hair that had settled on it. He turned it between his thumb and forefinger before letting it spiral to the floor. It was as if the rogue strand were the source of all the trouble, the hair in the soup, the fly in the ointment. "I fear so," he said. "I have to be realistic." He looked up at me. "So do you. This unholy mess has kicked you firmly in touch for the foreseeable future."

He looked so sad, sapped of energy. Neither angry nor supportive, just preoccupied with the weight of being senior partner, the merger, Keenes baying for blood. And me. But did I weigh him down in my capacity as godson or as a troublesome employee?

"I need a defense, Charles, a good attorney, this isn't my field. I was thinking of maybe using . . ."

He held up his hand to silence me, the hint of a sympathetic smile bending his lips ever so slightly.

"We have already chosen your attorney," he said. "Pablo Tochera of Schuster Mannheim. He's very good and Jim McIntyre trusts his judgment completely."

"Don't I get a say in the matter?"

Charles squinted, as if he was having trouble focusing on me from a distance of two feet. "Jim is very concerned by what's happened. It's important that the situation is managed by a strong team and one led by an attorney who knows what he's doing. Schusters is the best—that's why we're merging with them."

"That's not what I asked, Charles."

"I had expected you to be more grown-up about this, Fin and realize that we all have the same objective. If you want to pay for your own attorney, then I can't stop you. I would speculate that your assets would cover about twenty billable hours. In other words a statistically insignificant fraction of what this matter will involve."

He had allowed my mother to choose the Cotswold cottage, which decorators to use, the kind of annuity she'd receive. Clay & Westminster had even let her pick, and had paid for, the basset hound she so desperately wanted to replace the husband, my father, who had left her—us—nothing. My mother was a grace and favor widow of Clay & Westminster. But at least she'd been given swatches of the shackles to select from.

"With respect, Charles, that's rather unethical. I should have a say."

Flicking his chin with one hand, he motioned to the folder on the desk with the palm of his other, as if he was cleaning a spill. "And you're going to report me to the Law Society, the New York Bar Association. For heavens sake, Fin, I'm trying to help. In any event, are you anticipating that your interests and those of Clay & Westminster may diverge at some point, that there may be a conflict? If so, you'd better spit it out now."

"I didn't own the car, Charles."

Charles grunted.

"Can't you bring yourself to say that you believe me?" I asked.

"What I believe is neither here nor there." He picked up the folder and dropped it back down onto the desk. "What matters is that we sort out this unholy mess—quickly. I have a merger to consummate and the futures of fifteen hundred staff to worry about." He lifted the folder again and I thought for a moment he was going to ding me with it. "My God. Your father came near enough to destroying the reputation of this firm. What is it about your family? Brilliant but . . ."

More chin flicks. "There is only one way you will scramble from this wreckage alive and that is to do exactly as you're told. Myers Myerling are confident they can keep your name out of the press for a few days. But it won't be for long and, in the meantime, Pablo Tochera will be working on your case. You must follow his instructions to the letter, do I make myself clear? I need hardly spell out the consequences for us all if Jim McIntyre takes the view that you aren't taking your medicine. This is about trust, Fin."

"Medicine?" I stammered. "I don't . . ."

Paula opened the door. Mendip seemed relieved.

"Sorry to disturb you," she said. "But Mr. Keenes was wondering when you would be through."

Keenes had sent Paula, so that his own secretary wouldn't get flattened if Charles got mad at the intrusion.

But Charles's face opened out; he stood up, smiling. "Hello, Paula," He shook her hand across the desk. This was the charming Charles.

"And how are you and that lucky husband of yours?"

Charles could be good at paying top market wages, he could be compassionate about sick leave and the like, but when it came to caring small talk with junior staff he usually got into a mess. He usually left that kind of thing to Ernie Monks.

Ernie would have remembered that Paula's husband was dead.

Paula's face froze. She glowered at me like it was my fault.

"I'll let Fin fill you in on what's been happening in my life before the next time we meet. He seems to know zilch too, but it might help you get some of your facts straight."

She left the room, slamming the door.

"Dear me," Charles said.

"Paula's husband, Doug, died of cancer six months ago."

"I see." He paused. "I'd better run along now."

"Paula's desk is outside my office in the open area."

Charles looked at me quizzically. "Don't be stupid," he said. "I'm not going after *her*. I'm going to see Sheldon. I won't be long. Stay here until I'm back, please. We can carry on with our little chat."

He edged his way around me and left the room.

I called Paula on the phone.

"Sorry about that," I said.

"Whatever," she said flatly. "I'm one of the little people, I know that."

"So am I, Paula."

"That's why I like you, honey."

"Can you call Pablo Tochera at Schuster and schedule a meeting with him for as soon as possible, preferably this afternoon?"

"Is this about the merger? I thought you were off the case."

"Thanks, Paula. No, it's not about the merger. My de-merger, more like. Is there anything you don't know about me?"

"No," she said and hung up.

I tore a sheet of paper from the virgin writing pad on the desk.

I drew a small circle and wrote *me* in it. My pen doodled around the circle for a moment, awarding it a corona. I screwed up the sheet and pushed it to one side, tearing off a fresh one.

First heading: "Potential Defendants." Second heading: "Potential Plaintiffs."

Under "Defendants": Me.

And my defense? Not my car.

Then JJ. His defense? None.

His insurers next—I didn't understand umbrella insurance. One for Mr. Tochera.

My insurers, Clerkenwell Associates. *Where was Paula with that phone number?* Their defense was easy. They hadn't really insured me.

Any others? Clay & Westminster might get a place in the pleadings. If it were argued that I was in the course of my employment when I met with JJ. So, if the argument held water, then their defense would stand or fall with mine. Wait. Clay & Westminster would have insurers. Add them to the list. Wait again. If it was claimed that I was in the course of employment when I met JJ, they might say the same for JJ.

I added Jefferson Trust. And their insurers.

It was getting to be quite a list.

What about the manufacturers of the car? McLaren. Some wiseguy might say there was a defect with the car; that it shouldn't have done what it did. Crazy. The car was perfection. The argument would never get off the ground, even in the zero-gravity environment of US litigation.

Over to the other side of the page. "Plaintiffs."

The victims, the estates of the deceased, the families. That was it, wasn't it? No. The City, bent municipal property, the cleanup. Hey, shouldn't they be on the list of defendants as well: What if the protection for FDR drivers was shown to be inadequate? A long shot, but a possibility.

There didn't seem to be any other obvious plaintiffs, but I knew that plenty would come out of the woodwork, professional litigants who were masters at concocting connections and causality, however bizarre or remote.

My eyes glazed over. And I was at the bottom of the mess.

There were some deep pockets: a clutch of insurers, JJ's estate, Jefferson Trust.

But, in the midst of it all, I would be a lightening rod. JJ was dead, I was alive. Insurers were faceless, Jefferson too. But I had a face. The system would give me horns and cloven feet; it could chew me up and spit out the pieces.

"Excuse me, sir, are you Mr. Border?" A messenger peered around the edge of the door.

"Yes."

"Mr. Mendip said he'll be a while yet, and you can go back to your office now. He'll see you later."

He looked around the room. "He told me to get his briefcase for him."

Under the desk, lurking but not hidden, was a cheap black

reinforced plastic thing. I'd have recognized it anywhere. Charles had had it for years; my father used to joke about it.

I toed it. "This one?" I said. The messenger's young, spotty face lit up.

The clasps were open. I was about to warn the messenger to be careful when he grabbed the case and pulled it from under the desk.

"Goddammit," he said, as the entire contents cascaded onto the floor.

"Is your name Kevin, by any chance?"

The messenger was on the floor now, starting to draw together the scattered contents. He looked up at me like I was psychic.

"How did you know?"

I got down on my knees to help him scoop everything back into the briefcase.

"Don't worry," I said. "He won't notice—he just chucks things in anyhow."

"You won't say anything, will you? First day of a new job, and I fuck up."

"The first day of what I'm sure will be a long and distinguished career at Clay & Westminster."

Kevin studied me, checking if I were putting him on. Then he grinned. "Thanks."

I had in my hand an airline ticket, a small pile of papers, and a ring-bound presentation document. I took a quick look; it was Clay & Westminster's own marketing brochure. I knew it well; I'd drafted the section on the New York office.

The other was a hand-written letter to Charles. I recognized the writing. It was from Ernie Monks.

It was a long letter, about five pages by the feel of it. It looked angry; the thick paper was heavily scored by the flowery swirls that characterized Ernie's script. And there were a lot of exclamation marks. I wished I could read just a few lines, but his writing didn't lend itself to a casual scan and I thought I was already pushing my luck. I tossed the ticket, presentation, and letter back into the case.

Kevin had swept up the rest: the cheap ballpoint pens, the aspirin, the Clay & Westminster standard-issue leather diary, a basic pocket calculator with the Price Waterhouse logo splashed over it, and an inhaler. I hadn't realized Charles suffered from asthma.

That just left a book in a small brown paper bag lying on the floor. I picked it up, intrigued by what Charles might choose to read on the plane or during negligible spare moments in his hotel room. Peering inside the bag, I could see that it was a paperback, very old and well-thumbed, and I could make out the title: *In Black and White*. I was about to take a better look when Kevin snatched it and chucked it on top of the other stuff. He scanned the floor to check that he hadn't missed anything and then closed the case, making a big performance of ensuring the clasps were tightly shut.

"Are you sure he won't notice?" Kevin seemed unwilling to believe that someone so important could be so careless about his personal belongings.

"Let me put it this way," I said. "If Charles Mendip had his appendix out, the only way he'd know about it was when he got the bill."

Kevin laughed. "And he's the chief guy, right?"

I nodded. "Scary, isn't it?"

He stood up. "Thanks again."

The phone rang.

"You coming?" It was Paula. "Keenes has been bitching all morning for your handover notes and I've got the Clerkenwell Associates number. Pablo Tochera says he can't do today. Tomorrow, his place at two. Oh yeah, Carol Amen called, wondering if you could make it for a bite at Starbucks downstairs. I told her that was fine, but you had a few things to clear up first, shouldn't be more than twenty minutes, tops."

"And where will I be dining tonight?"

"Hell do I know?"

My handover notes would never be finished. They would always be susceptible to some further refinement. I typed out an e-mail header to Mendip and Keenes, pausing over the appropriate contents for the "Subject" box.

I typed in "Freelunch." Fuck 'em. It was accurate enough; I'd just donated my entire career to date to Messrs. Lamberhurst, Silverman, and Wardman. I attached the file with an electronic paperclip and hit "send" before I should have a change of heart.

It was 2:00 P.M. Seven in London, and too late to call Clerkenwell Associates. They'd have to wait until tomorrow, along with Pablo Tochera.

Too much for tomorrow, not enough for today.

I called Schuster Mannheim's main switchboard.

"The office of Pablo Tochera, please."

Music. "The Sting," for Christ's sake.

"Hi, Mr. Tochera's office, how may I help you?"

"This is Fin Border and I have a meeting scheduled for tomorrow afternoon with Mr. Tochera. The timing's not good, I'm afraid. I really need to see him today."

"Mr. Tochera's schedule is full, sir. There's nothing I can do."

"Kindly inform Mr. Tochera that Mr. Mendip, senior partner of Clay & Westminster, reckons that the grieving relatives of fifteen dead people will be snapping at my ass by tomorrow, and that in his professional opinion a powwow today is better than one when my butt has disappeared."

"I beg your pardon, sir?"

"Just tell him, okay."

I hung up.

Paula was standing in front of me.

"Naughty boy. You could get in trouble for stuff like that."

"More trouble than I'm in right now?"

Paula handed me a sheet of paper. "JJ Carlson wasn't at Harvard."

It was a news item off the net. Paula had summed it up well. JJ had attended a short summer program, but beyond that, Harvard had no knowledge of him and had never awarded him an MBA.

Harvard had been one of JJ's favorite topics over a Jack Daniels, the Shangri-la of his youth. He was as near as he ever got to being poetic when he described the place, as if he could still touch every venerable stone, still hear its wise heartbeat.

"Can I keep this?" I asked.

"Sure, it's easier to carry around than the PC."

*     *     *

Carol sat at a table, little bigger than a quarter, in the Starbucks a few steps away from the Credence Building. In front of her was a mug of coffee and a muffin, less one bite. There was another coffee and muffin laid before the empty chair.

She smiled as she saw me. "Not exactly power lunch. But okay?"

"Perfect," I said. It was.

"You look beat."

"You look beautiful."

She acted bashful, like a child. I wanted to hold her.

I gave her the page of news.

She gave a startled gasp.

"He set me up, Carol."

"What do you mean?" She was almost inaudible.

"He bought the car in my name, used most of my money, and borrowed the rest with me as the borrower. That car cost a million. But that's nothing compared to the lawsuits that will flow from this thing. I've already had the first shot across the bow from an insurance company."

"Oh my God."

"And they've taken away my client base, handed it over to my hungry colleagues. I'm in the garden, but it's a fuck of a long way from Eden."

"But you've done nothing wrong." She displayed the same wounded indignation as my mother.

"I'm not sure that's the point. For some reason JJ has whipped up a legal storm, and I'm in the middle of it . . ."

"My God," she said again, a tide of hair obscuring half her face. She didn't bother to sweep it aside; she just stared at me with one unblinking chestnut eye.

"Did you know that JJ used cocaine?" I asked.

"No," Carol replied rather too quickly. I could understand the swiftness of her response: She was still a lawyer, the chief investment banking counsel for Jefferson Trust, and in some respects responsible for the legal consequences of a banker's actions. On her desk might lurk a piece of paper similar to mine, with the same two headings and the same list of potential parties.

She tiptoed her hand across the table and took hold of mine.

"You still act for Jefferson Trust, you know," she said. "We're the client and nobody tells us which attorney is on or off the team. Not if they want to keep the account, they don't."

"I don't want to compromise you, Carol."

She squeezed my hand and stood up, swallowing the last of the coffee. "We can talk about this later. I better get back to the office."

"When will I see you?" I asked.

"Tonight. Dinner, my place. We can talk." She puckered her lips and blew me a kiss. "Maybe I can console you a little."

# THIRTEEN

**M**y call to Schuster Mannheim had paid off.

At four-thirty, I sat down with Pablo Tochera, my very own McIntyre-approved attorney, in Conference Room B.

He was a clean-shaven and dapper Puerto Rican with the contours of a man who liked his food and couldn't find the optimum trade-off with his evident vanity. His eyes darted around like pinballs.

He was an ulcer waiting to happen.

He was studying the letter from Marshall, Forrester, Kellerman, and Hirsch.

"This is a difficult case, Mr. Border."

Gee, I hadn't realized. But I wanted to hear his take. "Why?" I said. "I didn't own the car."

"Even assuming you didn't own it, there may be an argument that you owed a duty of care to stop Mr. Carlson taking the wheel while under the influence of cocaine."

"Like in the 'dramshop' cases," I said.

Tochera raised a respectful eyebrow and put down the Marshall,

Forrester letter. "I'm impressed. You know about those cases?"

Only vaguely. The proverbial purveyor of whiskey serves the paralytic customer his fiftieth dram and then helps him to his car and waves him on his way to death and mayhem. Jesus, it was a little close for comfort.

"But you need to establish the duty of care first," I said. "I don't see it in this case. And anyway, I didn't know JJ was high."

"Or had reasonable cause to suspect he was high," Tochera added.

"Precisely." I'd liked his response, but there was a reticence that troubled me. The eyes never landed on me; they scoured the corners of the room. Scouting for dust maybe.

"I agree with you about the question of duty," he said. "But someone might try and make new precedent with this case. That leaves us relying on the evidence." He wasn't yet standing on my side of the line.

"But what about proving that it wasn't my car?" I asked. "Showing how I was set up. You're going to get the documents, aren't you? Have them tested. Get investigating agents. Identify the people at the McLaren showroom, at Delaware Loan, depose them, find out how JJ did it?"

"Sure, all in good time."

We didn't have any bloody time. Now was the time. "Mr. Tochera," I said, "I'd like to feel that you were fired up, itching to fight in my corner."

He smiled at me patronizingly, but still the eyes strayed. "Of course. Your sentiment is only natural, but, as I said, this is a complex matter and litigation hasn't even been threatened. We can keep the police in a holding pattern for the time being. We need to see the kind of moves that people make, then we can establish the right strategy."

Bullshit, Mr. Tochera. This was about who was picking up the tab. Mr. Tochera was the piper and I wasn't paying him. I could guess who was calling the tune.

"I shall be maintaining close contact with Mr. Mendip regarding the conduct of my representation," I said smoothly.

Tochera stiffened. "I'll bear that in mind, Mr. Border."

I flattened my now well-creased map of defendants and plaintiffs on the table. "This case will breed parties like rabbits," I said. "I hope you're not offended, but I thought this chart might help."

Tochera's eyes were now actively avoiding the paper as well.

"I've been doing this kind of thing for a while now," he said. "And I wouldn't tell you how to draft an offering memorandum."

I drew my scrap of paper slowly toward me. "Point taken. I'm sorry."

He patted me gently on the back. "Sheesh, that's okay. This is kinda shitty, I know, but we'll be with you every step of the way. Relax a little. Let us handle things. That's what we're here for. That's what Mr. McIntyre and Mr. Mendip want and, believe me, that's what you need."

For the first time, his eyes met mine. He grasped my shoulder. "Okay, guy?"

I nodded guardedly.

"So here's the deal," he said. "I'll take a statement from you now—that'll take an hour. Then tomorrow I'll draft a response to Mr. Richter of Marshall, Forrester and get to work on just the kind of things you've been lecturing me about. We'll have a look at your chart some other time."

When Tochera had finished with me I took a detour on the way back to my office. It was time to visit the Clay & Westminster Human Resources Department.

The appellation of "Department" was another of Keenes's bureaucratic conceits. It was a tiny room with two locked cabinets presided over by a battleax called Barbara. She also ran the library, hence the soubriquet that Lamberhurst had given her: the Barbarian.

Getting a file off Barbara usually took a subpoena signed by the President, unless the incumbent was a Democrat; so I was surprised when she handed over Paula's personnel file with little more than a tasteless question about whether I'd seen any more good wrecks recently.

The file contained healthcare paperwork mostly. Doug, Paula's late husband, had used up a lot of paper and money. Poor Doug.

Paula's file didn't deliver much on his behalf for posterity. Admittedly, I'd never really asked about him, but the subject had somehow seemed off limits.

Then there was a pile of incomprehensible shit about her 401K Plan. I'd never understand pensions until I was drawing one.

Her offer of employment. Standard letter.

Her antecedents. I scanned them and snapped the file shut. There was only one section that interested me and it hadn't taken long to read, but it explained a lot.

As I left Barbara's kingdom, Keenes nearly ran into me.

"Bloody hell, Fin, can't you stay at your desk for more than five minutes? I've been looking for you everywhere."

"What's the point of staying at my desk? I don't have any work. You took it all and doled it out like Father Christmas. Remember?"

"Watch your lip. Anyway, you have some work now. Mendip wants to see you at the Regent Hotel at eight tonight."

"What's it about, Sheldon?"

He was already walking away from me at speed. "You'll find out," he barked over his shoulder.

"Mendip's errand boy," I muttered and headed for my office.

Back at my desk, I leaned on my elbows and studied the chart so pointedly ignored by Tochera.

There was a potential defendant missing.

I added Schuster Mannheim to the list. In parentheses, I scribbled: "Contingent on the merger with C&W."

If Clay & Westminster had a problem, then Schuster Mannheim would have a problem too. If the merger went ahead, that is.

Jesus. In five seconds, JJ had whipped up a black hole that had the potential to suck some very large objects into its vortex. He must have been very angry about something. But what had *I* ever done to him?

Paula came in.

"I want to take off now," she said. "Your schedule isn't enough to keep a high-flying bitch like me satisfied."

"You're not quitting, are you?" I asked.

"No. At least not yet. I just meant I wanted to go home, you turkey."

Thank God. "Sure," I said. "But I'd like a quick word first."

She tilted her head suspiciously.

"What about, counselor?"

"I know where you worked before you came here."

She performed a slow hand clap. "Well done, Fin. It's only taken you five years."

"Why didn't you tell me that you'd been with Schuster Mannheim? And don't say because I never asked."

"You never asked."

"Why did you leave them?"

"What does the file say?"

I hesitated. "Nothing."

"Then let's leave it at that, except to say that I wasn't fired and that I have good reason not to be overjoyed about the merger."

"But why the problem? Your position will be secure."

"Just like yours." She raised her eyes to the ceiling and exhaled sharply. "I'm sorry. That was cheap. Forget I said it." She smiled. "You're a decent guy. You shouldn't be going through all this, but it's taking it out of me too. That's why I want to go home now."

"Paula," I said as she started through the door. "Can't you even tell me who you worked for at Schuster?"

"Good night, Fin."

I called Carol and left a voicemail telling her I wouldn't be at her place until late as I had to pay an urgent visit to the Regent Hotel.

# FOURTEEN

It was still hot at seven-thirty that evening when I stepped into the fiercely air-conditioned lobby of the Regent. The perspiration inside my shirt turned cold.

The Regent lay halfway down Wall Street, just past the Stock Exchange. Once the home of Harry's Bar, it was now an exclusive hotel with room rates for those not on a budget. It was smart without being over the top, the kind of place Charles Mendip would like. As long as the food was good, which it was.

I was half an hour early but wanted to get on with it. I crossed over to the reception desk and asked to be put through to Mendip's room. The receptionist told me to ring 225 and pointed to a courtesy phone on a marble-topped table nearby.

I picked up the receiver and dialed the number. Then I glanced around and saw the elevator doors at the other end of the lobby open and disgorge a bunch of men in suits. One of them was Sheldon Keenes—his blond mop a beacon among the other heads. As I felt Mendip's voice vibrate the receiver, I quickly cradled the phone and moved behind the protective cover of a large spray of silk flowers in a massive Roman-style urn.

Two of the men seemed to have nothing to do with Keenes, and they strode purposefully toward the main entrance of the hotel and out into Wall Street. The other two remained with him, one facing out: Indian, youngish, and rather brash—the glint of jewelry as he gesticulated with his hands. The other had his back to me, but there was something familiar about it.

Sheldon appeared quite relaxed, draping his arm across the young man's shoulder. He seemed to be making a joke. The young man laughed and poked Sheldon in the ribs as if to say, you old dog, you. His companion wasn't so easily amused. Somehow the neat band of hair fringing his bald patch told me that his face was impassive, unmoved by Sheldon's witticism. This was a man who had mastered intimidation from any angle.

Sheldon's expression switched from levity to sincerity. He shook each man's hand vigorously. I sensed that he had promised them something and that they were to be left in no doubt that whatever it was, it was receiving Sheldon's full attention. The young man shot a furtive look around the lobby and then followed his colleague, like a puppy, through the hotel entrance. I could still see them as they stood on the sidewalk. The young man talked excitedly, while the other retained an impassive, uninterested air. He hadn't turned around once and I still hadn't seen his face. But I didn't need to. It was no use kidding myself that I didn't know who he was.

Sheldon turned and jabbed the elevator call button.

I picked up a copy of *Time* magazine and started leafing through it. I concentrated on not reading it for about five minutes until the elevator door opened once more and Sheldon emerged again. He marched straight for the entrance and went out into Wall Street.

I lifted the courtesy phone and dialed Charles's number.

"You're early. Come on up."

When I got to 225, Charles was waiting, holding the door open, wearing his scruffy suit, jacket still on. He didn't approve of jacket removal for meetings, even when the meetings were in his boudoir.

He led me into a drawing room decorated with classical prints and ornate furniture. There was a massive floor-to-ceiling cabinet that I took to be the in-room entertainment system. Unless opera or choral music was on offer, the doors of the cabinet were likely to remain firmly shut for the duration of Mendip's visit.

On the glass table in front of the couch was a tray loaded with the paraphernalia of afternoon tea.

"Sorry about the mess," Charles said, moving the tray onto a side table nearby. "I had guests."

I didn't say anything.

He poured and handed me a glass of mineral water, motioning me to sit down on the couch.

He looked at me. Anger? Sympathy? Anxiety? I detected traces of all three in his complex face.

He sat down opposite me, resting his elbows on his knees, steepling his fingers, rapping the knuckles of his thumbs against his top teeth.

Point of entry, I thought. He's groping for a point of entry, the opening shot.

"I could never fathom whether your father loved or hated India." The first volley.

Mendip paused. I would keep my powder dry for the moment.

"But you," he continued, "your perspective: I would have expected that to be clear-cut. After what happened to your father, what it did to your mother."

It *was* clear-cut. Mendip must've lost the plot if he was confused on that score. I began to wonder if we had the same subject in mind.

He unclasped his fingers and gave his chin a series of flicks with his index finger. "So why have you painted yourself and, more impor-tant, me, into a corner in this way? I'd tried to keep the whole thing away from you and in one afternoon you've managed to wrap your arms around it. Bloody breathtaking."

"You've lost me, Charles. I don't understand a word you're say-ing."

Mendip scowled, a lip-chewing scowl. "Less of the innocent schoolboy act. I'm not a bloody fool."

He wasn't a bloody fool. I knew that. My father had said he was one of the cleverest men of his generation. Ernie Monks had said the same. And I'd seen nothing to make me disagree, but Mendip was talking in another language and I didn't have a basic phrase book.

He sighed. "Well, you've got your way." He was behaving as if he'd lost a fight with me, a fight I never knew we'd fought.

"What are you talking about?"

"Carol Amen was very eloquent on your behalf; she's made a lot of senior people in Jefferson Trust eloquent on your behalf. Now the Indians think it's a good idea, positively insisting on you handling the deal. Can't change their minds about it. Of course, I haven't said anything about your spot of bother. Maybe I should have, they're bound to find out anyway. Too late now."

A deal. An Indian deal. The deal she'd mentioned at the cemetery. Shit, no. Hell's bloody bells, no.

"I don't know about any deal, Charles. Still less about one in India."

Charles affected incredulity. "Did you think it would be easier if you were out of the country? That the JJ thing wouldn't follow you? Bloody naïve if you *did* think that, Fin. Bloody naïve. I don't even know if we can get you out of the country." He took a small scrap of paper and stub of pencil from his jacket pocket and jotted something down. "I'd better get Terry Wardman onto that one," he said.

This was madness. India. If it were the only place in the world with oxygen, I'd still fly in the opposite direction.

"Humor me, Charles. Just pretend for a moment that I don't know what the hell you are talking about. Incredible as that might seem. Humor me."

"The stockbrokerage. The one that Jefferson Trust wants to buy. For fifty million dollars. The Bombay one: Ketan Securities. That one, Fin. Humored you enough, have I? You may be my godson, but that's as far as it goes, laddie."

So that was the deal. Jefferson Trust was to buy a Bombay stockbrokerage with me as the attorney on the transaction. Carol must've thought she was doing me a favor getting me on the list of parties. I hadn't told her about my father, the Fall. If I had, she would've moved heaven and earth to keep me off the file. If she really liked me, that is.

"I don't know how to say this in a way that will make you believe me," I said. "I know nothing of this."

Mendip reddened. "I think the last few days have unhinged you. It's the only explanation for your bizarre behavior. You've abandoned rational thought and will do anything to escape, even if it means going to Bombay. Frankly, you baffle me."

I shook my head. "Of course I don't want to go to Bombay. Take me off the damn thing. Blame me. Say that I'm in shock. Do you whatever you want, but take me off the bloody thing." I was starting to panic. On top of my visions of death on the FDR and my looming emasculation at the hands of bloodied victims and slavering insurance and loan companies, the video of Bombay was beginning to play in my head. But this wasn't a cozy tour around a vibrant city, pointing out the landmarks and making vacuous observations on the legendary hospitality of Bombay's inhabitants, its kaleidoscope of cultures, its exotic cuisine, and how it was the destination of choice for the discerning and sophisticated traveler. This was a video of the worst week of my life, the epilogue to the Fall.

"The die is cast," said Mendip flatly. "It can't be uncast. Whether or not you were the author of your involvement, you're now involved and can't be uninvolved."

"I can't go. Surely you of all people understand that?"

I listened to myself and then listened for the ghostly laughter of my father, the post-Fall father, the one I couldn't call Dad anymore, the one I could barely speak to when he had called from Bombay, drunk, stoned, whatever. Rambling. He'd compromised, he'd said. He'd choked on the half-eaten file, poisoned himself on a Bombay breakfast of scam and eggs. And something else, something he couldn't say. He needed me, right then, by all the millions of gods that crowded the millions of Indians, he needed me. I'd said nothing. He'd wept, implored. I'd hung up. I told myself he'd fallen too far; he'd exiled himself before he had even left for Bombay. For me, the Fall had happened in a neat house in Hampton Court, not in the heat and confusion of Bombay.

"You *will* be going," Mendip sighed. "Because I say so." His voice was both languid and menacing. "You're on a space walk, Fin. And I control the life support systems. If you don't go to Bombay I'll switch them off, every last one. And cast you adrift."

"I didn't know making threats was your style."

"It's a fait accompli, one engineered by you." He shook his head. "My God, if only I'd known what you were doing."

This was mad. "But Charles . . ."

He held up his hand. "McIntyre agrees that there is no going back. So do the others."

The others? The client?

Mendip leaned forward, near enough to hear the gentle wheeze of lungs that would need Ventalin if they were overtaxed. "You will have to do it, Fin. You must be seen to cooperate, to act in the collective best interests of the firm. I'm sorry, but do you think the partnership will allow the continued underwriting of your mother's entire existence: the house, the annuity, the thousand little courtesies and services rendered that you never hear about and she takes for granted? Do you think they will tolerate our continued attempts to prevent the world from finding out what really happened to your father? Do you think they will support my support of you if you behave like a spoiled child?"

The partnership would let Mendip do what he liked. He'd made them rich; he was about to make them richer. He could make me partner here and now or he could stick a grenade up my ass and pull the pin and, either way, they would say, huzzah, for he's a jolly good fellow. He could buy my mother a Caribbean island and they'd say bloody good idea, if Mendip told them that it was a bloody good idea. It was Mendip who had disseminated the story that my father had died of typhoid. They had all bought it; nobody questioned it, at least not out loud. They'd buy the true story, if he told them to.

"I don't know what it would do to your mother. It's realpolitik, not a threat." He allowed himself a sip of water.

Wasn't it? It would kill her if they pulled the rug from under me.

"Look, Fin," Mendip said, his face furrowed by concern, fake or real, I didn't care. I knew what was coming: the hand-wringing, the date-rapist's remorse, the grin-and-bear-it. "You'll be in and out of there in no time. A quick deal. A pissy little stockbrokerage, for God's sake. Standing on your head stuff. Then there's your future ahead of you. A great future."

Just transact. Nothing wrong in that, perhaps. Jefferson Trust wants to buy a stockbrokerage. So what? Perfectly reasonable and legitimate. Fifty Gordon's and tonics on the plane, keep myself topped up after landing, and I might never know I'd been to Bombay. It wasn't even a half-eaten file; no reason to think it was scam and eggs.

But the afterward, the real afterward. What about that?

"And what about the JJ business, Charles? When that becomes too fraught, will you ditch me?"

"Of course not, I've already told you," he said. "Just do as you're told and let the professionals get on with their work. It's about trust."

"I'm not convinced that Pablo Tochera has my best interests at heart."

"Don't be bloody stupid. You don't seriously think you're the one with most to lose, do you?"

Whatever happens, you won't be on the scrap heap, Charles Mendip. My place there already had a "reserved" flag stuck in it.

"That's my worry, Charles," I said, the chart at the forefront of my mind. "There are so many others with so much to lose, I might get lost in the crowd."

"Stop fussing. You have Pablo Tochera and you should consider yourself fortunate. This thing could go on for years and any skirmish over your dining table and cuff links will be a sideshow, over in the blink of an eye. Just let us deal with it."

"You've expressed my concern better than I could have."

I'd been reduced to the blink of an eye. It made me think. My father had been rich once. He had been in the top ten of Clay & Westminster and, in his prime, their top biller. But he had pissed it all away in two short crazy months. When he'd gone for the Fall, he'd traveled first class.

Charles reached inside his pocket and pulled out the inhaler. Leaning back, he put the snorkel-like end in his mouth and gave a firm jab on the cartridge.

"I have enough to contend with as it is," he said when he found his breath. "Let Mr. Tochera deal with the Carlson matter and you handle the Bombay transaction. McIntyre isn't happy with this turn of events but I have interceded on your behalf. If you don't like the arrangement, then I can do no more for you."

"So when do I start?" I said.

Mendip shut his eyes. Thanking God, was he?

His eyes flicked open. "Tomorrow morning," he said. "Nine sharp, round at Jefferson Trust. Ask to see your standard bearer, Carol Amen."

"What about local counsel in Bombay?" I asked as if I didn't already know the answer.

"Askari & Co.," Mendip said.

Downstairs I'd seen the back of a head. Five years before I'd seen the front. It belonged to Sunil Askari, principal of Askari & Co., Bombay. There were bigger firms in India, more prestigious firms, but in Charles's lexicon of Indian lawyers, Askari really *did* begin with *A* and he didn't bother with firms starting with any other letter of the alphabet.

"You know what Sunil Askari thinks of me." Askari had worn his contempt for me like a badge. "You know what he felt about my father. Can't we use somebody else?" I recalled the imperious Askari lolling in a high-backed chair, a copper-colored Churchill, lecturing me—in precise Oxford tones—that my father's behavior had come within an ace of causing an international incident, that he had nearly ruined the reputation of Clay & Westminster and Askari and that I should be grateful for both his and Mendip's intervention, which had saved everyone from calamity. The fact that my father was dead was a relief, as far as Askari was concerned.

"Don't be absurd," said Mendip crossly. "Of course we can't use someone else. Only Askari & Co. can navigate this transaction in the timetable set by the client, which, by the way, is bloody short. And, anyway, Sunil would never forgive me if we switched horses. You won't have much contact with him in all probability."

Mendip stood up. I thought he was signaling an end to the audience and I started to get up, but he motioned me to stay seated. "I appreciate what you must think of me right now, but believe me, the future—*your* future—doesn't lie in Bombay, it lies with Schuster Mannheim."

He picked up that day's *Wall Street Journal* from the table. He came around the back of me, dropped the paper on my lap, and put his hands on my shoulders.

"Look at that," he said.

I scanned the front page. There was a largish piece on the JJ affair with recriminations from Miranda Carlson about how the culture at Jefferson Trust impelled JJ onto the FDR. The article made brief reference to an editorial deeper in the paper that begged to differ. There was a much larger piece on the Schuster Mannheim merger with Clay & Westminster. A eulogy for the deal and the vision of the firms' respective senior partners.

Charles straightened his jacket. He was preening himself.

"We've got it right," he said, beaming. I could appreciate why, by and large, he should be pleased.

But had JJ put a bomb under the whole thing?

Charles evidently didn't think so. "This is the perception, Fin," he said, "this is what people really think of the merger. And it's the reality as well. You know that I'm not usually prone to hyperbole, but this combination is unquestionably the most important in legal history. In our own little world, it's the War of Independence, it's the October Revolution. And it's the likes of you that will benefit immeasurably from it."

"I don't see how," I said gloomily. "Schuster knows the trouble I'm in, after all, they're acting for me. I shouldn't think they hold me in particularly high esteem."

Mendip took the paper from me and folded it neatly before placing it back on the table. "You're right, they don't," he said. "They think you're a perfect pest. But they've also seen your track record and, in time, they will admire you for the great lawyer I know you to be. I'm sure Jim McIntyre will alter his current somewhat jaundiced view."

Jim McIntyre was a man whose reputation suggested he rarely changed his mind about anything. And for the first time it really struck me that Mendip was scared of McIntyre—taking away my clients, knocking me off the merger was more likely prompted by him than by Keenes. Only someone as powerful as McIntyre could have forced the issue.

"And after Bombay," I ventured hesitantly. "Will I be able to return to the New York fold?"

I wanted to come back to New York. However vague its draw upon me was, it was real. Maybe I hadn't scaled the Empire State Building or joined a social conga line of actors, dentists, therapists, and lawyers. But I'd looked through the rear window of a cab at night and seen the Met Life Building bestride Park Avenue. I'd seen a man dressed as a tomato on Fifth Avenue. I'd rummaged through the antiques and bric-a-brac in a thousand stalls around West 25th on Sunday morning. I'd eaten in a hundred SoHo restaurants. Noodles in Chinatown, pasta in Little Italy, steak at Peter Luger, fish at Docks. Baseball with fucking JJ.

And, of course, Carol Amen.

Mendip wandered over to the door and opened it. "Let's get Bombay over with first, shall we?" He gently propelled me into the hallway. "I must get on now. I'll speak to you later. Remember I'm behind you. We both have jobs to do, so let's do them."

I tried to read his expression: There was a smile, but the eyes were as hard and gray as ballbearings.

# FIFTEEN

**Y**ou look terrible." Carol drew me into her apartment. I watched her face, fed on it.

She wasn't aware that her best efforts on my behalf had been a curse.

She poured some wine and curled around me on the couch. T-shirt and drawstring shorts again, a welcome reprise. I could smell her, a chemistry of soap and shampoo working with her own fragrance. I could see her muscular strength, the slight ripple of forearm as she stroked her hands down her legs. And the passion: her brimming eyes, the pink-tinged cheeks, maybe the work of wine. No; something deeper.

"I got you some work," she said. "It isn't big but it's interesting and we'll be working together on it. It took all afternoon to swing it. There are some people at Clay & Westminster who seem pretty pissed with you." She wasn't triumphant, there was no high-five—too much had happened for that kind of display. Her voice was quietly satisfied, as if she had delivered something important, understated, that would

speak for itself and find its own place in the hierarchy of the good and
bad stuff.

She put her hand to my cheek and gentled my face toward her. "I
wasn't expecting an eruption of joy, but . . . Bad meeting, huh?"

I nodded. "Bad meeting."

"Well, it's over now."

*I don't think so, Carol.*

"Anyway." Her voice brightened, still strained but gamely trying
to break out of the gloom I'd brought in with me. "Shall I tell you
about the deal?"

"I know about it already."

She looked a little hurt, as if she'd wanted to watch me unwrap
my present.

"A stockbrokerage in Bombay." She wasn't going to let me spoil
her moment. "Ketan Securities. It's been in the hopper for a while and
I don't know any real details. You know how it happens, the soup
simmering on the back burner just boils over. The bankers are produc-
ing a deal pack as we speak." Her eyes scanned my face for some sign
of reaction, something encouraging maybe. "Clay & Westminster had
already been iced to act if called on. So it was just a matter of getting
them to name you as lead guy. And they have."

I said nothing.

Anxiety began to leach into her expression, like she was beginning
to sense that something was badly wrong. "It'll get us out of this place
for a while." She was still trying to sound upbeat. "Exotic location,
expenses paid, first class all the way. You, me." She had a vision, I
could see it in her wide eyes: her and me strolling down Marine Drive,
the people, the smells, the sun setting over the Arabian Sea. Big bedroom, mosquito nets furling in the breeze, giant vats of mango juice,
full of ice cubes, clinking like Tibetan bells. The two of us naked on
the big, big bed. She wouldn't know Marine Drive or what the rest of
Bombay looked like, but she'd have the vision all the same; it would
excite her. In another life I would have been with her all the way, but
in this one, I couldn't join her. She needed to know.

"My father died in Bombay."

Carol let her hand fall from my face.

"No," she whispered.

I could see the mortuary slab, my father on it. In an ice-cold crypt, a big, dirty refrigerator of a place. My father, held in the suspended moment of his dying. I remembered myself saying: Not my dad, this is not my dad. My dad wouldn't let the vultures eat away half of his face. My dad's left eye didn't usually hang out of its socket, semi-chewed like a discarded pickled onion. My dad's body is muscular, tanned, not like this scrawny chunk of meat that looked like it had been through a threshing machine. My dad wouldn't have fallen so far, so quickly.

"I'm sorry. I didn't know."

Of course she didn't. I'd never told her and people didn't tend to regale clients with details of my father's last journey. "It's okay, it's not your fault." I stroked her hand, proof that I meant it.

"Your father was a lawyer?"

I realized I hadn't even told her that much.

"He was a senior partner of Clay & Westminster," I said.

"The boss."

"Not quite, he was on the way there. It was really either him or Charles Mendip. But they were good friends, going way back to university. If there was rivalry, it didn't show. They shared a vision of where the firm was headed."

In hindsight I could see that my father, Dad as he then was, didn't have so much a vision as an assumption about my own future: join the firm, climb the ladder. Not much pressure exerted on me, though; there was no need, I just toddled along behind, happy to hang on to his well-tailored shirttails. Ambition had never been one of my foremost attributes. University, good degree, law school, sure, but locked squarely, almost unquestionably, in the slipstream of Dad's simple assumption. We never really talked about it—that's how assumptions were supposed to be: assumed.

And then the Fall began, the descent. "He inherited something from another partner who'd died. Not money or a gold watch, mind. A file, a deal, a client." The legendary half-eaten file, the legacy of a half-finished meal. He should have known better. After all, he had counseled me enough times on this score.

"He spent a lot of time in the Gulf: Oman, Jordan, Bahrain, places like that. Then India." From time to time he'd return to our neat house in Hampton Court, where he'd brood, as if our home was a transit lounge and he had to fill in the time between flights. And drink. He'd never drunk much before, the odd glass of claret, but somewhere in his travels he'd found the taste for it. My mother watched; she just stayed in the background, silent. Maybe she was praying a silent prayer. It didn't work.

"He told me he'd made a miscalculation."

A miscalculation. For a lawyer, that usually meant undercharging a client, finding ten hours of billable work after the invoice had been sent. But that was the word he used, *miscalculation*. Euphemistic to the end.

"I couldn't figure out precisely what kind of miscalculation. He had been back in the UK for only a few hours and was drunk. He was incoherent. He seemed to be in despair."

Gold, he'd said. Havala—the middle-men traders, Non-Resident Indians. Bombay breakfast of scam and eggs. It didn't mean anything to me then, except the gold, of course. I knew what gold was. He spat out the name of the client, like it was a swear word. The name hit me, carried in a spray of scotch. He'd cursed himself: How had he let himself be drawn in, be compromised? He asked me to take an oath. The melodrama, the drunken melodrama of it. Don't compromise, he'd asked me to promise. Never. He was my dad and so I promised. He then relaxed and even laughed, he told me that it wasn't too late for him, he could turn the tide. He was smarter than them, than *him,* whoever "him" was. He'd reclaim the high ground, in his drunkenness he was defiant. But he hadn't realized he had a long way to go yet, that he had only just begun to fall.

"Two weeks later he went back to Bombay." Then there had been the telephone call, his desperate voice, someone I couldn't recognize as flesh and blood, not my dad, not even my father. "And the next time I saw him he was dead."

"How did he die?" Carol asked.

Being alive, being alive killed him. Alive with whatever he'd become, he couldn't face it.

Or maybe I'd killed him, just by hanging up the phone.

Click—you're dead.

"In the end it was an overdose," I said. "But he was so full of every kind of poison, he would have died soon enough anyway. He just hastened it, deliberately or not. Who knows?"

The Bombay police had found his body at the gates of the Parsee funeral precinct: the Towers of Silence, the resident vultures sitting on him as if he were a couch. Scandalous, the potent embryo of an international incident. But capable of being hushed up. Swept under a sprawling Indian carpet.

I let Carol hold me. She felt warm.

"They said it was typhoid. Everyone, well, everyone outside the loop, believed it. They still do." Mendip had said it was typhoid, so it was typhoid. Things like that could happen in India, even to great men. A great leveler of a place. Sure, Mr. Mendip, if you say so.

"I can get you taken off the file, if you want," Carol said. "It would be easy."

I sat up and drank some wine. I sucked it through my teeth, savored the bouquet, felt the tannin adhere to the enamel.

"No, don't do that," I said, "things are complicated enough as it is. Anyway, it's time to pull my head out of the sand and face a few things."

She didn't argue, merely leaned over to refill my glass. "What did your father do that was so bad? Did you find out?"

"Not really. It just sort of evaporated, disappeared behind the veil of his death."

The truth was that I never tried to find out and nobody had bothered to tell me.

Actually, the truth was that the Fall wasn't about gold, havala, or Non-Resident Indians. For me, the truth of the Fall was in Hampton Court, not in Bombay. It was the fleeting vision of a teenage waif, a nymph dark and half-naked, flitting between the bedroom and bathroom in a house supposedly empty except for my father—mother seeing her own mother in Leeds, me destined for a friend's stag weekend. My father should have been alone in his study sucking on his scotch, brooding, planning a comeback, booking his ticket to Bombay, whatever. As I'd driven to a drunken weekend of male bonding, I thought of him. Dad. Alone. I turned around and came back home—a long-needed gesture of solidarity.

Home to a quiet house, study empty, bottle empty on its desk. Then the sound of Victorian water pipes, the clunk and groan. Silence. Footsteps, upstairs, the cliché of pitter-patter, a child's footsteps. The bedroom door ajar and there she was, like some forest creature, a wood nymph. Breasts no bigger than walnuts, but a knowing face. One glimpse of me and she'd gone—whoosh—into the bathroom, a billow of black hair and spindly legs. And then heavier footsteps, grown-up. My father coming along the landing, seeing me. Shocked. Pleading with me as I swept downstairs two steps at a time. It wasn't what it seemed, he yelled. Jesus, he said *that*. Top of the letterhead of Britain's greatest law firm and he said *that*. He tried to grab me, but I just wanted the front door and out of there. I fought him off. His momentum was his downfall. Literally. He cleared the last five steps headfirst.

And that was the Fall. When Dad became my father and not even that. For me, the rest was detail.

Carol let my head sink onto her chest as she stroked and kissed my hair. She then maneuvered me so she could kiss me on the mouth. Her face was wet; her eyes were shut, creased in some profound agony. Mine or hers? I wondered.

"Do you want to go to bed?" she asked.

# SIXTEEN

When I woke up, Carol had already left. There was a note on her pillow telling me she'd had to go in early to prepare for the inaugural Bombay meeting at nine o'clock. There was breakfast neatly set for me in the kitchen. She told me to get my passport and bring it to the meeting so she could arrange for an Indian visa.

I peered at the clock radio on her bedside table. There was time for breakfast. Suddenly I was ravenously hungry.

The global headquarters of Jefferson Trust occupied a massive glass tower on Liberty. The piece of brass that grudgingly admitted the company's presence could have easily fitted onto the cover of *Euromoney* magazine. The security arrangements were reminiscent of the border controls of a small and belligerent Eastern Bloc country prior to the collapse of the Berlin Wall.

After being vetted and tagged I was taken up to the thirtieth floor and handed over to a receptionist presiding over Jefferson Trust's warren of meeting rooms. From her I was released into the care of a navy-blue-suited flunkey, who delivered me to the meeting room with views across to Jersey City one way and the Statue of Liberty and Ellis Island the other.

Carol was sitting at the huge table, absorbed by a thick file of paperwork. Sitting next to her was someone who looked barely into his twenties, eyeing a spreadsheet and running his finger down a line of figures, tut-tutting as he went. I took it he was unimpressed with what he saw.

Carol looked up and smiled at me. It seemed a natural smile, designed neither to hide nor betray. I smiled back.

"Fin," she said warmly. "Let me introduce you to Chuck Krantz. He's the investment banking analyst assigned to this transaction and has been going over the accounts and earnings projections."

Chuck Krantz stood up and shook my hand stiffly. When he said that he was glad to meet me, I didn't exactly see it dancing in his eyes.

"We were just talking about the timetable for this thing when you came in," Carol said.

"I figure we can tie this up in a few weeks, assuming no deal-breakers or antsy regulators," Krantz said.

"Chuck and his colleagues have prepared a deal folder. I've only just seen it myself." Carol pushed a large plastic comb-bound file across the table toward me. Its cover announced that the contents were strictly private and confidential. In the middle of the page, in large red type, were the words: *Project Badla*.

"That's for you," she said. I didn't open the binder, nor even read the five-line executive summary that was likely to adorn the first page and which would tell me in a nutshell what the deal was about. A brokerage, Jefferson wanted to acquire a stockbrokerage. In Bombay. What else was there to know?

Chuck Krantz threw me a hostile glance. "Here's the deal: Jefferson Trust has good coverage in the emerging markets in Europe and the Far East. We do business through local joint ventures, green field start-ups, and sometimes through acquisition of Grade A domestic outfits."

He wasn't telling me anything new. Emerging markets. A jungle full of money if you could find the best tree, a jungle full of trouble if you couldn't. Scam and eggs.

Krantz turned to Carol for belated permission to hold forth. She blessed him with a nod.

"Sometimes we change strategy for a particular market. We only do this for sound commercial reasons." Krantz paused for a moment as if challenging Carol and me to allege that Jefferson Trust would do something other than for sound commercial reasons. When he seemed satisfied that no contradiction was forthcoming, he continued.

"After thorough analysis, we have concluded that we should adopt an alternative strategy in India."

Again he paused. Jesus, this guy needed an audience. What did he want us to do—cheer?

"So instead of dealing through local brokers and banks," Krantz continued, "we're going to buy a well-established stockbrokerage for ourselves and consolidate our position with a meaningful rollout of our brand name in India. We aim to quadruple our profits from the region over two years and become its number-one foreign bank and broker."

Krantz looked at us expectantly.

Carol and I said nothing.

Shrugging, he pointed at the cover sheet of the document. "What do you think of the code name for the project? Badla. Cute. I was pleased with that. Do you know what it means, Fin? Let's see if Clay & Westminster know jack shit about India."

We knew. My father would have known. I knew.

Carol looked nervous: This was as much a test for her as for me. If I looked bad, she looked bad.

"*Badla* is when you purchase shares." I made like I was thinking hard; I didn't want to appear a smartass. "And you don't pay for them. When the time comes to settle, you roll over into the next settlement period. It's expensive: You pay a Badla rate of interest. It was a particular favorite of bull market players, and when there was a rising market it was wonderful. When the market fell, it was pretty catastrophic for those caught in the turning tide. It was outlawed—after the big scam of the early nineties. But then they allowed it back when the market went flat and lost its fizz and they needed to kick-start it."

Krantz smiled, clapped his hands once, and turned to Carol. "All right. The guy knows something—you had me worried for a while."

Carol looked relieved.

Krantz flipped open the binder and motioned us to do the same. "Let's look at the deal now," he said.

It seemed straightforward enough. A medium-sized brokerage with about a hundred employees. It wasn't Grade A—Krantz was right about that—all the good ones had gone years before, bought by Jefferson's competitors. They were entering the game very late and I doubted whether the two-year objective of becoming number one was achievable. Still, that was their problem and the tut-tutting of Krantz over the figures when I'd come in the room showed that he knew it was a problem too.

"So the purchase price is fifty million," I said.

"Yup," said Krantz.

"All cash? Or do you want to use some stock? Will there be an earn-out period and what about handcuffs?" I was on autopilot.

"Slow down, Fin. Okay?" Krantz held his hands to his temples in mock bewilderment. "Some stock," he continued, "small percentage of earn-out—ten percent of consideration, max. And, yes, plenty of heavy handcuffs. We don't want these dudes thinking they can take a walk too quick."

"Stock could be a problem," I said.

Carol nodded.

"Then fix it," said Krantz simply.

It wasn't that easy, but the point could wait. "Client base?" I asked. I could guess.

"Foreign institutions, a mature domestic mix: individuals, corporates, banks. Usual franchise. And then there's a big NRI following." He paused to see if I knew what an NRI was, another test.

"Non-Resident Indians," I said absently. The offshore guys. A reservoir of money: many billions of it. A well-heeled diaspora of twenty million people. "What Exchange memberships does it have?" I asked.

"Bombay, National, and Ahmadabad." Krantz's voice was deep

and confident. He'd obviously gotten a very good grade in his MBA.

"Okay," I said. "That means we'll need their consents, along with those of the Stock Exchange Board of India and Reserve Bank of India. We can get local counsel to take informal soundings and check that we aren't going to hit any brick walls with the bureaucrats."

"One of our guys has already tested the temperature," Krantz said. "Everything seems fine."

"Who was that?" I asked, trying to sound interested.

Krantz acted uneasy and unfolded his hands, running one of them through his gleaming black hair.

Now I *was* interested.

"JJ Carlson," he said quickly and quietly, as if he was hoping I wouldn't catch the name.

If I managed to hide my surprise, Carol certainly didn't. She looked shocked and I thought she was going to say something, but seemed to think better of it and kept her mouth shut.

"Was this his deal?" I asked. "Did he negotiate it?" I couldn't believe that Jefferson Trust would be pressing ahead with a JJ transaction after what had happened.

"I'm not sure that's relevant for you to know," Krantz said.

I looked at Carol for a cue. She smiled weakly, lost in her own thoughts.

"Let's turn to the documents," I said. Pursuing the JJ angle would get us nowhere for now. "We'll need a sale and purchase agreement, new company statutes, arrangements for the key employees—the handcuffs. A new corporate structure, and, of course, the due diligence pack: legal, accounting, and general mop-up stuff. If we're fiddling with corporate structure a lot, we may need novation agreements for certain long-term arrangements with third parties. What else did you have in mind, Carol?"

"A final set of accounts with auditor's sign-off and usual warranties," she responded instantly. Her brain was back in the room.

"Of course," I said. "Who are the accountants and attorneys?"

"CFN are the accountants and Jaiwalla the lawyers. Who can we use for our outside counsel in Bombay?"

"Askari," I said.

"Make sure you use the best," instructed Krantz.

They weren't the best. "Bombay's finest," I said.

"What about the sellers of the business?" I asked. It was a relevant topic to cover: Proprietors who had spent a lifetime building up a business could be awkward as hell when it came to selling their baby, even if they were to be made multimillionaires in the process. It was a parent thing: Letting go could be damned hard and sometimes they—subconsciously perhaps—wanted to drag out the process with crazy conditions or requests. They were selling control, but didn't want to relinquish control in return for the money. It was our job to make sure that the client got what he was paying for. On paper at any rate.

"Did JJ or someone from management meet with them?" asked Carol.

"Of course someone has," Krantz snapped. "You don't think we'd pay fifty million for a business without meeting the principals first."

I winced. It was a pretty stupid question. Her mind must have taken another little excursion. I tried to cast her a look of support and sympathy. But she just acted flustered and twirled her pen between her thumb and index finger.

"If you look at page fifty of the pack," Krantz said crisply, "you will see that the owners have a very good reputation and checks have been made to corroborate this." He ran his finger down the margin. "There are three main family shareholders: father and two sons. Pop just counts the money in some serious real estate in the best part of town, while the sons run the business, one looking after the sales, trading, and research and the other doing the corporate finance work. It's the sales and research we're after; the corporate finance is good for a few contacts and being able to offer a turnkey service, but otherwise it's too niche and marginal. They've got two office properties, one in a place called Narriman Point and the other somewhere I can't recall—it's mentioned somewhere in here. There's a whole heap of useful shit in this pack. You two better make sure you read it well and quick. I expect you to be in Bombay in a few days."

"Time out, Chuck," said Carol. "There's a lot to do and it needs to be done properly."

"Listen Carol," Krantz said hotly, "management want this deal done real quick and I'm telling you that delay is out of the question. The Indian market is part of our core growth strategy, but it isn't the core of the core, if you get my meaning. We don't want to waste too much time on this thing. If we were going to buy something there we should have done it five years ago, not now. But I guess that's by the by. The message is: no holdups, no screwups."

A crazy timetable. But there was nothing unusual in clients setting crazy timetables: It was their prerogative.

"Will you be coming out to Bombay?" I asked.

Chuck looked shocked.

"Hell no. It's a shit-hole, and anyway I have some very large transactions to work on. Nope, I'm sure you and Carol can handle it, no sweat. I'll be contactable in the office or by e-mail or cellular the whole time. Like they say, I'll call you if you need me." He gave a good laugh at his macho banker witticism and waited for us to follow suit. Carol was stony-faced and I just made like I was studying my Project Badla folder. To some Bombay was a shit-hole. To me it was hell. I tried to concentrate on the fact that to eleven million people it was home.

"So what's next?" asked Chuck. He seemed to be directing the question at Carol, but she was miles away.

"I'll take a look at the folder," I said, shouldering the question. "Then I'll send over a draft timetable and list of documents together with a first cut of the due diligence questionnaire and some of the key documents."

"Sounds good." Krantz flicked an irritated glance at Carol. He stood up, shook my hand, and thanked me. "If you'll excuse us, I just want a word with Carol about something else."

I had no choice. Time alone with Carol would have to wait until later. She waved her hand.

As I reached the door, she called out to me. "Did you bring your passport, Fin?"

My subconscious had been praying that it had been forgotten. No visa, no visit.

I handed it over.

"You ever been to Bombay before, Fin?" Chuck asked.

"Just the once," I said and quickly made my exit.

# SEVENTEEN

**A** hot mist pressed itself against the outside of my twenty-fifth floor window. I could dimly make out the shape of the Brooklyn shore rising out of the East River, a soft charcoal gash in the gray.

I'd just come off the line with Tochera, who had told me that he'd drafted a response to Marshall Forrester's request for input from me. I asked to see it. He said, no need, I can summarize. Fuck you, Mr. Richter.

He'd spoken to Clerkenwell Associates in London. They *had* written a highly customized policy for a very fancy premium, paid up front. Me as owner and the insured. One other named driver: JJ Carlson. Beats me, Tochera had moaned, with the whole thing based on misrepresentation, it's invalid, so why bother?

JJ's daisy chain of chaos. Someone would try and claim on it, they would contest it: either on the basis that it was real, that I had signed the form, or else by reference to some desperate, screwy jurisprudence. Whatever the basis, it was another energy source for JJ's vortex.

I diverted my phone calls and placed the Project Badla folder in front of me. I took a copy of the International Securities Association

Handbook from my carefully assembled one-shelf library and opened the fat paperback at the India section and laid it next to the folder. I then opened a new file on my PC.

I made my way through the Badla folder and sketched out a timetable and strategy as I went. There were moments when I forgot the fact that the subject matter was anchored in Bombay—during those moments I enjoyed myself. I could see the legal structure of the deal as clearly as if it were an architect's plan laid out in front of me. I sensed the shape, texture, and length of the relevant documentation: I would write these from scratch, I rarely used precedent. By the normal standards of legal agreements, the paperwork would be concise and intelligible—even to the layman. It was what I did: clearing a path through the chaos of others, while leaving my own chaos untouched.

But then the reality of Bombay would nudge the fluent stroke of my brushes and I would linger vacantly over a tiny corner of my canvas, unable to proceed without massive effort.

There were other distractions from my work. Paul Lamberhurst and Alf Silverman both paid me visits to fill in some background or get clarification on the files that life's slot machine had rained on them. Lamberhurst could barely hide his delight. In his aristocratic drawl, he managed to promise to steward the files well on my behalf before almost skipping from the room. Alf Silverman was more diplomatic. He was a US attorney specializing in antitrust law, or hatchback counting, as Ernie had called it. He seemed to appreciate that it was my misfortune that had served him up a good helping of free lunch and was fairly up-front about it. But I could still detect his thrill at being able almost overnight to clock up a calendar of quality billable hours without any effort on his part.

Terry Wardman, the third dysfunctional musketeer, didn't pay me a visit at all. I wasn't surprised: I doubted whether we had exchanged more than sixteen words in the past five years. If it weren't for the fact that I knew that Ernie thought so highly of him, he probably wouldn't have registered on my radar screen. After all, he wasn't even a qualified lawyer—he was a Legal Executive. But he was an expert on matters regulatory. An encyclopedia. Maybe I'd ask him for some background material on India, pick his brain.

At around 5:30 P.M. I closed the Badla folder and pressed the print button to spew out the work I'd done so far. It would appear at the printer on Paula's desk; she'd see it and she'd bring it in. We'd hardly spoken to each other all day.

I called Carol and got through straight away.

"You okay?" I asked.

"Krantz gave me a hard time over my performance at the meeting," she said.

"I thought he might."

She laughed nervously. "I can deal with him—he's only a baby banker."

A pause.

"How about you?" she asked. "You were dead to the world when I left this morning. I was worried you wouldn't show. I wouldn't have blamed you."

"Let's eat out tonight," I said. "If you're free, that is. You choose."

"Cellar Americana. You know it?"

It was a hip place on a corner in the middle of SoHo. There were tables on the sidewalk and, at that time, the air would be pleasant and the atmosphere a contradiction of buzz and relaxation. We could watch the people go by and drink good white wine and engage in conversational foreplay away from the dark clouds over my future.

"In one hour," I said.

"Perfect."

Paula came in with my Badla product.

"Busy guy," she said dumping about fifty pages of material in front of me.

I felt the crisp warmth of the freshly printed paper and turned over a couple of sheets to see how it looked. It was shaping up.

I checked through it for another half hour and was about to make my way to Cellar Americana when Paula came back into the room.

"I give it about five seconds before Mr. Monks comes to see you," she said. "I think he's been drinking."

The door swung open.

"Eyelash."

It was Ernie, and Paula was right. His face was smeared and blotchy, although he seemed fairly steady on his legs. He wore a beautifully tailored summer suit of a gray whose lightness verged on cream. He asked politely for Paula to leave the room before he slumped into a chair.

"Bloody hot," he said, pulling a freshly laundered white linen handkerchief from his jacket pocket. He dabbed it gently across his forehead.

He did his grieving moon impression. "I need a chaperon," he said. "Can't face it on my own."

"I'm afraid I already have an appointment." Ernie could be very persistent in his quests for company.

"Cancel it," he said flatly.

"It's a client, Ernie. I can't." Carol was a client.

"You don't have any. Charles snaffled 'em."

He didn't get this one, Ernie. She hid during the roundup.

"Tomorrow, Ernie," I said firmly. "We can go out tomorrow. I really can't duck out of my appointment tonight."

Ernie moved from grieving moon to hurt child. "Just fifteen minutes. Not even that. Nine hundred, widdly wee seconds. Escort me, support me. When we get to where we get to, I shall release you into the night, free as a bat to flit amongst the gas lamps."

"Where are you going?" I asked.

Ernie brightened. "Good, that's settled," he said, slapping his massive hands together like a playful seal.

"I didn't say that."

"As good as," Ernie retorted. "Just to the Regent. Not a millimeter beyond."

"You're not staying there, are you?" I didn't want to go to the Regent. Too much risk of running into Keenes or Mendip or, worse still, Sunil Askari—although he was most likely already on a plane back to Bombay.

"Good God, no." Ernie seemed shocked by the suggestion. "Not enough chintz for me. Too cold. More for the likes of Charles."

"I won't go in the hotel, Ernie. I mean it. To the door and that's it."

Ernie frowned. "You negotiate like your father. A luscious villain. Very well: the door and no more."

Dad had been a great negotiator. He could have sold slaves to Abraham Lincoln.

"After that, I have to go," I said emphatically.

"Go, go," he said, now a tragic diva. "Desert me, I will not hold you back."

"I'll see you downstairs in five minutes," I said. "I must make a quick phone call."

I called Carol on her direct line. Voicemail. "Fuck, fuck, fuck," I said out loud.

"Language, counselor." I looked up. Paula was standing in front of me.

"Sorry," I said sheepishly. "Could you do me a big favor and try and get hold of Carol Amen and tell her that I might be a bit late for my meeting with her."

"Meeting or date?" Paula teased. This woman was incredible.

"There's no getting anything by you, is there?"

Paula laughed. "No. I'll get hold of her for you. And you better get after Mr. Monks before he winds up walking into the street and getting himself knocked down."

"You're an angel," I said, blowing Paula a kiss. "And tell her I won't be long."

I stopped at the door. "It's our little secret, Paula. Okay?"

She tapped her nose. "What is?"

# EIGHTEEN

**E**rnie was sitting in the back of a Lincoln Towncar with its engine running. I climbed in beside him and turned to see him take a big slug out of a hip flask before poking it under my nose. The pungent vapor of scotch nauseated me.

"No thanks, Ernie."

When Ernie hit the scotch, he meant business. Blues Booze, he called it. For him, gin was merely the warm-up act.

"They're having a bit of a do," said Ernie.

"Who's having a do?"

"Clay & Westminster Merger Committee—of which I am the most decorous member—and the senior shits from the Shyster Guggenheims. Charles has called us together for an evening of hands across the water. Or rather, Budweiser in their case and malt in mine."

"Christ, Ernie. You might have told me. If I'm seen even on the edge of a gate-crash, I'll be in worse trouble than I am already."

Ernie shook his head sadly. "Trouble with insurers and Bombay buggeration, I hear. Don't ask me for advice, I'm not sloshed enough to play the lawyer. Anyway, I don't know the details, they don't tell me anything these days. There was a time when I could have helped you. But not now." He took another swig from the hip flask. "You just stay lurking in the shadows of the backseat when we arrive. They'll all be upstairs anyway. Now hold my hand, I'm maudlin and need the touch of innocent flesh."

It was crazy—sitting in the back of a limo holding the hand of a fifty-five-year-old man in a cream suit. But I had provided this gentle service several times before and never come to any harm, so what the hell.

"They're scared," he said, his eyes shut, his tongue glossing his lips in languid sweeps.

"Yes," I said.

"But McIntyre shoots cowards." Ernie raised his hand and cocked his thumb. "Pop pop. *Next* . . ." The driver turned around in startled surprise at Ernie's outburst.

Ernie giggled. "He's a fucking haddock with a beard. Your daddy didn't like beards, did you know that, Eyelash?"

"No."

"Ah well. The possum's no longer with us. Can't protect us from the raging bearded haddock."

He subsided in his seat. I thought he'd gone to sleep.

"I'm scared too," he said suddenly and sat up.

"What of, Ernie?"

"Not 'of.' 'For.' For you, Eyelash."

"That's kind of you, but you've said there's nothing you can do."

Ernie frowned. "I did say that, didn't I? Rotten of me, pusillanimous." He yawned like an elephant seal and swept his handkerchief over a fresh tide of sweat on his forehead. He then turned to me and cupped my face in his hands. His palms were big enough for my head to seem like a crystal ball comfortably resting in their generous embrace.

"Your father was a wonderful man and a wonderful lawyer," he said, "and you have inherited his elegance of intellect. Sometimes we forget the aesthetics of law, its inherent beauty." His eyes ranged over my face. He really was scared, he was *showing* me his fear.

"I became deputy senior partner of a small firm," Ernie continued. "A few mavericks, a studio of artists, if you like, commissioned by people we admired and were interested in. Charles knew the future lay in a different direction—multinationals, banks, widget manufacturers. Unbeautiful but profitable. I don't blame him, though. He's a decent sort—been good to me. And to your father. And you. He's trying to protect you, you know."

From whom, from what?

Ernie tilted my head in his hands. "The picture's got bigger, Eyelash. It's more difficult to stand back from, see its whole. You know, like those pictures made up of dots. It takes a special perspective to see the picture for what it is. Take my advice, don't just stand back, take two steps sideways. Standing back is for Johnny Average, the plodder. You're better than that. But don't ignore the dots, Eyelash. Once they think they've got the picture, people always ignore the dots. But you won't, will you? Dots can provide bearings. They can be coordinates."

We had pulled up outside the Regent.

Ernie gently released my face. "Thank you for coming with me, Fin," he said. "It was a kindness and I know it was a burden for you. I would have asked Terry Wardman to do the honors, but he wasn't around." He grinned. "Anyway, you are much, much prettier."

"Driver," he suddenly shouted, "take my friend to his appointment with destiny." With that, he heaved himself awkwardly out of the car, slammed the door shut, turned inelegantly on his heel, and tottered into the Regent.

I told the driver where I wanted to go and sat back. Maybe I could inhabit a better world for a few hours. Tomorrow, the real world would come flooding back, invasive, unwelcoming, fueled by aggression and vitriol, overpopulated by cops, attorneys, and tabloids.

Tilting the center armrest down I let my arm dangle lazily over it. I felt something on the seat.

It was a black wallet, thin and floppy, made of the finest kidskin, monogrammed with the initials EM. I flipped it open and took out a VISA card. Mr. Ernest Monks. I leaned back in my seat, shut my eyes, and quietly mouthed every expletive I knew.

I was due to meet with Carol in fifteen minutes. We were attorneys, Carol would understand. And "Fin the Quartz" was in a Queens cemetery, buried alongside JJ.

As we pulled up outside the hotel again, I told the driver to keep the engine running. He nodded and smiled and informed me that, had he known the urgency, he would have offered to return the wallet after dropping me off in SoHo. Why the fuck hadn't I thought of that?

I got out and started to make the dash for the hotel entrance. Then I saw them. Standing next to a limousine a mere few yards away were Mendip, Keenes, an unsteady Ernie Monks, and another man I knew from pictures in the press to be Jim McIntyre. Could I still drop the wallet off at reception and get back to the car unseen?

"Eyelash." It was Ernie. He released himself from the group and came toward me, the others following closely.

"You promised to behave, Ernie," I heard Keenes hiss.

"Had my fingers crossed, you little Nazi," Ernie replied savagely.

Ernie wobbled dangerously. "Managed a whole minute with the Shysters, Fin. A *whole* sixty seconds of polite piffle." His bottom lip bulged in a guilty pout. "Then exception was taken to my thrilling parodies of Hollywood stars."

He grabbed me by the breast pocket of my suit jacket. "Come up and see me sometime. I need you. Sometime soon," he slurred, in a ghastly impression of Mae West. Keenes pulled him off me and I thought Ernie was going to take a swing at him. But he just rocked on his heels and looked sullen.

Beyond them, McIntyre shot me a deadly glance and then turned to a furious Mendip. He said, "This guy needs a bed, Charles." I assumed he was talking about Ernie, but the hostility seemed directed at me.

Charles put his arm around Ernie. "I think there's been enough excitement for one evening." His tone was surprisingly gentle. "You're an old fool and your own worst enemy." Charles patted his back and Ernie nodded humbly. It seemed that all the fight had gone out of him, as if his now crumpled and sweat-stained cream suit merely housed a large balloon filled with tepid water, gin, and scotch. Ernie allowed Charles to escort him away without any further physical or verbal resistance.

Keenes was standing next me. "I've got Ernie's wallet," I told him. "He left it in the car."

"We'll talk about your part in all this in a minute," said Keenes coldly. "I'll return it. Meantime, wait here." He snatched the wallet from me and went over to the car where Ernie had now been stowed and tossed it carelessly onto the backseat before muttering something at the driver. Mendip leaned against the car, deep in discussion with McIntyre, and without pausing, straightened himself, slammed the door shut, and allowed the car to speed off down Wall Street.

From down the sidewalk, Keenes crooked a finger at me.

"What in the blazes do you think you're playing at," he said.

McIntrye gave Mendip a friendly tap on the chest. "I'm going back to the party, Charles," he said. "I think you've got an internal issue to resolve here. Don't be too long. You and I've got to say a few words to the folks and then let them hang loose and relax."

Mendip nodded. McIntyre went back into the hotel without looking at me.

"Well?" Keenes glared.

"Ernie asked me to accompany him here from the office," I explained evenly. "He left his wallet in the car and I came back to hand it in to reception. That's it."

"You're a menace," Keenes said.

"What the hell was I supposed to do?" I replied. "You know Ernie, you know how he can be. It's not my problem, not my fault. Ernie's your management issue not mine. I've got enough on my plate as it is."

"That'll do, Fin," said Mendip quietly. "Let's put a line under this. Stay away from Ernie from here on. He always seems to be drunker than usual when you're around. But he's very much part of the Clay & Westminster family and we must make allowances. You are part of that family too; but you're making it difficult for us to help you."

Some family.

"Shouldn't you be in the office preparing documents for Bombay?" Mendip said.

"That's precisely what I was trying to do when Ernie whisked me away," I said.

"Good." He reached out and straightened my tie. "And don't you ever ever use my name to try and gain access to people. I know what you said to get the meeting with Tochera brought forward."

His face spoke of censure; if so, what were his hands saying?

Mendip turned around and strode toward the hotel entrance. "Come on, Sheldon," he said over his shoulder. "I've got a speech to make and you've got to listen, not heckle, and show extravagant appreciation."

Keenes poked his finger in my ribs. "You may be part of the family," he whispered, "but you're the bloody black sheep. Just like your father."

I went back to the car and told the driver to head for SoHo.

My call to Carol's cell phone was greeted by the answering service. I left a message to say I'd be late.

I got the number for Cellar Americana from information and called them.

"Miss Amen has left a message for you," a waiter told me. "Hold on a second." In the background I could hear the sound of people enjoying themselves. "Here it is. She couldn't wait, she's sorry, something came up, will call tomorrow."

"That all?"

"That's it, sir."

"Take me to Battery Park, please," I told the driver.


I walked into the lobby of my apartment block and nearly made it to the elevator.

"A special delivery for you, Mr. Border." The jolly doorman. "You guys lead your lives at one hell of a pace." He handed me a FedEx bag.

He touched my arm, like he wanted to get my attention. "I was thinking maybe I would try the banking game. You got any advice, I could sure use it."

I stared at him for a moment. Early twenties, sharp-looking, probably make a good banker. "My advice, just fucking forget it," I said.

I tore the FedEx bag open in the elevator. I didn't want to read it in my apartment, my domain.

It was from a firm of attorneys, but not Marshall, Forrester, Kellerman, and Hirsch. A small Manhattan outfit, a one-man band: Jack Kempinski. A tough name, rugged, gritty, seen action on the legal eastern front, ate tank traps for breakfast, Brit attorneys for lunch. He said his client was Miranda Carlson. JJ's death had left her and the children destitute. He had advised her that JJ's death was entirely my fault, that I was a dope peddler, had gotten JJ high, and put him behind the wheel of a death machine. I was a pusher, a wrecker, a dangerous desperado who deserved to be deleted. Financially and professionally ruined first, then deleted. And he was just the guy to do it.

My chart needed amending, another plaintiff to be added, one that I hadn't planned on.

I paused at my front door.

Miranda destitute? Why? JJ was rich. Sure, everyone would be after a slice of the estate, but that could take years. For now Miranda was rich. But if that were the case, why was she running to an ambulance chaser like Kempinski?

Inside the apartment, I went straight to the refrigerator and took out a can of beer. Out of the kitchen, my footsteps clacked mockingly on the wooden floor.

I checked the voicemail.

"You'll have the letter by now." At the cemetery, Miranda's voice had seemed weak, enfeebled by the rain, dissipated by the vast terrain. Now it was almost flat, barely making it through the little plastic mouthpiece on the phone.

"You must have known all along. You were his attorney, you must have known. He had nothing, left us nothing. He wasn't even an employee of Jefferson Trust. He was hired through some kind of consultancy arrangement—I don't know, I don't understand these things. Some offshore thing. Jefferson Trust doesn't, won't, say he even existed for them." She stopped talking, but she hadn't hung up, I could hear the short ragged breaths, a little mouse cornered by the cat. "And you knew all along, didn't you? Well, you're the lawyer, Mr. Border, and I'm going to use your precious law to destroy you." It went quiet until the answering machine told me I had no new messages.

I took the chart out of my pocket, looked at it for a moment, screwed it up into a ball, and threw it on the floor.

JJ's vortex raged in my head, roaring, spinning, sucking, sucking me into its void.

I went to the bedroom, took off my suit coat, and chucked it carelessly over the back of the chair. There was a light tap—something had fallen to the floor. I switched on the light and saw a small cardboard folder lying by the bureau, little bigger than a credit card. At first I thought it was an old receipt holder from a fancy restaurant, but when I picked it up I saw it contained a brass key. It was for a room at the Plaza. 567 was scribbled untidily on the inside flap. I looked at it for a while, trying to figure out some logical reason for its presence in one of my jacket pockets.

Ernie had grabbed at my suit. He had asked me to come up and see him sometime. Sometime soon. It was Ernie's room key; he'd slipped it into my breast pocket before he had allowed himself to be driven away.

He'd said he needed me. Drunk as he was, perhaps I needed him even more.

# NINETEEN

It was around eleven-thirty when I walked into the lobby of the Plaza, dodging and weaving through the tide of people making their way out after functions or dinner. For the most part they were well-dressed, some in tuxedos, whereas I was in Levi's and a burgundy, cotton Barneys short-sleeve. But there were still some tourists in their dreary travel-wear milling around gawking at the gaudy splendor of the Plaza public areas.

A bellboy eyed me suspiciously as I got in the elevator. I pressed five and he disappeared from view as the big brass doors clunked shut in front of me.

The heavy-duty doorknob of 567 had a Do Not Disturb card dangling from it. I pressed the buzzer firmly. I knew I'd have to give several buzzes and allow a fair amount of time for Ernie to make it across the room.

I buzzed again and waited a little before putting my ear to the door. I was sure I could hear some music; classical—choral, perhaps. But I could hear nothing that signified a stirring Ernie.

There was the sound of conversation coming from around a corner about thirty feet along the hall. I lifted the Do Not Disturb card and slid the room key into the slot, turned it, and entered the room, immediately shutting the door behind me.

Before even appreciating that I was in total darkness, I gagged. The smell was terrible. Violently organic. I fumbled for a light switch, located it, and found myself standing in a small hallway that led into the main suite. I went into the next room and switched on the light.

A large drawing room. Its sumptuous furnishings appeared undisturbed, the cushions still well-plumped. Elaborate ashtrays were unsoiled and, apart from a dirty glass and a half-full bottle of cask-strength malt whiskey standing on a sideboard, there was little evidence of occupation. But the music was louder and the smell was stronger.

There was a pair of double doors that I guessed led into the bedroom. I opened one gingerly and found myself in another unlit room, whose darkness was filled with a choir only a few decibels short of deafening. I found the light switch.

The bedroom. A suitcase unopened on a stand; passport and wallet on the bedside table, the bed itself turned back for the night, its good-night chocolate resting unopened on the pillow, its sheets crisp and undented. The doors to the entertainment unit were open and I could see that there was a CD player on a shelf below the TV. I turned down the volume; some strange sense of decorum prevented me from switching it off altogether.

A strip of light ran along the bottom of what I imagined to be the bathroom door. Turning the handle gently, I let the door swing open. I staggered back; here the smell was overwhelming. This time I couldn't control myself. I sank to my knees and retched. Nothing came; I hadn't eaten since God knew when.

Beyond the entrance to the bathroom, a lake of filthy liquid slicked the floor. It was punctuated by islands of solid matter, anonymous, disgusting. I could also see a foot and the shin of a hairless leg.

I forced myself to walk into the bathroom.

The mess was everywhere. And in the middle of it was Ernie Monks. He was slumped against the sink, his head just below the lip of its rim, a cheap wig of long black hair tilted bizarrely over his temples.

He couldn't slide all the way to the floor because there was a leather belt around his neck that had been lassoed over one of the big chrome faucets.

Ernie stared at me, his eyes vacant and bulging. His mouth was open, and filled with a tongue the size and color of a small eggplant. The rest of his face was stretched in a macabre facelift, thanks to the contorting effects of the leather belt straining around his throat and up behind his ears.

He was naked, and I couldn't help being struck by the fact that he was completely hairless—apart from the dumb wig—not a tuft, not a strand, anywhere on his marble-hued body. I touched his left hand. His skin felt like cold tire rubber. And then I glanced at his pelvic region: His penis and scrotum were bloated and purple, a knot of twine poking out from their base. Jesus. Like a tourniquet on the end of a sausage.

I wanted to release him, to cover him. This wasn't the real Ernie. This wasn't real at all. This was the Madness of Queen Ernie the Third, as he had once termed one of his own lapses of good taste.

But I knew I wouldn't go near him again as I edged back toward the door. The price of his dignity was too high for me. I felt guilty as I nudged the light switch off, to at least afford Ernie's corpse some temporary privacy. It was a small gesture, and not nearly enough.

In the bedroom I tried to think. My first inclination was to call the police or at least hotel security, but then I started to see the future and imagine myself once again in the center of events. The police, Mendip. I had done nothing wrong, except be in the wrong place at the wrong time. Again.

Ernie was dead; there was nothing I could do for him.

In a short while, he'd be found. My interference would add nothing to the process except more additions to my now discarded chart.

What had happened here? The finale to a dark struggle. It was too near to the event to get a grip on the steps that might have led to this scene. A gone-wrong sex game? I didn't think so: Ernie wouldn't die from something so banal. A pickup that had turned on him? No: Ernie had invited me to his room—he wouldn't want me to find trade in his boudoir. None of it made sense: the wig, the twine, the shaved body. Maybe when I hadn't showed up quickly, Ernie had started on a fatal ritual, perhaps hoping that I'd appear to stop it in its tracks before it was too late. No, no, not that either.

My brain registered the music, a coping mechanism maybe. A Palestrina Mass, one of Ernie's favorites. *"Sicut lilium inter spinas,"* sang the sublime alto voice. "Like a lily among thorns."

The CD player was set to repeat. I switched it off but left the CD in its tray. To the left was another small shelf with a few books stacked neatly on it: the Zagat restaurant guide, Henry James's *Washington Square,* leather-bound with an EM monogram embossed on the spine, an anthology of T. S. Eliot poems. And the latest Jackie Collins. There was another book tucked behind his little library. I lifted out the slim paperback carefully. It was *In Black and White,* by Rudyard Kipling. Inside the flyleaf was a white envelope with the name *Terry* written on it, in Ernie's appalling script.

I'd been in the suite for too long. I slid the book back behind the others, but kept the envelope, thought for a moment, and then folded it and stuck it in the back pocket of my jeans. I jerked a tissue from a box on the dressing table and made a quick sweep of the room to remove at least the most obvious prints. It was futile, I knew. My dabs were sure to be somewhere and would be found, if the police decided to treat the place as a murder scene. And, anyway, nothing would get me back in the bathroom. I hadn't touched anything in there, had I? Only Ernie.

I switched out the light in the bedroom and moved quickly through the drawing room before hesitating at the suite entrance. I turned out the last light, wiped it, opened the door an inch or two, and peered one way down the corridor. It was clear. I opened the door a little farther and poked my head around the other. That was clear too. I shut the door quietly and walked toward the elevator.

# TWENTY

**D**ots. I'd tried stepping sideways—two steps—like Ernie suggested. Still blasted dots. Not bearings, not coordinates. Atoms of chaos.

On the desk in front of me, lay a newspaper with my name in it.

"You okay?" It was Paula.

No. Ernie's dead, he died in a Bosch-inspired hell. And my own life is a small, vulnerable, expendable box in an overcrowded PowerPoint presentation. My chart has become more sprawling than the Kennedy family tree and won't fit on a single sheet of letter-size paper anymore.

I turned the newspaper around for Paula to read. "I don't get a headline yet," I said. "But they place me at the scene." There was a quote from the dog walker, a picture of him even. "They ask the obvious questions and, by tomorrow, they'll have learned that it's my name on the McLaren registration documents. Tomorrow, I will be the devil."

Paula didn't read the piece. "I've already seen it."

I folded up the paper and dropped it in the wastebasket.

"Pablo Tochera called," Paula said. "Your phone was off so I thought I'd leave you in peace for a while."

"That was nice of you."

"This isn't," she said, handing me an envelope.

I didn't take it. I kept my hands flat on the desk.

"Your resignation?" I whispered.

"Uh-huh."

"Does it contain an explanation, Paula?"

Tears were leaking down her cheeks. "Leave it, Fin."

She was too important, too pivotal. To me. But what about *her* life? What was pivotal in her life? Or rather, why was it so important that Schuster Mannheim play no part in it?

"Please, Paula . . ."

She threw the letter on my lap and left the room, barging into Charles Mendip on the way.

"Oh my God," she muttered through her tears. "Not you. Jesus, not you."

Mendip shut the door and sat down, impervious to the chill welcome.

I put Paula's envelope in my pocket along with the one I'd taken from the Plaza.

Mendip glanced briefly at the newspaper in the wastebasket and frowned.

"Ernie was found dead this morning in his hotel room," he said flatly.

I affected a look of shock—it wasn't difficult: All I had to do was to conjure the image of Ernie's face as he hung suspended from the sink.

"What? That's terrible," I said. "What happened? I can't believe it." I supposed that this was what I'd say if the news were hitherto unknown to me.

"A heart attack," said Charles. "We'd been warning Ernie for years: the drink, the smoking, the candle-burning. It was bound to happen sooner or later. Still, he was one of a kind, a big person in every way." He stopped for a moment and looked away from me and I thought I heard him mutter, "Bloody fool." He turned his back to me.

"But I want to know about last night."

"What about it, Charles?"

"You were with him. What happened?"

"I've already told you."

Charles gave an impatient wave of his hand. "I know what you said. I want to know if there was anything else. Did he say anything peculiar? Did he seem ill? Did he behave oddly?"

"Ernie always behaved oddly," I said. "But no more oddly than usual. I suppose he seemed tense, the jokes were less thick and fast, and a bit more gallows than usual, but not dramatically so."

Charles sat back in his seat and flicked his fingers against his cheek. They rasped more than normal and I realized he hadn't shaved. That was a first, in my experience.

A heart attack. Ernie's memory would be better served with a heart attack, just like my father's had been better served with typhoid.

"Nothing else?" Charles probed.

I shook my head.

"You didn't see him again last night?"

He wasn't going to get anything more out of me unless he confronted me with a photograph of me retching on a Plaza suite carpet. "No, I did not," I responded emphatically. "What are you driving at?"

"You are in a great deal of trouble, Fin, and I'm trying to help you. You and I know what an old rogue Ernie was and I am simply making sure that there is nothing else that involves you, or that you know about."

"I thought you said he had a heart attack. What could possibly involve me?"

Charles eyed me sternly. "Just checking."

I asked some questions normally associated with the passing of a human being, like were relatives coming over, was the body to be flown home, when would the funeral be held?

"Ernie's body was only discovered about two hours ago," Charles said. "It's a little premature for arrangements to have been made in such a short space of time, don't you think?"

They'd gotten JJ underground pretty damn quick. But I let the point go.

Mendip tapped his pen on a piece of paper with a few lines of handwriting on it. "A communication to all staff will be made later today. In the meantime, I would be grateful if you made no mention of your liaisons with him."

"They weren't *liaisons*," I said angrily and then, sarcastically: "Will I be able to attend the funeral?"

"No," Charles said flatly. "Not after your performance at Carlson's."

Apparently being shouted at by a widow for no better reason than my mere presence disqualified me from one-third of life's great religious ceremonies. That left weddings and christenings to look forward to.

"Is there anything else?" I felt an overwhelming need for Charles Mendip to be out of my room.

"Is Project Badla on track?" The pissy little stockbrokerage, he was worrying about a pissy little stockbrokerage.

"Yes," I said, without disguising my contempt.

He glanced at the newspaper again. "I think you'll find you'll be going to Bombay sooner than expected. The clients are in a hurry. And with your name now in the papers, it may be better for you to be out of the country for a while. Although, as you know, Bombay would not have been my destination of choice."

Nor mine.

Mendip stood up and remained motionless for a moment.

"Charles. What's going on?"

His breathing came with difficulty; his eyes seemed suddenly glassy.

"Don't dissolve into a jibbering wreck like your father," he said. "If you do, I can't help you."

He seemed to loosen himself.

"This is difficult for all of us," he muttered as he left the room.

I called Carol's number and got through.

"Everything all right?" I said. "I was worried about you when I got your message at Cellar Americana last night. You didn't call."

"I had to go up to my mom in Scarsdale." She sounded distant. "My father had pulled some shit on her and she was upset."

"I'm sorry."

She gave me a brief and distracted tour of her parents' divorce. She made it sound like a natural component in her rite of passage: measles, adolescence, losing virginity, parents' divorce.

"I saw the piece in the papers about you," she said. I sensed her need to shift away from her own life. She had to be crazy to want to go near mine.

"I expect you're relieved they made no mention about the car being in your name," she said.

"They will."

"I guess." She drew a deep breath. "What else is happening? How you doing on the Badla documents?"

Fuck the documents.

"One of our most senior partners died last night," I said.

"Oh my God. What happened?"

"A heart attack." The Mendip version, even for Carol. For now, at any rate. "He was a good friend," I added.

"I'm sorry."

"Yeah. Some people have a bullet with their name on it. With Ernie Monks, it was more of a howitzer shell." I could see his body lying in its organic fallout.

"Ernie Monks?" Her voice was brittle.

"You've heard of him? I'm surprised; he never worked with Jefferson Trust. To be frank, he wasn't that fond of Americans." He hated them. He often said so—along with women, cheap wine, and anchovies.

"Yes, I've heard of him," she said. "You know the Cloisters?" The question seemed to come from nowhere.

I knew of the Cloisters, though I had never been there. It was an obscure corner of the tourist map and my sightseeing itinerary had been rather in abeyance lately. "Up at Fort Tryon?" I said.

"I'll see you there at three this afternoon." It was an instruction, not an invitation. "Go to the Cuxa Cloister, it's near the middle of the complex. Cuxa—got it?"

"What's the matter, Carol?"

"Just be there," she said and hung up.

# TWENTY-ONE

Ernie Monks and his death had spooked Carol.

Why?

At three, maybe I'd find out.

I took a clean sheet of paper and one of those pens with an extra-fine point. Maybe the chart would fit if I wrote microfiche style.

It didn't take long to reconstruct the contents of the ball of paper now lying on my apartment floor.

I then added Miranda Carlson as a plaintiff. Would the children have a separate cause of action? I wondered. One for Pablo.

I made supplementary notes to the entry for Jefferson Trust. If JJ wasn't an employee then maybe they could wriggle out of any liability based on his actions. What did his business card say? Most players had some version of *president* on them, others a variant of *director,* a few carried *chairman* for the ego trip.

I remembered now. JJ's had nothing. Just a name and some telephone numbers. Not even a reference to Jefferson Trust. Maybe, in invisible ink, *Master of the Universe.* JJ didn't really need a title; his brain, his physique, his boundless confidence; all of these were his call-ing card. Titles were for little people.

Delaware Loan, my alleged lenders, were slotted between the plaintiff and defendant columns. Where did they fit in? I'd heard noth-ing from them. Strange. They had supposedly lent me nine hundred and fifty thousand dollars. Either they didn't watch the news or this sort of thing happened to them all the time. Maybe they assumed that my Chase Manhattan account was overflowing.

Shit. Chase Manhattan. They deserved a mention. They could go in the defendant's column, with me as plaintiff. Good God, here was a suit where I was on the right side, except that it had cost me fifty thousand for the privilege.

I slipped the revised chart into my pocket and left the room.

Time to visit Terry Wardman.


Terry's door was open and he was in; I could see the back of his head as he sat poker-straight at his desk in front of a window looking out on a view of other offices looking in on him. I watched him for a moment. He wasn't moving at all, as if he were a Victorian gentleman waiting for the camera to finish a long exposure for a starchy portrait. His phone rang but he didn't react. After a few rings, the call switched to voicemail.

I patted the breast pocket of my jacket to check that the letter from Ernie's hotel room was still there. I knuckled the side of the door.

He didn't respond.

For only the second time in five years I went into his room. It was just as I remembered it, pristine and serious, like a laboratory. The entire wall was a library of black lever arch files with white labels neatly noting their contents in a delicate italic type. It was a geography lesson in the world's securities regulation: files on the SEC in the US, the FSA in the UK, the COB in France, the CNV in Spain.

I coughed and Terry turned around.

His tight gray features betrayed nothing—neither knowledge nor ignorance of Ernie's death, neither joy nor despair, just the penetrative powers of little blue eyes that could suck the legal nourishment out of turgid mounds of material that the world's regulators had an unquenchable capacity to produce.

"Oh, it's you." His voice was featureless north London, un-influenced by his years in the States. He turned back to his desk and minutely rearranged a blotter pad. For most attorneys, a desk was a childhood sandpit where they could abandon themselves with their toys and make an unholy mess. But Terry's desk was a field of open space: a computer monitor, a keyboard, a telephone, and a blotter inhabited only by what he happened to be working on that moment. All other papers would be sorted and stored in the Clay & Westminster blue files and hung in the credenza that skirted the wall.

"Have you heard the news?" I asked.

Terry seemed to be inspecting his fingernails, his spotlight eyes searching for flecks of dirt in their well-manicured curves. "Yes," he said simply.

"I'm sorry," I said. "I know that you and he were close. He was a good friend to me as well."

Terry drew breath audibly and turned his attention from the actual nails and started a quality check on the cuticles, rubbing each one until he seemed satisfied that there was no immediate threat to their health. When he'd finished, he laid both hands flat on the desk.

"Good friends are hard to come by," he said at last.

Ain't that the truth.

"I gather you have problems of your own," Terry continued. I couldn't see a newspaper in the room. "Ernie mentioned something. Not by way of gossip, mind. I know what people thought about Ernie, but he was trustworthy, didn't let his tongue wag. Anyway, he said something about you having a cross to bear, but he didn't go into detail. If that's right, I'm sorry for it, though there was a time I would have rejoiced in the fact."

I couldn't imagine Terry rejoicing about anything, still less any-thing to do with me.

"I'm afraid I don't understand." I pulled up a chair and sat down.

"You know that I'm not a qualified lawyer, don't you," said Terry. I nodded. We all knew it—Terry's Chip, it was called, a legal executive among fully-fledged attorneys. He was paid a ton of money, but he wasn't officer class, wasn't a true member of the club.

"When your father was still alive," he said, "I asked Charles Mendip for a year's leave to get myself qualified. I needed enough time to bring myself up to speed with the main body of law." He waved his hand at the row of files along the wall. "My niche is too specialized, you see. This is all I know. I needed to cover the basics, real law."

"Didn't he give it to you?" I asked.

"He said that he had no problem with it, but that there was another senior partner who wouldn't budge, said I was too important to let go for that length of time."

"Flattering, but rather unfair," I said.

"Perhaps. Perhaps not. I understood it was your father who wished to stifle my career development."

I was astonished. To my knowledge, my father had never particularly concerned himself with the aspirations of employees. He was like Charles; the development of the client base and doing deals were his overriding motivations. It wasn't that I thought my father would be incapable of insensitivity to staff member who wanted to get on; it was just that I didn't think he would care one way or another.

"I'm sorry." It was all that I could think to say. I didn't feel any urge to defend the memory of my father.

"Which is why I haven't sought your company for the last five years."

Perhaps that explained the mild animosity I'd sensed coming from him; although he seemed to avoid most company, and I just figured that I was perhaps slightly more out of his field of vision than the rest of the office.

"Why didn't you simply ask Mendip if you could have time off after my father died?"

"When I was refused permission, they sweetened the pill with a great deal of money, which I took. It didn't seem right to ask again. Anyway, your father's death wouldn't have made any difference."

"Why?"

"Because I know now that it wasn't your father who vetoed my leave, after all."

A part of me felt a relief at this news. "Who was it then?" I asked.

"Mendip probably. Ernie wasn't sure." It didn't sound like Mendip's style either.

"So Ernie told you," I said, stating the obvious.

"He told me last night, actually. He rang me shortly after he'd got back to his hotel, still fresh from his altercation at the Schuster Mannheim reception. Said he was listening to angels and swigging malt, you know Ernie. He spoke warmly about you, how you'd escorted him when he couldn't find me. He told me that it wasn't your father, and said I should speak to you. And that's what I'm doing. Apparently I'm fulfilling a dying man's last wish."

The vision of Ernie flooded my head. I rather doubted that speaking to me was his last wish.

Terry turned away from me. "I wish I'd been with him," he said. For the first time in the conversation there was a trace of emotion in his voice.

I pulled the envelope from my pocket. "This is for you, I think."

Terry reached out his hand without looking at me. I heard him fastidiously unfold the letter on his desk, keeping the piece of paper close to him, as if he were guarding a test paper from the roving eyes of cheats in an exam.

"It would appear that your secretary, Paula, has handed in her notice," he said. "Most unfortunate, but hardly my concern, I think."

Shit. I took hers back and gave Terry the one from Ernie. To my surprise, Terry found my error amusing. There was a gentle smile on his face.

He studied the letter. "Where did you get this?"

"I'd rather not say for now," I said.

Terry frowned, seemed that he was about to pursue the point, then relaxed. He was more interested in the letter's content than the history of its delivery. "Do you know what it says?" Terry waved his hand over a page of Ernie's scrawl that looked even more impenetrable than usual.

"No," I said.

"I *think* it's a reference, bless him," he said, handing me the letter. "Take a look for yourself."

I scanned it quickly. In the main it was gibberish, sentences didn't start or finish with anything like an approximation of English grammar, words were mispelled and misused, much of it was nearly illegible. But, at its core, there was a sense to it and I agreed with Terry that it looked very much like the attempt of a man trying to recommend, to whom it might concern, the virtues of another man—his work, his integrity, his intellect, his dedication.

"Christ, I wouldn't like to be going for a job on the back of this," I muttered.

I turned the letter over. "What's this stuff, do you suppose?" Hundreds of numbers were scrawled on the reverse. They looked like arithmetical calculations, but with no total, no solution.

Terry looked briefly. "Don't know," he said.

"Maybe he was doing his final accounts," I suggested. "Or maybe this was just a scrap he'd picked up to use. You know how he was, how he used to slice up old envelopes and draft letters on the back for his secretary to type."

"Perhaps," said Terry, taking back the letter and looking at the text again. "He believed he was trying to save me," he said.

I gave him a quizzical look.

"You see," said Terry, "Ernie knew that the merger with Schuster Mannheim would be bad for me. He was very worried about it and told me that he had even written to Mendip on the subject, put it in black and white. He was right to be worried: I'm not qualified and I don't try to ingratiate myself with the right people. In short I'm in no position to play the politics required to have real prospects in the enlarged firm."

I wasn't about to argue with him. His future was pretty bleak under the Schuster Mannheim banner. When they cottoned on to what he was and what we paid him, they would want him out and quick.

"So this was his way of trying to help me." The emotion was back in Terry's voice and for a moment I thought he might even cry, but he coughed slightly and straightened up. "Of course, it's no earthly use to me, silly old fool. But a beautiful gesture. He must have been terribly ill when he wrote this."

He folded up the letter carefully and replaced it in its envelope and stuck it in the top drawer of his desk. "I shall treasure it," he said.

"Will you look for another job?" I asked.

"Perhaps. I haven't really thought about it. I do the work and that's all. No plan. The last time I planned anything I wasn't allowed to pursue the matter. Planning's not my forte. At the moment I seem to be spending a large part of my time arguing with the US immigration authorities for Green Cards, visas, and whatnot for the other ever-mobile members of this firm. After the merger I expect they won't need my rather subtle skills. They'll just ring up, say what they want, and it shall be given."

Terry sat there quiet for a while, not looking at me, not looking at anything. "Show me the other letter again," he said abruptly. I pulled Paula's resignation out of my pocket and handed it over. He studied it. "She likes you," he said. I was about to say something stupidly bashful and modest when Terry leaned forward in his chair and brought his face near mine. "She likes you a lot," he whispered forcefully.

He gave me back the letter. "You know she worked for Schuster Mannheim before she came here?"

I nodded.

"Did you know she worked for Jim McIntyre?"

Jesus.

"Of course, he wasn't senior partner then. He was head of corporate, but already well on the way to the top spot."

"Did he fire Paula?" I asked. "She wouldn't say and her file doesn't show anything."

"It wouldn't." Terry smiled knowingly. "When I said that Ernie didn't gossip, that wasn't strictly true. It appears that McIntyre went through a bad patch in his marriage and problems with the bottle. And he turned to Paula for support. He took her up to some monster house on the Long Island North Shore, Oyster Bay, I think, and presented his credentials, as it were. She wasn't having any of it, brave girl, and told him where to go. There was a bit of a scrap, with Paula threatening to scream harassment, and McIntyre alleging fraud and extortion. Anyway, the upshot was that Paula was prevailed upon to leave Schuster with $70,000 in her pocket. From what Ernie said of McIntyre's behavior, Schuster was very, very lucky to get off so lightly."

"No wonder she felt she couldn't stay," I said.

"She'll be all right, she's a very strong lady," said Terry. "But what about you? I know you saw the Carlson suicide. That must have been horrific."

It was indescribable, so why describe it? "I'm going to Bombay next week," I said. "It might help to put it out of mind."

"I know. Mendip wants me to make sure you can get out of the country. Shouldn't be a problem, if we're quick about it."

"Pity."

"Where your daddy died. I can understand your reluctance."

Terry pointed to his shelf. "You're welcome to my material on India. It's pretty much up to date, although I expect you know everything already."

He stood up and ran his finger along the line of files. "Here." He pulled it out and handed it to me.

It was heavy, the steel rods of the lever arch couldn't have held any more.

"Watch it in India," he said. "Ernie had an expression for it, just as he had an expression for most things."

"What was that?" I asked, knowing what I was about to hear.

"Bombay breakfast: scam and eggs."

# TWENTY-TWO

I took a car to the Cloisters. Up the West Side Highway, all the way to Fort Tryon Park, around the folly that necklaced the rocky outcrop overlooking the Hudson. A chunk of land was given to the Metropolitan Museum of Art by a Rockefeller to house their medieval art collection. And on this chunk, they'd built the replica of a monastery.

The driver asked if I wanted him to wait. I squinted up at the squat medieval tower rising from the thick walls of familiar Manhattan stone. The sun shone fiercely on the place and I fancied I was a noviciate monk checking in to my Tuscan Benedictine hideaway for the rest of my unnatural life. I could tell the driver he could wait, if he had sixty years to spare. Then I saw the fleet of M4 buses; this was their last stop. I'd take one home when I was ready and save myself thirty-five bucks.

I was a little early, but didn't want to hang around outside in the heat, where I could be seen.

A tunneled flight of steps took me into a cool hallway where an intense-looking student sat reading Homer's *Odyssey*. She put down her book and awarded me a totally disarming smile and welcomed me into a cavern that reminded me a little of my college chapel. I sauntered aimlessly around for a while, gawking unintelligently at the icons, the statues of saints, the faces of gargoyles, the tapestries. There was even a whole chapter house that had been imported stone by stone and reassembled. Everything looked strangely comfortable in its 1930s home, hostage from a genteel pillaging around the remnants of medieval Europe.

It struck me that I hadn't been to a museum in four years. I hadn't even been to the Met itself, let alone its weird annex up on these remote Manhattan heights. I figured Carol was a museum-goer, a lover of galleries, concerts at Lincoln Center, that kind of thing. The books and pictures in her apartment spoke for her. I imagined her cross-legged on the floor of the classics section of a Barnes & Noble bookstore, checking out the latest translations of Greek poets.

I looked at my watch. It was three o'clock. I made my way hurriedly along the posted directions to the Cuxa Cloister, not bothering to look at the relics on the way.

Although the Cuxa Cloister was deep in the complex, the sun was still high enough to stream into the little courtyard, bounded by an arcaded walkway, deep in shadow at one end and bathed in sunshine at the other. I took one circuit of the arcade, half-admiring the capitals and their carvings: scrolling leaves, apes, pinecones, lions, leaping men, and other stuff I couldn't identify. I couldn't see Carol anywhere. I looked out into the courtyard itself, symmetrical flower beds and paths spreading from a centerpiece basin, an old font, perhaps. The carpet of plants was too short to hide anyone and the place was empty.

"Fin."

I turned around. Carol was standing in a shadow. She emerged, wearing the same shades as she'd worn at the funeral. Her hair was tousled carefully and shone like an ad for conditioner. If this had been a real monastery, she would have represented a clear and present danger to a monk's vows.

I gave her a light kiss on the mouth. Her lips puckered only slightly in return.

My arm swept across the view.

"Nice place," I said. "What made you choose it?"

"It was nearby," she said absently, her gaze following my arm.

Nearby?

Canada felt nearer to Wall Street than this place.

She sat down on a wooden bench. I joined her.

She stared out into the courtyard. Every detail of the blue and yellow flowers was picked out by the sun; it was an utterly still life. No wind could find its way into this basin of tranquillity. My mother would have loved it; she'd know the names of all the plants, their full Latin names; she could've conversed with the monks of antiquity as they glided around their garden and admired God's handiwork and maybe felt a touch of pride at their own human talents. Of course, *this* garden could not have been planted more than sixty years ago, but it still had the timeless feel of the bygone age it was supposed to represent.

Carol rocked slightly, rhythmically, like she'd done that night in her Tribeca loft. She rubbed her hands, as if she were washing them. Her nails were chewed, and there were scratches on the backs of her hands.

"The guy who died," she said.

"Ernie Monks."

"Yeah. Him." She rubbed her hands some more and then gripped the edge of the seat.

"What about him?"

"Well, maybe it's not so important, maybe I just got carried away." She looked like someone who'd gotten on the wrong bus and was too embarrassed to ask to get off until it reached a scheduled stop.

"Why not tell me anyway and then we'll see."

"JJ knew him."

"Knew Ernie Monks?"

"Uh-uh."

"I don't think so. Ernie actually said he didn't know him."

"They knew each other."

She said it with conviction. But she had to be wrong.

I shook my head. "JJ and I used to talk about people at Clay & Westminster, Ernie included. Particularly Ernie—he was an extraordinary man. JJ never said he had met him. There would be no reason to hide it, would there?"

"Maybe there was a reason. I don't think Ernie Monks liked JJ. I think that maybe they didn't like each other."

"Ernie never said anything. He knew what had happened to JJ, he knew I was there. But he never said anything, Carol."

"He knew him." She hesitated. "They met each other," she said. "They had a big argument."

"Where? What about?"

"I'm not sure, India maybe, some of the words they used . . . they were used by Chuck Krantz. And by you. *Badla* was one of them. I don't know, Fin, I feel kind of stupid. But there's JJ's death, there's Bombay, and now there's Ernie Monks. I just needed to hear myself talk about it, out loud, see if it made any sense. It doesn't. Forget I said anything."

"You were there? When the argument took place, I mean?"

"What are you getting at?"

"Either you were there, or someone reported it to you."

"Yeah, I guess." She seemed annoyed. She might have tried to close the subject but it was still buzzing around like a fly that wouldn't go away.

I didn't want the subject closed. "Well, which? Were you there, or did you hear about it?"

"What's with you, Fin? I'm not your goddamned witness." She took off her dark glasses and wiped them on her shirt.

"You asked me up here," I said.

"I wish I hadn't."

"I'm glad you did. I think what you've said is significant. I don't know why yet, but I think it is."

"They met, that's all. They argued. People meet and argue all the time. It's no big deal. Except that JJ killed himself and Ernie Monks had a heart attack."

"I don't think Ernie died of a heart attack or, if he did, it's a highly misleading explanation of his death." I described the scene in Ernie's bathroom.

Carol brought her hand to her mouth. "Jeez, that's horrible." She moved her hand away and placed it on my knee. "You were there, you saw it for yourself," she whispered.

I nodded.

"God, how awful." For a moment she looked bewildered. Then she seemed to make up her mind about something. "I was there," she said, "I mean I was present when Ernie Monks and JJ argued."

"At the office, at Jefferson Trust."

"No. At JJ's apartment."

That was crazy. "A meeting at JJ's place with Ernie? And you? It doesn't make sense. What was it about?"

"Ernie Monks didn't know I was there."

I was missing something. The dot picture was too near. Two steps sideways. Still dots.

"I was hiding in the bedroom while JJ and Ernie Monks argued in the living room."

I could see the picture now. The dots had gone.

Carol sighed. "JJ and I were lovers."

"I see," I said slowly. I didn't really see at all, the whole thing jarred. The tap of a tuning fork with metal fatigue. The investment banker and his attorney.

"Were you lovers when he died?" I finally managed to ask. If I'd slept with her the day her lover was buried, it would somehow make it worse.

She shook her head. "No. We broke up some weeks before. Finally."

There were enough supplemental questions to fill a passport application form, but I wasn't sure that I wanted to ask them.

"If I asked you, would you tell me about it?"

"Are you asking?"

"I don't know." It was my turn to rock in my seat.

I turned to face her, but her dark glasses blanked me. "Do you know why he killed himself, was it because of you?"

A meandering line of chattering schoolkids made their way along the arcade and stopped in front of us to be lectured by an enthusiastic guide. She got animated about the likely daily rituals of monks in the twelfth century: prayers, meditation, gardening, farming, tending the sick, and scholastic work; she took the kids a world away from the unfettered capitalism coursing through the skyscrapers a few miles south. But I remembered that monasteries could be cauldrons of intrigue and unbridled greed and that it was perhaps only a coarse habit that separated them from Wall Street.

The line of kids moved on and the chatter faded away to a gentle hum drifting out of an adjoining enclosure.

Carol stood up and ran her hand along one of the ancient columns supporting the arcade. "I don't know if it was all down to me. JJ had a whole heap of problems. I knew he used coke, like you said, and other stuff too, really weird and obscure. He had money troubles as well. I think the thing with Ernie Monks shook him up; they hadn't just argued, I think it had gotten physical. JJ had a nasty scratch on his face when he came back in the bedroom after Ernie had left." She paused. "But maybe JJ's death was all down to me. He told me he just couldn't face losing me. He was scared, he said. I was the only thing that kept the fear at bay."

"I'm sorry," I said and found myself thinking of my last conversation with my father, when he'd called from Bombay. It seemed like you could kill someone just by doing nothing. Death by lethal rejection.

"You don't have anything to be sorry for." The dark glasses stared at me. "I realized the whole JJ thing was crazy," she said. "There was a time when I loved him, you know. But then he scared me, people around him scared me. We split up. But he drew me back in and the second time it was harder to leave."

Second time? Dates, Carol, dates. Would they coincide with her shifting attitude toward me over the years?

"If we had been discovered," she said, "it would have meant big trouble. What with him being married. Jefferson Trust doesn't like that kind of thing. So it had to finish. I've worked hard to get where I am and, in the end, I'd stopped loving JJ. It just wasn't worth it. But it was hard, all the same. Letting go, that is."

"I understand."

"No, you don't, you couldn't." She sat down again and took my hand. "Jesus, what have I done?"

"You had a relationship. You ended it. He died. Like you said, he had plenty of other problems. Don't punish yourself."

"What have I done to you, I mean."

She'd made me happy. In the worst week I'd had in five years, she'd made me happy. "You've done more than I can say without sounding like an adolescent. All of it good. Well, apart from Bombay. That was a shitty thing to do, but you meant well."

"I used you, to protect myself."

"You haven't used me, Carol."

"I have. When I tried to break up with JJ the second time, he wouldn't accept it."

"If you tried to ditch me, I wouldn't accept it either."

"Just listen, will you? JJ wouldn't accept it. The only thing that would make him believe it, he said, was if there was someone else. So I told him there was someone else."

"Was there someone else?"

Carol paused. "In a way, yes, but I wasn't actually seeing him."

"You mean you weren't seeing him yet."

"Right."

I heard myself groan. "You told him you were seeing me."

"You're smart."

"No, I'm not. I'm stupid." I felt numb. I'd been Carol's wire-cutters, her escape plan. Her way out of Camp JJ.

"So that's why JJ had me along for his suicide?"

"I guess."

"And why he put the car in my name. And stole fifty thousand of my dollars. And made me a borrower to the tune of nine hundred and fifty thousand."

The guy must've really loved Carol. And really hated me.

But why whip up such a colossal firestorm? Everything about JJ was big, so he wasn't likely to go out with a whimper.

Carol took off her dark glasses. "I'll tell the cops what happened, and the insurers, and the folks at Clay & Westminster, anyone you want. I'm so sorry, Fin. If I'd had any idea, I'd have found some other way of getting free."

I should have read the writing on the wall. A badass with spray paint had seen it coming. *Shit happens.*

"And what would happen to you if you told them?" I asked.

"I don't know."

I knew. Be fired. Her termination letter wouldn't spell it out, it wouldn't say: Fired for fucking a married man who killed fifteen people and framed respectable outside counsel. But she'd be pushed, all the same. Unemployed and unemployable thereafter.

I looked at her. She was crying.

I held Carol close to me. "I'm not sure telling everyone would help anyway. Think about it. The moment they cotton on to the fact that we are an item, they'd tear us to shreds, tell us we made it up, that there was something deeper, worse."

Carol pulled away from me and dabbed her eyes. "They don't need to find out about us."

"These things tend to get out, in the end. That is if they continue. And I'm not sure I want us to be a secret indefinitely."

Carol stroked my face. "I'm bad news, I think. I'll speak to the police and then you can straighten things out."

She wasn't bad news and, anyway, I knew it wasn't that easy. Manelli wouldn't buy it, nor would the insurers, nor the press. And certainly not Miranda Carlson. I'd need proof of what JJ had done. Carol's tearful confession wouldn't work on its own.

"Is your career important to you?" I asked.

Carol nodded. "Sometimes I think it's all I have, all I am. I feel defined by it. My parents aren't rich or smart and when I made Harvard, they turned cartwheels of joy. When I joined Simpson Thatcher they turned some more. And when I got to Jefferson Trust, I thought they'd spin out of control." She laughed. "But it wasn't just them. I felt good too. I feel proud to have made it this far. I know I shouldn't be saying this to you, but I don't know what it would do to me if I lost all that."

"Then wait," I said. "Don't do anything for now. Don't tell anyone. Work on Badla, come to Bombay, and take it from there. Okay?"

"But what about you, what about your lawsuit, your loan?"

"Schuster Mannheim is working on it." I wanted to imagine Pablo Tochera sweating blood on my behalf. I had a chart. And I had the truth on my side. Why didn't I feel the confidence I wanted to express?

Carol straightened up and uncreased her skirt. "He could be generous, you know. He did a lot of charity work. He even endowed a school in Bombay."

For me, there couldn't be a good side to JJ anymore. I didn't want to hurt Carol unnecessarily, but I didn't want that sick fuck JJ to get any positive airtime either. "Most charitable work is either self-aggrandisement or a guilt trip. There're not too many genuinely good people out there." I didn't know if this was true; I'd never done much more than give a dollar to a vagrant or sponsor the kids of work colleagues to do something wacky for a good cause, but it sounded like a reasonable statement under the circumstances.

"I've learned that emotions and motivations are very complex things," she said.

"I just want you to tell me you aren't going to the police." A straight yes or no.

"For now," she said.

"And where do we stand?"

She wouldn't look me in the eye. There were three or four sparrows thrashing around in the font in the middle of the garden. Her eyes were on them, the carefree little bastards.

"Oh, Fin. I need to think."

She stood up. "I've got to go now. Wait a few minutes before leaving." She walked briskly along the arcade and then turned sharp left and out of sight.

The sparrows were growing frantic; their twittering echoed around the cloister. Then one of them flew off and the rest followed. Silence.

Ernie knew JJ. Ernie scratched JJ on the face. JJ killed himself. And Ernie? What the hell had happened to him? India seemed to be the exchangeable currency between them. What half-eaten file had they choked on? Or was it just that JJ liked fast cars and hated me? And that Ernie went one weirdness too far in a Plaza suite bathroom. I could hear my father laughing again; maybe he was dancing with his wood nymph in a shady pool in another world, just like the sparrows in this one.

I got up and made my way out of the Cloisters. As I reached the foot of the tunnel of stairs and squinted into the bright sunlight, I half hoped to see Carol waiting for me, as she had stood at the chapel of rest after JJ's funeral. But she wasn't there.

# TWENTY-THREE

I turned off the phone and ordered Paula *not* to keep me posted on anything that Clara might turn up on the net. I was at work. I *needed* to work. And Project Badla was my only outlet.

I faxed Jaiwalla & Company, attorneys to the sellers of Ketan Securities. I told them what I wanted: all Ketan's corporate documents, all their dealings with the regulators, all their material contracts, lists of clients, staff details, banking details, lease details. The whole shebang. I attached a thirty-page questionnaire, covering every legal and accounting aspect of their business. I even had a stab at asking them economic questions: Who were their competitors, what was the breakdown of their client base, what were the prospects for the Indian market? Where did they see the threats? Where were the opportunities?

I sent them a draft memorandum of understanding, a draft sale and purchase agreement, a draft set of corporate statutes, draft employment contracts with built-in handcuffs. A share option scheme, the format I wanted for the accounts, a paper on tax issues, the kind of letter I wanted from Ketan's accountants, their lawyers, their banks, their bloody hairdressers. I was going to bury them with paper. I didn't want to give them a chance to send drafts to me first. I wanted to be in control. If Jefferson Trust wanted to buy a Bombay stock-brokerage, then so be it. It would be done properly, no compromise. This wasn't going to be a half-eaten file. I would give Jaiwalla so much to read, they wouldn't have the time to write anything for themselves. They wouldn't be able to compromise me.

I did a group distribution on the fax: to Jaiwalla. Copy to Sunil Askari at Askari & Co. Copy to Carol and Chuck at Jefferson Trust. Copy to Keenes and Mendip down the hall. I wanted to deplete an entire forest of paper. I was the phantom fax-man.

At 3:00 A.M., I switched off my light. The office was utterly quiet: no Paula, no Keenes, nobody, except the security guard who'd be swinging his flashlight around, nosing into offices, hunting for intruders between drinking coffee and watching porn on the portable DVD player I knew he had.

Outside, the moist heat intensified the pungent fish smell that haunted the district. The trucks would be moving in now, dumping the catch for the next day, spilling slime and ice over the rough cobblestones. I was tempted to take a detour through this incongruous scene—I'd done so many times previously, after a hard night's work. Not tonight, I decided, a brisk unromantic trot directly to Battery Park and then bed.

At the apartment block, I slunk past the concierge. I didn't want to hear about any more special deliveries. Maybe I should have let Carol go to the police and see if she could call off the dogs.

No. It wouldn't be right. It wouldn't work either. Anyway, it was a strategy that could be used later if all else failed. Yeah, but why use it any time if it won't work? I shook my head. Write another chart, bozo. I was getting confused. I was tired. I wanted to sleep the sleep of an attorney who had just done some good hard work.

I didn't even remember getting into bed.

# TWENTY-FOUR

It was 10:00 A.M. when Pablo Tochera rang me.

"It's Saturday, Pablo," I said through the wooze.

"Gee, I didn't know. I must lodge a complaint against Jim McIntyre for his barbaric work practices."

"How's it going?" I asked, sitting up. The blinds were drawn, so I couldn't tell whether I might get uptown to Central Park and pretend I had a normal life for an hour.

"I've gone ten rounds with Manelli over what he wants to charge you with."

"And what *does* he want to charge me with?"

"Everything from standing on a street looking like a dumb Brit all the way to Murder One."

"Why doesn't he get it over with and show his hand?" Then I'd see whether I needed to deploy the Carol defense.

"You've got them climbing up each other's butts. They will charge you when they're sure they will nail you. And they're close now. Manelli's sounding more relaxed by the hour, says when he next pays a visit, the only bargain he'll cut with you is not to demand the death penalty."

"There isn't a death penalty in New York, is there?"

"You're behind the times, guy," Pablo sneered.

"So what should I do?"

"Beats me. I don't generally do criminal work."

Fucking hell.

"What happens if I leave the country?" I asked.

"Sheesh. Stop there. You trying to get me jailed?"

"Okay." I didn't know the ethics issues for him. "What about the investigation work? How's that going? Finding the witnesses. Finding the truth?"

Pablo started coughing. "Sorry, guy," he said at last. "One too many cigars last night. Jesus. Julia—that's my wife—she busts my chops about the smell. Witnesses, you said. Well, to be truthful, there are a few technicalities in that regard."

"What kind of technicalities?"

"Jim McIntyre wants it done in a particular way and I, well . . . you see . . . I have some issues to resolve. I shouldn't be telling you this."

"What issues?"

"Jesus. You're going to get me fired. I knew it the moment McIntyre put me on this file. Issues. Yes. He has some cost concerns."

"Wait a minute." I got out of bed and started pacing the length of the phone cord. "It's in everyone's interests that it's proved I wasn't the owner of the car. Surely."

"That's what I said, but I'm not sure he sees it that way. I sense there are issues if JJ Carlson was the owner."

"What has that to do with costs, for Christ's sake? Anyway, Schuster Mannheim are *my* attorneys."

"That's what I said."

"Well, say it again," I shouted. "A bit louder. LIKE THIS."

"Okay, okay. Calm down. Talking with McIntyre isn't easy. And he doesn't take kindly to raised voices. Listen, I'm between a rock and a hard place. I'm partner material and this thing is fucking up my chances and then some."

"That's your problem, not mine. If you won't act for me properly, I'll find someone who will."

"Listen, I don't like to kick a guy when he's down, but you won't find anyone out there who can spell their own name who will act for you. You're very bad news. Anyone looking at the background material will know that they will be fighting the whole of New York City anytime now. You're going to be the most unpopular guy on the Eastern Seaboard when the shit starts flying. Believe me, I've thought it through. I'd hand you to someone else, if I could, if McIntyre would let me."

"This is crazy." I was shaking with anger.

"I'll call again when you've calmed down a little. Maybe I'll have some good news for you."

"Yeah, right," I said and slammed down the phone.

It rang immediately.

"YES?"

"They said you hadn't showed up at the office," Carol said.

"It's Saturday."

"This is New York. You're an attorney."

I held the phone against my shoulder for a moment. I put it back to my mouth. "I'm sorry, Carol. It looks like I'm being gutted and stuffed for someone else's dinner."

"It's okay," she said calmly. "It's good to scream sometimes. It's cathartic."

"I'm not screaming now," I said. "What are you doing and why aren't you doing it with me?"

"Listen, we need to get to business here. I've just been going through your fax to Jaiwalla. You want to crush them with paper?"

"Just doing my job. Isn't it okay?"

"Hey, I was kidding. It's great, very impressive. More to the point, Chuck Krantz thinks you're a class act. I think he'd hire you instead of me, given the chance."

"When are we going to India, Carol?"

"Now," she said. "That's why I called."

"How soon is now?"

"Like now, now. Delta Airlines flight 106, JFK direct to Bombay.

Leaves JFK at just after eight tonight. We arrive Bombay tomorrow night, about eleven. Two seats, first class, already booked."

"Jesus."

"I told you. I can take you off the file, go to the police. If that's what you want."

No. Thirteen hours on a plane next to Carol was all I wanted right then.

"Stick with the arrangements," I said. "I'll come, assuming I'm not arrested beforehand."

"And you need to pick up the tickets," she said. "They're with Paula and she's at the office waiting for you. She thought you might prefer a call from me rather than her. I like her."

On the way out of the apartment block, the jolly doorman was slouched over the counter. I avoided his gaze.

As I walked through the outer door, I could hear him mutter. "Asshole motherfucker," was how it sounded.


"The chief wants you," Paula said, as soon as I got into the office.

"Chief of what?" I was beholden to so many people, any number of chiefs. "You mean Mendip? Is he in his cubicle?"

"Yup. You want breakfast?"

"You're an angel. When I'm through with Mendip we'll talk."

Mendip looked like he was ready to go. He had his wheeled suit-case and an ancient garment bag.

"You leaving us?" I asked.

He didn't look up from the mess of paperwork on the desk. "Just for a day or so, to deal with matters arising from Ernie's death." Ernie was now a "matter arising" on a partnership subcommittee.

Mendip looked up at me. "You're going to Bombay this evening." His eyes were bloodshot and he'd cut himself shaving; a small scab had formed in the center of his chin.

"I know," I said. "Carol Amen told me."

Kevin, the messenger, came in. "Can I take your things down to the car now, Mr. Mendip?" He looked at me nervously as he carefully maneuvered Mendip's baggage. I winked at him. He grinned. "Hi, Mr. Border, how you doing?" He left the room without spilling a thing.

"Just get on and do the deal," Mendip said. "Don't mope; don't go in search of things that may disturb you. Read a book or something. And I suggest you don't tell your mother where you are. You'll only upset her. She's your mother, so it's up to you, but that's my advice. Anything else?"

"Yes. What the hell is going on here, Charles?"

He nudged me aside as he tried to get out of the room. I could hear him wheeze as he passed by. "Nothing," he snapped. He paused. "Remember, just do the deal. Don't inflame Sunil Askari, you know what he's like. Ring me if you have problems. Peggy in London will know how to get hold of me."

He hesitated and then shook my hand before leaving the room.

I returned to my office. There was a bagel and coffee on my desk and Paula stood by with a large envelope in her hand.

"The tickets?" I asked.

"Tickets, passport, and visa," she said, handing over the envelope. "There's a voucher for the Taj Hotel. No currency, though. You can get it when you arrive. A driver will meet you at Sahar Airport—that's the airport for Bombay."

She paused. But before I could say anything she was off again. "Health. I've been talking to the Jefferson travel people about that. It's too late for any inoculations, but your certificate for typhoid and some other real nasty diseases seems okay, just so long as you don't travel outside Bombay into rural areas." She tossed a large box of pills onto the desk. "Malaria. You better take one now. You should have started a week ago. So just don't invite any mosquitoes into your room."

She stopped again. Momentarily. "But I guess you know all this. I think you've been there before, haven't you?" She stared at me. I looked at my feet. Her eyes were too strong for me, too honest.

"Yes," I said.

"I figured."

I ripped open the envelope and spread the contents across the desk. It was all there, just like she said. "I wish you could come with

me. You could do the deal and I could sip gin and tonics and lob pis-
tachios into my mouth."

"I got better things to do, honey."

"Like what?"

"Like figure out what I'm going to do with my life."

"Would you hang around here for a little longer, while you do
your figuring?"

She looked agonized by my request.

"I need you here," I pleaded. "I need some Stateside eyes and ears.
The knives are out for me and maybe you can tell me who's wielding
them. I need someone I can trust."

Paula shaded her eyes with her hand. Maybe if she couldn't see
me, I'd go away.

"I know what happened, Paula," I said. "About McIntyre, what
he did to you. I found out."

She unshaded her eyes. "What do you know, who told you?" She
looked scared; her voice had lost its liquid bass undertone, a frightened voice.

"That McIntyre propositioned you. That Schuster Mannheim
paid you off. That you were a victim."

"Who told you?"

"I can't say." It occurred to me that Terry Wardman hadn't actually bound me with any express duty of confidentiality. But I'd assume
he had, for the moment.

"Propositioned me." Paula laughed bitterly. "You could put it that
way. That would be a lawyer's way of putting it."

She hunched her shoulders, as if she was shrugging someone off,
as if McIntyre was in the room with us. "He did a tad more than
proposition me."

"What he did, what he did exactly, isn't my business, though you
can tell me if you want. I just need you to know that I know. And that
I support you completely."

Paula smiled. "That's nice of you. I appreciate it."

I unwrapped my bagel and took a bite.

"You packed?" Paula asked.

"Nah. I'll do a few things here, then go back to the apartment, throw a toothbrush in my briefcase, and head off to Jefferson Trust around three-thirty."

"What's that?" Paula pointed to Terry's file.

"Background on India. Terry Wardman lent it to me. Looks useful."

Paula pursed her lips. "Mr. Wardman's a nice guy. Kinda remote, maybe. But nice. You've been talking to him, haven't you?" Her eyes told me that she knew Terry was my informant.

She handed me a folded piece of paper.

"What's that?" I asked.

"See for yourself." I unfolded it.

The Saturday *Times of London* crossword.

"You're amazing," I whispered.

She made her way to the door. "I'll stay," she said. "Until they formally announce the merger. I'll stay until then."

"Thanks."

As she went through the door, Paula wagged her finger at me. "Go on and take that pill. I don't want you getting sick in that place."

If Paula had been my father's secretary perhaps he would have lived.

# TWENTY-FIVE

I looked out of my apartment window. At America, or at least my little bit of it. The water, New Jersey, the piers thrusting into the Hudson, the edge of Ellis Island. A couple of tower blocks and some low-rises. That was it. The horizon defied perspective, seemed too near, mocking my close-packed five years of Manhattan-bound existence. You could have seen a lot more of this place, the horizon seemed to say. But now it's too late. Show's over.

I sipped my beer and surveyed my living/dining room. I wouldn't be remembered for my lavish entertainment, my sparkling soirees; the procession of beautiful people gliding across the wooden floor, entranced by my talent for conjuring up more and more breathtaking feats of social magic.

On a small table stood a stunted line of framed photos, desolate as a late-night bus stop. Mother—featured twice, once in her glad rags at Ascot, once asleep in a deck chair in our garden, exhausted from pruning and deadheading. Me on a wind-surfer, hitting the beach in Corfu. Granny, liver-spotted, just before she died, smiling strongly, a false-toothed smile, smiling for all of us, like we weren't capable of doing it for ourselves. A misty shot of the Brooklyn Bridge. And Chuff, the smelly basset hound, the one paid for by Clay & Westminster, forever shadowed by my mother with her air freshener. He'd outlive us all.

I looked at the photo of the Brooklyn Bridge again. Just the bridge—no people. I realized that there wasn't a single photo of me in New York. When friends visited from England, I was the one holding the camera. If there were any of me, I hadn't seen them. Five years in a place and no evidence of it, apart from an impending sprawl of lawsuits.

I opened the drawer beneath. A few keys, a can opener, an AOL CD ROM—early version. And another framed photograph. A nice frame, bird's-eye maple, something like that. My father. Same beach in Corfu. Blue Hackett shorts, little round John Lennon sunglasses. Tanned, glazed, muscular, pointing at the camera. Saying something, I couldn't remember what. But it would have been smart and funny. Dad was funny on vacation. He could make us all laugh with his well-remembered jokes, his stories, his easy way with strangers. By the end of a trip we would always have a long list of new friends, new Christmas cards, new do-not-bend envelopes bursting with vacation photos. In the gathering gloom of Hampton Court, though, these trophies of his social skill looked strangely out of place.

I took the photo out of the drawer and set it up alongside the rest. Somehow his smiling presence made the little group look less wretched. He cheered them up, inflated them.

If I had not hung up on that final call. If the "click—you're dead," hadn't happened. What then, I wondered? Would it have been different? Would the events of the last week have happened to someone else?

I recalled the scampering wood nymph: mute, grotesque, beautiful. She'd been a harbinger. I should have recognized her for what she was.

# PART II

# TWENTY-SIX

Delta Air Lines, Flight 106.

On time.

But we weren't. Not if we wanted to catch the flight with a comfortable margin, without chasing the 767 down JFK's runway number one.

We scanned the boards for our check-in. Letters of the alphabet, numbers, hieroglyphs. The language of airports.

The man at the check-in desk saw our panic as we approached and looked at his watch. He shook his head.

"You got any luggage to check in today?" His eyes were reproachful as they scanned his computer screen, his fingers dancing across the keyboard.

"Nope," Carol said.

"Then you're just okay." He sounded disappointed, as if it was good for first-class passengers to learn they had to organize their lives a little, once in a while, just like the rest of us.

He took our passports. He handed Carol's straight back to her. Mine he opened at the page with my US visa and held it flat with a stapler while he attacked his keyboard. He peered at his screen.

How would I feel if he pressed a button under the counter and immigration officials showed up, polite but implacable, telling me that the US was my home for the time being? More hammering on the keyboard, a hand sliding under the counter.

He pulled out two boarding passes.

"You're all set. Go straight to Gate 42. You have preassigned seats, 2A and B. Have a good flight."

We ran.

"This is your fault," Carol hissed as we made our way to the head of a long line at security, ignoring the hostile glares along the way.

It *was* my fault. A call from Raj Shethia, a junior counsel from Askari in Bombay. Sunil Askari's gopher. Up at 6:00 A.M., Bombay time, to tell me that everything was set for our arrival.

"You could have spoken to him from the car."

*I could have, but I didn't.* He just wouldn't stop talking. The guy was excited, wanted to go through *everything*. It hadn't seemed right to cut him off.

Our hand luggage emerged from its chamber full of x-rays and slid onto the rollers.

We were off again.

"What time did he say? For the meeting." Carol hurled the question over her shoulder.

"Eight A.M. at the offices of Ketan Securities."

There would be virtually no time for rest before the factory gates opened.

Another passport inspection at the ramp. Maybe they'd called through from check-in. Stop that man.

"You guys sure cut it fine." The stewardess smiled as she snapped off a section of boarding pass and handed the smaller stub back, together with our passports.

We found our seats and sat back heavily, looking at each other. Carol mouthed the word *asshole* at me and hit me with the in-flight magazine. She then turned to look out of the window.

When we reached cruising altitude, we arranged our nests, clogging our living space with stuff from our bags that would end up in dark recesses around our seats, unused and most likely left there.

Carol took her sleeper suit out of its plastic bag.

Suddenly she pointed at the two black files at my feet.

"You going to do some work?"

At the start of a flight I was always committed to the prospect of work, but it usually just didn't happen.

"I might try." I'd see how endless the next thirteen hours turned out to be.

Carol caught the attention of a stewardess. She quickly scanned the entertainment guide and, leaning across me, pointed out the film she wanted. She had almost chosen it at random. "Can I have this video?"

"Sure, Miss."

I looked at the movie menu. Nothing appealed.

"You know that the Bombay film industry is the largest in the world," I said.

"No shit?" Carol didn't sound interested.

"Bollywood. It makes thousands of films a year. Soppy musicals, mostly."

"People like musicals. I guess that's why they make so many, Fin. Why so patronizing?"

Was I? Maybe I was.

I picked up my sleeper suit and amenity bag. "I'm going to get changed."

When I got back, Carol had laid out her seat flat into a bed. All I could see of her was a small tassel of hair poking from the blanket she'd wrapped around herself. She was shut in and I was shut out. Her movie lay on the armrest.

I flipped out my TV screen and put on the headphones. The news. I pressed the program key quickly.

Then the food started to arrive. White linen was placed before me, an armory of silverware, condiments, a saucer of scrolled butter.

Two hours catered for.

I nursed a brandy balloon half full of Remy XO. I drained it. I would sleep now.

But I couldn't. I tried all the positions, the seat was perfectly accommodating, but sleep wouldn't come.

I sat up and looked around. Everyone else was either watching a movie or sleeping. I set my seat upright and picked the two black files off the floor.

The deal file, Project Badla. I put it back down; I knew its contents, I'd written most of it.

Terry's file. A small white sticker on the spine: *India, Reg. & Misc.* Regulatory and Miscellaneous, I guessed, opening it.

A table of contents. Christ, the man must've had seventy files in his room. Were they all indexed? Probably.

The first part, the *Reg.* part. I scanned the list of items: the stock exchanges, listing rules, capital raising, the money markets. The menu snaked down most of the page. Worthy but boring.

I knew the devil was in the detail. A fitting residence for the Prince of Darkness. Nobody ever went there, except attorneys.

Part two. *Misc.* Just one item: press cuttings. Living, breathing material, at least by comparison.

I heaved over Part One and started to riffle through the newspaper articles, all neatly photocopied with the date and source noted in black ink on the top of the page. *Times of India, Times of London, New York Times, Financial Times, Time* magazine. *Wall Street Journal, Herald Tribune,* and its racier international counterpart, *America Daily, Asia Week.* Bombay, Delhi, Calcutta papers, and a whole lot more places I'd never heard of.

Coverage of deals mostly, some with Clay & Westminster involved, others that Terry must have found interesting, instructive. Worthy of his archive. Then a separately tabbed section.

*Scams.*

Dozens of them. Scams about illegal political contributions, scams about funding of insurgents, scams on the stock market, scams in forests, scams on public highways. Scams with names: the Bofors Scam, the Urea Scam. Scams by Non-Resident Indians. Scams against them.

Then the dark roots of scam, the offshore havens. The real ones first: Cayman, Cyprus, Antilles, Mauritius, Liberia. Then the made-up places, conjured by mad conartists who wanted their own realm and some sucker to pay for it: Utopia, the Kingdom of Enen Kio, Melchizidek. Crazy. How were people duped by these shysters? But they were. The lure of above-market returns, secrecy, and more besides.

And then, *Gold.* The glint of a word. Just a short article, more of a

snippet. How Indian workers in the Gulf—waiters, engineers, taxi drivers, servants of the oil-rich—were used as couriers for running gold into
India. How they would take their maximum allowance back home with
them, then hand it over to middlemen—the havala traders—who would
then sell it into the market. The couriers were paid a few rupees, the
financiers of the gold made a fortune. Nod and wink illegality, low-grade
villainy. The Indian government got the customs duty on the gold brought
in, so they didn't appear to mind too much.

But my father had minded, it seemed. He had minded himself into
a despair of indigestion; an inedible compromise nestling like gristle in
his half-eaten file.

I couldn't quite believe there wasn't more to it. Had a marginally illegal traffic of gold really driven Dad to the steps of the Towers of Silence?

I turned to Carol. Sleeping soundly.

Our lives had joined in bed. Where else did they join?

JJ Carlson. For each of us, JJ had been a catapult into another world
where the old assumptions didn't hold. It struck me that the events of five
years before—my father's Fall—hadn't made me reevaluate anything. It
had been *his* problem, not mine. Something for my mother to sort out,
not me. But now . . . The power to damage that had lain dormant all this
time, was now stirring, was teaming up with JJ, coalescing with the contemporary, whispering with the conspirators in my chart. It was saying
that it was time to conclude unfinished business.

I asked for a Coke. I let the bubbles bruise the roof of my mouth.
Cleanse it. I sucked on the ice.

I looked at Carol again. Maybe she wasn't sleeping at all. Perhaps,
under the Delta blanket, her eyes bulged with terror, her heart pumped
guilt, and her intestines knotted as terminally as a child's shoelace. She
seemed to edging away from me and a torrent of something was washing away the bridge between us.

"Are you awake?" I whispered as loudly as possible.

She moaned slightly and twisted her body into another position.
Then nothing.

Terry's file slid off my lap. I didn't reach down for it; there had
been enough work for one flight.

Finally, I felt like I might sleep.

# TWENTY-SEVEN

**Y**ou're weird."

Carol held out an orange juice in front of me. Her hair was scraped back into a ponytail, she had makeup on, and she'd changed into jeans and T-shirt, her sleeper suit now discarded on the floor.

"Why weird?" I managed. I felt like shit and the orange juice didn't help much. Acid poured on acid.

She seemed to check that nobody was looking and ran her hand along the stubble on my chin.

"We spend five thousand dollars for a seat up front that turns into a queen-size bed and you sleep upright." She laughed. "Is it some Indian thing, like a bed of nails?"

I looked at my watch—I'd slept nearly nine hours, best sleep in a week.

"You missed breakfast or second dinner or whatever," she said. "Anyway, I got you this orange juice to revive you." She twitched her nose. "You smell of booze a little."

I called the stewardess and asked for another Coke. I let the bubbles blitz away in my mouth.

"Did you watch your movie?" I asked.

Carol nodded.

"Any good?"

"Uh-huh. What I needed, at least."

The plane dipped slightly, the engines altered their tune.

Carol pulled up the blind. It was black outside.

"I guess we're coming down."


I'd forgotten how hard it could rain. By comparison, New York managed only a thin drizzle. This was the real thing. A chain mail downpour.

Our driver waded across the road outside the arrivals hall of Sahar Airport, parting a sea of people and water before us, trying to hold an umbrella above Carol, ignoring me. Young boys skipped around us like tadpoles, offering porterage, Chiclets, hotels, cars, their sister, anything our foreign hearts desired. Our driver cursed them, swatted them away. We edged through a flotilla of yellow and black Ambassador taxis, their drivers supervising the loading of impossible cargoes of luggage and humanity.

Five years earlier, I'd sat with my mother on the bench-hard backseat of one of those cars and tried to explain where we wanted to go. The driver had told us where *he* wanted us to go. The impasse of savvy local versus gullible new arrival.

This time it was simple. We were going to the Taj Hotel. The driver knew it, we didn't have to explain anything. But the chaos was the same, the smell the same: damp barbecue laced with spice and sweat.

We got into the car, a Mercedes S Class. A huge metal haven made cozy by the sound of crashing rain on its roof, its enormous single windshield wiper only affording us stroboscopic visions of the drenched world outside.

"This is neat," said Carol as the driver accelerated through a barrier of slow-moving trolleys.

It didn't feel neat to me.

I wanted to talk: not the guidebook talk of an old Bombay hand pointing out smudged landmarks through the driving rain. I wanted to talk about Carol and me, where we were headed. I wanted to talk about Project Badla. JJ. My chart. My father. My fear. I wanted to fill our big German car with the comforting noise of talk. But I couldn't. The driver sat in his seat like a huge black microphone, a recording machine that would carry the talk to somewhere it shouldn't go. Paranoia? Maybe, but it gagged me nonetheless.

Carol looked out of the window, rubbing circles in the condensation, her neck turning with anything that caught her interest. Totally absorbed. I loved the way she folded herself into whatever she was doing, how her body found just the right position and how that position resulted in contours that made me want to hold her.

After a while she sat back, shook her head in disbelief. "How do all those people live like that on the streets?"

How indeed? How could Carol or I have any real conception of the day-to-day struggle of the poor in a city like Bombay?

"They just do, because they have to," I said.

"I expect that a lot of them come in from the rural areas, don't they? They're lured by the city." She paused. "But why do they stay? Why doesn't someone tell them not to come in the first place?"

I didn't know. It was stupid, that's all, but there was even less for them in the countryside.

Maybe every society had its own analogy. I said, "Why do waitresses from Kansas pack up and go to LA, expecting to walk into Paramount and pick up the lead on the first day?"

Carol thought for a moment. "They believe in the dream," she said. "And sometimes it really happens. Like those diets you know won't work but buy into all the same. Like lottery tickets. People will always buy into hope, however hopeless."

Maybe she was right. I conjured the image of Pablo Tochera crying "eureka" and chewing his nails while he waited for me to arrive at the hotel. Then he'd call me and tell me he'd sorted it out. All of it. A more realistic scene would be one with Pablo clutching his stomach with one hand and his heart with the other in the back of an ambulance on the way to the ER. A direct result of my telephone call to him from the gate at the airport to tell him where I was going.

Carol rubbed a circle in the condensation on her window and went back to world watching.

"Look. A beach," she said after a while.

That would be Chowpatty Beach. We were getting near the hotel. I leaned over Carol's shoulder and looked through her porthole: a wasteland of hard compacted sand, the sea invisible beyond it, the heights of Malabar rising from one side of the sandy cove, the lights of the millionaire apartment blocks winking confidently above the tree-tops.

She pointed at the heights. "What's that place?"

I could smell her as my chin rested on her shoulder. After a thirteen hour flight she still smelled good.

"Where the rich live. The Hanging Gardens are up there too."

"The Hanging Gardens," she repeated in a whisper. "How exotic."

And next to the Hanging Gardens were the Towers of Silence. Dark stone amphitheaters for the Parsi dead. Hidden by a dense screen of trees, seen only by priests and vultures.

My father had wanted to die in one of these crumbling cauldrons. What madness had made him want to go anywhere near the place?

Carol sat back again and stared ahead of her, through the windshield.

"I'm sorry," she said.

"What for?"

She touched my hand, withdrawing quickly. "This. Bombay. Your father. It must be really hard for you. I should have been more sensitive."

"It's fine," I said. "I can cope with it."

Fifteen minutes later we drove along the huge floodlit frontage of the Taj Hotel. Carol craned her neck to get a view of a crazy three-domed Victorian cathedral to the hotel industry.

The car pulled up under the canopied entrance. It was nearly 2:00 A.M. but the place was still buzzing. An army of turbaned porters opened the doors of a constant flow of vehicles ferrying returning party-goers and new arrivals while an aggressive PA system screamed out the numbers of cars for those people who wanted to leave. The whole place was steamy and breathless.

We stood on the red-carpeted steps while our luggage was assembled and taken away.

Carol was restless. "We need to talk. But not now."

"When?" I asked.

"Not tonight. No sneaking up to my room. And don't wait for me to show up in yours either. All right?"

I froze. I had sensed something like this coming, but it still paralyzed me.

"All right?" Her eyes were pleading. She looked pale now, almost ill. I wanted to say that I was the right medicine for her.

I shrugged. "You're the client."

A small man in a gray suit stood nearby and seemed to be watching us, tentative and shy. He didn't look like a member of the hotel staff, a bit too scruffy, too unsure of his station. He tugged at a weedy mustache that made him look older then he probably was.

He approached us.

"Clay & Westminster and Jefferson Trust?" He held his hands stiffly by his sides, like they were holstered but ready to draw in a handshake should we show signs of drawing first.

"A bit of them," I said guardedly, signifying my knee-jerk distrust for a local I didn't know, but who seemed to know me.

The man grinned and the hand flew from its holster.

"Raj Shethia, assistant to Mr. Askari. I am here to ensure that everything is satisfactory. Miss Amen, I am so pleased to meet you. Mr. Border, you look exactly as I imagined from our telephone conversation."

He was excited and now that his hands had escaped they wouldn't keep still, a blur of gesticulation.

"Please, please, inside." He ushered us up the steps into the hotel.

"The flight satisfactory? Delta Airlines. American. Tip-top."

We moved toward the reception desk, the lobby was as chaotic as the arrival area.

"And the car? A Mercedes. I personally arranged it."

"The car was great, Raj," said Carol.

Raj Shethia blushed at the use of his first name, unsettled by instant familiarity from a woman. "I will register you," he muttered, and hurried over to the reception desk.

Carol was unabashed, still enthused. "Bombay changed its name to Mumbai, didn't it?" she said. "You know, like Peking to Beijing. I like the old names better. Is it okay to call it Bombay still?"

"Either's okay," I said, not caring. The place may have decreed a name change, but in all other respects it seemed the same.

# TWENTY-EIGHT

The rain had stopped and a few banners of cloud floated in the morning sky. The world had regained some clarity after the brawling weather of the night before.

As I made my way along the promenade toward the rusty brown basalt of the Gateway of India, small birds dive-bombed the breakwater boulders on the shore below while, high above me, black shadows circled. *Craa-craa-craa.* I'd forgotten the noise of those black shadows. Despite the heat, I shivered.

I'd already spoken to Pablo Tochera that morning. There had been no "eureka"—no heart attack either, which was something. He had been distracted, disgruntled, edgy. Another round with Detective Manelli. No charges yet, but soon, real soon. The first stirrings of a class action by the victims, a warning letter from the Borough of Manhattan. What about the documents, Pablo, what about the McLaren showroom? Delaware Loan? Sheesh. Nobody identified, nobody interviewed, no forensics in my favor. Why not? It was a crazy fucked-up world was all I could get out of him. I didn't need a four-hundred-an-hour attorney to tell me that.

I stood next to the Gateway, a somber Arc de Triomphe, and peered up into the dark crook of its arch.

I wheeled around suddenly. Somebody had touched me.

"Mr. Border, sir."

It was Raj Shethia. He stepped back swiftly. "I hope I did not surprise you." He looked scared, as if I was going to beat him up for intruding on my reverie. "I saw you from the hotel and came out to greet you."

I smiled, holding out my hand in greeting rather than attack. "I was just taking a stroll. A postbreakfast constitutional." I made it sound like the routine of an English gentleman, something that Raj Shethia might expect, perhaps. I never walked and normally had breakfast at my desk. Who the hell did I think I was?

Raj shook my hand to breaking point. We both looked up at the Gateway.

"Before the airplane," he said, "this was the first sight to greet visitors to Bombay. From the ships, you see."

I knew. All the guidebooks said so.

I scanned the bay, where dark freighters and old tankers squatted in flat water the color of milky tea. There were no proud cruise liners scything toward the jetty. No P&Os or Cunards. No excited passengers hanging from the deck rails, confetti and ticker tape snowing into the bow wave.

Raj looked at his watch. "We will be leaving for the office shortly. I should ensure Miss Amen is ready."

As I started to follow him back to the hotel, he noticed me looking up at its facade. "Do you like the Taj?" he asked.

In other circumstances I might have, but now it appeared like a swollen English seaside hotel, self-important, oversized, and matronly. On the inside, it was sumptuous enough, but too many balconied walkways skirted deep canals of dark space, both giddy and claustrophobic. My room was okay, though. Maybe I should have been more grateful; five years before, I had shared a mildewed cell of a room with my mother in a hotel that boasted not a single star.

Carol was waiting at reception. She wore a gray skirt cut well below the knee. She had kept her hair simple, her makeup pastel and lightly applied. A cream silk top completed the spartan ensemble.

"This place is amazing," she said. "You seen the dining room?"

I shook my head. I hadn't. A pot of coffee in my room and then my walk.

She looked disappointed, like I had spoiled her party. She'd recall why soon enough, I reckoned.

Raj led us out to the Mercedes.

We drove into a Victorian sprawl near the Stock Exchange Building, where streets, stalls, vehicles, and people vied for decreasing swing space. Our Mercedes was like a hippo in a birdcage. Carol was utterly absorbed by the circus around the car and for twenty minutes she was a carefree tourist.

The car stopped.

"We get out here." Raj rattled off some instructions to the driver. I tried to discern where in the mayhem of stalls and buildings the Ketan Securities offices might be. On one side of the street it was all storefronts and trestles laden with fruit and vegetables, partially obscured by carts and taxis, the other dominated by a single building entirely splinted by a network of scaffolding.

Raj aimed his umbrella at an alley separating the shrouded building from its healthier neighbor.

The gap between the buildings was little more than a crack, but the scaffolders had still contrived to put up their shaky climbing frame along its entire length and we picked our way around the steel struts whose bases were sunk in half an inch of bilge water.

"Mind the drain," warned Raj. Down the center of the alley, a river still swollen from the previous night's rain flowed glutinously toward a sea of slime. It reeked of rotting vegetables and shit and even the rats seemed to be giving it a wide berth.

Raj stopped at a large steel door, pressed a buzzer, and shouted into it. After a moment, the door swung open, bathing the dark alley in a harsh fluorescence.

We made our way along various strip-lit hallways and up and down countless small flights of steps. People pressed against the wall as we passed, smiling warmly or eyeing us as invaders. By the time we stopped in front of an imposing oak door I had lost track of where the consensus might be.

The world beyond the oak door was in complete contrast with everything we'd seen en route: a vast teak boardroom table, five men seated around it, a place setting in front of each of them—blotter, paper, pencils, water pitcher and tumbler. Three giant marble ashtrays paraded down the middle.

Four of the men stood up. One stayed precisely where he was. The sleeve of his suit strained as his arm crooked awkwardly over the back of the chair. He stared out of the window, at a jungle of greenery punctuated by orange and red fruit, and blinding flashes of flowers in full bloom. Frenzied birds, exotic and mundane, flitted a few inches above the canopy.

Sunil Askari was not birdwatching. He was showing his contempt for me.

What the hell. I looked at the others.

It was easy to see who was in charge, the patriarch. White-haired, slim, and over six feet; teeth like an ad for floss. He wore his age effortlessly, a Bollywood elder statesman who had kept up with his personal trainer.

"Welcome, welcome," he said. The welcome seemed primarily aimed at Carol, who moved forward nervously to shake his hand. I thought for a ghastly moment she might curtsy.

He bade us sit. "I am Ashish Ketan." He splayed his fingers on the table in the shape of a tepee, the gold Rolex and nugget of a ring apparently weightless on their muscular host.

Then he waved a hand vaguely at a youthful, black-haired version of himself. "This is Parves Ketan, my eldest son and managing director. My other son, Damindra, cannot be with us—he is running the business as we speak. I like to think of Ketan Securities as a shrine to perfection and you will appreciate that this is a full-time occupation for my family and employees."

Everyone nodded.

His hand waved in another direction. "Mr. Sunil Askari, senior partner of Askari & Co., one of Bombay's most prestigious law firms and one which owes its greatness entirely to its distinguished senior

partner. Jefferson Trust is most fortunate to have retained their services."

Askari was seated normally now, perhaps content that I was
placed at the opposite end of the table from him.

He smiled and, with unconvincing modesty, brushed aside the
compliment with a shake of his imperious head.

Ashish Ketan then briefly introduced his own attorney, a bilious
and sweaty man from the not-quite-so-distinguished firm of Jaiwalla
& Company. Ketan didn't bother drawing our attention to the
Jaiwalla bag carrier or Raj Shethia.

There was a short pause and Ketan turned to Carol.

I noticed her scribbling on the pad in front of her, not a doodle,
but a nervous cluster of words and dashes and asterisks. A speech.

"Jefferson Trust is very excited about the prospect of bringing
Ketan Securities into our fold." She sounded assured, not even glancing at her notes. "Our chairman, whom I believe you've met"—Ketan
inclined his head to show he had—"sends his best wishes and has
instructed me to do everything to ensure a speedy completion."

She hesitated. "Chuck Krantz sends his apologies. He wanted to
be here, but has to make preparations for the acquisition back in New
York."

Yeah, right. Chuck Krantz thinks Bombay is a shit-hole and he's
got better things to do.

Carol sprinkled a few more platitudes across the table and then
relaxed, content with her performance. The audience also seemed very
pleased, Ashish Ketan staring at her as if she were his favored daughter and Parves Ketan only a micro-dribble short of a drool.

Ketan senior nodded at Askari, who snapped his fingers at Raj.

Until that moment, Raj had been a coiled spring, which at
Askari's signal uncoiled in panic. A small buff folder was passed to
Askari, who had perched a minutely framed pair of reading glasses on
the end of his shark-fin nose. He glowered briefly at Raj and then
peered down at the file.

"Applications for regulatory approval have been lodged and are
proceeding well." This was news to me—these bits of paper were for
Jefferson Trust, my client, to sign, and I hadn't seen any.

"Have we seen them?" I asked. I sensed the room reel in shock that I had dared to interrupt Sunil Askari.

He didn't look up. "Our mutual client, Jefferson Securities, has seen them, approved them, and signed them."

I glanced at Carol. She was blank; I was sure she hadn't seen them, she would have told me otherwise. It was a liberty. Nothing should have bypassed Clay & Westminster and certainly nothing should have bypassed the senior investment banking counsel of Jefferson Trust.

I didn't press the point. I'd pick it up later—offline.

"If I may continue . . ." Askari surveyed the room, his eyes never landing on me. The others kept their eyes away from me too. Already I was a leper.

"Clay & Westminster have provided draft agreements."

He steadfastly refused to mention my name. "But we were obliged to amend them to reflect the proper Indian legal position."

"How far have you gotten on the questionnaire?" I asked. Thirty dense pages, each question maybe needing a pine tree or two to answer.

"It is ready."

It couldn't be. A half-assed stab, maybe. But ready? No way.

Askari removed his glasses, as if by doing so he'd reduce me to no more than an irritating blur. "You seem surprised, Mr. Border."

"I am. And impressed if—"

"If what?" It was Ketan senior. I couldn't see his teeth; he wasn't smiling. "Impressed if we did it. That was your thought, was it not? You wonder if business people in India can match your Anglo-Saxon professionalism?" The tide against me was obviously at full spate.

"No, sir, of course not. It was just rather a lot of material to cover in such a short time, that's all."

"And that we wouldn't know our business well enough to answer your questions?"

"No, please—"

"Or that we wouldn't anticipate the questions you might pose?"

"Good God, no. I'm sorry if I've offended you."

Ketan junior tapped his Mont Blanc on the blotter. "Mr. Border does not have a high regard for us, I think."

"This is absurd," I said.

Ketan senior stood up, clutching at his ring as if he were going to wrench it from his finger and hurl it at me. "So now we are absurd."

Askari groaned. "Mr. Border is too much of the lawyer and not enough of the diplomat." He gave Carol a comforting smile. She looked petrified. "He has had a long flight and perhaps got dehydrated."

Ketan senior snorted. Maybe for him, dehydrated meant hungover.

"I can only apologize if I caused offense," I said. "It wasn't my intention."

Ketan senior and junior ignored me.

Askari seemed triumphant, his initial mission accomplished. "Where was I?"

For the next two hours I was the bad smell in the room. On the rare occasions I tried to offer input, I could almost hear the snap of clothes pins on noses. The entire strategy for bedding the transaction was settled—anything substantive was for Carol and Askari, the rest for me and Raj. Tea was served; to me, last and grudgingly. Plans for the evening were finalized; my presence was not required.

And Askari got happier and happier.

As we stood to leave, Ketan senior pointed to Carol's skirt. There was a splash of dried mud on the hem.

His eyes rested threateningly on Raj. "How did this happen? It is but a short journey and the rain has stopped."

Raj explained about the waterlogged alleyway.

Ketan was horrified. "You came in that way?"

"It's nothing really," Carol said, dusting herself down. "I've plenty of spare clothes."

Ketan rattled something off in Hindi and Raj froze. Presumably he had been told that entering the building via the anus was bad navigation, and incompetent pilots had to walk the plank.

Everyone started to leave. As I began to join them, Askari stood behind me. I could hear his teeth clack, like he was sharpening them.

"You will go with Raj Shethia to the data room at Nariman Point, where you can see for yourself that the questionnaire has been answered."

Askari was supposed to be my lawyer, not the other way around. I wanted to tell him to fuck himself. But there was another way, I realized. I could keep my thoughts to myself. There would be no more sharing.

Askari must have noted my expression. "Each of us must yield to a superior force," he said. "Even I am answerable, beholden."

I turned away from him without answering, choosing to watch Carol lap up the Ketan schmooze; but before I cut Askari, I'd noticed something in his expression, the fizz of pepper on Ernie's cigarette end, the fear.

The data room was on the twentieth floor of a stained seventies cereal box with a better view over the Arabian Sea than it deserved.

I'd expected to find an abandoned paper recycling plant by way of documentation. But no. File after file of neatly tabbed documents, cross-referenced into the questionnaire I'd sent them. I walked down the length of the table, inspecting the material, as if I were a visiting head of state reviewing a guard of honor.

Askari had been right. It looked like it was ready.

"Who put this together?" I asked.

Raj bashfully tugged at his mustache. "Me, sir. Me and the gentleman from Jaiwalla & Company. Under the guidance of Mr. Askari, of course."

"Of course."

At random, I picked up a file of correspondence between Ketan Secuirites and the Stock Exchange Board of India. Usually regulators were whining about something, focusing on the minutiae and missing the murders. But these letters seemed full of praise—for management, for systems, for client care. Prize pupils, it seemed.

"This is pretty impressive."

Raj waggled his head in the Indian way.

I was cross with myself about the incident in the meeting. "I wish they hadn't misunderstood me back there."

Raj's hands started waving. "It is just a storm in a cup of tea. It will pass."

I sat down. "We'd better go through this now."

I picked up the first file. *Answer to Question 1. Corporate History and Structure.* I read it. Bloody perfect, bar a few trivial supplementary questions I could raise out of sheer devilment.

Raj went out of the room to organize tea and came back followed by a vision in a red sari carrying a tray laden with cups and Hobnob cookies.

Raj picked up one of the cookies. "English. I thought you would like them."

"Do you live in central Bombay, Raj?" I asked.

"In a chawl, sir."

"What's that?"

"Accommodation for people like me, sir. In town. Very convenient. But I'm saving for something better and soon will have it. Mr. Askari is very generous, you see."

Yeah, like Ebenezer was.

"How long have you worked for Askari & Co.?"

He paused, like he was counting the years. "Since I left school. My parents had died long before and he took me to his bosoms."

He started to reach into his breast pocket for something, but seemed to change his mind and withdrew his hand empty. "My sister too," he said. "Mr. Askari paid for her education at a fine school in Bombay and then arranged for her to go to America to finish her education."

I guessed he had a picture of his sister in his wallet, but had second thoughts about showing me.

"That *is* generous. Why did he do that?"

Raj seemed taken aback. "Because Mr. Askari is a good man. He helps people, many people." He wasn't impressed with my apparent cynicism, my belief that the world's agenda was not primarily for the mutual benefit of its inhabitants.

I wanted to appear interested, I'd insulted enough people for one day. "What's your sister called?"

"Preeti."

Great name and I told him so.

His eyes were as forlorn as a spaniel's. "But she is in America and it makes me sad. I have no other family."

"Why don't you join her? Plenty make the jump from here."

Raj toyed with a file. "Mr. Askari needs me here."

Another hour passed. Five more files, all clean as a whistle. A few desultory points to raise. These people could teach an international law firm and a major investment bank a thing or two.

Raj let out an enormous yawn and scratched his stomach. The guy had good reason to be tired if he had put all this together. "More tea?" he asked. I echoed his yawn and nodded.

His raisin eyes narrowed and he smiled impishly. "A beer maybe?"

"How decadent. Why not?"

"Kingfisher or Kalyani Black Label? Or perhaps I can find some Heineken."

"Kingfisher." As my mother had tossed in her mogadon-induced sleep I had sat at the end of the bed in our squalid hotel room, swigging Kingfisher. I'd just come back from the mortuary and hated everyone and everything. Except her. And the beer, ice-cold and indiscriminate in whom it pleasured.

Raj started to leave the room.

I halted him.

"Do you want some money for the beer?" I asked. Beer was expensive, taxed to kingdom come by the spoilsports in government. I was on an expense account.

Raj was solemn. "I am treating you, sir."

"Thanks," I said. "And my name is Fin."

Raj grinned and left the room.

I dragged another file toward me. The label said *Question 18: Material Contracts*. No doubt another six inches of perfection. This was getting tedious; these bastards had no sense of fun. There was nothing to whet the jaded palate of a forensically minded attorney.

Material contracts were supposed to be agreements outside the normal course of business, deals that should be highlighted to a prospective purchaser as they might contain something unusual. These looked pretty pedestrian: a few expired joint ventures, a sponsorship agreement for a cricket tournament, some fairly juicy incentive packages for senior employees. And the last one: an order-routing agreement, a deal whereby a number of parties had promised to put all their stock purchases through Ketan Securities in return for certain favors. Risky in India, but probably not fatally so. And one couldn't get too hung up on the odd gray area. Still, it was something I could ask about.

Unlike the other documents, this agreement had a messed-up front cover, as if something had gotten onto the photocopier glass and smudged badly.

At the foot of the page I could see a small swirl of gray smudge and at its edge the letter *A*. About half an inch away, there was another distorted letter, maybe an *i*.

I realized something. Idiot. Why hadn't had I seen it earlier?

Legal agreements normally had the name of the law firm that drafted them written on the front. I flicked back through the Material Contracts file. None of the documents referred to their draftsman.

Liquid Paper, Snopake, Wite-Out. The smudge was undried masking fluid. The person copying, probably Raj, had gotten careless and hadn't waited for the stuff to harden.

Who would have been the lawyers? They should have been Jaiwalla & Company or their predecessors. But common sense told me that the smudged name was Askari & Co. I didn't know of any other Indian law firms with an *A* and *i* juxtaposed in this way. I looked at the date of the agreement: a few months old. Askari should have told us they'd acted for Ketan Securities so recently. The potential for a conflict of interest was huge. Maybe Askari *had* told us or, rather, Charles Mendip, and Charles had waved it through. But Carol didn't know, I was sure. She would have said.

And somebody was sensitive about who was whose lawyer and when. Why else white-out their identity?

Raj came back, weighed down by a large, clinking paper bag.

He took out two bottles and rifled through his pockets until his hand emerged with a bottle opener.

He waved the opener in the air. "Bloody brilliant Boy Scout, Fin."

I applauded and shoved Material Contracts out of the way.

"How many bottles have you got there, Raj?"

He adopted an air of secrecy and tapped his nose. "Enough for present needs."

The beer was good and Raj was on his second before I was even halfway through my first. I wasn't going to get drunk, but Raj could get smashed out of his skull for all I cared; in fact it might suit me.

I waited for him to start his third bottle. "If I needed to study a document back at the hotel tonight, could I take it, as long as it was returned tomorrow morning?"

Raj tried to look grave; but the froth on the end of his mustache, like cuckoo spit on grass, mocked the effort. "I have been told to knock the bloody block off anyone who messes with the data room." He paused and grinned. "In your case I would ask you politely not to."

If I wanted a private viewing, I'd need to make my own arrangements.

I reimmersed myself in the files, making sure I studied every line carefully. I was interested in the order-routing agreement, but I left it alone; I didn't want Raj to think I was intrigued by it. He was there more to watch me than help me. After all, he'd put most of the stuff together so there was little else for him to do except swill beer and answer any questions.

I looked at the accounts again. Normally it was the fine print that interested the attorney, the notes to the profit and loss account or the balance sheet, where, on a good day, one could spot cracks in the superstructure. But with the sign-off from reputable auditors and some cute window dressing, it was usually pretty difficult to get one's fingers in the cracks.

I left the fine print alone. I went straight to the headline of the profit and loss account. Turnover was big. The profit was also big and had been so for a number of years. The results were good by any standards. This was a valuable business. More valuable than appeared at first sight because the accounts deducted some large amounts for exceptional items, which brought the profit down. Add those exceptional items back in and it looked like Jefferson Trust was getting the business for a song.

I checked around the exceptional items—this time I had to refer to the fine print. They looked real enough, but when I mixed my smattering of accounting knowledge with a healthy dose of skepticism, I reckoned the exceptional items were a sign of someone trying to keep their reported profits artificially low. Possibly for the taxman, possibly for another reason.

I cross-checked by scanning the working-capital statement setting out the cash flow for the business. Huge. And plenty of headroom between cash and bank facilities and the needs of the business, the acid test of good working capital.

Another couple of hours didn't provide any further insights, even with my antennae set to max sensitivity. On the face of it, Jefferson Trust was doing a cracking deal. But I reckoned this brokerage had two faces.

I yawned.

I needed to get outside. It would be hot and sticky, but I wanted air, not AC. And I wanted the order-routing agreement to myself.

"Can we take a break?" I asked.

"Sure. No problem. What would you like to do?"

Raj was on his sixth beer. He looked relaxed. It was probably the first decent down time he'd had in a good few days. But, Christ, didn't the guy need to piss? Six beers. He was a camel. And I wanted him out of the room.

I faked a sneeze. And another—just enough to justify the request for some tissues.

Raj got up and went to the door. "I will get you some."

"Thanks," I said. "I'll think of somewhere to go while you're out. No hurry."

As soon as he'd left the room, I grabbed the Material Contracts file and flipped it over to the last document, the order-routing agreement. I removed it from the clip and was going to take it over to my briefcase when the door opened.

It was Raj. "Is toilet paper acceptable? There are no paper tissues in the gentleman's."

Toilet paper would be perfect, given I'd nearly shit myself.

I casually leafed through the agreement for a moment before answering. "Sure."

He disappeared again, but I wasn't going to risk his coming straight back to ask if I wanted pink or blue.

I stuffed the agreement down my trousers.

Where could I go for an afternoon diversion?

Did I dare? Would I ever be *ready* to dare? I doubted it. My mother had never spoken in detail of her visit to the Towers of Silence. But she had dared, had braved it within three days of my father's dying there. She had slipped away from our squalid bedroom and made the pilgrimage, returning a few hours later looking like she'd left most of her soul in the place.

Raj came back with an entire toilet roll. "It is the air conditioning getting into the nasal passages. I expect you will be sneezing a lot."

I wondered if I'd condemned myself to sneezing fits at five-minute intervals to maintain the subterfuge.

"Can I borrow the car and driver and go somewhere?"

"Certainly, Fin." The words were positive, but he sounded coy. "Where is it you would like to go?"

When my mother had returned to our hotel from the Towers of Silence, she told me that it had sucked her dry and that she had then needed to go to a good place, a simple place, an antidote to the Towers. She wanted something less spiritual, more grounded in noble earthly endeavor. She said she'd found the very spot and that it had given back some of her soul.

"Versova," I said. "I want to see the fisherfolk at Versova." A pure trade, my mother had said, fishing; a view inherited from my father, who maintained that fishing and waiting tables were the only two honest occupations.

Raj looked surprised. "A strange destination. Why not the Elephanta Caves or the museums, or I can take you out to Kanheri Park or show you a film studio?"

I didn't want his guidebook. I knew where I wanted to go.

"Versova," I said, rather too firmly.

"Very well," Raj said. The smile was back. It seemed that I would have to try harder if I wanted to offend him. "I will call the driver to ready him. He will take the most direct route, most assuredly. He is a very good driver."

I didn't want a direct route. "There's somewhere else I'd like to visit on the way."

"That is no problem. Where?"

I couldn't say it. Shame? The need for privacy?

"The Hanging Gardens." A stone's throw from the Towers, a short walk.

Raj gave me a strange look, as if sensing a hidden agenda.

"Okay," he said, sticking the bag of beer and the dead bottles into an empty storage box.

I couldn't go sightseeing with an order-routing agreement stuffed down my pants. "I'll need to go back to the hotel and change first."

Raj shoved the box under the table. "There, safe as a sound." He stood. "I will wait in the car while you change. Then it shall be the Hanging Gardens and Versova, my friend."

This was supposed to be a solo pilgrimage. "Are you coming with me?"

"My heavens, of course. What kind of host do you take me to be?"

I wasn't ready to insult the only person in Bombay who seemed to like me.

"That's great. Thanks," I said.

He gave me a slap on the back. "We go." I let him lead the way, not wishing to betray my ungainly waddle with the order-routing agreement bracing my midriff.


I called Carol's room when I got back to the hotel. I didn't expect her to be there. But she was.

"How's it going?" I asked.

"Great." The voice was hard.

I heard a beep. "What was that?"

"A heart monitor. I'm going to do some exercise."

"Not thinking of jogging around the block, are you? I'm not sure that Bombay's ready for that."

An icy silence.

"They have a gym," she said at last. "I'm going to ride the bike before dinner."

This was ridiculous. I felt as if I was cold-calling someone chosen at random from the phone book. I needed to clear the air.

"Hey, I don't know what happened in the meeting. Wires got crossed or something."

"They thought you were patronizing and they didn't like it. I didn't like it either." I guessed it was the voice she used to converse with attorneys on the other side of a deal, attorneys for whom she had a low regard.

"Come on, it wasn't like that," I said. "I respect these people. I wouldn't set out to insult them." It was like they'd been waiting for me to leave a gap through which they could snatch an insult and be offended by it.

"Just like you respect their soppy musicals." I remembered my comment about Bollywood. She had a good memory when it suited.

"That wasn't patronizing either," I said.

"You should look it up in a dictionary. You seem to have lost touch with the meaning of the word."

"They were determined to have me insult them."

"For Christ's sake, Fin. That's bullshit. You should stop looking around corners, expecting the bogeyman to jump you."

"What about Ernie Monks and JJ?" I remembered the look on her face as she'd stared out into the center of the Cuxa Cloister. "They were your bogeymen up at the Cloisters."

"Shadows, Fin. And whatever JJ may have done, he knew a good deal when he saw one, and he knew how to put it together."

"Like the deal he put together for me with Delaware Loan?"

Carol paused. "I told you I would go to the police if you wanted. The offer still stands. Is that what you want?"

No. I just wanted Carol back. It looked like I might have to wait a while. "Let's leave things the way they are."

"Then just calm down." Her voice had softened. "I know it can't be easy, what with your father; but you won't gain anything by alienating everybody. They're pissed with you, don't piss them off anymore."

"Okay," I said.

"They showed me their operation." She actually sounded cheerful. "It's pretty impressive."

"Are we talking the appendix? Or the heart bypass?"

"Yeah, yeah, very funny," she said. "Behind the crazy front of that building, away from the hallways, they've got a state-of-the-art trading floor and fantastic space for their analysts. Then there's a small area for investment banking. All cordoned off nicely, so no trouble with ethical walls. It's a very professional setup. And buzzing. The client base is superb; it's a great franchise. I can see why JJ was attracted to them."

"Good value for fifty million, then?"

"Uh-huh, I reckon."

"Perhaps a little too good?"

Carol sounded irritated. "What are you driving at?"

"Think about it. The foreigners bought most of the stockbroker-ages years ago, paid a big premium for them. Ketan Securities stays untouched. Maybe they wanted to keep their independence, whatever. But now they're selling. The last quality item on the shelf—you would have thought they could command top dollar."

"When did you become an investment banker?"

"When I learned to divide a purchase price by the current year's profit before interest and tax."

Carol clicked her tongue. "I know what a price earnings ratio is, you jerk. Don't start patronizing *me*."

"Well, what is it?" I asked. "The PE. For Ketan Securities, I mean."

I thought I could hear her brain whirring. "A ratio of around ten, ten and a half," she said. Near enough.

"Now extract the exceptional items," I said.

"Shit, Fin. I don't have the file in front of me and I don't keep exceptional items in my head."

"After exceptionals," I said, "the price earnings ratio comes down to five. Who says lawyers can't count? Anyway, the going rate would be more like fifteen going on twenty. Even without accounting for the exceptionals, it's a great deal for Jefferson Trust. With them, it's a bloody steal. You're right, JJ knew a good deal when he saw one."

"So Clay & Westminster are going to advise Jefferson Trust not to do the deal because it's too good. Great."

"You know that a purchase at an undervalue should make you suspicious. It's a red flag. You're an international securities lawyer, one of the best. I shouldn't have to spell it out."

Carol hesitated. "A good deal doesn't mean undervalue." There was doubt in her voice. "I guess I was surprised they turned out to be so good. But their future earnings, they're worried about them, we're worried about them. And remember, Mr. Investment Banker, you buy a business on prospective earnings, not past ones."

Maybe that's what the textbook said. "Ashish Ketan didn't sound like someone who thought his shrine to perfection was about to fall down about his ears."

"He's proud, that's all. After all, he's selling a business. How would you expect him to sound?"

"Greedier, for starters," I said.

"Maybe he just wants to sell out to those who'll do the best for the business, protect its franchise, look after the employees, be a good partner. Maybe his talk about a shrine to perfection isn't just bullshit."

"I doubt it."

The heart monitor beeped again. Maybe when I raised her blood pressure, it sounded an alarm.

"Sometimes people have good motives, you know," she said.

That used to be one of *my* assumptions as well. "Like for example JJ endowing a school in Bombay," I suggested quietly. "Maybe he just did that to show what a great guy he was and get some sucker to sell him a prize stockbrokerage on the cheap. Come bonus time—if he'd lived—he pockets another ten million and the few hundred thousand he's put into a poxy school looks like a good investment."

"Jesus, you're cynical."

"I'm a lawyer."

She sighed.

"So are you," I added.

"I'm going to the hotel gym, sleep, then dinner with the Ketans. What are you doing?"

"I'm going out with Raj. I may want to talk to you about it later. Can I see you then?"

I could feel the pain coming down the line. She probably felt guilty about me, but guilt wasn't enough; she was trying to keep her life on the rails—she'd offered to derail for me, but I'd let her stay on the tracks. It looked like she wanted to rejoin her career path and I was a dangerous detour.

"I . . ."

"Think about it." I didn't want to hear her say no to me. "Have a good evening."

I took a quick shower and dressed in chinos and polo shirt. Before leaving the room I placed the order-routing agreement in the safe. I was bad at remembering PIN numbers so I made do with the year of my birth.

# TWENTY-NINE

At least it wasn't raining, but the sky hung like waterlogged canvas over our heads, promising to split and spill later on.

Raj and I wandered up and down a network of gravel footpaths skirting flower beds that seemed to have little by way of flora in them. Watching the dive-bombing sparrows, I wasn't surprised; any seed would be lucky to germinate under that kind of sustained attack. So much for the Hanging Gardens.

Had my father been here? Before he made his way to the Towers of Silence perhaps. I stared at a bench occupied by an old man humming a tuneless mantra through a mouthful of betel nut. Maybe on that very bench, Dad had reflected on where his life had taken him. From near the top of the letterhead of a great law firm to the edge of an abyss. Did he have a bottle of booze with him, a special cask-strength malt he'd managed to save for his last drink? Or was it some local hooch that washed down the pills or accompanied the self-administered chemicals that finally overpowered his already bug-infested blood?

"The Towers of Silence are near here, aren't they?" I asked Raj.

Raj pointed. "Over there."

It was a wall of dull greenery on the horizon of the Hanging Gardens. Dad would have known the way without asking; he would have checked and prepared beforehand, he'd have drawn a line on a city plan and achieved his destination without deviation or hesitation.

Suddenly I didn't care what Raj thought, what anybody thought. "I want to see them, the Towers."

Raj seemed startled. "You cannot go inside, it is forbidden."

"I know. Just the outside. The steps to the entrance."

Raj shook his head. "It isn't a good place."

"I know."

Raj hesitated, then shrugged. "Come. We will need to take the car."

On reaching a busy intersection at the foot of a steep road surrounding the Hanging Gardens, our driver hairpinned up a narrow driveway bordered by neat rockeries and plants. A quarter of a mile brought us into a parking lot with a small fountain in the middle of it.

Raj pointed to a white building that looked like an open-fronted village hall. "That is where they hold funeral services for the dead before they are taken into the Towers of Silence—only the priests are allowed in there."

"This isn't it," I said rather impatiently.

Raj bridled. "It is, sir. I have brought you to the Towers of Silence. Just as you asked."

Maybe. But it didn't accord with the description given by Sunil Askari of where my father was found. It didn't accord with my own vision of the place: It didn't brood, the paint on the clapboard buildings was fresh, the flower beds neatened by the hand of man rather than nature. It was almost as if Pinelawn Cemetery had been transported to the subcontinent.

No, this wasn't the place.

"There is another entrance," Raj said with an anxious tug at his mustache.

Into the car, back down the driveway, up the hill, around the

Hanging Gardens, and back down the other side: a new stretch of quiet road, lined by the millionaire apartment blocks on one side. I looked up at the other side. Dense green foliage hung over the edge of the wall, thirty maybe forty feet above me, like wild hair sprouting from the scalp of a giant.

The wall curved away from the road and a shoulder-high parapet separated us from an area of scrub from which an unpaved track snaked somewhere beyond my line of sight. An ugly black pipeline ran alongside the parapet, dark ooze leaking from its crude rivets.

"Behind the trees," said Raj, pointing. "That is the start of it. It stretches for many acres."

I peered, trying to penetrate the wall of green. I had a sense of the huge stone cliff, but nothing was defined. It was designed to hide and confuse.

We descended farther and met the unpaved track that ended at the roadside. No barrier; one could walk right in, it seemed.

The car stopped and we got out.

"Can we go in?" I asked. Whatever the response, I was going to.

"It's okay. It takes us to the gates. Then no farther."

The path went through the deserted area of scrub, short harsh grass growing through a cindery soil, the odd oily puddle. It was more of a barren lot next to an oil refinery than the outer precinct of a sacred burial ground.

We were silent as we walked. I knew I was now on the path my father had taken. It must've been at night; his body was found in the early morning. Why the hell did he come here?

Raj stopped. "Up there." He didn't point. There was only one way to look.

A long flight of steps, a dual carriageway of flagstones leading up from the path into foliage, but this time I could see the top. Set into the wall was a large dirty yellow door, metal most likely, brown around its edges, like a skin graft that hadn't taken too well.

The steps, the door. Vision merged with reality.

"Behind the door are the Dakhmas," said Raj.

"The what?"

"A *Dakhma* is another word for tower."

I'd never really thought about the place as something in its own right, only as a stage upon which my father had played out his final act. For eighty thousand Parsees, the Towers had a significance that drew nothing from a crazed man who wanted to die there.

"There are seven Towers," continued Raj. "Some very ancient, many hundreds of years."

"Towers," I whispered. "Like crematorium chimneys."

Raj shook his head. "Oh, no, sir. Not like chimneys." He seemed to be scouring his brain for an apt metaphor. "A big pan . . . no . . . vat, that is a better word. Like the ones we use to cook biryani at weddings. A stone vat of strict measurement; I do not know exactly how big: maybe one hundred feet across, perhaps more. And inside, there is a sloping floor all the way round on which the dead body is left for the vultures to eat. Then the bones fall into a central pit. There is lime in the pit so that everything disappears. It is most hygienic." He frowned. "Or so it is asserted. Although sometimes—and I hesitate to say this—the rich people of Malabar claim that the vultures occasionally drop pieces on their balconies." The vulture air raids on the great and good seemed to trouble him for a moment, but then his face cleared. "But the Dakhmas were here before them and so they must accept such things, I think."

I followed his gaze up the steps. "The ground is made sacred by Parsi priests and only they may enter."

I focused on the door. It didn't look like the threshold of something sacred, more like a prison.

"Death is a temporary evil and should be handled by the proper officials so that it does not become permanent."

My eyes wouldn't leave the door. The avenue of foliage drew them and held them. "You seem to know a lot," I said.

Raj was uneasy, tugging at his mustache again. "Everyone knows these things."

He moved a few paces sideways and stopped, staring at the ground.

"Here," he said. The pool of filthy water and slime just below the first step swallowed his shoes. A bubble of trapped air burped from the gloop.

"Here what?"

Raj avoided eye contact. "He died here. Your father."

I had already sensed it, but still I grew unsteady. I gripped myself and moved toward the puddle. I put my hand in its slime, rubbed it into my palm with my fingers, and wiped it off on my trousers.

"You saw it?" I whispered.

Raj shook his head violently. "No, no. Askari told me."

"Told you what?"

Raj shuffled his feet, I could see the slime wash over his socks and the cuffs of his slightly too short suit trousers.

I reached for his jacket. "Tell me."

His eyes looked so sad. "There is no need for that," he said. "There is little to tell, but Askari will destroy me if he knows I spoke with you about your father. He does not like these things mentioned."

I let go and brushed him off. "I'm sorry." I vaguely waved my arms at the surroundings. "This. My father. I'm sorry. I won't say anything to Askari, you have my word. But I must know what you know."

"He had been taking many drugs, I think."

I knew. The morgue officials had said massive dehydration resulting from ulcerative colitus. The scrawl on the death certificate declared likewise. But Askari had drawn *his* version of events from the shocking lexicon of drug abuse prevention campaigns, building his description of my father until he was no more than a grubby test tube brimming with narcotic bile.

"And he was very ill. Maybe delirious."

That was kind of Raj, excusing my father because he didn't know what he was doing, that he hadn't the intention lawyers insist upon before guilt can be established. Lack of *scienter,* the Americans would say, no *mens rea,* guilty mind, the Brits would echo. And then exonerate him. "What did Askari say?"

"That he was the devil," Raj replied without hesitation.

"Because he died here?"

Raj wavered. "It is difficult. I do not wish to speak ill of him. He is your father and you honor him."

I didn't honor him. For five years he had been dormant dust on the floor of my memory. But JJ's death had broken in and . . .

Raj gently touched my shoulder. "Maybe your father did not come here with the intention of dying."

"You mean it was an accident, not suicide?"

"Your father was very angry with Askari, blamed him for many things. Wrongly, says Askari. Askari says that your father did not understand India and our way of things and that his lack of understanding drove him to foolishness: drink and drugs and the ladies. Askari tried to help him and bring him out of his foolishness."

There were certainly the drink and the ladies, or rather the girl. I had seen them for myself.

"But your father would not listen and he got very depressed, would not listen to reason. He was mad with anger at Askari and wanted to hurt him. Askari believes that he died here to insult the many clients of Askari who are Parsi. He believes that your father wanted to destroy Askari & Co."

I looked around me at the dark cinder track, the flagstones, the tough grass, and, behind me, a gray hut.

My foot dug hard into the slime, the ground underneath was firm. A hard place to die. Someone would have to be beyond reason to die here, beyond blame perhaps. Beyond shame. And yet he *had* shamed us. He had shamed us on two continents.

There was a flapping noise; one could almost feel the air move with the beat of something powerful.

A vulture settled on the steps near the entrance to the Towers.

"The vultures are still kept busy," Raj said. "But there are not so many of them now. Some of the Dakhmas are in use, others are idle. Many Parsis simply burn their dead now. Fire is considered adequate."

I shivered.

"In fact, fire is sacred to the Parsis," Raj prattled, "they see it as an earthly infestation of Wisdom."

Manifestation, not infestation. But maybe infestation *was* more accurate.

Jesus. Fire or vultures. What a choice. I remembered the cruel ridges, embankments of purple swollen around the deep wounds on my father's naked body. And of course the pickled-onion eye hanging from its socket. But the hair had been brown and soft, still healthy, as if just washed. "My father was mutilated by vultures," I whispered.

Raj nodded. "I know. Askari feared that this was a sacrilege also. The vultures here are for the Parsi dead, not outsiders."

At the end, Dad had been on the outside of everything: me and Mum, Clay & Westminster. Himself. He had tried to gain access, one phone call to the interior, me. But I'd bolted the door. Click. Only the vultures would commune with him.

I suddenly recalled the small brown mole on Dad's cheek. In the morgue, I'd seen the skin all around the mole lacerated and punctured, but the mole remained intact. It was as if his distinguishing feature needed to be preserved, the medium of instant recognition, no matter what happened to the rest of him.

"He must have been very lonely," Raj said.

I was numbed, couldn't even nod.

I wondered if my mother had stood where I was standing and, if so, what had passed through her mind. Or had the actual event been too recent, making her unthinking and numb like me? She had been alone, I supposed, so she could perhaps have drawn comfort from a leaf-rattling yell, a primal scream.

"What had made my father so angry with Askari?" A breakfast of scam and eggs, the half-eaten file.

Raj was cautious. "Some business, I do not know what. Your father thought it bad, Askari didn't agree. Maybe you should not think too harshly of Askari. He did much to keep the honor of your family."

Honor to the outside world, maybe. But inside . . .

I turned away from the steps and wandered over to the hut and peered through the window. I could see nothing, a room filled with blackness. I tried the door. A giant rusty padlock would deter any opportunist without a crowbar at hand.

I felt my shoes sink into a mulch of reeds around the hut's base.

There was something poking out of the reeds, almost camouflaged by the base plank of the hut. It was shy, but definitely there. I went around the side and knelt to take a closer look.

It was a cross, a crude thing made from two slats of wood no more than a few inches long. I ran my fingers over it, the wood smooth with the constant slow shower of slime, a knot of fragile string holding it together, rotten and fragile. But in this dark eave no wind would disturb it, no casual passerby observe it. Only someone coming to the death scene of his father might notice it.

"Are you all right, Fin?" Raj called out but stayed where he was.

"Yes, yes, fine."

"What are you doing?"

What *was* I doing? Touching a shrine. A splintery memorial erected by my mother.

I stood up. "Coming."

Raj looked worried. "I thought you had fallen over, collapsed maybe."

I wiped more slime off my hands and onto my trousers. "No, I just felt bad, needed privacy for a moment. That's all."

Raj nodded sympathetically. "I never knew my father, so his loss meant little to me. For you the anguish must be terrible."

I hadn't known my father either, it seemed.

I smiled. "You're a kind fellow, Raj."

Raj bowed his head bashfully.

I took a sideways glance at the hut. My mother had laid Dad to rest here with a simple cross. Back in England, he lay in a plot in a Cotswold churchyard. There was nothing more for me to do in this place. What I should have done lay in the past, five years ago, when I'd received the phone call.

But at the moment of death, what was in my father's head then? Suicide or accident? A legal definition divided the two words, but here they were joined together by another word: *shame*. A *scienter* of shame, a *mens rea* of shame.

My mother had honored him. With a cross. Yes, but she hadn't known about the wood nymph.

I turned and faced the steps up to the Towers again. A vulture slouched on the stained stone, eyeing the intruders.

"Let's go to Versova," I said.

\* \* \*

My mother had been right. The place *was* an antidote. To some extent anyway. No matter how picturesque, a beach at twilight couldn't completely scatter the convention of demons debating noisily in my head.

As Raj and I wandered onto a busy foreshore, trailed by a chattering caravan of small children, the sight of small boats being tended made me hanker for the noble simplicity of the effort to put food in the stomach; not for prestige or partnership, or even wealth. Just to stay alive. If one could only keep the objective stark and simple, then life might not be tainted by impurities.

I knew that this was naïve. A Westerner's fantasy of a pastoral idyll. The woman leaning against the blue hull of a little boat, attaching floats to a net, would give anything to have what I had, with or without the clutter that went with it.

"They catch bombil," Raj said. "And dry them on those." He pointed along the shore.

In the fading light I could make out a network of frames, small black strips hanging down from them.

A fish gallows.

"They make Bombay Duck from the bombil fish." He didn't clarify this local contradiction.

A gentle breeze rippled across my face. The air was pure fish concentrate, much more pungent than the smell of South Street Seaport; this was the real thing. An eloquent reminder of what this strip of land was for.

Nearby, laughter rose from a small group of men. They were playing a game of some kind. I couldn't see properly. They squatted in a circle, under a bombil frame, their hands waving, their fists thumping the sand in excitement.

The light was disappearing fast. There was no sunset to speak of; dull clouds hung overhead. Would the fishermen go out if it rained too hard? The boats didn't look substantial—no problem while the Arabian Sea quietly slapped tiny breakers on the beach, but in a real swell?

"Are you thinking about your daddy?" Raj looked at me as if I were in the last stages of a terminal illness.

Actually I had momentarily banished him from my head. I was watching fisherfolk, thinking of them. I had found a bit of Bombay where India evoked something other than pain for me.

I smiled at Raj. "I was thinking that it wouldn't be a bad thing to be a fisherman." I half expected Raj to turn on me, explain the brutality of the life, how these people made no money, how they were exploited, and how their existence was a living hell.

"It is very noble, I think," he said.

It was dark. Lamps shone, on the beach and farther away, on the water. Points of light moved slightly with the gentle swell: bobbing, bobbing, bobbing.

I asked Raj if they fished at night.

I could imagine the nocturnal bombil hunt, the highlight of a daily cycle that had remained unchanged for thousands of years and would carry on long after Clay & Westminster, Jefferson Trust, and the whole of Wall Street had crumbled to dust. Well, maybe the fisher tradition wouldn't survive that long. But I liked to think so.

"I don't think they go out in the night," Raj said. "Bombil are office hours fish."

Raj certainly knew how to burst a visionary's bubble.

"Shall we go back now?" I said.

"You want some dinner?" Raj asked.

I desperately didn't want to hurt his feelings, but I needed to be alone. A compromise, perhaps. "I'll tell you what. We'll have a small bite in the Taj restaurant and then I'm going to bed. I'm feeling kind of tired. Is that okay?"

Raj put his hand on my shoulder. "No problem."

We turned and made our way up the beach, through the line of shanties and to the car parked in the world of traffic and tinpot commerce. We had crossed a boundary into bustle and it was hard to believe that a few yards behind our backs a woman was attaching floats to a net in the tranquillity of a fishing community.

# THIRTY

I had hoped that a few envelopes would be poking from under the door of my hotel room when I returned. Bottles, stuffed with optimistic messages, washed up on my shore.

Nothing. The beach was clean.

It was only eight-thirty; Carol wouldn't be back yet, hardly left even. But I called her room anyway and got her voicemail. I didn't leave a message.

I had watched Raj wolf down a biryani, but hadn't touched a thing on my plate. He knew I wanted to be left in peace and ate with ulcerous haste. He wiped his mouth and told me I was a good chap. He told me I could go to his chawl anytime I liked, day or night, if I needed a shoulder. He was sorry that it did not have a phone, but one day . . . With that he bounded out of the hotel restaurant.

Clinging to a cold Kingfisher, I removed the order-routing agreement from the room safe. For a moment I hadn't been able to remember the year of my birth, my head was full of vultures, mud, and the image of a little wooden cross.

At the desk, I flicked through the first few pages of the agreement. In one sense, it was standard enough. In return for advice and good service and a heap of other incentives, the broker received the exclusive rights to the client's share dealing.

But the scale of the thing was utterly inconsistent with a business only worth fifty million. The parties to the agreement were anticipating around a billion of activity. And the client was an unknown, not one of the big institutions; not a Goldman, not a Fidelity, not a Citi; not a Jefferson. Some dingy, offshore dog.

I turned to the signature pages. The front cover usually named the key players only and mopped up the minnows with a dismissive "and others." You had to go to the back to find the hangers-on.

Tom, Dick, and Harry. All offshore. Obscure bastions of vested interest.

Then a Dutch company, or perhaps the Netherlands Antilles. Whatever, it was the name that seized me. Huxtable BV.

It came back to me through the haze of half a decade. The name of the half-eaten file. The name launched at me in a mist of scotch by my father. His Bombay breakfast of scam and eggs.

And who had signed on behalf of Huxtable? The squiggle of black gave no clue to the identity of the Mont Blanc– or Dupont-wielding signatory. Unless, of course, one had seen the signature before. And I had.

I would have recognized the mark of Ernie Monks anywhere.

I opened a second beer and picked up the phone. I dialed Paula's home number; it was around seven-thirty in the morning for her, and I might catch her before she left the house for the city.

"You awake?"

Paula groaned and snuffled. "I've got no makeup on, you know."

"I'll avert my eyes." I allowed a few moments for Paula to gather herself. "You listening?"

"Nope."

"Good. Now get a pen."

"I already got one. What's up?"

"Call Marty Smith at Callaghan's in the Netherlands Antilles and get him to do a search on Huxtable BV. I want the result yesterday."

Huxtable could have been Dutch, but I was sure it wasn't. Holland was too nice a place to be home to a company like Huxtable.

I wanted Marty to use the heavy-duty scalpel, to dig deep. "Get him to find the ultimate shareholders, if he can. It may be tough, but he can charge what he likes for this one."

"Anything else?" Paula sounded fully awake now.

"Yes. I want you to trawl through the office records to see if anything shows for Huxtable, if we ever billed them for anything. You might find something logged under Ernie Monks or . . ." I hesitated. "Or my father."

"Sure," she said, displaying no surprise or curiosity. "And what cost center should I charge Callaghan's to? You know how Keenes gets with this kind of thing. He'll be all over the bill if you're not careful."

She had a point, a good one given the time of day in the US. I thought about it. "Charge it to the Schuster Mannheim merger file." The expense tab on the file was astronomical and there was no client to fuss about it. I could've stuck in the bill for a new suit and nobody would notice.

"Naughty boy," Paula said.

"It'll be you that processes it, Paula."

"Will that mean I don't get a going away gift?"

"Read back the name of the company to me, so I know we're on the same page."

She spelled out a name. Microsoft.

I grunted. "Very funny."

"I know how to write down a name, counselor; even one with three syllables. Hux-ta-ble. There. Happy?"

"No." I paused. "Today, I visited the place where my father died."

I heard her intake of breath. "That must've been tough."

"Yes," I said.

"It's kind of hard to say this now, but your mother called at the office."

"Did you say where I was?"

"I didn't have to. After five minutes of shadowboxing, she figured it out. She's a smart lady. Sounds real sweet too."

"Oh no."

"I got the impression that she might follow you out there."

"Oh Christ, she mustn't. I'm not sure she'd survive a second time around."

"I told her you'd be back in New York any minute."

"Well done, Paula."

"None of my business, Fin, but I think you should have told her. She sounds pretty grounded."

*When she's not on the pills, Paula. When she's not airborne on the wings of those little white fuckers.*

"Mendip said I shouldn't," I said lamely.

"He family, counselor?"

My godfather. He owned the family house, the family purse. "You're right, I should have spoken to her," I said.

"Well, like I said, it's none of my business. I'll get back to you when Callaghan has something."

I tried my mother's number, letting it ring until I got a harsh, high-pitched monotone.

What would my father have done? Before the Fall. When he was still the Clay & Westminster Executive Committee member with a first from Oxford, when he could have charged by the word rather than the hour. When he seemed to have the answer to everything. Which tome would he have pulled from the shelf, blown the dust from, opened at just the right page? His law always seemed to be the old, immutable law. He rarely paid heed to new cases, relying instead on the tablets handed down from the mountain, but still he always seemed to be one step ahead.

Until the half-eaten file had caught him out. Until he'd compromised.

I slept a short sleep filled with faces, dirt, and flying feathers.

Consciousness only really returned when I heard the flushing of the toilet, when I watched the frothing tide of puke and water sucked from the gleaming porcelain to start its short journey to the Arabian Sea.

My neck rested on the rim of the toilet bowl, as if I were waiting for the executioner.

At length I got up, brushed my teeth, and returned to the bedroom.

I tried Carol's number again.

"Uh." I'd woken her.

"How was your evening?"

"Fine."

Silence.

"I visited the Towers of Silence with Raj." I could have gone on.

Carol let out a yawn. "Was that such a smart idea?"

Smart? Smart wasn't the issue.

"I've been reading an order-routing agreement," I said. "There's a whole lot more to Ketan Securities than meets the eye, and it has some very strange clients."

Carol groaned. "Jesus, Fin, it's late."

I looked at my watch. It wasn't that late. "Can I come and see you?"

"No." There was no hesitation.

"Why not?"

"Because."

"What kind of answer is that?"

"Look, I'm sorry. I guess you've had a shitty day, but we both need some rest. We have a full day tomorrow."

"Haven't you heard what I'm telling you? Ketan Securities stinks. Our job should be to find out how full of shit it is—"

"Like I said, you need some rest. Good night."

The line went dead.

# THIRTY-ONE

The Askari & Co. S Class Mercedes dropped me outside its somber Victorian headquarters at nine the next morning.

A hundred years of accumulated grime stained its entire frontage, windows included. I'd seen it before. Just the once, when I'd visited Sunil Askari with my mother.

I climbed the stone steps into the reception area. It hadn't changed. It was like a railroad station: people and packages, ebb and flow, announcements and waiting, waiting, waiting.

And at the edge of it all stood a man in khaki with an ancient Lee Enfield 303 slung over his shoulder. It was the same guy as five years ago; slightly fewer spots, more facial hair, but unmistakably a grown-up version of the dopey adolescent I remembered.

Raj was leaning against the receptionist's counter, waiting for me. He looked smart. Today's pants went all the way down to his worn but shiny shoes. There was a flash of steel at his wrist.

"Morning, morning." He put his arm around my shoulder and turned to the receptionist. "This is a very important attorney from

New York. He is our client. He will have an office here during his visit and every convenience must be afforded to him."

The receptionist smiled and waggled her head while wiping the area where Raj had been leaning with a large red cloth.

He led me down a corridor. "You like the suit, ya?" He stood in front of me to allow me to admire it. "Pierre Cardin. Very chic."

I said I liked it very much.

He stuck his wrist under my nose. "And the watch. Omega Seamaster, as used by James Bond." He lowered his voice. "A fake, but a very good one, don't you think?"

I couldn't help but agree.

"I'll take you to your office now. Everything is ready for you."

We passed into an enormous room. Nothing here had changed in five years.

"This is where all the clerks and junior attorneys work," Raj said.

It was a great hangar of a place; a sea of desks, all occupied and loaded with piles of papers tied in red treasury tape. Around the desks were more piles of papers, so tall that they nearly obscured the men and women working at the desks. The room testified to the labor-intensive essence of legal practice on the subcontinent.

Down one side of the room ran a long counter, over which a conveyor belt of young women in saris moved new and finished work to and from the legal factory floor.

Aside from the swish of the ceiling fans, there was curiously little noise. Where were the ringing phones? Where was the office banter?

I could never love the law enough to work in a place like this.

We left the room and squeezed along a dark passageway lined with gray filing cabinets. Raj stopped at a gap in the gunmetal and opened a door.

The room reminded me of the windowless cubicle used by Mendip back in New York. A single table, a schoolroom chair. Blank gray walls.

"Your office," Raj announced. "I do not have such a thing. I work in the main room. It is fine, but one day I will have my own office and that will be grand."

If it was anything like this, Raj would be better off where he was.

Askari had assigned me the least officelike office in the building. There was a phone, a barrel-sized wastebasket, and a dozen or so draft documents marshaled neatly on the table. I glanced at them. No Liquid Paper or Wite-Out this time. *Askari & Co. SA/950.* Sunil Askari, file reference 950.

Raj looked guilty. "I hope you are not offended by the work carried out on your drafts. They were indeed excellent."

"Who made the amendments?" I asked.

Raj made as if to tidy the already tidy deck of documents. "I did." I could barely hear him.

"Then I'm not offended in the least."

Raj beamed.

I pointed to the front covers. "Surely they should have the initials RS on them."

Raj stopped smiling. "I don't think clients would appreciate that."

"One day you'll be senior partner," I said.

He seemed shocked by the suggestion. "There is a ceiling for me. I am a Dalit."

Untouchable. The caste system: the rich man in his castle, the poor man at his gate. Immutable, divinely ordained roles and status, changeable only in successive lives. But wasn't the President of India a Dalit? Raj turned away from me and shuffled some papers.

The topic was obviously as untouchable as the subject matter.

"Askari wants me to do some things for him," he said at last. "So I must leave you here. Lunch will be brought to you at one. If there is anything else you want—tea, coffee"—he winked—"or beer. Then call reception." He pointed redundantly at the phone. "Dial 0."

"When will you be back?" I asked. "Or shall I just leave when I'm through and see you tomorrow?"

Raj waved his hands excitedly. "Good heavens, no. I will be back in the afternoon. Then I hope you will let me entertain you this evening. My treat."

"Sure. But it's my treat this time."

And then I was alone.

My first inclination was to sweep up the documents into a bundle and head back to the hotel, where at least there was a window and minibar.

But no. It would be noticed, commented on, cause trouble. Not just for me, but maybe Raj too. Something made me feel protective toward him.

It would be late evening in New York. My hand curled around the phone, then I drew it away. I'd give Pablo Tochera until morning.


I worked my way through the pile of documents.

Most of what I'd originally written had stayed, but the changes made by Raj looked sensible enough. No point scoring, nothing persnickety, just solid matching of circumstance to law.

Except in one respect.

I went back to the sale and purchase agreement, the cornerstone contract for Project Badla.

Clause 5. *Exclusivity.* The keep-out-the-riffraff clause. Normally this outlined what was to happen to client lists after the sale, which part of the business kept which accounts, where the income was credited. In this type of deal it was important, because a part of the fifty million was to be deferred, depending on how well the business performed after it was bought by Jefferson Trust. That meant if other parts of Jefferson Trust appropriated Ketan clients, then the take for the sellers could be slashed.

I'd expected a scuffle around the exclusivity clause. But what was being suggested in the amended Clause 5 confused the hell out of me.

Ketan wanted all Indian clients to be the exclusive domain of the Ketan business. Fine. Next, they wanted all the non-Indian clients for trading in Indian stocks. More controversial, but still not surprising. Then they said it was okay for Jefferson to keep the income generated by clients listed on a schedule at the back of the document.

I looked at the list. It was a who's who of every major institution in the world. Nobody seemed to be left out of the party.

Jefferson Trust should be cracking open the champagne in celebration. On the one hand Ketan had said in Clause 5: We want all the clients. Then in the schedule they'd said: Oh, fuck it, you can have them all back again.

Why?

Take it from the top, I told myself, first principles. Ketan had the domestic Indians. Okay. Then all the big guys were handed over to Jefferson on a plate. Weird. Who did that leave? The minnows. The flotsam of no-hopers, bobbing on the massive ocean of the financial markets.

They weren't all minnows, though, were they? The order-routing agreement proved that. Unknowns, but with billions to spend. Offshore fat cats in shades. Ketan Securities wanted to keep control over them, not let nice respectable Jefferson Trust dirty its hands.

I remembered a statistic in one of the newspaper articles in Terry's India file. There were around one hundred and twenty billion dollars of assets outside India but owned by Indians. The Non-Resident Indians.

Gold had been a sideshow. Huxtable and Ketan were playing for bigger stakes, their slice of the cake owned by patriotic Indians who might want to wash their goodies in and out of India. To do this they needed a kindly lock keeper who could crank the handles and make sure that the waters flowed in the right direction, and at the right depth.

I had to persuade Carol to listen, to see that Ketan Securities was little more than an industrial-scale financial laundry. Jefferson Trust would own it, but have no control. The Ketans would keep that for themselves.

I tried to track her down at Ketan Securities. Out, sir. With the Ketans, sir. A message? Certainly, sir.

And what did Charles Mendip know about Ketan Securities? Maybe no more than what Askari told him. But there was Ernie's signature on the Huxtable agreement. The signature of Mendip's right-hand man. Should I confront him, point out to him that he'd told me to do my job, tell him I *had* done my job? Ask him what the fuck was going on.

Again, my hand neared the phone.

It rang.

"Sheesh, you're a tough guy to find."

"I'm not hiding, Pablo," I said.

"I'm sorry, really sorry," Tochera said.

"About what?"

An intake of breath, the prelude to bad news.

"Have they charged me?" I asked.

"How the fuck should I know? I haven't spoken to Manelli for over an hour."

"What, then?"

"I . . . Christ. Look, I can't go on acting for you, Fin. I've told McIntyre it's making me sick. I've asked him why he's telling me to do my best for you and then . . . Jesus, I'm shooting my mouth off, here. If this continues, I'll be lucky if they let me clean the trainees' Allen Edmonds."

"Allen Edmonds?"

"Shoes, Fin."

"And cutting loose from me will help, will it?" I felt a fly tickle the scab on a small shaving cut I'd given myself that morning. I swatted it. It circled once and returned to the same spot. "Jesus, Pablo. McIntyre put you on my file in the first place. Why should he think you're partnership material if you run to him with a doctor's note when a case gets tough?"

"Fuck you. I've tried my best; I haven't been home for a week. Julia sent me a postcard yesterday; told me the weather was good on the Upper East Side, would I like to join her. Sheesh. This isn't what I signed up for."

"This is litigation, and you're a litigator," I said. "What's the problem?"

"This is a whole heap more than litigation."

"Elaborate. It's the least you can do."

"Someone else can handle your case better than me," Tochera said, his voice calmer now. "I fucked up, though you won't get me to say that in company. McIntyre will assign someone who can provide the right coverage. McIntyre knows my strengths and weaknesses. He wants me to play to my strengths from here on. And I can't do that on this case."

"This is totally unethical," I protested. "I want *you*."

"Why? You just said I was unethical."

"McIntyre's unethical." My mouth was caked in dried saliva. "You . . . You . . . Well, I don't want you for your ethics, anyway."

"I'm sorry, Fin," he whined.

"You've said that already."

"I've got to go. I just wanted to tell you face-to-face. Well, you know what I mean."

I didn't know what he meant at all. But the smell of his fear filled my horrid little room.

"When will I know who's acting for me?" It was either that or trying to get hold of someone like Jack Kempinski, a one-room, one-photocopier attorney, and instruct him over the phone from Bombay, explain my situation and give him a swift résumé of the assets with which I could remunerate him. A very swift résumé.

"McIntyre will call, I'm sure." Tochera didn't sound sure at all.

"Could you put me through to him?"

Tochera hesitated. "I'll try."

Music. *The Marriage of Figaro*. Schuster Mannheim was preparing for the wedding with Clay & Westminster.

The music stopped mid-bar. "He's away from his desk right now. I've left a message for him to call you."

"How can you do this, Pablo?" I had no pride; he couldn't help but hear the desperation in my voice.

"I'm sorry. It's just not possible to explain. Good-bye."

I tried to get through to Charles Mendip. He was away from his desk too.

It looked like I was on my own.


As promised, Raj showed up later that afternoon.

"Successful day?" He asked lightly.

I didn't reply as I slid my pen into my pocket and stood up.

Raj frowned. "You need cheering up, my friend. I will take you to some jolly places." He picked up my briefcase. "I will carry your bag to the car and you will go back to the Taj and change into your chinkos first."

"Chinos, Raj."

He giggled. "My heavens, yes." I caught a goodish breeze of beer.

# THIRTY-TWO

I felt like a bag of cement. Christ only knew how many beers and buckets of curry were thickening into an impregnable dyke between my small intestine and all normal exit routes.

"I will ask for some Paan," Raj said, empathizing with my bloated condition.

He carried on talking and drinking and mopping his plate with chapati. Since Raj had collected me from the hotel at seven, he had talked all evening. Above the racket of a restaurant filled to capacity, he had yelled his life story, elaborating on the loss of parents, his love of cricket, the luck of his sister, the generosity of Askari, and how he, Raj Shethia, last of the male line, was going to break out of the grim squalor of his chawl and find a nice apartment. And maybe, just maybe, go to America.

And find a wife. Oh yes, sir, a fine woman to bear me children. She will come to America with me and we will have American children. So that the Shethia name can expand into an American future under American citizenship. He was certain, as certain that the Paan would ease my distended stomach.

The Paan arrived. A chrome lazy Susan—a "Paan daan," Raj called it—sectioned into bowls of betel nut, cumin, coconut, caraway, aniseed, and stuff I didn't recognize. He smeared honey across an olive-green leaf—banana? I wasn't sure—and carefully applied a strip of pure gold foil over the honey before tipping a teaspoon of each item from the lazy Susan onto the leaf. Then he rolled it up into a tight package, a green owl pellet.

I sniffed at the package.

"All at once, Fin," Raj said. "Crunch, crunch."

I popped it into my mouth and bit hard. It was like chewing a forest floor.

But then an almost narcotic wave swept over me: pine, eucalyptus, Listerine, and cognac all at once.

And my stomach eased.

Raj was laughing. "Good, ya?"

"Good," I managed.

I began to relax again, more confident now that I wouldn't explode. I even asked for another beer, conscious that I was about six behind Raj, who had somehow stayed fresh and dapper in his well-worn Pierre Cardin suit and fake Gucci loafers.

"So where precisely does your sister live?" I asked. Raj had made vague reference to New York.

"I do not know exactly. Her school moves her from place to place, to ensure a broad education."

"So how do you write or call, if you don't know where she is?"

"She has a PO box, so I can write, and she telephones me every few months. She tells me how happy she is, how one day she will be a model and I will see her on the cover of *Vogue* magazine."

"She must be very beautiful."

Raj smiled and nodded. Then he tapped his head like he'd just remembered something important. This time he got his wallet out and flipped it open.

"It is an old photo. Taken before she left Bombay."

A girl, fourteen, maybe fifteen, in a school uniform—lilac, a crest on the jacket, a small elephant deity with four arms—with wild eyes and wild hair that the photographer had tried to tame without success.

The kind of wild thing that was all legs, and fast; fast enough to run from a bedroom to a bathroom in a split second, fast enough to betray only a flash of face, but one that would stick in my mind for a lifetime.

The face of my father's wood nymph.

My stomach tightened, the effect of the Paan evaporated. And suddenly I felt drunk too. The photo swam in front of my eyes. The elephant on the crest seemed to leer at me.

"Beautiful, isn't she?" Raj stroked the picture and slipped the wallet back into his pocket.

"Did she ever go to England?" I heard myself ask.

Raj pursed his lips and tugged at his curried mustache. "No. Why do you ask?"

Because my father was a colonial villain who had pleasured himself with her at a Victorian house in Hampton Court, then tossed her in the garbage.

"What is the elephant crest on her jacket?" I asked.

"Ganesh," Raj said. "A very important god. We have big festivals here in his honor. He is the god of good luck. It is good to pray to him."

"What's he like at getting insurance companies off your back?"

Raj seemed to take my question seriously. "He is also the god of removing obstacles."

Then his lips curved into a sly smile. "I shall take you to the bazaar now."

Shit. Haggling over souvenirs larger than my suitcase was the last thing I needed.

Raj must have sensed my reluctance. "Not the usual kind of bazaar, Fin. This is more interesting, I promise."

Hell's teeth, not the red-light district, please. I'd visited more rancid, overpriced bars in the world's capitals than I cared to remember; evenings of moronic antics with hostesses who hated you and had to submit to indignities like drunken tongues licking lime juice out of their cleavages or sitting on the laps of businessmen whose wives didn't understand them. Then the instant replay in the taxi back to the hotel, the mutual tales of what we could have done, if only we dared. The next morning's hangover and the crumpled VISA slip for a thousand bucks.

"I'm sorry Raj, I don't really think . . ."

He looked crestfallen. "Very good place. High-class. Tip-top."

He stood up and swayed, I could see he was very drunk. The silly dolt didn't know what he was doing.

"Okay," I said, sighing.

I stood up and then realized how drunk *I* was.

At the door Raj dipped his hand into a wooden bowl and scooped up a handful of Khyber matchboxes.

"Here. Take these," he said.

"I don't smoke, Raj."

"Take. Take. A souvenir."

I stuffed them into my pocket.

In the cab, Raj snored while I watched the street distractedly, feeling the nausea of a stomach overladen with curry and beer. Or maybe it was guilty anticipation of where we were going.

He jerked awake and looked about him. "Thieves' market." A clotted vein of a street, furtively crawling with people picking their way through the vehicle parts and other untraceable proceeds of crime.

Then it went dark, as the shanties closed in on us. The houses melted like dark glaciers into the potholes and garbage. The bulbs were no longer white.

The car stopped.

"Stay close to me," Raj said.

Sound advice, I thought, stepping into a bog of rotting vegetables and watching shifty groups of men staring at the barred windows of garishly painted slums; the dull light hinting of shadows of women inside; women caged and for hire.

"Here?" I asked.

Raj crooked his arm in mine. "Goodness, no. These are the whores for layabouts and millworkers." He spat.

I looked up at the upper floors, many with white billboards, like bar signs protruding from them, proclaiming that help was at hand: Dr. This and Dr. That, specialist in VD, in skin diseases, in HIV.

"Where are we?"

"Falkland Road, Kamatipura," Raj said, virtually dragging me along the street, pushing aside those who got in the way.

Reeperbahn, Wanchai, Pat Pong, Rappongi. As an observer rather than participant, I'd witnessed the various red-light galleries. But this was something else. There was a purity of purpose in this place. Sex unadorned, the release of semen as a need, not a pleasure. No neon, no enticement, no packaging. The uncut heroin of sex.

"You see," explained Raj, "the ratio of men to women in Bombay makes such places necessary. And for most, these men cannot afford to marry or they are on the move all the time, truckers. So"—he waved his free hand at the barred windows—"this is the only alternative."

I felt an icy thrill, horror cut with the mentality of the Peeping Tom. "I shouldn't be seen around here."

Raj laughed and squeezed my arm. "Chilly out, Fin. It is completely legal, well, nearly. And if someone sees you, then you should be asking what they are doing here. Their gun is your gun too."

And the experience wasn't sobering me up either. My legs were sandbags, my arms as pendulous as two snakey coils, my vision the texture and angle of a sixties movie.

Suddenly, Raj pulled me into an alley, pitch-black, only the sound of scurrying rats signifying a way ahead. We turned a hairpin, Raj seeming to know when it was coming. There was light at the end of this stretch of tunnel.

We emerged into a small courtyard, surrounded on three sides by squat ramshackle tenements, the fourth occupied by a detached house, a crazy distorted timber structure, painted electric blue.

Raj whispered into the ear of one of the two mammoth bouncers standing side-by-side at the foot of a flight of steps leading up to the entrance. They didn't move and ignored Raj.

"We can go in," Raj told me, patting the folded arms of a bouncer and receiving a death threat stare in return. He ran up the stairs, with me close behind, expecting the bouncers to reanimate and lock me in a vice as I squeezed between them.

Inside the house, the light was leaden blue and red, muting edges, obscuring reality, while thick incense clogged the nose and brain. Females aged fifteen to fifty sat on couches or beanbag chairs, reading film magazines, filing nails, or just staring ahead of them. A few men wandered among them, gripping tumblers of booze incongruously swaddled in delicate paper lace doilies. The walls depicted scenes from the Kama Sutra, and torn chiffon hung from the ceiling, some weird take on the seven veils.

I could see Raj sweat and fidget as he spoke to an elderly twig of a woman, guarding another flight of stairs ascending lopsidedly into the building's upper reaches.

Raj beckoned me. I followed him upstairs, feeling more nauseous with every step as the soles of my shoes stuck to the threadbare carpet.

We turned left at the top of the stairs into a thin hallway. I looked to my right. There was just a large door, sealed with a huge rusty padlock.

Raj giggled nervously. "Behind that door isn't for us, my friend."

Not one splinter of this place was for me, I told myself piously.

The hallway suddenly got busy and we wove among men and women who had finished their few moments of bliss, and were now vacating the cubicle for the next shift, like train cars emptying at a station.

Some doors stayed shut, and from behind them I could hear unambiguous thrashing and groaning.

I was glad to reach the end of the hallway.

We found ourselves in a brightly lit room, like a library, floor-to-ceiling shelving on two sides, the timber slats sagging dangerously under a mass of books. And ahead of me, a curtain of glass beads, leading perhaps to a balcony. The slight tinkle of glass on glass betrayed a gentle breeze.

An enormous woman sat slumped in an armchair. A ring-encrusted hand dangled lazily over the arm of the chair and foraged in a copper tray of pistachio nuts perched on a wooden stand. Henna tattoos snaked around her fingers and over her knuckles before making their way up her arms and under the sleeves of a gold sari, where they were swallowed by the deep folds of her whalelike interior.

With long red fingernails, she raked a brittle mane of golden hair while her sandals scrunched in the gravel of pistachio shells.

She eyed us haughtily.

"Good evening," she said at last.

Raj shuffled like a child in front of a headmistress. "Baba Mama, this is a visitor from America. He is English."

No names. People didn't have names in this house.

Baba Mama smiled. Midas teeth—a row of gold, preened by a gold toothpick that chiseled away at shards of nut, which, when dislodged, she spat from the side of her mouth, obligingly, away from us.

"And the weather?" she said. "Is it cold in New York?" She mimed a shiver and drew a tartan rug up to her neck as if I had brought an icy blast with me.

She'd guessed I was based in New York. Was it merely a guess?

"It's summer. It's hot, though not as hot as here."

She nodded slowly and then shifted her hair almost an inch. She seemed unconcerned that we should know it was a wig.

"And are you ready to enjoy our services?"

I wasn't and never would be. "I think we are visiting to pay our respects, as it were." I saw Raj wince and stare down at his fake Gucci loafers.

At that moment a servant came in wielding a steel tray with three small shot glasses filled with a clear liquid. Baba Mama took a glass and tipped the drink straight down her throat, exposing gold all the way back to her abrasive larynx. Raj took a glass and did the same.

I held the glass and hesitated.

Baba Mama stopped smiling.

"I hope you like it." It didn't sound as if she cared whether I liked it or not. I just had to drink it.

I did.

I remembered as a child being told never to rifle among the bottles and boxes and packets that lurked under the kitchen sink. They'd kill me if I even touched them. Someone had distilled everything under the sink into a thimbleful of concentrate and just given it to me to drink. I would have given a thousand bucks for an owl pellet of Paan to dull the taste.

But Baba Mama was smiling again. Raj was smiling too. I couldn't. Standing up was about all I could manage.

"Where were we?" Baba Mama asked. "Ah. My girls and you; I

remember now." She adjusted her wig. "You see, we have rules here. The rule of law, inherited from our past. Our colonial masters, the great justice of the white man. It is what separates us from our past."

She allowed a pause for us to take in the grandeur of her historical perspective.

"And there is a particular rule," she continued. "It provides that anyone who honors us with a visit must choose one of my lovely girls and pass time with her, behind closed doors. They need not do the business; they may converse and drink tea if they wish. But it is not for anyone to deny that they have spent time with one of my lovely girls and so feel, mistakenly, superior to other gentlemen."

Baba Mama was becoming a blur. I leaned forward to try and reclaim a sharper vision and felt myself start to fall.

Raj steadied me. He held me for a moment and then slowly withdrew his hands to see if I could stand unaided. He watched me like a window dresser eyeing a rogue mannequin.

Baba Mama ignored my little drama. "It is a good rule, and stops gossip and the unwarranted superiority of gentlemen." She waved her hand in a grand gesture. "It prevents"—her hand circled and circled like a plane in a holding pattern waiting to land—"what is the word?" She stared at Raj.

"Horridness?" Raj ventured.

Baba Mama scowled. "Hypocrisy." The hand settled back into the tray of pistachio nuts.

She peered at me. "Come here."

I was glued to the spot.

"Bah," she said, "I will come to you." She heaved herself out of the armchair, shifting her huge bulk with surprising grace as she scrunched over the carpet of pistachio shells.

She held my chin in her hands. I could feel the gold of her rings press into me.

She raised her head and stared at me, her piggy eyes ranging over the contours of my face. "We had a gentleman in here once who looked very much like you." She let go of my face and returned to her chair, tucking in the tartan rug around her tightly as if the room had turned cold. "He came to a bad end, I believe."

Suddenly I was thirsty, a desperate thirst. I asked for some water. At least I thought I did. Nobody seemed to hear me, though. So I asked again and then again. I sensed I was shouting, but they still ignored me. They were talking; I could see lips move. But hear no sound.

I had to move, prove I had a body. I lurched and felt muscles tense and then relax. I lurched some more and found myself moving at speed across the room past Baba Mama toward the glass bead curtain.

I burst through it. I wasn't expecting a noise, but the yielding ropes of glass shrieked as if I'd destroyed an entire display of crystal in a New Year's sale.

The balcony was occupied. Three women in cane chairs sat around a copper table loaded with tumblers of beer and packs of cigarettes. The women were weaving or sewing, I couldn't tell exactly, I just saw hands at work and twine and thread looped around their fingers and trailing to the floor under the table, where they ended in untidy balls of fiber.

I rocked on my feet. Two of the women remained focused on their task. The third turned her head and I looked into her face.

It was the face of a man. Framed by a fringe of luxuriant black hair were the unmistakable features of an old, old man, cheeks sunken by toothlessness, eyes large, mournful and bloodshot, stubble sprouting on the chin and below the nose. Lip gloss and eye shadow merely emphasized both age and masculinity.

"Fuck," I wanted to say and maybe did. I didn't hear the response as massive arms circled me and I was dragged back into the presence of Baba Mama.

Whoever had pulled me off the balcony was now pinioning me against the bookshelves, my face pressed hard against the spines of the books. I could smell old paper and taste bitter dust.

Distantly, I could hear Baba Mama. "Take your friend to a room now. Let him have value for his rupees."

No. No.

Raj was laughing. I opened my eyes onto a line of swastikas. Little Nazi dancing wheels receding to the horizon at the end of the bookshelf.

I felt myself being spun around and my arm placed over the shoulder of Raj. "It is time to leave Baba Mama alone." He sounded jovial.

And then I heard the voice of my father whispering in my head. "Tell Raj about Preeti. Go on: Wipe the stupid smile from under that stupid mustache of his."

When I opened my eyes again, I was staring at a forty-watt bulb dangling from a ceiling of gray-stained Styrofoam tiles.

At my side knelt a girl. She was thin, almost emaciated, eyes deep and tragic, and her skin, despite its blackness, showed the ravages of acne or something worse.

She was naked.

So was I.

I looked down the plateau of my chest and could see my penis, semierect and unsheathed.

Christ, please, no. Tell me I didn't. Tell me that much at least. I didn't feel like I'd felt with Carol after we'd made love, but our union hadn't taken place in a squalid box on a filthy mattress, bathed in the light of a forty-watt bulb.

I sat up and pulled my shirt across me, trying to wipe away the sweat that drenched me. Sweat from sex? It was hot enough to make a sleeping salamander leak buckets, so maybe it didn't signify anything. But how could I be sure?

"Did I . . . I mean we. Well, did we?"

The girl looked at me blankly and brushed her hair.

She then picked up a little notebook and wrote a number on a page with lots of numbers already on it. Five hundred, she wrote.

I owed her five hundred rupees. Eleven dollars. Jesus.

She closed the notebook. It was a school notebook. It had a crest on it. A little elephant with four arms.

The door creaked open and Raj's grinning face appeared.

"I told you it would be interesting," he said.


As we passed the two bouncers outside, a random thought flitted across my dizzied consciousness. The Nazis hadn't been the first ones to fly the swastika.

# THIRTY-THREE

I was woken by a loud hammering on the door. I looked at my watch. Middle of the night. Only two hours since I'd collapsed in my hotel room.

The knocking was insistent, frenzied.

My head nearly disintegrated as I got up and slid my robe on.

It was Carol, her face barely a shade darker than her white T-shirt.

I noticed the shadows of sweat down her back as she pushed past me and sat heavily on the bed.

She started to sob. I poured a glass of water and sat down on the bed beside her. As she sipped I stroked her hair, soft as a cat's fur. "When you're ready," I said.

The choking sobs became less intense, the gaps between them increased. She raised her head and groaned.

"They know," she said, shaking her head hard and pressing her palms under her eyes to wipe away the tears.

Know what?

She finished the water and clutched the empty glass. Her knuckles whitened; she was holding the glass so hard I thought it might fracture. I gently pried it from her fingers.

Her body went limp and she curled up on the bed in a fetal position. I was prepared to be patient, but I wasn't going to let her take a nap before she told me what was going on.

"Tell me, Carol. What's happened?"

She uncurled and sat up against the pillows. "*America Daily* will be running a story."

A single sob gripped her and she held her breath for a moment. "About me."

"What will it say?"

"Miranda Carlson has found out about me and JJ. I don't know how, but she has. It will be a big story."

Jefferson Trust's chief banking attorney the lover of FDR smash banker. She was right; it would be big and ugly. Pictures of Miranda and the two kids. A mug shot of Carol, only the prisoner numbers missing, but the readers' minds would supply them, sure enough.

"Who knows this is on the way?" I asked.

"Everyone." She gave the pillow a vicious thump. "*America Daily* people have been calling around for backup and quotes. They called me; someone must've told them I was here. Jesus, the guy was almost bubbling with excitement, wanted all the background: where, when, how many times, did I make JJ kill all those people, did I know Miranda, the kids. It was sick."

"What did you say?"

She chewed her lip. "I'm still an attorney. I said no comment and hung up."

She took my hand. "They asked about you too."

I felt my heart jolt.

"They know that the car was in your name. They kind of implied we'd run off to India together . . ." She clenched her fists, her face; a whole body clench. "Oh, Christ. I should have gone to the police and saved you and me a lot of pain."

"You've done nothing wrong."

"Nothing wrong?" she hissed. "Jefferson Trust doesn't see it that way."

"You've spoken to them then?"

"The general counsel called me. He's married, four kids. A Baptist preacher. He could hardly speak. Wants me on the next plane to New York. I tried to explain, but he didn't want to know, said I could tell it to the chairman."

She lifted her head. The face was raw, ravaged by desperation and despair. Strands of hair were stuck across one eye and over her cheek.

"I'm ruined," she said.

"Shh." I removed the hair from her face. "Take it one step at a—"

"And you. Look what I've done to you. Let me call the police now."

It wouldn't be that simple. We were Bonnie and Clyde.

She gripped my arm. "I guess you're wondering why I've been kind of shitty. Well, distant anyway."

"You fell in love with Ashish Ketan and couldn't bear to tell me."

In spite of everything, she laughed. "No. Though he's kind of cute for an old guy."

"Why then?"

The smile fled. "Chuck Krantz reckoned we were seeing each other. There was a rumor, someone in Starbucks saw us and tried to add it up and got the right answer. Anyway, Chuck called me. Told me to get on with the deal, no distractions. And if I was out of line he would tell the general counsel and allege that Clay & Westminster only got deals because I was sleeping with you."

"And you and I know that it's because I'm a great attorney."

"Yeah," she said. "Anyway, I got scared, lost track of priorities."

We fell silent. I could hear the rain had started again, not hard yet, but it would be.

"Of course, Chuck's threat is rather academic now," I said.

"I guess."

The phone rang.

"This is Brad Emerson from the *America Daily.*" A sentence delivered at a hundred miles an hour. A journalist's sentence. I cupped the mouthpiece.

"They just found me too," I said.

I let my hand go, still watching Carol, who was rocking gently like she'd done in her apartment after we'd made love.

I had a problem with journalists at the best of times. "What do you want?"

"You're a hard guy to track down. We've had to run a piece without your input, so I'm giving you an opportunity to tell it your way for a later edition. You know what I'm talking about; you're not going to make me sweat it out of you, are you? That'd be a waste of our time and I know how busy you international attorneys are."

"When will it be in the paper?"

The guy laughed. "We're a real-time outfit now. Printing is fly-by-wire and we can update anytime on the Web. To answer your question, the Asian hard copy is out around now. It'll be in tomorrow's in New York. Now you can answer some of my questions."

"Up yours," I said and hung up.

"Was that such a good idea?" Carol asked.

"Ernie Monks always told me that hacks need oxygen to breathe, and I wasn't about to open my valves."

Carol looked unconvinced.

"Anyway," I said. "There's nothing I could say that would make it any better."

"Hold me," Carol said.

I held her, feeling her damp T-shirt, the sweat turned cold by the AC. I prayed she wouldn't recognize the smell of whorehouse on me, detect the incense, the booze, the cheap scent and draw the only possible conclusion. I felt infected.

"You should get changed, you'll get a chill," I said.

"Sure, Mom."

"When's your flight?" I asked.

"Just after seven this morning. Air India to JFK." She nuzzled into the base of my neck like a frightened pup. "You know what the general counsel said? He told me to travel coach, so that Jefferson could get a refund on the first-class ticket. I don't think he cares about the money; he was delivering a message about where I was headed." I could *feel* her voice, her warm breath a breeze bending my chest hair. She couldn't help but arouse me.

"Do the Ketans know you're leaving Bombay?" I asked.

"I didn't say anything. I took the *Tribune* call at their house and returned to the table as if nothing had happened. It was a great performance, although I don't know why I bothered. Anyway, someone from Jefferson Trust will call them, I expect. By tomorrow I won't be their golden girl."

"You're probably better off out of it."

Carol sat up. "Why do you say that?"

"Like I've told you, there's something very wrong with Ketan Securities."

"Not the Ernie Monks and JJ thing again. It doesn't show anything."

So far it was just dots, no picture. But I was sure there was a picture in there somewhere. "There's more."

"Like what, Fin? More shadows?"

"Like the purchase price, for starters. You must see that it's too cheap."

Carol needed more before she'd join my three-wheeled bandwagon.

"Then there's the fact that Askari & Co. were Ketan's attorneys until about five minutes ago. They're not on our side, you can be sure of that."

"How do you know?"

"The name was whited out from the agreements."

Carol looked more interested, but not on board yet.

"Go on."

"The exclusivity clause keeps the toxic stuff in the hands of the Ketans and there's a material contract that stinks. Ketan has entered an order-routing agreement with a number of people. You know, so they can get the business and maybe give a discount."

"Fin, we handle soft dollar arrangements all the time. What of it? Sure, it might be on the edge, but it isn't such a big deal."

I shook my head. "I don't much care if it is illegal. It's the size of the thing. Massive. Disproportionate to the value ascribed to it. And the parties smell. These people are launderers. If I had a career, I'd stake it on that fact."

I started to get off the bed and go to the room safe, but Carol grabbed my hand.

"I don't want to read an order-routing agreement right now."

I stayed put. "You remember I told you how my father got involved in something bad, something that finished him?" There was the matter of the wood nymph too, but that could wait.

"Gold and stuff. Havala, you said."

"He was working for a client. A company called Huxtable. They're a party to the order-routing agreement."

Now she was interested.

"And Ernie Monks was the signatory."

"You're kidding?"

"Something's rotten in the Shrine of the Ketans. My guess is that a few years ago there was a small operation to run gold and it got bigger. There's a reservoir of money outside India held by non-residents— NRIs. And Huxtable and Ketan are their bag carriers, acting as an illegal conduit for assets in and out of India. And now that Jefferson is acquiring Ketan they get a foothold in a huge and respectable bank. Jefferson keeps the kosher activity and the Ketans pursue the illicit trade on an expanded basis."

"But where's the backup, the proof?"

"Not in the data room, that's for sure. That material was put together under laboratory conditions. Maybe at Ketan Securities. Maybe Askari. Who knows? Maybe in a file somewhere at Jefferson Trust."

Carol shook her head sadly. "I don't think you are going to be on this case long enough to find out."

I'd reached a point where the picture was coming into focus, and so was a promise to myself: that this was one cause I couldn't abandon. Whatever had happened, it drove my father to his death. It was my case now. It should have been my case long ago, but the wood nymph got in the way. My father's crime had put him beyond the pale, guaranteed that I'd hang up on his first plea for help. But now that Huxtable was a factor in my own file, I figured that my father's could be reopened.

In India, everything was connected with everything else. The events of the last two weeks were merging with those of five years ago, even though the contact points were weak, and the weld as yet incomplete.

"What about Clay & Westminster?" Carol asked. "You going to tell Charles Mendip?"

"He's away from his desk," I said. I looked at my watch. Two A.M.

"You need to head to the airport in two or three hours," I said. Carol's face started to collapse. "That is, if you're going to obey orders. Are you?"

The tears started. "I have no choice."

I dabbed her face with my robe and nodded.

She was shaking. "What will my parents think? Christ, they're going to wake up and read a paper that makes me out as . . ." She couldn't find the words and sobbed instead.

I drew her to me again. "They sound like okay people. You can explain."

"Why did I ever look at that man? It could have been you and me all along. Why are you Brits so fucking inhibited? Why didn't you say something, make a pass? You don't know how easy it would have been."

"If only," I whispered. If only.

"JJ was energy, you see," Carol said. "Brain energy, body energy. He *glowed*. He seemed to understand how to harness it. I know it sounds crazy, I know what he did on the FDR, but he was gentle with it, kind. He was able to control the power, wield it where he thought it might do some good; the schools, hospitals, that kind of thing."

I couldn't stop myself from asking: "Why did you leave him?"

"Like I told you, he started to scare me. I began to see that he was having trouble controlling the energy, like it wasn't really his, you know, like he was a nuclear reactor but the fuel rods weren't his. He was scared of himself. The first time we split up, it was his doing. It hurt, but he told me that I should get out, he wasn't safe to handle, volatile material. But then he came to me after a while." Carol caught her breath, seemed to choke a little. "He needed me, he said. I was the only thing that was real in his life. Nobody had ever said that to me before. I believe he meant it too."

"So what went wrong?"

"The drugs. The moods. And you know what was weird: He could buy a forest in Chile, but couldn't afford to get me a soda. He talked about the kids a lot, Miranda as well. He was worried they would be taken from him. Shit, it was him fooling around, but it was more than a divorce that scared him. There was something, someone else: His brother, the one at the funeral; he would brood about him, watched for him. He seemed to think that whatever it was, whoever it was, would take me too, but that's another story. JJ said he wouldn't be real without me. He would cease to exist. I didn't like that, Fin, being someone's life support in that way. It wasn't healthy. I wanted to make him happy, me too. But I wanted to love and be loved without all that other stuff getting in the way. His kind of love was making me ill."

She got up and poured herself another glass of water, draining it in one draft. She came back to the bed.

"Of course we know now that in many ways he wasn't real," she said. "No Harvard MBA." She tossed her head back and shook her hair. "But MBAs don't make people real. Or unreal. Do they?"

"He wasn't really an employee of Jefferson Trust either."

Carol touched my lips. "So you found that out, huh? I remember the bitching we had over his business card. I fought with him over that one."

"It may affect Jefferson Trust's liability," I said.

"Fuck Jefferson Trust's liability," she said, then kissed me hard. Her tongue probed my mouth.

Mine probed right back.

She pulled away for a moment. "You know, I was thinking of you all day. Even before the *America Daily* thing, I'd planned we would be doing this." She let us both fall back on the bed, lying on our sides, facing each other, locked hard. "And this." She ground her hips into me. I pushed myself hard against her. "And this." She unthreaded the cord on my robe and ran her hands down my back, over my buttocks, and then moved one hand to my front. "I want you so badly. I want you the way it was . . ."

I started to ease down her shorts, caressing her soft skin, exploring her wetness, my hand acting on its own, without orders. It was the great escape, a world beyond remorse and recrimination, beyond grim memory.

But it was delusion. The world of a few hours earlier wouldn't go away that easily; the voices, smells, and images of a whorehouse weren't going to be banished like an unwelcome Jehovah's Witness. The voices were armed with a warrant. They spoke of physical and moral corruption, a baton of depravity handed to me and which I'd held on to, for whatever reason. They said I shouldn't have gone to Baba Mama's. Period. It wasn't Raj's fault. I could have said no and stood by my refusal. But there had been a part of me that had thrilled at the prospect, in spite of my self-righteous distaste.

Carol studied my face closely, a shadow of confusion darkening her own. "What's the matter?" Her eyes were trying to glean something, a clue to the conflict between my mind and the rest of me. But, as the battle raged in me, I wasn't giving anything away about its origins.

I pushed Carol gently away. "I can't. I . . ."

She stared at me. Her face was receding, plunging into a depth of sadness never before explored, where the pressure seemed likely to crush her.

I tried to pull her back to me, but she recoiled.

Without another word, she ran from the room.

"Carol," I shouted, but stayed on the bed. Frozen.

I picked up the pillow and hurled it against the wall. I picked up Carol's empty glass and hurled that too. It shattered against the bathroom door.

I stared at the phone. Hurl it or dial it?

I stabbed at the keys. Voicemail. I just screamed her name down the phone and waited.

"For God's sake, pick up. Please." I was desperate. I hung up and called again. Same voicemail, same scream, same plea. Same silence.

I retrieved my robe cord and ran out of my room and down to the floor below. I hammered on her door. Then listened.

I could hear her weeping.

Again, I rapped on the door, shouted. She never came. Down the hallway, a man's head appeared inquisitively from a doorway.

Back upstairs, I lay on my bed, one hand stretched across the phone in case it rang. I tried not to think, reflect, or analyze. With my eyes shut I could see my father, with them open, the painful white of my remaining pillow. Open, shut, open, shut. Breathe. Ragged. Breathe again, asthma. Where's my inhaler? Shit, shit.

You don't have asthma. Charles Mendip has asthma. Breathe again. Smoother this time. Open and shut eyes. No, keep them closed. Just breathe. Don't sleep. Keep away from the Dakhmas. Don't let the mooching vultures in.

But I did sleep and the vultures were there, padding lazily on the raked floor of a Dakhma, looking for meaty chunks.

Sometime later, I found myself sitting upright in the bed, nursing a glass, swirling water around the inside of my mouth, slaking the nightmare.

After a while I looked at my watch.

I called Carol's number again. Voicemail.

I called reception.

"She's just checked out," a distant voice told me.

# THIRTY-FOUR

I called reception again some time later, and asked if *America Daily* had showed up yet. No newspapers until seven.

I scalded away the grime of Baba Mama's under the shower and then asked room service for a pot of coffee.

The phone rang.

Please, not the press.

"Alone, are we?" It was Mendip. "Not brought back some dark fluff from the brothel to keep you company?"

How did he know?

"I . . ."

"Save it. No one can hear you in the wilderness, and that's where you've put yourself, my lad."

"Then why did you call?" I felt like hanging up. But he was right about the wilderness.

Mendip grunted. "You were supposed to keep your head down, Fin. Do the deal and come home. But instead you chose to insult some very respectable and powerful people and then go philandering in a Bombay sewer. Retracing your father's Via Dolorosa?"

"They're not respectable people."

"More respectable than you, though that wouldn't be difficult." He was growling now. "Is that the best you can do? I wouldn't reach for the Schuster defamation lawyer; you've no reputation to protect."

I wasn't going to be deflected; not this time. "And I suppose it's not a disgrace that Askari had been acting for the Ketans until very recently."

"Good God. So what? I cleared it myself, it's not a problem."

"And the price for Ketan Securities. It's a blatant undervalue."

"Don't be ridiculous," Mendip retorted. "Since when was fifty million dollars a trifling sum? In any event, you have no basis on which to appreciate the valuation issue. There are all kinds of factors at work here."

"Like an order-routing agreement with a scumbag Antilles company for which Ernie was the signatory? You cleared that too, did you?"

"I'm not going to debate the matter with you. I haven't got time. I have a merger to save. How do you think Jim McIntyre is feeling right now? Did you think of that?"

McIntyre was probably playing with himself in anticipation of sharing an office with Paula. Either that or he was busy instructing the coffee machine to be my next Schuster attorney.

"Ketan Securities is a can of worms," I said. "And Jefferson Trust shouldn't be buying it."

"They know exactly what they're buying. Keep your nose out of it."

"Carol Amen didn't know."

Mendip paused. "Miss Amen is history."

I remembered Carol's sweat-stained back as she'd fled my room.

I should have followed her, stopped her.

"So am I, it seems," I said. "Pablo Tochera has been called off my case and nobody's prepared to say who is minding my interests," I said. "What the fuck's going on?"

Mendip's breathing was ragged. I heard a rustle followed by the whisper of his inhaler.

The breathing cleared. "I warned you, Fin." Another jab at the inhaler. "You're to go back to London."

"I thought you said I was in the wilderness."

I imagined myself in England, sitting across a Cotswold kitchen table from my mother, the old Roberts radio leaking Mozart, our hands wrapped around mugs of cocoa. The two of us numb after another losing bout with Bombay.

"And what if I don't want to come back?" I asked.

"Of course you want to come back," Mendip snapped. "I'm in New York for a few more days to finalize the merger and then I'll be in London. Stay in a hotel, stay with your mother, I don't care. But just get the hell out of Bombay and be in England when I get back. I'm trying to help you, for God's sake."

He hung up.


It wasn't until nine that *America Daily* arrived.

The photo of Carol was terrible. Maybe she should have been grateful; nobody would stop her on the street. The words painted an equally cruel portrait; unrecognizable, a wide-screen, surround-sound Jezebel.

And then me. No photo, but an artillery bombardment of narrative. A high flyer in New York, owner of an F1, a Svengali who had as good as cast the cokehead JJ into the flowing torrent of the FDR. And lover of JJ's lover, the despicable Carol Amen.

Then the quotes: unguarded statements made by people woken by the rottweiler Brad Emerson, their defenses down. A senior guy at Jefferson Trust, a "no comment" merchant. Tight-lipped, lawyerly evasion from Mendip and McIntyre. And Miranda. Nothing sleepy about her response. It was lucid and venomous.

I tossed the paper into the wastebasket.

I went to the room safe. The order-routing agreement was still there, scrolled untidily among my tickets, money, and passport. Even if I did manage to return it, someone was bound to notice that it had seen some action outside the data room.

I took out my airline ticket, passport, and money and stuffed them in my jacket pocket. I would be needing them if I was going to follow Mendip's instructions to insert my tail between my legs and return home.

But I had formed a mental agenda. First Paula and then those nasty little swastikas.

I called Paula at her home number. The line was busy. So I went down to reception. As usual it was busy, and it took a few minutes to get their attention. "Where are the good bookshops in Bombay?" I finally got to ask a desk clerk.

"We have a most excellent one in the hotel, sir. The Nalanda."

They wouldn't have what I was after. I didn't want an overpriced paperback novel or a photographic guide to the temples of India.

"Any others?"

The clerk took out a map and turned it the right way up for me on the counter. He then took a pen and marked two Xs on it.

"Here is the Strand in Pherozshah Street. Very good. Or what about Bookpoint in the Ballard Estate?"

"That it?"

"You could try Dr. Dadabhoi."

"Who's Dr. Dadabhoi?" I asked. It sounded more like somewhere I could pick up the hippy's handbook and a few back copies of *Rolling Stone*.

The clerk laughed. "Dr. Dadabhoi is a road, not a gentleman. There are many bookstalls there."

"Mark it on the map, would you?"

The clerk carefully outlined a length of street with his pen before folding up the map and handing it over. "Happy hunting, sir."

There would be nothing happy about this hunting trip. "Thanks," I said, and turned to find myself staring into the petrified face of Raj.

If a mustache could speak for its owner, then Raj's was fluent in a hundred languages. The clump of coarse hair was sad, matted and deranged. The rest of him was a sodden accompaniment. It must have been raining hard outside and he wasn't carrying an umbrella.

"We need to talk, sir." He looked around nervously. "But not here."

He walked swiftly toward the main entrance. His once pristine

Pierre Cardin was baggy and soaked, leaving a slick of water in its wake.

I followed him.

He made his way out of the hotel and over the road to the piazza surrounding the Gateway of India.

I stopped under the canopy over the hotel entrance. Rain was hammering on it and, beyond, the world was awash.

Scanning the forecourt, I saw an umbrella rack nearby and grabbed at one of the handles.

"I'll be back in a moment," I said to an enormous white-turbaned Sikh at the door who seemed ready to floor me.

Racing across the road, I caught up with Raj.

We went around to the seaward side of the Gateway, where there was less chance of being spotted, but every chance of being snatched by one of the waves crashing against the pier and swirling around our feet.

I opened the umbrella, a bright yellow monstrosity advertising an electronics company. The wind immediately plucked it from my hand and swept it out to sea.

"You are in the newspapers," Raj shouted.

"I know."

Raj clutched my arm. "Mr. Askari is very cross. He says you are the devil."

"I had a feeling he didn't like me," I said.

"He is very cross with me as well." Through the waterfall pouring down Raj's face, I could see his eyes widen.

"Why you? You've done nothing." Except take me to a brothel and maybe let me poison my bloodstream. That and talk to me about my father.

"He is saying that he will throw me back on the streets. He says he will bring my sister Preeti back from America and throw her on the streets with me. He says I am ungrateful."

"Why the hell should he say that?"

"I allowed a document to be taken from the data room."

I pretended I couldn't hear.

Raj grabbed me by the arm and pulled me around to the side of

the Gateway, the leeward side, a haven from the wind. I would have
to hear what Raj said now.

"A document has gone, Fin. And he is blaming me. He thinks you
took it but that I must not ask you. You are the devil and I must stay
away from you."

"Why does he think that a document has gone; why should he
think I took it?"

Raj shuddered. "Askari knows everything."

Askari knows a document is missing, Mendip cornered me with
my visit to Baba Mama's. Baba Mama knew I was from New York.
All of them drinking at a river of information. Where was its source?

"What kind of document was taken?" I asked.

"A material contract, a share dealing agreement. Not important,
Askari says, but he is angry at the impertinence." Raj looked like a
bedraggled floor mop that had come to the end of its useful life. "Did
you take it, Fin?" I couldn't lie to him.

"If it was so unimportant, why is Askari rattled?"

"I don't know."

"Is it because it might contain something that, if you knew where
to look, might not be so good?"

"I don't know," Raj pleaded. "I'm only a clerk. You must ask
Askari."

"And why is Ketan Securities so cheap? Any thoughts?"

Raj looked astonished. "Fifty million dollars, Fin? It is a won-
drous sum of money." I conceded that this point was unlikely to go
far with someone whose annual income was less than most people's
monthly mortgage payment.

"Here's a question you *can* answer. When did Askari & Co. stop
acting for Ketan Securities, stop being their attorney of choice? Five
minutes ago, Raj? Ten minutes? When?"

Raj blocked his ears like a child. "Oh God, you must stop asking
these questions."

I wrenched his hands off his ears. "If you want the document back,
just answer the questions. Askari will never know what you said and you
can tell him you've found the document in the data room, or maybe in the
box of beer bottles. You'll think of something. Just answer my questions."

A look of hope came over Raj's face. "You have the document?"

I nodded. "You can have it right now, if you want."

He hesitated. "There is bad stuff in it, but I don't know what. Non-Resident Indians, perhaps, moving their property, here and there, in ways they shouldn't. There are men who rule Askari, people who frighten him. Maybe one man more than others, a shadow, Fin. I do not know who he is. Askari will not breathe his name." His mouth snapped shut.

A shadow. Who? I looked into Raj's squirrel eyes. He didn't know, that was for sure, didn't want to know either.

"And Askari & Co., when did they act for Ketan Securities?" I asked.

Raj clutched at his temples. "Always. Fifteen years, maybe more. They still act for them." He slumped against the railing. "There, I've told you. I can say no more. You can beat me but I'll say no more."

He hadn't told me much more than I'd already guessed, but I reckoned he'd earned a crumpled order-routing agreement for his trouble. The poor guy was in a state of near collapse.

I patted him on the shoulder. "There'll be no beatings. I'll get the agreement for you. Wait here."

Raj nodded weakly.

I used the side entrance of the hotel to get back to my room; I didn't want a confrontation with the burly Sikh doorman.

In the elevator, other guests backed away from me, like I was a rat escaped from the sewer. When I got to my floor, I hurtled down the balustraded landing, nearly sending a porter with a trolley cart of mini-bar refills over the rail and into the depths below.

My room had been made up while I was out. Tidy bed, huge bolsters nestling at its head and a laundry bag at its foot, waiting for a new consignment of tropically matured underwear.

The wardrobe door was ajar and I opened it fully. I tapped in the year of my birth on the room-safe keypad slinking in the shadows behind my socks. *Whirr click.* I yanked the little door open.

Empty.

My hand dredged the dark interior. Nothing.

For a moment I stood transfixed, before running to my briefcase and tearing it open. Everything seemed in order; nothing missing, so far as I could tell.

I ransacked the room, but I knew it was hopeless. I hadn't imagined putting the document in the safe and I hadn't forgotten taking it out again. Someone else had gotten it. Floating in the river of data had been my safe number.

Shit: my passport, money, and airline ticket. Then I remembered. I patted my jacket pocket. Lumpy and soggy, but my travel arrangements were still intact.

I ran to the spot where I'd left Raj. He wasn't there. I circled the Gateway twice; the seaward side was even more treacherous than before, and I didn't fancy a third round trip. I wandered across the rain-swept piazza, deserted except for a man selling balloons in the shape of hot dogs. He started to follow me and I wished I had an umbrella so I could swat him away, or at least burst one of his blessed balloons.

The order-routing agreement and Raj had disappeared at the same time. The agreement was, in the final analysis, just a piece of paper, but Raj was flesh and blood. And my fear was that the flesh and the blood were about to be separated from each other.

Back in my room, I wondered what to do. Call the police? And say what? Yeah, right. A hero of the *America Daily*'s front page implicated in the death of a Wall Street banker is worried about a friend who has gone AWOL.

Stay your hand a while, I counseled myself. Cool it.

My hand stayed where it was for half an hour.

I then called Askari & Co. and asked for Raj.

"One moment, sir."

It wasn't one moment.

"Hullo." It certainly sounded like Raj.

"You okay?" I said. "You did a disappearing act on me. The order-rou—"

"I'm sorry, but I got a call on my cell phone and had to dash along."

He didn't have a cell phone; he'd told me at the Khyber Restaurant.

"I'll come to the office," I said. "And we can go over what to do next. I finished the drafts and we can discuss them."

"No." The tone was uncharacteristically firm. "There are some documents you missed, I think."

There weren't. The day before, I'd played with a full deck. Raj would know that. Raj was telling me something, and I sensed he wasn't alone.

"Okay," I said.

"Did you like the fishing people?" He sounded jovial, as if he was keen to reminisce about our seaside stroll.

"Sure."

He sighed. "I have asked my friend whether they fish at night. It would appear that I was wrong in my first conjecture. They fish at night. The best time to fish."

A nocturnal bombil hunt.

"Think of it," he said. "For thousands of years they knew the best way to catch fish. There is much that the West could learn from them."

"You're so absolutely right, Raj," I said. The relief coming down the phone was palpable. "I shall remember the fisherfolk when I go back home. I'm due to leave Bombay, you know."

"Oh." Raj sounded desolate. I could picture him tugging at his mustache.

I laughed. "Probably tomorrow morning. I would never be able to pack all my souvenirs in time to get a flight today."

"Yes, yes." He sounded relieved. A night fishing trip was still a possibility.

"Will I see you later on?" I asked.

A pause. "I don't think so. We can speak after you land and discuss outstanding issues."

"Well, Raj, it's been a pleasure. I'm sure we'll meet again soon—"

"Assuredly," he said stiffly. "And be a bloody brilliant Boy Scout, ya?"

Be prepared. Good advice.

"You bet," I said.

\*     \*     \*

Mendip wanted me in London. I wanted to be in New York. Neither of us wanted Bombay.

I called Delta. Their schedule didn't work for me. I called Air India. There were flights to London and New York around the same time the next morning. New York at seven-ten. London at five-fifty-five. That worked.

"I don't know if I'm going to London or New York," I explained. "Can I book two seats?"

"Certainly, sir. If you pay for two seats."

It figured.

I swapped my first-class coupon to New York for a seat on the London flight. And I bought a one-way to New York—in coach—on my credit card, and arranged for collection at their desk at the airport.

My bets were now hedged.

I showered and changed and called Paula again. Still busy. I called my mother. Still not answering.

I called down to reception to ask for a car to take me to the airport the next morning. I didn't want an Askari car. If Raj wasn't safe, then the same would go for me. I ordered a car for 2:00 A.M.; that would be consistent with the London flight, should anyone be interested.

I ordered another car. For right away. Not cash. It could go on my hotel account.

"Where do you want to go?" I was asked.

"Pherozshah Street, the Ballard Estate, and Dr. Dadabhoi Road."

"Is a Mercedes all right, sir?"

Perfect. Perfect to go looking for swastikas.

# THIRTY-FIVE

The rain had eased to a dribble when I emerged from Bookpoint empty-handed. The Strand bookstore had been no good either. It was going to be hard finding swastikas in this town.

For the West, swastikas meant Nazis. For the East, it meant good luck. West met East in the works of Rudyard Kipling; he used to have the swastika emblazoned on the spines of his books. He might have employed a different symbol had he known that Hitler was around the corner.

I remembered my father's bookshelves. An early set of Kipling, just like the one in Baba Mama's. If she had a set of Kipling, then I reckoned she might have *In Black and White*. That meant three people with the same book: Mendip, in his briefcase, Ernie Monks, in his hotel room, and Baba Mama, somewhere in a brothel. And the volume they'd chosen was at the obscure end of the Kipling catalog; not like *The Jungle Book* or *Kim*. This was advanced students' reading, an oddity in cheap paperback. It didn't even warrant a swastika. But the book obviously meant something to them, though God knew what.

"Dr. Dadabhoi Road, please," I told the driver.

As we glided through the traffic, exhaustion gripped me again and I dozed. No dreams this time, though.

We slowed to a crawl. There was a crowd in front of us, heads turned all one way, necks craning to get a view. An accident maybe.

We edged forward. Suddenly there was brilliant light and an array of large metal stands topped with outsized umbrellas. An army of men with bulletin boards rushed around warding off the crowd and screaming into walkie-talkies. A truck with thick cabling threading from its rear rumbled like a plane waiting for take-off.

"Ah," the driver said, sounding excited. "They are making a fil-lum."

He brought the car to a halt. I peered into the center of the chaos. Lights, camera, but precious little action. There didn't appear to be an actor in sight.

The driver turned to me. A lecture on Bollywood? I waved him off.

The car picked up speed and the driver was silent until he drew up to the curb.

"Here," he said and pointed at the head of a dark arcade, a pipeline leaking people into the street and drawing in as many replacements. And over the entrance the yellow *M* of McDonald's. This wasn't going to be the great library of Alexandria.

Still . . .

I asked the driver to wait and joined the procession entering the arcade.

Each side was lined with stalls. Only some sold books, the rest peddled dark glasses, ancient electronic equipment, coins, flashlights, belts, posters of deities, Indian singing stars, and Britney Spears. Those that *did* sell books, were, for the most part, little more than shoe boxes with a few moldy scraps in them. A few were more ambitious with giant stacks of old software manuals and magazines. Popularity seemed to signify a measure of quality: One or two stands were virtually inaccessible due to the crowd around them. Prying my way through a couple, I found teak bookshelves lined with volumes in alphabetical order, presided over by white-shirted, bookish men who barked warnings to any browsers who looked as if they were going to make off with the merchandise.

But no *In Black and White*.

I was near the end of the arcade and the far end of my tether, exhausted by the crush, drained by fending off the urchin children who scrambled in the undergrowth of an adult forest, tugging at pants, looking up, big-eyed and imploring, begging with remarkable eloquence.

And then there was Mukherjee's Antiquaria; a stained white linen banner slung between two arches declared what lay below. The throng around this pitch was more animated and unyielding than any I had so far encountered. But I fought my way to the front and faced a white-bearded man, stout and smiling, stationed behind a trestle loaded with books. Mr. Mukherjee, I presumed.

Among the Dickens, Austen, and Shakespeare, I could see the glint of a swastika.

I shouted, "Do you have *In Black and White* by Rudyard Kipling?"

The old man's eyes lit up as he reached under the trestle and produced a dirty green paperback just like the one I'd seen in Mendip's briefcase and Ernie's hotel room.

I felt an elbow in my stomach and tried to wrench myself around. This was crazy, worse than any rummage sale I'd been to with my mother as a child.

The old man held the book up for me to see. "An original copy. Very valuable, very rare."

This was going to cost.

"How much?"

The man looked sad. "I do not think I want to part with it."

Save me the heirloom shit. Everything was for sale here.

I tried to reach into my jacket for my wallet, praying the pickpockets hadn't been at work.

The man sighed. "Three thousand rupees."

That *was* a lot. But what the hell. I managed to extract my wallet.

I found myself in the midst of a new wave of jostling. A man tried to push me and as he did so I heard a muffled crack. The man fell heavily onto the trestle and it split in two, sending him and a hundred books crashing to the ground. He just lay there, a large pool of red expanding across his stomach, vivid against his white shirt.

There was shouting to my left, and I could see the crowd bend and part like a field of grass with a dog running through it.

For a moment the crowd around the stall froze, but then they got the point. The man in the white shirt had been shot. The panic started: screaming, shouting, and shoving. I felt myself being twisted in all directions by the mass of bodies and every time I moved my head someone would yell in my ear.

But Mr. Mukherjee stood statue still, *In Black and White* held aloft in his pudgy hand. I buried my elbows into the bodies next to me and thrust forward, suddenly finding myself leaning over the corpse. I grabbed the shoulder of an onlooker for balance and plucked the book from Mr. Mukherjee's hand. I then turned and head-butted my way through the tide of people that was rushing to see what had happened, into a more sparsely populated area whose inhabitants sensed something momentous unfolding, but didn't know where to catch it.

By the time I'd reached the end of the arcade I was trying to act casual, against the cramping tension in my limbs.

The Mercedes was waiting and I told the driver to head for the hotel.

As we drove away, the driver craned his neck to look back at the arcade. "Is something happening in there?"

I didn't follow his gaze. "Somebody fainted, I think."


I sat on my bed.

That shot was meant for me, meant for me, meant for me.

Someone wants to kill me. No repetition. I needed a train of thought, a way through the mire. They wanted to kill me with a gun and some poor bastard who had tried to take a closer look at Mr. Mukherjee's library got between me and a bullet.

Wait a minute, it was a big step to infer that the guy who got shot wasn't the intended victim. No. That shot was meant for me, meant for me, meant . . . Shut the fuck up and think in a straight line, not a circle.

I'd seen my father dead, Ernie dead, and somewhere in a heap of twisted metal, JJ Carlson. But this was different. I was now a target. Take aim, fire. Missed the first time, but what about the second? And who was pulling the trigger? I couldn't believe we had come to this.

I was shaking. Have a drink.

After three miniatures of Remy, I was still shaking. I opened the window. It was raining again and I let the warm shower beat against my face.

The phone rang.

"Wake ya?" Oh God, what a wonderful sound. Paula.

"Someone just tried to kill me."

"Jesus." She paused. "You hurt?"

"No. But I don't mind admitting that I'm scared. I need to get out of this place. I don't know what the hell's going on."

I looked at my watch: five o'clock. Christ, where had the time gone? The seconds ticked by and there was no sound coming down the line. "You still there?"

"Yes." The voice was choked, distorted, but she was still on the line. I wondered if my father had held the phone to his ear after I'd hung up. Did his voice rise in panic as he asked me to answer, give a signal of my presence? Did he hammer violently on the cradle like people do for some reason when the line's dead? What did he feel like when the fact of his solitude hit him?

"They shot some poor bastard standing next to me," I said. "He just wanted to buy a book, for God's sake. And they shot him."

I needed things I could understand, concrete things. "I'll be on a flight to New York tomorrow. Only you know that and Terry Wardman will when I call him. Okay?"

"Sure." She was great; there wasn't a trace of terror coming over the line now. Her calm was infectious.

"You got any news for me?" I asked.

"Your guy in Antilles knows how to move quick, although he says the fee will blow our minds."

"And?"

"Huxtable is creepy. His words, not mine. He says the accounts are as black as ink and will tell you squat. The directors are all locals:

attorneys and trustees. But the shareholder list is more revealing. A few companies with weird names. Indian, he reckons." She listed the names, and I jotted them down on a Taj Hotel notepad. "And a more recent shareholder, Saracen Securities."

Ernie's client. Oh God. The one that Ellis Walsh hadn't liked, but his client Reno Holdings seemed to have eyes for.

"Your guy reckons that Saracen is Turkish. He says that anything with Turkey and India on the same brass plate is bad news. Just a tad better than Russia, maybe."

"Did you check if Huxtable features in any client records?"

"Yup. And it doesn't show anywhere. If it was there, I'd have found it. I nearly blew my PC to pieces in the search."

"Anything else?"

"Yes. The name of Askari & Co. figured heavily in some of the documents among the Huxtable papers. Someone called Dakma as well, not a director or shareholder, but his name seemed to come up more than others. That's d-a-k-m-a. No, wait. There's an *h* in it. D-a-k-h-m-a."

Dakhma? Dakhma wasn't a person, it was a thing, a black ugly thing.

Paula continued: "He says he dug deep and stuck his neck out to find stuff you normally don't get to see. He says you owe him."

He was right, I did. But I still didn't have anything tangible. The only smoking guns were real ones on Dr. Dadabhoi Road. And now I didn't even have the order-routing agreement; I needed to reel in new bits of paper to wave around. Night fishing for Raj's missing documents.

"You've done great, Paula."

"I know."

"One more thing," I said. "Terry Wardman's home number; you got it?"

"I always keep the Clay & Westminster home directory next to my bed, in case I get lonely." I heard a rustle of pages. "Here it is."

"Thanks. I'd better be moving along."

"Fin." I could hear the concern back in her voice. "Don't get yourself hurt. I don't think I could handle that."

"I'll be careful. And when I get in to New York I'll call you and let you know where I am."

I'd forgotten to mention my forthcoming appearance in the New York edition of *America Daily*. "You may read stuff about me in the papers tomorrow, about Carol Amen too. Don't believe it." I gave her the gist of the piece.

"Won't they stop you at Kennedy?"

"I think that depends on Terry Wardman."

# THIRTY-SIX

I stood behind a water vendor opposite the offices of Askari & Co. The owner of the cart was lying on the shaft slung between the huge leaky barrel of water and an emaciated donkey chewing happily into a bag hanging around its neck. I could hear the cart owner's snores above the din of the street.

It was almost dark and I was clutching a bulky envelope like it was a comfort blanket.

People were leaving Askari, the clerks, the drones. Back to their homes for meat and rice and tea; a beer maybe. Most of them would live somewhere a notch above a chawl and a visit to Kamatipura or Baba Mama's would be unthinkable. Why was Raj different, what kept him under? Sunil Askari kept him under: his so-called benefactor, the man who held the purse strings for Preeti and kept Raj in squalor as recompense.

Five years ago, I'd met with Sunil Askari here around this time. The end of a working day: He hadn't wanted his staff to see him with a lowlife like me. He'd been furious, asking why the hell I'd brought my mother. She'd insisted on coming, I'd said. It was my father who was dead, but it was her husband.

Anyway, we hadn't stayed long.

I looked up at the third floor of the crumbling Victorian facade and scanned the windows. There it was. The statue. A bust of Shakespeare. Horrid thing, my mother had said, reminds me of a classroom.

I was waiting for the light to go off. I'd soon know whether Askari was the creature of habit he had claimed to be.

I shifted the envelope to the other hand; it was starting to darken with my sweat. It had the feel of containing something important, something eagerly awaited by the addressee, a sale agreement maybe, or some massively significant forms to sign. Back then, Askari had given me forms to sign, release papers for my father's body. He had influence, he had explained. Most people had to sign at the morgue, but he could swing it in his office. The forms had upset my mother. Why all the paperwork? she'd asked; he's dead and that's it. Just let us go home. Askari had wagged his finger at her, the pedagogue strong in him. Things had to be done properly, he'd said. He shouldn't have wagged his finger, he really shouldn't. She hated that. She hated everything when she was on the wings of her little white pills.

And then she had lunged at him, over the desk and at his throat, elegant and deadly in one swift, grief-induced movement. Askari had tipped out of his green leather swivel chair and lain pinned to the floor. Boy, did he know how to swear. My mother didn't like that either; she was going to choke the curses from him, silence him. I managed to pull her off before she could kill him, though. It was harder than I'd expected; she had the strength and desperation of a wounded animal. My mother had stared at us both for a moment and then run from the room.

The light in Askari's office was still on, but the statue was gone. Weird. Did he tuck it into bed every night? Tell it a story, read it a sonnet, maybe?

Then the light went out. I looked at my watch and smiled. Six-thirty, almost to the second.

I crossed the street and walked a hundred feet or so away from the front entrance of Askari & Co. I then turned into a narrow alley and made my way through the sludge until I hit a T-junction into another alley.

The channel was dark, but up ahead a dull light spread across it and glistened against the mold on its outer wall.

I clutched the envelope tight. It didn't contain a sale agreement or a massively significant form to sign, but that day's *America Daily* retrieved from the wastebasket in my room.

I walked toward the light.

It was an alcove at the rear of Askari, where mail was delivered, where tradesmen had to go, so as not to mess up the reception area and put off clients. It was here that I'd finally tracked down my mother after her dash from Sunil Askari's office. She had been huddled against the wall, covered in grime and shit from the alley. Silently sobbing, she had offered no resistance when I had lifted her gently to her feet and we had retraced our steps through the building, followed by the scandalized gaze of employees and clients.

Two men sat on stools, smoking and drinking tea. They looked relaxed, the day's hustle pretty much over.

"Excuse me," I said.

They stood up.

"I want to deliver this to Raj Shethia, please."

"You can please do that at the front, sir," said one of the men.

"The man at the front said I should come here," I explained.

They both shook their heads, appalled at the indiscretion of the front desk—what could they be thinking? Heads will roll.

"You can leave it with us, sir," one of them said. "We will ensure it gets to Mr. Shethia."

"If you don't mind, I need to hand it to him personally. It's very important." I tapped the envelope as if to prove the point.

Both men looked doubtful.

"Call him," I said. "Tell him Mr. Findlay is here."

One of the men got up and went inside the building and entered a small booth full of clipboards where a giant black telephone sat solidly on the desk.

I smiled at his companion. "I don't want to be a nuisance, but could I have a glass of water?"

He eyed me carefully. I needed a trump. "I won't get another drink until I see Mr. Askari later tonight."

The man waggled his head and smiled back. "Of course, sir. I will get you one. In a jiffy."

The power of the name of Askari.

He went inside and disappeared. The other man was still on the phone, facing away from me.

I breathed hard, starting to sweat.

The floor just inside the building was of uneven wooden planks, the kind that would sound like a drum when a shoe hit it. I eased off my loafers, feeling my socks soak up the bilge, like bread in gravy.

I edged into the building and tiptoed as swiftly as I could along the hallway. I didn't look behind me.

I was inside and no one was screaming, *"Hey you."*

The place was quiet and ill-lit. But I guessed there'd still be people about, cleaners and lawyers working late—although with Askari gone, they might not feel the need to hang around. And the guard, of course. However old his Lee Enfield might be, I still didn't want it stuck in my face.

My goal was the stairwell, the hub of the building. Using the worn map of my memory, I moved carefully along the hallways that I thought would take me there. I became increasingly aware of the silence of the place. I was expecting to hear footsteps, voices. I was ready to parry anyone who emerged from the shadows or from around a corner. I had my half-baked story prepared, rehearsed. But I saw no one, nothing. Not even the office cat or ghost.

Suddenly, I was at the stairwell. I looked around me, listened hard. Still nothing. I went up the old wooden staircase and entered a carpeted hallway, the start of Askari's domain. I was holding my shoes, still fearful of the clack of leather against wood, and could feel several splinters working their way into the soles of my feet. I put my shoes back on.

Askari's office was at the end of the hall. I passed a series of closed doors, no light showing from under them; the other partners must've left for the day. I patted my pocket. The souvenir penknife I'd bought from the hotel shop was still there. I might need to pry a cabinet open.

The door to the office was ajar and light spilled through it from the street. I could hear the hum of traffic and shouts of traders drift in from the world outside, but still nothing from the building itself.

I looked around the room. There was something wrong. A desk with two phones, the green swivel chair, a gunmetal filing cabinet, and some shelving. A couple of straight-backed chairs for guests. A portrait of a stern and gloomy Askari on the wall, presented by the Law Society of India in gratitude for services blah, blah, blah.

But the shelves were empty, except for a pewter tankard and a ball of elastic bands. The desk was bare, the floor around it clear; none of the usual clutter of the busy lawyer.

I went over to the filing cabinet. The drawers moved freely when I pulled them. Empty. Not a blasted thing. The place had been cleared out. Why?

There was no point in hanging around in there.

I walked back to the stairwell and went down to the second floor. I headed toward the open hangar-like space. In the hollow of the counter that ran its length were files; I'd seen one of the girls rummaging among them as Raj led me through the day before. She had pulled out a buff folder, similar to one that Raj had in his hand. I'd start there in my search for traces of the steaming trail of dung that Ketan Securities, Huxtable, and its grubby shareholders must have left in their wake.

I took out my penknife, and felt it slip through my fingers. Shit, the shakes again.

Then I heard the *clack, clack* of shoe on wood, getting louder, coming my way. Running would echo badly now I had my shoes back on. I looked around me. A door. I tried the handle. Locked. The *clack, clack* was closing in.

An armchair, an old thing, maybe an orphan from a partner's office. I pulled it away from the wall and crouched behind it, pressing the back of the chair as firmly as possible into me. It felt like a pathetic hiding place. But the light was dim and maybe, just maybe . . .

I saw my penknife lying in the middle of the hallway, a prize to tempt a passerby to stop and wonder and then see a dumb-ass behind a chair looking like a frightened rabbit. It was too late to retrieve it.

The noise was on me. I prayed. For the first time since I was a child, I prayed.

There were two of them. They were running and I couldn't see them properly. Maybe they were the same two that I'd foiled out back. If so, they'd been drinking something besides tea in the meantime. There was a strong smell of booze. And the smell of something else, something I couldn't place.

They were excited, chattering and laughing as they ran, their gritty, breathy voices making them sound like euphoric hooligans who had just roughed up a derelict and were making their getaway.

As they passed, one of them kicked the penknife; I heard it skitter across the floor and clatter into the baseboard.

They checked their pace, arrested by the noise. Then one of them got angry and swore at the other. They continued on their way.

I drew a desperate breath as I heard them career down the stairs, two or three steps at a time.

I emerged from the behind the chair, listening, scouting around for my penknife. The guy had given it one hell of a kick; it could have been anywhere.

A pair of double doors led into the open space. It was so different from the day before. Empty of people, an echoing cavern. And hot. I looked up; the ceiling fans were still. Their blades reminded me of the crossbeam frame used to control puppets. I imagined a giant hand manipulating every move of the room's occupants. And above the hand, the face of Sunil Askari. But it looked like the puppet master had gone home for the night, and taken his puppets with him.

Directly opposite me was a gap in the counter. This was the only route to and from the workstations.

I went through the gap and saw that the counter had sliding doors. A simple sticker announced: *A* and *B*. The client files. In alphabetical order. I yanked at one of the doors. Locked. I dismissed the idea of going back to the hallway and looking for my penknife. There was bound to be something on a desk, a letter opener, maybe. I could improvise and, anyway, the door felt flimsy enough.

The letter *H* would be my first port of call. About twenty feet away, I reckoned.

I went back through the gap and walked down the outside of the counter.

I sniffed the air. There was definitely a smell, growing stronger, of burning. And now I could see light flicker at the other end of the room.

A plume of flame, capped by a mushroom of smoke, rose to the ceiling.

The two men. Fire-starters. Now I could identify the other smell: lighter fluid, kerosene maybe. In this powder-dry environment of paper and dust, the place would be an inferno in no time.

I vaulted over the counter. *G* to *K*. Somewhere behind this weedy brown strip of plywood was Huxtable. I glanced around for something with which to pry it open, then the obvious hit me: You fool, this place is going to be ashes any minute. The door shuddered as I gave it an almighty kick, but it didn't budge.

Looking up, I could see the flames tracing a path down the room; they were happy, crackling and roaring as they gathered pace, gorging on the nourishing tinder. The smoke had snaked up the wall and was now spread over almost the whole ceiling. Soon it would reach the other end, come back down again, and then fill the whole room.

I gave the door another kick. A long split appeared. I stuck my fingers in the narrow gap and pulled. The door flew off in a shower of splinters.

I looked inside at the neat rows of hanging files, all labeled. I ran my finger along them. End of the *G*s, start of the *H*s. Horrocks, Hosni Industries. Dammit. The end of that cupboard. That meant Huxtable was in the next one.

My throat tickled; the smoke was getting greedy for space. I coughed. An echo? I could have sworn I heard another cough from nearby.

I stood up. There it was again. I walked around a desk next to me. Nothing. Then the next desk. Another cough. I looked down.

A giant red caterpillar, squirming and writhing. And coughing. A human being, trussed in red treasury tape. Mummified in it.

I knelt down and could make out a few coarse hairs poking from the head end of the package. Raj's mustache. I could hear him groaning. The tape was so tight I was surprised he could breathe.

"Hold still, I'll get this stuff off you."

I pulled at the cotton tape and could see soon enough that it was at least three layers deep. I managed to create a small gap around his mouth.

"Thank you, sir, Fin. Sorry."

The guy was about to be roasted and he was sorry. I scoured the place for some kind of blade. There was nothing.

My penknife. The flames were near, cackling and popping, having a real party. The smoke was getting thick. There would be no time to retrieve the penknife.

I clawed at the treasury tape. Jesus, they'd done a good job. They must have saved this one for an Olympian red tape merchant, the Bureaucrat-in-Chief.

"I'm going to carry you." At school, I'd been to an open day at the local fire station and had a fireman's lift performed on me. It was a piece of cake, I reckoned.

"No, Fin, you can't."

Oh ye of little . . .

I pulled at him, but he only rose an inch or two. He was held by guy ropes of red tape. Like Gulliver waking in Lilliput. Dozens of lengths of tape stretched taut to the desks and chairs around us, where they ended in fierce knots.

They really wanted Raj to die.

I started on one of the knots. Difficult, but not impossible. It came loose and I went to the next.

"It's no use," Raj moaned.

I ignored him. The second knot yielded and I moved on to another.

The flames were virtually on us; I could feel my hair singe, the salty, gritty taste of ash in my mouth and throat.

"Preeti," Raj said.

"What about her?"

Another knot fell away.

"Will you make sure she's all right?" Raj sounded desperate.

"No need," I said. "I'm getting you out of here." A rivulet of flame was just about touching Raj's head and I leaped over to try and smother it with a thick folder of papers. As I swatted the flame, I noticed the label on the file. *Huxtable BV.* The cardboard was scorched and as I smashed it down on the flames, dozens of sheets of paper densely covered in typescript numbers flew out, hard copy e-mails by the looks of them, but otherwise unintelligible. As they scattered, an updraft caught them and they spontaneously combusted in midair.

Raj moaned again. "It's hopeless, Fin."

My eyes followed the ten or so guy ropes that still stayed anchored to the furniture. Around us, a small semicircle of desks and chairs separated us from the wall of orange flame that popped and shrieked, exalting in its liberty, gnashing on the abundant diet of oxygen, dust, and paper. Searing heat proclaimed its approach. The flames didn't have a particular destination—they were about to consume everything.

Raj was right, it was hopeless.

"How do I contact Preeti?" I asked. "You said she only called you."

He started coughing; I could see phlegm and spittle gather around his lips, staining the tape. "There is the box address," he managed. "9735. A place called Bayville."

"I'll check her out. You have my word."

He seemed to relax, like he was ready to burn, ready to die. What had this poor bastard done, except to be employed by a cunt?

"Do you think me a bad man?" he asked.

I let the Huxtable file fall to the floor and held his head, feeling my own back start to burn. "No, Raj. You're a decent man. In a hard place, you're decent." People like Raj were the flattened wildlife under the wheels of ambition's juggernaut; their passing unmourned, almost unnoticed. And unthanked; their contributions and sacrifices submerged in the euphoria enveloping the successes that they helped create: the successes of Askari and those of his clients.

And this was his reward.

"Thank you." I aimed the word at where I was sure his ear would be. He had to hear me.

"I'm sorry I took you to Baba Mama's," he managed, his mouth a grotesque gash in the tape. "They made me. Askari made me, but even his hand was forced. And do not be afraid that you did something with the young lady. I forbade it, sir. They are dirty girls . . ."

The dynamic of the fire altered, the rush of heat seeming to still for a moment and then switching directions, pulling, pulling like the undertow of a receding wave.

Then the surge. The room revolved as I traveled on the crest of a blast, flung away from Raj's tethered body.

I found myself lying in a pile of charred papers, my body crooked against the leg of a table. Ten feet from me was a ball of flame with something resembling a large, blackening hot dog at its center.

I turned away.

The smoke thickened into an impenetrable fog. The flames suddenly seemed to be all around me. If I moved the wrong way I'd end up like Raj.

The gap in the counter, that's what I needed to find. Find that and then it would be a short step to the stairwell and a way out of this inferno.

First I had to find the counter. I crawled in what I took to be the right direction and found myself pressed against another table.

I couldn't breathe; drawing in air was like sucking on brick. I turned and crawled the other way, beginning to thrash as my hands sank into burning paper and molten plastic dripping from the seats.

Something crashed to the floor nearby, plaster from the ceiling or a fan blade maybe. This is it, I thought. I should have been getting on a plane to New York in a few hours. In New York, I'd emerge into the sunlight, if Terry managed to do his thing. And then, armed with a stack of material in my hand baggage, I was going to sock it to these fuckers.

But it wasn't turning out that way.

I started to slump and was surprised that there was nothing between me and the floor; no desk, no chair, no counter.

I had found the gap.

I crawled a few yards. The smoke was still thick, but the heat a little less intense.

Then I heard shouts and footsteps. I headed toward them and found myself falling. The smoke cleared a little and I took a breath. I felt myself fly through space. Maybe I was dead.

A fireman broke my fall.

There was a loud clang as the oxygen tank on his back hit the deck. Through his mask I could hear him scream in pain and anger.

He tried to grab me.

I didn't need rescuing; I'd just rescued myself. I flailed my arms and carried on down the stairs, through the line of firemen behind him.

I emerged from the building at speed. There was a big crowd outside: police, soldiers, firemen, and onlookers. A few stretched out their arms, as if to take me, to comfort me. I charged at them.

There was a loud explosion and a shower of glass and debris rained down, scattering the crowd.

I ran like hell down the road and into the first alley I came to.


It was a good five minutes before my lungs would accept the gift of oxygen.

Raj was dead. Poor bastard. But I was alive. Burnt, but alive. My back stung where the blast had thrown me off Raj and I tried to crane my neck to get a look at the damage, my hands attempting to feel its extent. My eyes were unwilling to give up crying, blinking, and stinging, but I forced myself to inspect an area of burnt linen jacket and burnt shirt beneath. Where burnt cotton ended and burnt flesh began, I couldn't tell. The only real guide was the pain. My right hand had suffered too; molten plastic from furniture had tried to mold itself on me, came away, and left a nasty mess.

I ran my left hand through my hair, only to discover that I had been left with half an inch of stubble that spread black ash on my palm.

I felt the bulge in my jacket pocket. I still had my passport, money, and a ticket to ride. But I needed to get back to the hotel to retrieve my stuff and head to the airport before someone cottoned on to the identity of a charred Caucasian racing out of the Askari fire and refusing, most impolitely, all offers of assistance.

The sirens wailed nearby. I could hear the crowd too; they sounded as if they were enjoying the spectacle.

The pain turned up a notch and I felt nauseous. I had to get back to the hotel.

At the end of the alley there was a small market, brightly lit and even now still boisterous. There was no choice. I slunk through it as best I could, conscious of the stares. Children leaped around me, sometimes touching me, and it took all my patience not to lash out at them.

Then suddenly I could see open road ahead, the yellow and black flash of taxis passing, like angry hornets. In a few moments I would be in the backseat of one of them. I felt myself relax, then warned myself not to, not until I'd made it.

Someone walked into the center of the narrow gap between the stalls. A glimpse of khaki, a lathi hanging languidly from one hand. A policeman.

I sidestepped between two stalls.

"Do you need help, sir?" A large, friendly face peered around a dead chicken hanging on a meat hook.

I stepped back and rammed my burn into the corner of the stall behind me. The pain tore through me. But I wasn't going to let it show.

"Actually I am lost. Perhaps you *can* help me." I heard my P.G. Wodehouse voice.

"You are hurt, sir."

I thought of the actorless film set I'd seen earlier en route for Dr. Dadabhoi Road.

I laughed the easy laugh of someone most definitely not hurt. "Oh, this mess, you mean. No, no. I'm an actor."

The man looked incredulous.

"No, seriously." I sidled up to him, glad of the pile of boxes of meat and vegetables cluttering up the back of his stall. They made a good screen. "We are filming something nearby. On location. An action movie."

The man's eyes widened. "Golly. I think I heard about this. Where is it happening?"

"That's the point. There was a break in the shooting and I went off for a wander and appear to have lost my way."

"I will ask around. I am sure we can find out where you were, and I shall escort you back there."

I picked some fluff nonchalantly off the jam on the back of my right hand. "No, thank you all the same. You see, I rather want to go back to my hotel now. The director has been so infuriating, and I've had enough for this evening."

The man nodded solemnly. The actor's sensitivity, he could understand that; he had read about that.

"I am assuming you are staying at the Taj, sir," he said.

"Of course."

He peered at me closely. "Are you a famous actor?"

"Have you seen *Lethal Weapon Six?*"

"No, sir, but I have seen the others on video."

I smiled. "Wait till you see this one; it's the best of the lot."

He brought his hand to his mouth. "Oh my heavens," was all he could manage.

"But shh, okay? I don't want to be pestered. I'm tired enough as it is."

"I shall take you to the Taj myself, sir."

The policeman was bearing down on us.

"A lift would be marvelous," I said.

"My car is on the street, follow me."

By the time we reached it, he knew my stage name, the plot of the film we were shooting, and the names of every other cast member.

By the time we got to the Taj, he knew my full list of credits. He was almost as impressed as I was.

"The side entrance please," I said. "Too much fuss round the front."

He pulled up exactly parallel to the discreet door. I autographed a piece of paper for him with a suitable expression of my gratitude and tried to hand him a thousand rupees for his trouble.

"No, sir, I couldn't. It has been a privilege."

I made him take it. He would discover how small a privilege soon enough.

As the pain drove its steel toe into a new foothold on my back, I wished Raj had been there to applaud my performance.

# THIRTY-SEVEN

I fell against the door of my hotel room and, as it unlocked and opened, I stumbled through and kicked it shut.

My hand and back were pools of sulfurous pain that bubbled and welled. I hardly noticed the splinters in my feet.

The room was dark. I staggered to the mini-bar, took out all the bottles of Bisleri water, and started pouring them over me.

Mistake. The paradigm of sting. Bees were bloody amateurs.

I yelled.

"Be quiet," my mother said.

I fiddled with the switch on the desk lamp and looked at the bed.

She was lying on the bedspread, hands across her chest, her face half obscured by a loose layer of silken gray hair.

*"What on earth are you doing here?"*

She sat up, peeling her hair back behind her ears. Jesus, she'd aged. Puffy crescents under her eyes, the color of gravy, her network of wrinkles increased fourfold in the year since I'd seen her. She had been beautiful. But now . . . she still was, but the beauty was frayed, an echo.

She put her hand to her mouth. "Good God, what's happened to you?" she said. I was tempted to ask her the same thing.

"A fire, Mum." I slumped facedown on the bed. A fire started by Askari henchmen. Why else would his office be so comprehensively vacuumed before the flames took hold?

My mother got up and started to inspect me, wincing at the charred cloth and flesh on my back. She gently lifted my right hand, peered at it, and slowly replaced it on the bed.

She ran her hand over my hair.

I resisted closing my eyes, though the temptation was nearly overwhelming. There would be pursuers, men in suits with guns, *lathi*-wielding men in uniform with big dogs. "We have to get going."

"Don't move." She went into the bathroom and I heard her whipping the towels off their rods and running the faucets.

She came back out with the bathroom wastebasket slopping with water, steam rising from it. She rummaged in a paisley-patterned overnight bag, the same one she'd lugged around Europe when I was a child and still featured on family vacations. Dad and I joked about it. Not about the bag itself, but its contents. She had everything in it. It was a challenge to come up with a situation for which her paisley bag couldn't cater.

She produced a small bottle of disinfectant and two tubes. One antiseptic, the other anesthetic.

Cautiously taking my shoulders, she eased me into an upright position and started to remove the jacket. As she slipped off the right sleeve it brushed over the back of my hand. I nearly fainted with the pain.

Then the shirt. I strained my neck to see what lay underneath. It was like removing the cellophane dividers from sliced smoked salmon.

"Someone died," I said.

"Shush."

The image of Raj came back to me, tufts of mustache hair pressed over lips, white teeth bloodied, from biting his tongue maybe, or perhaps it was dye from the treasury tape. Surely I could have saved him? He was bound in stuff made to keep a few bits of lousy paper together. It should have been as easy as tugging at the ribbon on a birthday present.

And yet, in the absurdity of his death, there had been a dark dignity, a sense that life would carry on in another form, that the ashes of Raj would remain part of something that mattered. His religion decreed a status for him and consoled him with the possibility of a better life next time around. Or was it simply that Raj was the kind of person that, when the flames licked over him, could focus on others: his sister, the wood nymph that now had a name. And me. He cared about me, despite the fact that I'd stuffed an order-routing agreement down my pants and gotten him killed.

The shirt was off and my mother started with the tubes of cream. She didn't have to warn me that it would hurt. I yelled out with the pain.

"There," my mother said, giving me a gentle pat on the shoulder.

I looked at my stinking socks. "There are splinters somewhere under the slime."

My mother waved her hand. "Lie down." She put on her reading glasses.

"There isn't time." But I still lay down.

Tweezers emerged from the paisley bag. She peeled off my socks, wiped my feet with a warm wet towel, and started searching.

"You said someone died," she said.

"Yow." It felt as if she'd drawn an arrow from me. She held up the tweezers to show me a small shard held between their jaws, an itty-bitty thing, no more than a quarter of an inch.

"Yes, somebody died," I said. I couldn't tell my mother that the somebody had a sister, once a visitor to Hampton Court, a plaything of my father's. And that I'd promised to make sure Preeti had a future.

"Tell me what happened," she said.

"Just pack. We have to leave."

"I've just arrived," she said.

Why, for Christ's sake? Why? I knew why: Distance was a curse for her and disaster the excuse she needed to come and confront it.

"I'll explain everything later," I hissed. "Just please get packed."

I eased myself off the bed, flung open the wardrobe, scooped out my clothes, and stuffed them into the suitcase. I then tore my shirts, pants, and jacket from their hangers and loaded them into my suit carrier. I left out a fresh shirt to put on just before leaving.

"Where are we going?" my mother asked.

Good question. Where *were* we going? It was now eleven; the car was booked for two; the flight to New York was at seven-ten. The flight to London was at five-fifty-five and Mum was going to be on it. First-class.

Choice: Get a car now or go somewhere else and wait.

Decision: Order another car. No, two cars. One for me, and one for Mum. She'd be safer if we separated.

"Wait a moment," I said. I called down to reception.

The receptionist started to take my booking and abruptly stopped. Someone else came on the line. "I'm sorry, sir, but it is a very busy time and all the cars are booked. A car will be available in about an hour."

"What about a regular taxi?" I asked.

"The rain, sir. Everything is topsy-turvy, I'm afraid. The wait is about the same, maybe a few minutes less."

For me, every minute counted. "I want two taxis. One for me and one . . . one for a Mrs. Holden."

I turned to my mother. "You shouldn't have come."

She sat on the bed with the paisley bag on her lap. She looked wrecked. Tears rolled freely down her face.

"I had to," she said. "You are all I have. When your father left us . . ." Her face creased and she covered it with her hands. I moved over and put my arm around her.

"Shh," I said quietly. "I know, I know. We'll pack and check out and find a corner of the hotel coffee shop. We can see who shows up from there and then, if we have a clear run, I'll go to the taxi first, you wait a minute or two and then follow. Okay?"

"What's happening, Fin? Didn't all this end five years ago? Why has it come back?"

"I don't think it ever really went away," I said. "It just hung around in the shadows, while I was busy ignoring it."

My mother started sobbing.

"Have you got everything?" We needed simple, discrete tasks, one at a time and in the right order.

"I'm so tired," she said.

"You'll soon be on a plane; you can sleep then."

She wiped her face and stared at me. "A plane? Where?"

"To London," I said gently. "Up front, in comfort. I already have a ticket and it can be switched to you at the airport."

"But I came here to, to . . ." She looked blank for a moment. "To resolve things. Resolve things, with you. We need to do it together. We've never really resolved anything, what it was that drove your father to that . . . that place."

"I think it was a corporation called Huxtable. That and Sunil Askari."

"Askari," she repeated, barely audible, her eyes burning.

"Look," I said, "we really must get out of here." I scanned the bedside table. The photo of Dad in Corfu. A snapshot of me on the same beach. It had been a good vacation; the dice had rolled double sixes for two weeks.

There was also a brown bottle of pills, the sleepy variety, the same as she'd had on the bedside table five years before.

And a small brass elephant, the size of a fist. I stared at it. Then it clicked. It was Ganesh. Ganesh, the god of Preeti's school crest. Ganesh, the god of a prostitute's account book at Baba Mama's. With four arms, two small white tusks peeking out from under its trunk and, behind its head, a sun halo with a spiked corona, just like the suns one drew as a child.

I picked up the little elephant. It was heavy, pleasantly tactile. On its base, there was an engraving. "Our everlasting gratitude," it said. That was all.

I put Ganesh, the photos, and the pills in the paisley bag.

"Anything in the bathroom?" I went in there and was arrested by my image in the mirror.

Mum had done a good job of cleaning up my face. But the hair. I looked like an escapee from a Victorian mental asylum. I turned around and tried to see my back. An irregular red lake rose from about the base of the ribcage to my shoulders.

The bathroom shelf was a mixture of my bachelor clutter and Mum's precisely assembled toiletries. I just swept it all into my hands and switched off the light with an awkward flick of the elbow.

I came back into the bedroom, chucked the stuff into the paisley bag, and eased on a fresh polo shirt. I felt the cotton implacably attach itself to my back.

"Let's go," I said.

My mother lifted herself from the bed with an effort out of all proportion to the hundred-and-ten pounds I reckoned her to be.

"You can't carry all that on your own," she said, taking the paisley bag.

I was about to shut the door behind us, when the nagging worry that had been muttering incoherently at the back of my mind thrust itself forward and screamed out its name.

"Shit."

I dumped the luggage and rushed back into the bedroom.

There was a letter rack on the desk and from behind the postcards and envelopes I removed my copy of *In Black and White*.

"Hold that," I said, handing the book to my mother while I opened my suitcase.

"What is it?" she asked.

"You ever seen it before?"

She stared at the cover doubtfully, perhaps suspicious of the profile of the knife-wielding, turbaned assassin guarding the book's contents.

"We had a blue set of Kipling," she said, "but I don't remember this. Where did you get it?"

She gave me the book and I put it in the suitcase.

"I'll tell you later. Let's get downstairs."


My mother was still sitting at the corner table in the coffee shop when I returned from checking out. The coffee in front of her was untouched and she was staring into the middle distance. She was the unhappiest person I'd ever seen. Except maybe for Carol when I'd pushed her away.

I sat down, realizing that we were in a room with one door and no view of approaching threat. If the posse showed up, then we were finished.

"We can talk if you like," I said.

"Not here." My mother scanned the bar with that air I remembered from her haughtier days. "On the plane, please."

There would be a plane for both of us, but not the same one. I wasn't ready to tell her that.

Instead I took *In Black and White* out of the suitcase.

I challenged the turbaned sentinel on the front cover. He wanted to keep his secrets secret. He was telling me to keep useless watch on the door and leave his little book alone. Beneath him was an elephant poking its head from a small banner announcing that the book was No. 3 in the Indian Railway Library, price one rupee. Not a godlike elephant this time, more the circus variety, capable of tricks and with sawn-off tusks.

Everything seemed quiet enough.

"Only half an hour, Mum," I said. She stared into space. I'd leave her to her astronomy for the time being.

I opened up *In Black and White*. It was a book of short stories, eight in all. About black men, said the introduction, the common people. I flicked through it, sensing nothing that would interest the disparate likes of Mendip, Ernie, and Baba Mama.

It was the sort of book Dad would have read to me at bedtime. Until I was eight he had been a loyal bedside visitor. Then his world had sped up and I only had his word for it that he came into my room every night to make sure I was okay.

The first story was a gutsy tale of unrequited revenge. It was only a few pages and read easily.

The next two stories were pretty good too.

Then the fourth story: "Gemini." I didn't get into the text; the heading caught my attention. Under the title was a native proverb: "Great is the justice of the White Man—greater the power of a lie."

The words of Baba Mama, the rules of her house, order and harmony wrought from the justice of the white man. A coincidence? There was no such thing as a coincidence in India.

I read the tale of twins, one switching with the other and ripping him off in the process. A cute story, but no hint of anything for my purposes.

Suddenly I was thirsty. The waiters were determined to avoid my plaintive hand signal. So I got up and went over to the counter to order a mineral water.

When I returned to the table, Mum was wearing her reading glasses and was turning the pages of the "Gemini" story. She looked different from a few minutes before, more composed somehow, more the mum of old. I smiled.

"It was a club, you know," she said. "A silly schoolboy thing."

"What was a club? What schoolboy? Dad?"

She shook her head. "No. Not your father. It was before his time, but he knew about it. The Gemini Club." She closed the book and handed it to me.

"And?" I said.

She took off the reading glasses. "It was one of those Oxford conceits. Dinner jackets, secret talk, and funny handshakes. Playing posh. The only thing was"—she laughed gently—"nobody wanted to play in their club, or maybe it was just too secret for the membership secretary to drum up members. So it was really just Sunil Askari and Charles Mendip and two others. Not much of a club. Too exclusive. But they took it very seriously: clandestine meetings, expensive meals. They claimed they did a lot of charity work. A bit of hanky-panky more like, your father reckoned. By the time he went to Oxford, nobody remembered it."

"Who were the other members?" I asked.

She shrugged. "Some American over on a Fulbright or a Rhodes or whatever they call those scholarships. The other was a German. I remember him; he stayed in touch with your father and visited the house a few times. Strange man, clever, I think, but an obsessive look about him, not healthy, I remember thinking. He was called Stein. I can't recall his first name. Conrad? No. But German anyway. Jewish, I think."

"Do you know any more about what the club did?"

"No more than I've told you. Silly and pretentious boys practicing for the grown-up world. Later, they sometimes roped your father into things. Only the charity stuff, or so your father insisted." She tapped her fingers on the paisley bag. "The brass elephant. It was a token of thanks for his help on some project of Askari's. Your father didn't say what, but the thing seemed to have significance for him. And it's a nice piece. I managed to salvage it from one of his drunken demolition sessions." She sighed. "There was so little left by the time he died. He seemed to want to destroy everything around him."

The face reverted to inconsolable sadness. "Perhaps if he had confided in me, I could have saved him. I was blind then. I saw only a drinking problem and hoped it would go away."

He'd confided in me. He'd sent up the flare, but I'd ignored the distress signal. He should have called my mother instead. Then maybe she could have done more than simply erect a cross after the event, like one of those sad shrines on the side of the road at the site of a fatal accident.

I looked at my watch. "It's time I went. Stay here for five minutes and then go out and ask for Mrs. Holden's taxi. They'll have the number and call it for you."

Was she listening? She had to listen. It was important.

"When you get to the airport, go to the Air India ticket sales desk. I'll be there. If I'm not, just wait for me."

She nodded. "Don't worry, Fin. I understand."

I held her hand and smiled.

"When we're on the plane together we can talk properly," she said.

Still I couldn't tell her.

# THIRTY-EIGHT

**W**ill you be needing an umbrella, sir?" It was the Sikh I'd robbed earlier in the day.

"Just a car, thanks." I returned his stony gaze pebble by pebble. "It's reserved in the name of Border."

The Sikh scanned a sheet of paper clipped to a lectern and screamed out a number before turning his back on me.

I waited for a good five minutes, but my cab didn't show. I wandered around the side of the canopied entrance and saw a fleet of taxis waiting for the call; there must have been fifty of them lined up, their drivers leaning against them chatting and smoking, taking advantage of a lull in the rain. The talk of taxis being in short supply was bullshit.

"Mr. Border, sir."

I wheeled around to see a uniformed driver standing next to a black S Class Mercedes. He came toward me. It was the Askari & Co. driver.

My heart quickened.

"They said you were waiting for a taxi," he said amiably. "I was expecting to take you, sir. Later, sir. I will be more than happy to take you now, however. I am freely available."

He stretched out and jerked the suitcase out of my hand and went toward the car.

"Change of plan," I said. "It's okay, I'll go in a taxi."

I saw my mother come out of the hotel and talk to the Sikh dispatcher.

She noticed me and did a double take.

The Askari & Co. driver appeared shocked at my taxi suggestion. "Goodness, no, sir. What would Mr. Askari say? You come with me. Bah, a dirty taxi. No, sir."

He pulled the suit carrier from my shoulder and hurled it into the trunk over my suitcase. The burn on my back shrieked at the violent passage of strap over raw flesh.

While this was going on I contorted my face in a way that I prayed my mother would take as an instruction to ignore me.

"Please," I said. "I *want* to take the taxi. Can I have my bags back now?"

My mother walked down the steps to a taxi that had appeared almost instantly after the Sikh had screamed out the number. She got in, but the taxi couldn't go anywhere. Its path was blocked by the Mercedes.

"You will be traveling in this car." It was a voice behind me, deep and honeyed and totally assured. I felt something stick into my lower back.

"Yes, it is a gun," the voice said. "Don't turn around and just get in."

It wasn't a voice to be disbelieved.

I opened the rear door to the Mercedes and sat down. The door immediately slammed shut. The driver was already behind the wheel and was pointing a gun at me, his earlier affability no longer evident. The other man sat in the passenger seat and rested his weapon in the gap between the headrest and the top of the seat. It looked so at home in that position, as if Mercedes had thought of every design detail, including a little gun emplacement.

The driver turned forward and eased the car out of the Taj fore-court.

I watched the gun. I wasn't used to firearms: a few wildly inaccu-rate sessions on the college firing range and a skeet shoot at some-body's house in Westchester where I had displayed my Brit ignorance by asking what kind of bird a skeet was. And that was it.

"Do you know who I am?" asked the gunman. I studied his face. It registered with me. New York somewhere. Yes: the Regent, with Sunil Askari, in the lobby. The excited fellow who had joked with Sheldon Keenes. The big teeth, the big jewelry. The slightly pock-marked playboy face.

"I am Damindra Ketan." Son of Ashish, brother of Parves. The keeper of candles in the Shrine to Perfection that was Ketan Securities.

"What do you want with me?" I asked. My voice sounded scared, childish almost. My back and hand throbbed.

"I have told you my name," Ketan said, "and that will do for the time being."

The rain started up again, powering through the headlights of the few cars around at that time of night.

"Your visit to India is over," Ketan said.

Silence was an enemy, in silence I couldn't proceed. Talk would be progress, a foothold from which to advance to a stage that might be better rather than worse. Silence was like the red treasury tape that had bound Raj. Apparently innocuous, but deadly. "What the hell do you want with me? Just tell me, for Christ's sake."

"Shh," Ketan said, placing a well-manicured finger against lips the color and shape of Brazil nut shells.

I peered out of the window. The rain thickened even more, the meager traffic seeming to glide on the slick road. We had crossed over the narrow promontory and reached the sea again. Luminous white horses fizzed on the waves. Was there stuff in spume that made it glow in the dark? Dad had once said there was.

As I had waited at the hotel reception for my account, I'd decided that I would go back to England. After New York. I couldn't stay with Mum on a permanent basis, but seeing her regularly wouldn't be so bad. I had started rehearsing negotiations to get Carol to join me.

Would I ever see either of them again? So much for advance planning.

We passed Chowpatty Beach. Blue plastic sheets covered a small carnival; a network of metal legs dug into the sand and rose into the modesty of its blue skirt.

If we had been going to the airport then we should have peeled away from the beach and into the hinterland. But we were climbing the first terraces of Malabar Hill. My stomach tightened and the burn on my back stung from each new release of sweat.

"Where are we going?" I asked. "This isn't the way to the airport." Dumb comment, of course it wasn't the way to the fucking airport. But again, I felt the silence smother me.

"I don't think you are as clever as your father," Ketan said. "He went to Oxford, I believe. Clever chappie." He shook his head sadly. "I couldn't, unfortunately. My father needed me to stay in Bombay and manage the business. Parves went, though. He said it was for us both. I did not mind. We got a good degree. Philosophy, politics, and economics."

I toyed with the idea of opening the door and bailing out, but the car was moving too fast.

With his free hand, Ketan picked at his teeth and inspected the result on the tip of his fingernail. "Sunil Askari hates you very much. I've told him not to get so upset. He is an old man now and should relax more. But he has added you to the two things that already consume him: firstly, your father and secondly, the modern scourge, as he calls it, of e-mail. Is it not strange the combination of sublime and ridiculous that can preoccupy an old man's heart? But I think that your father is his overriding obsession and he sees much of him in you. In many ways your father was such a stupid man." His face displayed a sudden interest. "Are you your father's son, Fin Border?"

"Why should you care?" I said.

Ketan shrugged and muttered something to the driver. The driver flicked me a brief glance and started laughing.

"Do you know where we are going?" Ketan asked.

"I've been asking you that," I said.

Ketan smiled. "But I think you can guess for yourself now."

I could, but the words were hateful to me, they scared me rigid. Twice in two days. "Perhaps," I said.

"Your father nearly committed a great sacrilege. And in his heart he succeeded in doing a great wrong. I am not a Parsi, but Bombay is a place of diversity and we respect each other's religions. It is a pity that your father should have chosen to die in such a manner. Mr. Askari was terribly embarrassed by your father's thoughtless behavior. Mr. Askari went to Oxford. He can't understand why an Oxford man would perpetrate such a thing."

"I don't think my father knew what he was doing."

"Maybe," Ketan conceded. "Mr. Mendip cannot understand either. Another Oxford man. He was there with Mr. Askari, you know."

I knew, Mendip the Gemini.

"And he is your godfather, I understand," Ketan said incredulously. He shook his head. "I'm afraid that Mr. Mendip has been rather sentimental in your direction and his friends have had to rally round and protect him from himself. And you."

Mendip: my mentor, my father's friend. I felt sick. The air in the car was cool, but Ketan was wearing a strong, musky aftershave and it was acting as a catalyst for my fear. Breaking the silence hadn't helped; no progress made.

Ketan withdrew his gun for a moment and wiped it with a handkerchief before replacing it in the arrow slit. "You should atone, finance a temple. Maybe an Atash Bahram. You know what that is? It is the most sacred of Parsi fire temples. It contains a fire from sixteen different sources, one of which must be started by lightning. The Parsi religion is an intriguing faith, don't you think?"

"Stop the car," I said uselessly. "I'm going to be sick."

The car lurched and rocked and I sensed the braking system rising to the challenge of mud and wet scree. We had turned off the main road and were slithering on an unpaved surface.

We drifted to a halt. The driver cut the engine and only the noise of rain could be heard.

I was going to be killed. They didn't want anything from me, except my death. Dr. Dadabhoi Road was a rehearsal, the blood-soaked man lying in a pile of books was my stunt double, merely a temporary stand-in.

"Lie facedown on the backseat," Ketan ordered.

I swiveled on the leather, careful not to rub my back or right hand against anything in the process.

Ketan leaned over the front seat. "Get on with it," he said viciously. He slapped his palm against the top of my back and roughly pushed me into a half-lying position. I screamed with the pain.

"Now put your legs up."

"Okay, okay," I yelled.

"If you move, I will shoot your knees."

I could hear both front doors open and slam shut. Then the moments were filled with nothing, except the noise of the rain beating on the roof of the car.

The door next to my head opened. I felt the warm rain gust into the car. My lower right arm was bent upward toward my neck. "Stand up." It was Ketan again.

I could feel his grip only an inch or so from my burn. One small slither and I would descend to another world of pain.

I moved around into a sitting position and then eased myself out of the car. The driver stood over Ketan with an umbrella in one hand, and in the other a thin blue plastic bag, the sort one gets in very cheap grocery stores. Ketan kept my arm twisted up by the nape of my neck. I felt the cold metal of the pistol barrel against the side of my head.

Even in the dark, even in the driving rain, I knew where I was. About thirty yards to my left I could see the outline of the hut, behind me the cindery path snaked back to the road, and above me I could sense the clifflike walls enfolding the Towers of Silence.

I moaned. "Why are you doing this?"

Ketan ignored me.

We walked toward the hut, and then slightly beyond.

We were standing precisely where Raj had stood when he told me what had happened to my father in this place. I felt the flagstones beneath my feet. I looked up and could see the first ten or so steps leading up to the door to the Towers, but no farther. Everything beyond was lost in a swirl of rain and darkness.

A cataract of water was dancing down the steps.

I started to shiver. My body stayed upright, but it jerked violently. "What is this?" Ketan shouted. "Some kind of trick?"

It was no trick; it was the sniveling realization of my impending execution. In the car, the thought had crashed around in my head, but it was locked in a padded cell, smashing uselessly against the cushioned walls, unable to commune with the rest of my brain, or my body. Now the thought was out, running riot.

Ketan rammed his fingers into the top of my right hand. A bolt of lightning to shot through me and I sank to my knees. Soon the pain would subside; it had to, it served no physiological purpose, so why persist?

Ketan took out a handkerchief and wiped his fingers, the blood mixed with the creams my mother had applied, a red ripple across the clean linen. He looked disgusted and handed the cloth to the driver, who put it in the blue plastic bag.

"The fire at Sunil's office hurt you." Ketan said. "That will appease him a little. You made him destroy what he loved most. He will never forgive you, but he will appreciate the poetic justice of your pain."

"Now stand up and remove your clothes," he then said.

I didn't ask if he meant every stitch, I'd just unpeel until he told me to stop.

I dropped my jacket at my feet, watching it turn black as it soaked up the slime. Then the shirt, like removing a bandage that had been superglued to my back. I tugged at it gently.

"I will show you how to do this properly." Ketan tucked his hand under the bottom of the shirt and yanked it up my back and over my head in one movement. I screamed.

He stood back. "My. Sunil will be pleased."

The shakes had gone; I knew I hadn't shit myself and somehow the knowledge of that gave me a little strength. I took off my pants and socks.

"Them too." Ketan inserted his fingers into the top of my briefs and snapped the elastic viciously against my skin.

I stripped completely. The man with the umbrella sniggered.

Ketan circled me, running his fingers across my back. I looked straight ahead, clenching my jaw. I wouldn't flinch, whatever he said, whatever he did.

"These injuries will serve as a respectable start." He pursed his lips. "We need only trouble you with a few more."

Ketan took the plastic bag from the driver and, after a quick rummage, removed what looked like a cheese-grater, flat-ended but well-ridged, for crude rather than delicate woodwork.

He swiped the grater over my shoulder blade. The sharp corrugations ripped into me.

I roared with the pain.

He swung the grater over my thigh.

I hadn't known that pain could be so cumulative. Somehow, I'd always assumed that one pain would cancel another out.

I sank to my knees again and realized that I was being flayed alive.

After a couple more passes, I slumped onto the flagstone. The water, that had already seemed so dark, turned even darker as my blood began to flow.

Ketan dipped the grater in a puddle of water, gave it a shake and handed it back to the other man. "You know," he said, "you look just like your father."

I remembered the morgue, the purple ridges and rivulets that criss-crossed his body. Where had they come from? The morgue attendant said vultures. It wasn't the vultures, it was their come-on, their hey-guys-dinner's-ready.

I tried to regulate my breath, find the core of being alive, and focus on it. While I could focus, I could survive.

Ketan took the plastic bag from his partner once more, in exchange for the gun. After another rummage he removed an airline amenity bag. He slid the zip open.

Kneeling on the ground beside me, he held a syringe up close to my face. "Soon the pain will be gone, and you will be with your English god and there will be no more terror, no more Towers of Silence. But for now"—he swiveled the syringe in his hand—"we judge you. The vultures can digest your sins."

He took out a small bottle of cloudy liquid. He held the bottle up and shook it. "Does your English god send people back to earth after they die?" He removed the cap from the end of the syringe, and withdrew the plunger to its fullest extent. "Who knows, maybe you will return as someone or something else. A priest, or a dog."

The driver moved closer and stood with the gun aimed at my temple. He knew that if I were going to make a move, it would have to be in the next few seconds.

Ketan stuck the needle into the rubber cap of the bottle and pressed the plunger down. He then withdrew it slowly. I was transfixed by the fluent passage of liquid from the bottle into the syringe.

I tensed myself. I was going to try and drive myself upward and pitch Ketan over and, in the process, try to get him on top of me so that the first shot from the driver got him, not me. After that, the plan got fuzzy.

From near the hut we heard a sound out of synch with the rain; wood cracking, something like that.

Ketan turned toward the noise for an instant and, as he did so, I grabbed his wrist and began to turn his hand.

He was strong and his other arm swung around and caught me in a tooth-rattling blow to the face. But I didn't let go.

There was another noise and the driver turned and ran into the pitch-darkness alongside the hut.

I heard a shot.

"You fucking dirty bastard," Ketan yelled at me, his lips drawn back in a bestial snarl, the rain snaking in wild rivulets down his face.

Ketan stuck his fist into my back. Against my bare flesh, his suit felt like armor.

I pulled my head back and rammed it with every last ounce of my strength against the bridge of his nose. Blood spouted instantly all over my face. I turned with him as he tried to pull away and found myself crouched on top of him.

The syringe was still in his hand. I twisted and pushed, and in the instant the needle was directed at him, I fell onto the plunger. Ketan groaned and I saw his eyes widen.

"Not that," he whispered. I pressed myself hard against his body and felt him thrash. I reached up and grabbed his hair and started pounding his head against the flagstone. *Slam, slam, slam,* time after time. Like he had swung the cheese-grater over me, a slam for each pendulum swing—plus interest.

I felt his body go limp, but still I slammed. "Stop, stop." I raised my head to locate the voice.

It was me. I was telling myself to stop. The human in me was trying to bring the animal to heel.

I lay there, my face pressed against Ketan's chest. It didn't rise and fall. I lifted myself onto all fours. His eyes were open, the whites of them vivid, the retinas staring upward toward the entrance of the Towers of Silence, his hair, glistening with rain and blood, pressed flat against his skull.

I sat up some more and, without taking my eyes off his face, I ran my hand down his chest until I came to the syringe, stuck in to the hilt like a plastic Excalibur. I didn't know where his heart was, but the needle had missed a rib and journeyed somewhere deeper.

I moved myself slowly off Ketan's corpse. With every ripple of every muscle, my burns burned, and the wounds from the grater seared my flesh.

I couldn't stand at first.

I was gradually able to turn my face to the sky; there was no moon, just diamonds of water falling onto my face.

I turned around. I could see a pair of legs protruding from the deep shadows next to the hut. No, there were more than two. I managed to stand up and staggered toward the hut.

The driver was lying on top of another body. His head was turned in my direction, his eyes, like Ketan's, staring into eternity. His skull was smashed, I could see pink sponge poking through a gap in the hair. I followed a thick trail of blood that coursed down the side of his head and along an arm that stuck out from under his body.

The arm was sleeved. Most of the material was steeped in blood, but there was a small clear patch. A floral pattern. I followed the arm to the hand and saw a woman's fingers, a gold band on the ring finger, a sapphire winking from an engagement ring nestling alongside.

My mother had always said that when she died, the rings had to go with her into the next world.

Then I howled.

I pulled the driver's body roughly off my mother and let it slump untidily next to her.

I buried my head in Mum's chest. "No, Jesus, no," I sobbed. I felt the rain pound onto her and could see a bloody swirl below her breast.

A single bullet was all it had taken.

I held her close to me, an inverted Madonna and child, rocking her in my arms, stroking her thin silk hair, sad strands smooth with the rain, like she'd just emerged from the shower and would comb out the conditioner and turban her head in a white fluffy towel.

Her eyes were shut, not like the others who had tried to keep their vision of this world. Mum had been ready for the next; prepared to take the journey. For me, her cub.

And nearby, glistening in the rain was the brass elephant deity. My mother's weapon. I'd been saved by someone else's god. I held it in my hand, wiping away a gobbet of something from the end of its trunk.

I went back to where Ketan lay and picked up my clothes. I tried not to look at him, but even in death, his piercing eyes drew my stare.

I could hear flapping. In the dark, there were even darker shadows.

The vultures.

They weren't having my mother, I vowed.

I went to the car and opened the trunk and found my suitcase and suit carrier under a dirty blanket. I got into the backseat and wiped myself down as best I could and eased on a set of fresh clothes. I checked through the sodden mush that had been my jacket. The ticket, money, and passport were still there, not in great shape, but retaining enough of their original essence to work for me.

Then there were the bodies to attend to. I dragged the driver and Ketan around the back of the hut. They would be found the next day, most likely. But not until the vultures had feasted.

The blanket was large enough to cover her small body. But she felt heavy as I struggled to the car. I could hardly breathe by the time I settled her along the backseat of the car. I'd thought about the trunk, but it would be so dark in there for her.

The paisley bag. Suddenly it seemed important that she should have it on her last journey. She'd need it, in case of emergency.

I wondered if her taxi might still be waiting. I thought of the walk down the path to the road. I knew I didn't have the strength.

The windows of the Mercedes were well tinted and, in this light, near enough opaque. No one would be able to see in, and I certainly wasn't going to sit Mum upright and strap a seat belt around her and pretend that she was some elderly dowager on a midnight jaunt.

I sat in the driver's seat and checked the lights, the signals, the automatic gearshift. I didn't want to be stopped because of some dumb-assed display behind a wheel.

A pack of Marlboro and a gold lighter sat in a small tray in front of the radio and CD console. I didn't smoke, but the thought that maybe it was time to start crossed my mind. No, Mum hated the smell of cigarettes.

I eased the car down the track and edged out onto the road. About a hundred yards up the hill I could see the parking lights of a stationary car. I covered fifty yards and stopped the car and got out.

It was a taxi, the driver reclined in his seat, snoring. I could see the paisley bag on the backseat.

I tapped on the window. The driver jerked awake, rubbed his face, and then looked terrified.

"I have no money," he said.

I waved both my hands to show there was nothing in them. "It's okay," I said. "You gave my mother a ride, I think. From the Taj."

He still looked doubtful. "Yes, sir."

"How much does she owe you? I will take her to the airport from here." I took out my wallet and withdrew some soggy rupees.

He seemed to relax. "She was a very nice lady, most polite, and inquired of my family and well-being."

I nodded, glad of the rain to shield my tears.

"We were following your car," he said. "When we stopped here she told me she would not be long. She seemed most anxious to see you."

"My mother decided she wanted to travel with me," I said.

The driver nodded. "It is important that a mother and son should spend time together. I tell this to my son. He does not talk to his mother enough. There are some matters which are for a father to discuss, but there are others that require the sensitivity of a woman, I think."

"Absolutely," I said.

The driver was staring at my midriff. I looked down and saw that a bloodstain the size of a fist had made its way from the injury on my hip onto the front of my shirt.

"You are hurt, sir," he said.

"It's nothing," I said. "I had a fall." I started counting money from the wad. "How much did you say my mother owed you?"

"Ah, yes, sir. That is one thousand rupees."

I handed him two thousand. Forty bucks to me. A month's wages to him. I pointed to the backseat. "Can I have my mother's bag, please?"

"Certainly."

"You have been very kind," I said, "and my mother asked me to thank you, and extend her best wishes to your family."

The driver smiled and pocketed the money. "Thank you, sir, and likewise."

I walked back toward the Mercedes, each step tearing me apart.

I heard the taxi's engine start up, and looked behind me to see it perform a three-point turn and head back down the hill.

# THIRTY-NINE

As I felt sand replace potholed blacktop beneath the wheels of the Mercedes, the rain started to ease. I turned the headlights to low beam and tried to detect movement in front of me. Between the huts, the boats, and the bombil frames, Versova oozed tranquillity. I'd driven beyond the main drag, where groups were still gathered, families eating and children playing football among the fish. I was now in a backwater of the backwater.

I'd driven from a borough of madness to somewhere more benign, but as substantive distance accrued between me and the Towers of Silence I felt that I'd taken some of the madness with me. My head was a storm of crashing emotions and objectives. The pain of my grief had become synonymous with my burns and gashes. That helped. Creams and unguents could be applied; the pain could be tamed. Action on my part could tame it.

I cut the engine and burrowed in the bulging paisley bag. On the top lay a mishmash of toiletries; then a skirt, a couple of tops, a hand towel, some underwear and a bra. They all found their way onto the passenger seat. Underneath lay what I was looking for. Pills, creams, gauze, bottles, small scissors, tape, the photo of my father, the photo of me, beesting spray, water purifier tabs, a pack of jelly babies. And there was more, but I'd found enough to give myself some rudimentary first aid.

I replaced her clothes, painfully removed my jacket, and then laid the last shirt and pants from my suit carrier across the passenger seat.

I looked back to the bundle that was my mother. She was so small. How had someone so small carried me around for nine months?

I got out of the car. Wet warm air shot through with the smell of fish. Still cloudy, no moon, no stars. I looked out to sea. A few bobbing lights.

I scanned the dark beach. I was a good distance from the main encampment to my right, but there was a single hut not far to my left. No light came from its window, but that didn't mean it wasn't occupied.

The prow of a small boat poked out from the far side of the hut.

I crept over and knelt below the lone window of the hut before raising myself very gently until my eyes reached the dirty glass. I strained my eyes and could see nothing, no embers of a fire, no night lamp, no flicker of TV. I held my breath and listened. Nothing.

Around the other side of the hut, I sized up the little boat. I gripped the prow with my left hand and it moved easily on the sand. Not noiselessly, but quietly enough.

Turning it around, I pulled the boat away from the hut and toward the shore. Now I felt camouflaged by the sound of breaking waves; not big rollers, but the last puny vestiges of a storm already exhausted out at sea.

We'd had a boat on most vacations. Nothing fancy, a small dinghy usually; Dad the skipper, Mum at the stern with her hand trailing in the water. Content. She said that when she was cruising in a little jolly boat with Dad in control, she was never happier.

I left the boat a few feet from the water and went back to the hut, where I started to root around in the junk lying beside it. Nets, floats, old pots, twine, kindling wood. And what I was looking for, a small metal cannister. I lifted it gently and sniffed. Kerosene.

I went back to the car and opened the rear door and pulled my mother's body from the backseat.

I took as deep a breath as my scrapes would allow. Two trips, I reckoned.

I let my mother gently down onto the sand, went back to the car and repacked the paisley bag, leaving out only the first aid stuff and my bathroom kit. I then took the bag out of the car along with the cigarette lighter from the tray.

I headed back to the hut to pick up the metal can and kindling before lugging everything down to the boat.

Then it was back to the car. Everything was in place. I picked my mother up again, feeling my back, hand, and hip explode in pain.

I started walking toward the waves.

I laid her in the little boat. A snug fit, made for her.

And yet, what was I doing? Gesture, ritual. Something to sanctify my mother's life. No. Not just her life. Life itself. Life: that spark in the eternal dark.

I looked down on her. She was still in the blanket. It didn't seem right. She needed to be free; perhaps she'd want to trail her hand in the water.

I peeled away the blanket from the top of her, stuffing the coarse material down each side of her body, a cushion against the boat's timbers.

Oh, Jesus, her face looked so sad, so uncertain, as if she still didn't know whether I was alive, whether her intervention had saved me.

"You did save me," I whispered. "Look: a bit worn, but alive."

I kissed her on the lips. Somehow I expected her expression to change, but of course it didn't. Death doesn't work like that.

I placed the paisley bag by her feet, gently lifted her arms and folded them across her chest. I wanted to cover the bullet's entry wound. Everything had to be just so. I spread the kindling along her sides, wedged them into the blanket material, and opened the metal cannister.

I hesitated. Would this be what she wanted? I looked up into the dark sky. Still no moon, no stars. And out to sea: bobbing lights. The stars had landed. Raj had said they didn't fish at night, so it had to be stars.

I poured the kerosene over the kindling, over the blanket material. Shaking the can, I knew there was plenty more. I hesitated again before pouring the rest of the pungent purple liquid over Mum's body. I was careful not to get any on her face.

Then, with the lighter clenched between my teeth, I stood behind the boat and started to push it into the water. The waves wanted to push it back to shore, but I was ready for them. The warm water washed over me, the salt drilling in to me, working its way into the burns and gashes. I wanted to run from it screaming, but clenched my teeth on the lighter instead.

Push, push, push, until the water broke over my shoulders. Then, holding the boat with one hand, I took the lighter with the other.

I should have rehearsed it. The mechanism was unfamiliar to me. A steel bar across the top of the little gold cartridge. A lever? I pushed it one way, then the other. Then tried to lift it up; it wouldn't budge. A wave narrowly missed breaking over my hand and drowning the lighter.

I ran my finger to the other end of the little lever and flipped it. It opened with a satisfying click. Underneath, there was a small, serrated cog. The flint mechanism. I flicked it. Nothing. No hint of a spark. I flicked the cog the other way. A small spark, but no flame. This time I flicked it hard. Bingo.

I set the flame against the blanket and saw a blue wave dance along the dirty material. The pyre was lit.

I gave the boat a shove and it started to drift away from me.

Suddenly I was gripped with the need to retain something; she was taking too much with her, too many objects of value to me, things that might anchor her and my father in my memory.

I swam frantically toward the boat and realized it was now moving away at a fair crack; a current had picked it up and if I weren't careful we might end up sharing these dark waters.

The boat was well and truly alight by the time I reached its prow; the blanket gave off thick smoke and the kindling crackled. I could see my mother's clothes were beginning to flicker.

The paisley bag was alight too, but only just. Without thought of the new burns that I was about to inflict on myself, I thrust my hand through the flames and yanked the zip open. I yelped and withdrew my hand, plunging it into the water.

Before I could make the rational decision to retreat, I plunged my hand into the bag once more. Then my fingers closed around the elephant and withdrew it.

I held Ganesh beneath the surface as I trod water and the pain began to subside.

I started to swim.

The current was strong and I was weak. The brass elephant felt like an anchor, but I wasn't going to let it fall into the depths. Either we'd both make it, or we'd both go down.

I battled with the current but seemed to be making no progress. I shut my eyes. There was no point in looking. The shore was invisible and I didn't want to know how near I'd gotten if I should fail.

My strength was ebbing away as the water pulled at my clothes and the swell swamped me with its every peak and disabled me with its every valley. From the shore, and even while pushing the boat out, the sea had seemed calm, but now in my desperation it felt mountainous. And down at my feet the current tugged and tugged.

I was beginning to go under. I clutched Ganesh and allowed myself what I guessed would be a final struggle.

And then the sea let go of me. I'd reached the gentle curve of the shore.


I lay on the beach, feeling the soft waves break over me. With one hand I clawed in the sand, with the other I clutched Ganesh.

At last I raised my head and looked around me. There was nobody. I turned to look out to sea: The bobbing lights held their position, and heading toward them was a silent, flaming torch.

I got up and glanced at my arm. The burn wasn't good, and would join the other two in tormenting me for the foreseeable future.

I went back to the car, stripped off my wet clothes, and dried myself on Mum's hand towel as best I could. The cheese-grater hadn't hit a main vein, but my hip was bleeding badly and took most of the gauze to staunch it. The rip on my shoulder was vicious but oozed rather than flowed. The other wounds were surprisingly superficial, and I felt that some generous dabs of cream and some gauze would do for them. The burns I left alone.

I slipped gingerly into my clean shirt and pants, and removed all but a few hundred rupees from my wallet. Then I walked to the hut and slid the wad of notes under the door.

I returned to the car and stood looking out to sea.

She had said she liked it here.

There was no noise, no vultures, no ambiguity. People living in a past too distant to be threatening. The Ketan family wasn't India, Askari wasn't either. Raj was. And so was this place.

It was a good place from which to leave. It soothed my anger; even the raw agony of my burns and gashes subsided slightly in the wake of their stinging immersion.

There was a cross at the Towers of Silence. There was a burning pyre in the Arabian Sea.

# PART III

# FORTY

Traveling coach meant a long line at immigration. The cheaper the ticket, the less welcome the alien.

Another flight had just arrived at JFK, swelling the line of people to join, to wait behind. And at the head of the line there would be uniforms ready to handle me with crisp authority. A night in a cell? More than a night? That would depend on Terry Wardman.

I fiddled with my immigration forms. Obsession had attended their completion. Not only had they taken my mind off the pain after a few fitful hours of sleep, but I'd been irrationally fearful of the threatened fine for fudging them.

A gentle tap on my back alerted me to the gap that had opened up in front of me. It missed my burn by a millimeter.

The wound sensed proximity and flared anyway.

I felt like a refugee.

There was another tap on my back.

I shuffled a few steps and mumbled an apology.

"Excuse me, do you want to enter the States or don't you?"

I turned to face the man behind me. English; one of my fellow countrymen. He looked beat, desperate to get to his hotel, call his wife maybe, get the kids on the phone and tell them he loved them.

He started to move around me. This time he brushed against the burn on the back of my hand.

I groaned.

The man stopped and looked at me. "Are you all right?"

I tried to smile, but burns, rips, and thirteen hours on a plane were having none of it. I could feel myself sway and the grip on my suitcase loosen. The noise of the case hitting the marble floor seemed to echo forever.

"I'm fine. It's okay."

"You don't look fine to me." He waved at the world of official-dom on the other side of the white line.

A uniformed woman moved toward us.

"I think this fellow is unwell and may need some assistance." He headed for the counter. English first aid: call for help and escape.

I tried to focus on the officer's name badge. If I could address her by name, then maybe she'd leave me alone. Sbarro, Slorro, Sharro. Dammit. I couldn't bring it into focus.

My gaze switched to her face. It was hard and unsmiling. Her eyes stayed firmly fixed on me as she knelt down and picked up my suitcase.

"Come with me, sir," she said, taking me by the arm and prying the passport and forms from my hand.

We went through via the cubicle for diplomats.

By the time we reached the other side, three more officers were waiting for us. One of them took my passport, glanced at it, and nodded.

"This way, sir," he said.


I'd been in the gray room for two hours. But the time wasn't wasted. A paramedic had come in and done a pretty good job of patching me up: my hand, my lower arm, my back, and my gashes. He gave me a shot for the pain, a shot for tetanus, and a shot of something else for good luck. He said he couldn't do anything for my hair, and suggested that I go to the emergency room before visiting my stylist.

JFK was a whole lot better than Heathrow. There they would have given me an aspirin and shoved a flashlight up my ass to check for an over-the-limit bottle of Johnny Walker.

The paramedic left the room. I stared at the two posters on the wall: one of the Statue of Liberty and the other of the Golden Gate Bridge jutting out of thick fog. I toyed with the laminated card on the table that was supposed to tell me my rights. But I didn't read it.

I didn't feel like I had too many rights. The door opened.

Detective Manelli came in. "They tell me you're not fit enough to answer questions." He circled me and nodded. "You look like shit." He pointed his finger at me like a gun. "*Peeoww.* Tomorrow. Eleven A.M. We'll talk. Your guy will be with you."

My guy? Terry Wardman? Someone new from Schuster?

Terry came in the room at that moment. He wasn't alone. Pablo Tochera was with him.

"Thanks, Detective," Terry said. "We want to be alone with our client now."

Manelli eyed me. "Sure. See you tomorrow, Mr. Border." He left.

"How are you feeling?" Terry asked.

"Better than before. What happens now?"

"We leave here," Tochera said. "You get some rest tonight and tomorrow we'll talk over the situation. Then, assuming you're okay, we go and see Manelli."

"What are you doing here?" I asked Tochera. "I thought you'd dumped me."

He glanced at Terry. Was anger the dominant emotion etched on his face?

"I'm not here," he said. Yes, anger, tinged maybe with fear. "At least not officially. If McIntyre knew I'd come, I'd be out of a job."

"Well, I'm glad to see you anyway," I said gratefully.

"They're going to charge you, Fin," Terry said. "Obstruction and a catalog of moving violations. Holding stuff, while the lawyers determine how to pin murder on you. They may add drug dealing to the list, although even they seem to appreciate it's a long shot."

"When, Terry?" I challenged. "When will they charge me and why didn't they do it straight away?"

He smiled at Pablo. "You've got Pablo to thank for that. As brilliant a display of bullshit as you will ever hear, but he's too modest to shout about it, aren't you, Pablo?"

Pablo didn't return the smile. "We called Manelli before the plane landed and told him you were coming back voluntarily and you just needed one night to get straight and then you'd talk to them." He shook his head. "It's going to take a shit-load of bail to keep you out of the cells."

I'd ask Delaware Loan for an advance.

Slumping back in the chair, I shut my eyes.

"Can you walk?" Terry asked. "Let's get out of here. You can stay with me tonight."

No. I wanted to be in my own apartment, my own space. I wanted to speak to Carol. See her if I could. But whatever, I wanted my apartment as a base.

My eyes fluttered open. "That's kind," I said, "but I'd rather have my own things around me tonight. I feel like I've been away forever."

"Not a good idea," Tochera said. "You're not a very popular guy right now. And when it gets out that you're back in town—which will be around now—you're going to have plenty of visitors. Press, lawyers, and relatives of the victims."

I stood up. "I just want to go to my own fucking apartment. Okay?"

I caught the wink that Terry flicked at Tochera. "That's fine," he said. "We'll go there first and then decide what to do."

"Give me a cell phone," I said. "I want to try and get hold of Carol."

Tochera looked doubtful. "Leave it till tomorrow, it could complicate things."

I found myself standing up, my face against Tochera's.

"Complicate things?" I hissed. "How could they get more complicated? And I suppose you can tell me where she is, how she is, put my mind at ease?"

Tochera edged away from me and turned to Terry. "Hey, cool it. I'm here to help. Tell him, Terry."

"That makes everything all right, does it?" I said. "You were my attorney. Christ knows what you are now. I was supposed to be a footnote in Manelli's report by now, a witness and no more. There should have been a dozen statements from a dozen people saying how they'd set me up. I should have been going to Manelli to pick up a medal from the City."

Tochera held his hands up defensively, his black button eyes resting on Terry, pleading with him for mutual professional support. "Please, Fin. It's not like—"

"INSTEAD," I shouted, "I'm going to be charged with enough to put me away for years, and that's just for starters. They're still figuring out what to stuff me with for the main course."

"Calm down, Fin. This isn't helping."

I grabbed at Pablo's suit; not hard, I had no strength, but I wanted him to feel me, maybe feel some of my pain, feel the desolation that was so bad it was physical.

"They killed my parents. Did you know that, Pablo? When you went scurrying back up your partnership ladder, did you know what these people have done?"

"Terry mentioned that your father was dead," Tochera said.

"But not how he died, and how my mother has joined him."

"I'm sorry. I didn't know," Pablo said. "How could I?"

Pablo turned to Terry. "I better go now. Julia will be worried." He brushed his hand gently against my arm. "Tomorrow at eleven, guy." He paused. "You shouldn't be so quick to judge people. Sheesh. You ain't the only one with problems."

Terry placed his arm across my chest as I tried to follow Tochera. "Leave it, Fin," he said gently. "Let him go. Don't burn that bridge until you know where you are."

"Let me try Carol," I said. Terry handed me his phone.

No answer at the apartment, not even voicemail. Nothing on her cell phone either. Her mother's? I didn't have the number and she was divorced, wasn't she? She'd have changed her name. I tried information. An Amen in Scarsdale?

None listed.

"Let's go," I said.


I woke up as Terry pulled alongside the Battery Park apartment block.

"What time is it?" I asked.

"Ten-thirty." He paused for a moment, then slightly hesitatingly asked, "Do you still want to stay here, Fin?"

More than ever. I would be able to think in my own space. "Yes."

I eased myself out of the car. Terry retrieved my suitcase and garment bag from the backseat and we went into the building.

The concierge to whom I'd offered advice about a career on Wall Street was behind the desk. "Cute haircut, asshole," he said.

I ignored him and went to my mailbox.

But the voice followed. "Filled with fan mail I expect, Mr. Border." Terry put his finger to my lips, seeing that I was about to end my short-lived policy of turning the other cheek.

"Roll with it, Fin," he said. "I'm afraid there will be plenty more of that before this is over."

The concierge had been right about my mailbox. It was stuffed.

"I'll take those." Terry decked my luggage and yanked the mail out of the box, opened up my garment bag, and stuffed the whole lot inside.

"We can look at them tomorrow," he said.

We went up to my apartment. At the door I hesitated.

"You still have a key?" Terry asked.

I did. Secreted behind what few dollars I had left in my wallet.

I opened the door and switched on the hall light.

The first name was JESSICA. In red. Where a framed map of Manhattan in the late 1890s had been. The map lay on the floor, glass and frame smashed.

The next was ABBY.

The next, EILEEN, then JAPHIRA. Harsh red, harsh strokes, Jackson Pollock splatters all around the letters.

Down the hallway, RAY, CONNOR.

Into the living/dining room.

SEPH, ROSA, SOL.

All the pictures lay on the floor smashed, smeared, and spattered. Grand Central Station was unrecognizable.

JOHN, CARLA.

The photographs torn to pieces, the frames twisted and flung aside.

PATTI, HARRY.

The overstuffed couch and chair ripped to shreds. The dining table splintered. The chairs broken and scattered. A screenless TV. A hi-fi bleeding wires.

DAVE, CHUCK.

A computer, disemboweled of mother board, processor, and memory. The floor was a lurid, stinking palette of the contents of my refrigerator.

YOUR VITIMS HAD NAMES YOU FUCKER.

The missing C in VITIMS somehow emphasized the blind fury and hatred that fueled every brushstroke.

I was hated. It didn't matter that I had done nothing to earn it. I was hated. It was that simple, that terrible. I hurt all over, but I stayed on my feet, feeling my shoes grind into glass, wood, cheese, olives, the debris of my fragile habitat.

I remembered Carol telling me about the graffiti sprayed on the FDR parapet. Shit happens.

Did anything *else* happen, I wondered.

"Do you want me to call the police?" Terry asked.

"No," I said without hesitation. "Let me pick up a few things and we can go back to your place."

Terry scrutinized the mess. "How did they get in? No sign of forced entry. Anyone else have a key?"

"Only the management," I said blankly. "It doesn't matter. Let's collect my stuff and get out."

I went into the bedroom. The only things in one piece were the light switch and lightbulb. Whoever had done this wanted me to appreciate their handiwork.

The bed was eviscerated. My clothes were scattered and torn, covered in red paint.

"We'll get some new clothes first thing tomorrow." Terry was behind me, hands gently on my shoulder, just a slight presence, so as not to hurt me. I was numb now.

"Let's go," I said.

On entering the apartment I hadn't looked behind me, I'd just swung the front door shut. Now I could see what was written on the interior panel.

AND YOU KILLED ME. GUESS WHOSE NEXT.

# FORTY-ONE

**D**ownstairs I could hear a commotion as the elevator doors opened. I walked around the corner from the elevator bank and into a wall of intense light sharply peppered with blinding flashes.

I couldn't figure out how many of them there were. I was facing an unintelligible sea of mouths shouting questions. Lenses and microphones were thrust into my face. I shielded my eyes and we just barged through, Terry gamely swinging the garment bag like a matador's cape.

As I passed the front desk, the concierge treated me to a blinding smile. "I tried to warn you," he said, "but your phone don't seem to be working."

We got outside but the entourage stuck to us, wasps around a picnic. "Don't touch him," screamed Terry. "He's hurt. Don't hurt him."

How hurt? Who hurt him? They shouted. Why'd they hurt him? Did you hurt yourself? Did you try to kill yourself? Will you try again?

We managed to get in the car.

Surrounded. Faces, flashes, mouths at the windows. Baying for blood.

Terry sounded the horn and edged the car forward.

The ones in front of the car got the message, looked uncertain for a moment and began to clear out of the way.

Terry rammed his foot down. It wasn't an F1, but I could see the crowd recede fast enough as I watched through the rear window.

We headed out of the city district.

"I want to go to Carol's place. Tribeca."

"She's not there, Fin," Terry said. "You rang, remember?"

"She didn't pick up. Doesn't mean she isn't there. Look, Terry, you've done enough. Just drop me off and I'll take it from here."

"Ernie wouldn't like it if I dumped you," he said.

"Ernie's dead. He let me go to Bombay, his fingerprints are all over this filth. Why would he give a shit?"

"Ernie had his own nightmare," Terry said.

We pulled up outside Carol's building. It seemed quiet enough, a few late-nighters rolling along the sidewalk, someone with their dog bending over to scoop up Lassie's pavement art. An ambulance screamed by, narrowly missing the passenger door of Terry's ancient Caprice Classic as I opened it wide onto the street without thinking.

Inside, the lobby was deserted. The building didn't have a door-man, no elevator either. We climbed three flights, the injury on my hip getting madder at me at every creaky step.

We stared at Carol's door.

A helter-skelter of blue plastic tape stretched across it. Police tape. A notice warned not to enter and a crudely fixed bolt and padlock put the lid on it.

"Jesus," Terry said.

Terry took out his cell phone and a business card. "I'll call Manelli."

I touched the tape as if it were a live wire, that it could transmit the news through my hand.

We didn't need any more phone calls.

On the other side of the hall a fire extinguisher hung on a wall bracket.

I lifted it out. My arms grumbled at the strain. I ignored them; the sheer bulk of it felt somehow satisfying.

"Don't call anyone," I said, beginning a pendulum motion with the extinguisher.

"Fin, no." Terry stepped smartly out of the arc traced by the red cylinder.

I stepped forward and let it crash into the police padlock.

The impact sent a seismic judder through me. The padlock stayed put.

I swung again.

This time there was a gratifying crack as the wood around the screws split.

"Kick it now," I said. "My legs aren't up to much."

"Don't be an idiot," Terry said.

I began swinging the extinguisher again. "I'm not leaving here until we've seen inside."

Terry pushed me aside and aimed a kick just beneath the handle. It looked like he knew what he was doing in kicking terms.

The door flew open.

Inside, the sight was pretty much what had greeted us in my own apartment.

The difference was that Carol had possessions that were really worth trashing. The furniture, the glass, the pictures, the clothes, the plants, the knickknacks. Everything had been caught up in a whirlwind of hate that had spun through her home.

And the same names on the wall; same red, same violent spatters.

I stood in the living room. The couch where we'd started to make love; upturned, bleeding red paint. I moved into the bedroom. The bed where she'd clung to me was now desecrated, shredded.

"Where is she?" I said out loud. Where had she run to? Mom? Or farther, out of town, out of state? Where was her refuge? She would be scared, confused.

I wandered, trancelike, into the bathroom.

Porcelain smashed; her unguents, creams, sprays, foaming scummy islands in the pool of water that spread across the floor.

I picked up an empty pill bottle, pocketed it.

Back in the hall, Terry was kneeling near a smashed telephone. He was gingerly poking around in the torn-up, red-stained paperwork that had been scattered across the floor.

"Anything there?" I asked.

He shook his head. "Utility bills, bank statements, and a whole lot I can't make out because of the paint."

I joined him. He was right, there didn't seem to be much, other than the ephemera of household management. It seemed so sad. As if someone was telling her she didn't have a home anymore. Look, he was saying, you've ripped my life to shreds. Now it's your turn.

I picked up one of the more complete pieces of paper. Maybe this held the answer to where she was.

"We better get out of here," Terry said. "Someone's bound to have heard the noise."

Scooping up a few more bits of paper, I got up.

"Okay," I said.

There was nobody on the stairs, nobody in the lobby.

As we reached the car, I could hear sirens approaching.

Terry didn't accelerate hard, a gentle coast to the junction at the end of the street and a seamless merge into a line of traffic. We were now just anybody in an endless line of bouncing, honking automobiles.

As we drove north, I shuffled the papers from Carol's floor. They were medical insurance forms. She'd had some routine checks, a few hundred dollars. But it was the account from somewhere called St. Cecilia's that interested me. It gave no hint as to the course of treatment. Just seven-fifty bucks a day. No itemization, an all-inclusive price. It didn't even say it was a hospital. A hospice? No, people didn't come out of hospices.

Why the hell had Carol been there?

An address in Fort Tryon; a mere censer-swing from the Cloisters.

Carol had said that she had been somewhere that was both good and bad. St. Cecilia's wasn't a hospital for the body. And the roller-coaster that had been her affair with JJ Carslon had left Carol needing a place that dealt with the mind and spirit.

A refuge.

"I have to see her," I whispered.

"You've got Manelli tomorrow, fix on that, Fin. One thing at a time."

"There isn't time for one thing at a time," I said. "Tochera made certain of that."

"You shouldn't be so hard on Pablo. He stuck his neck out for you."

"He stuck my neck out."

"No," Terry said firmly. "Not just yours. He's in a tight place. He doesn't know why McIntyre put him on the case in the first place. It isn't really his field, and he doesn't know why McIntyre was so happy to take him off it. He was obstructed every step of the way, and he's diligent, but there comes a point . . ." Terry took one hand off the wheel and waved it vaguely. "He's astute, he has an attuned sense of fear, both his own and others. He's compassionate too."

"How do you know so much about him?"

"People like me have plenty of reason to be grateful to Pablo Tochera."

"People like you?" What did he mean? Legal executives? People who wear glasses?

The penny dropped. "He does work for the gay community," I said.

Terry nodded. "Everyone assumes that in a place like New York, gays have an easy time of it. That isn't necessarily so, and there are plenty of people whose lives are better because of Pablo Tochera. You don't think that any ordinary attorney could have got you out of JFK in anything but a police car?"

"I thought it wasn't his field," I said.

"Not when on official Schuster business. But when he's wearing the pro bono hat . . ."

"And does McIntyre know how Pablo spends his evenings?"

"He didn't," Terry said. "But Pablo believes he does now. I think that what's frightening Pablo so much. He has good reason to be afraid."

Even with the little I knew of Jim McIntyre, I had no trouble believing that Terry was right.

"You still got Ernie's letter?" I asked. Sure he had; he'd said he would treasure it and Terry wasn't the sort to say what he didn't mean.

"Of course."

"I've been wondering about the numbers on its reverse," I said.

Terry nodded. He kept his eyes on the road looking out for drivers and pedestrians to whom he could bestow courtesies, letting vans out of parking spaces, allowing taxis to swerve in front of him, waving jaywalkers across his path so that the vehicles in the other lanes had to brake sharply and curse him.

"I think those figures are code," I said.

"It's possible," Terry said, betraying neither surprise nor skepticism. "I was never convinced they were merely Ernie's accounting entries. He was a lawyer; he couldn't count."


Terry's apartment lay two blocks behind Central Park West. A hip address, but not as hip as JJ's aerie overlooking the Park itself.

In his own habitat, I appreciated how different Terry looked from when he was in the office. Sheldon Keenes wouldn't allow informal dress, so everyone wore suits. For some, the contrast between the uniform and casual wear is hardly noticeable. With Terry, the change was more profound. Sure, a black jacket, black T-shirt, and rimless spectacles perched on the bridge of a petite nose made him more Madison Avenue than Wall Street. But it was more than that. In the office, he didn't seem complete, the fact that he wasn't a qualified attorney somehow diminishing him. But here—since I'd seen him at JFK, in fact—I'd recognized that he was a whole person; there was nothing missing.

He moved like a black cursor on a white computer screen as he led me through the apartment. Everything was white, except for a few splashes of color on the wall, pastel blobs and squares. Inaccessible art, expensive. A bronze male nude, abstract, but recognizable, followed us with its distorted eyes.

And a tiny white bedroom, more of a box room with wall-to-wall futon, overlooked by a giant photo of Maria Callas, mid-aria at full soprano throttle. There was nothing else in the room save for a black telephone next to a single pillow at the head of the futon.

"Bathroom's down the hall," Terry said. "Don't worry about blood on the sheets. I'll understand."

He plumped up the pillow and then stood up straight. His whole body seemed in a state of hesitation.

"What did Ernie look like?" he asked at last.

"He didn't die from a heart attack," I said.

"Of course not," Terry snapped. He unzipped my garment bag and started to remove my smelly, crumpled possessions as if they were priceless artifacts. He stopped unpacking for a moment and smiled at me. "I'm sorry."

"It was like he had been strangled," I said.

Terry's eyes burned with both fear and hunger for knowledge.

I hesitated. "He was shaven. Not a hair of his own on him. But there was a wig. He was wearing a wig." I remembered how it had slid down his forehead, like some shaggy guinea pig trying to eat his face, and how I had arrived in time to stop the furry bastard before it reached Ernie's eggplant tongue.

Terry looked up at the ceiling and I heard him catch his breath.

"We can talk tomorrow, if you like," I said.

"No," he said quietly. "Now." He continued to unpack.

My mind panned over the bathroom scene. "I had the sense of . . ." What was it? Deliberation, premeditation, a grotesque order, a perverted still life. No, it wasn't like a painting. It was about a human being as part of a process.

"Ritual," I said. That was it, part-performance, part-sacrifice. Something choreographed.

"His testicles were tied tightly with twine," I said.

Terry stopped mid-movement and shut his eyes. He whispered something I didn't pick up. It sounded Indian.

He opened his eyes and motioned me to lie on my side and he started to undo my shirt buttons.

It was as if he was in a trance, but still his hands kept working: delicate, sensitive, precise.

He eased my arm out of one shirtsleeve without adding to the pain.

Terry stood up and pulled out a pack of cigarettes and lit one up. He didn't offer me one. "Ernie was a complex man," he said, exhaling the words with the smoke.

"A giant intellect, who allowed himself to be a figure of fun," he continued. "But he wasn't funny, really. He once said it was like he'd got on the wrong train to work and he could see another alongside him—the right one—and, as the journey progressed, the correct train peeled further and further away. He had laughed and said that he'd written a stinker to the Railway Users Association to ask for his life back by way of refund."

Terry pressed his fingers against his eyelids. "Cigarettes. They play havoc with the contacts."

"But why the twine, the wig?" I asked. "If he didn't set the scene, then who did and why?"

Terry shrugged and carefully flicked ash into a little silver box he pulled from his pocket. "Who knows, Fin. But I know that right now he'd want you to get some sleep and sort out your own mess in the morning. He loved you, you know. I know you lost your clients, I know you went to Bombay—and he didn't stop it. You have a choice, Fin: Either draw the conclusion that he didn't really care about you or accept that life is complex and that sometimes people take a wrong turn." He shrugged. "I don't know—I'm not the qualified attorney, you are. I thought they weren't supposed to be so judgmental."

Suddenly a new wave of exhaustion swept over me.

I turned over onto my front and closed my eyes.

# FORTY-TWO

At ten the next morning I was in Fort Washington, a stone's throw from the Cloisters, scanning the frontage of a high-gabled building smothered by creepers and shrubs at its lower reaches, but whose dark brown brick soon gave way to a half-timbered glory of yellow plaster and railroad tie-sized oblongs of black wood from which dozens of mullioned windows sparkled in the sun.

Terry had left the apartment just after dawn, telling me that Pablo Tochera would be along later. I hadn't waited for him. I needed to see Carol and I wasn't convinced that Detective Manelli could afford to give me compassionate leave to do so, now that my picture was on TV and in the papers. Whatever Terry said about Pablo, he didn't yet have my unconditional confidence.

From the outside, the building wouldn't concede that it was St. Cecilia's. But the street number matched. Maybe the neighbors didn't want the fact that they abutted a genteel madhouse advertised. And to keep the peace, the good sisters of St. Cecilia's had obliged.

As I pressed the discreet bell, I wondered whether this was a fool's errand. I had some old medical insurance forms and an empty bottle of Prozac look-alike from Carol's bathroom floor.

A smiling man in T-shirt and jeans opened the door.

He let me into a high-beamed hallway reception area; from the lofty windows arms of moted light reached down to a floor laid with a threadbare and uneven blue carpet.

Deep and frayed comfy chairs lined the wall, within easy reach of large oak coffee tables laden with bright magazines. No newspapers, I observed. In one corner was a cart with coffee, cookies, and bottled water.

It felt safe. The paintings and poems of incumbent and previous residents pinned to notice boards were, for the most part, competent and displayed psychoses under some measure of control. The few people wandering around in tracksuits appeared spaced-out but comfortable.

"I've come to see Carol Amen," I told a cheerful-looking receptionist who was performing lightning keystrokes on a switchboard, cocking her head as incoming calls flowed into her ear from a near-invisible set of headphones.

"I'm Fin Border," I added.

Her eyes narrowed, like the name meant something but she couldn't place it. "She expecting you?" she asked before tapping a few keys on her switchboard. "Please hold," she trilled into the little rod in front of her mouth.

"Yes, she's expecting me," I said.

The receptionist glanced at a notice board on the side of her little booth.

"She's got group in fifteen minutes, then dance therapy." She looked up at me. "You sure she's expecting you, honey?"

I smiled confidently. "I'm sure."

Another attendant in jeans and T-shirt appeared and was sent to check with Carol as to my bona fides.

"Make yourself at home," the receptionist said. "Take a seat, have some coffee."

With a magazine—the latest *Vogue*—open on my lap, I stared into the middle distance. I could guess what had driven Carol to this place. Had it worked the last time? And what about now?

*   *   *

Somehow I'd expected Carol to be a shuffling shadow swaddled in a dressing gown or an ill-fitting tracksuit, her hair matted and lank.

But her hair shone, her face appeared fresh and natural. She wore a tracksuit, but it wasn't ill-fitting. It perfectly framed her sensuous athleticism.

As I stood up, she motioned me to remain seated and joined me on the couch at an ambiguous distance.

"You look great," I said. But as my hand touched hers in a gentle squeeze, I felt the clamminess. Close, I could see that clever cosmetics masked the pallor of her face, the sadness. Now that she was sitting, her body crumbled inside the tracksuit.

She managed a smile. "You look terrible," she said. Before leaving Terry's apartment, I'd attempted some superficial work with my hair, trying to spread it out a little, dispel the post-bushfire scrubland look.

I now found myself fingering my stubble self-consciously, as another resident chose a spot immediately in front of us to read a magazine and slurp loudly on a cup of coffee.

"Is there somewhere more private?" I asked.

"We don't have secrets in here," Carol said flatly. "This *is* private."

"I've missed you." It sounded so lame.

Carol's face hardened. "I'm here to deal with my own feelings, not yours."

"I'm sorry."

"It's not about blame either," she said.

"Then what is it about?" I asked. I was up against an unscalable wall of therapy textbooks, where the grouting of small talk was scraped away and discarded.

"This place has firemen, bankers, housewives, storekeepers, and rock stars," she said. "They have failed marriages, jobs they hate, drugs, drink, anorexia, phobias about cheese. You name it."

She shut her eyes tight. "For some people here, it's about replacing existing things with new things. For me, it's about filling a space. I'm trying to fill the void left by Jefferson Trust, JJ, other stuff." She looked at me. "Anyway, I'm trying to find things over which I can exercise some control."

"And are you finding those things?"

She looked up at one of the high windows for a moment. "I don't know. But this seems a good place to start."

Carol's expression then gave way to what I took to be one of sympathy. "I saw the news, Fin. In here, we're discouraged from letting the outside world in, during the early stages, at any rate. But I saw it. Saw you. How are you coping?"

Coping? It wasn't about coping anymore. It was about fighting. Destroying the destroyer, or be destroyed.

"They killed my father, they launder money for NRIs, they . . ."

Carol held her hand to my lips, stemming the torrent of desperate words. "I'm sorry," she said, her voice breaking. "I shouldn't have asked. I don't really want to know: about your father, about Mendip, Askari, the Ketans. Any of them. Knowing about them won't help me. I had a Detective Manelli in here, asking about JJ. About you. You were right, Fin. I told him the truth—all of it—but he didn't want to listen. He's convinced you owned the car, that you and I add up to more than a couple, and that you're using me. He was quite sympathetic, but the truth for him is built on a different foundation. Maybe he'll go away, maybe he won't. At the moment I'm not sure if I really care. We're supposed to focus on our own truth in here." She stood up.

My truth *was* her truth, I wanted to declare. But, more than anything, I wanted to share with her what had happened to my mother. I badly needed that moment of vented grief. But as I watched Carol's face crumple, I wondered if that would be possible in the near future. Hers was a managed, professionally orchestrated isolation. She was being allowed to disintegrate and reassemble herself under laboratory conditions.

And the truth for her was that she still had a mother.

Carol wiped her face with both palms. She looked so wretched. "And don't ask about us. *Please.*"

She started to walk away but stopped and turned to me, then looked around the room: at the other residents, the high windows, the poems and pictures on the wall.

"I don't know if this is the right place," she whispered. "More of a space to get better in, than a place that makes you better."

"I always thought of you as someone who didn't need to get better," I said.

"We all get sick sometimes. The trick is to know when you need the pills or just a place to hide."

I was suddenly conscious of the avid attention of the coffee-slurping audience. I wanted to tell the man to piss off.

"You've been here before but you're back," I managed calmly. "The things that happened didn't go away, did they? This place won't make anything go away."

"I talk to the therapists and, you know something: So little of my distant past seems to inform my present. Sometimes I think that's all they want to work with, that and the pills." She smiled. "In many ways, my childhood is too boring to account for how I feel right now."

"There's enough contemporary material to make up for any shortfall in early life. The world has irretrievably changed for us both, Carol. You don't need a therapist to tell you that. And I think you already know it."

Carol sat down again. "I just want the fear to go away," she murmured. "It hangs over all of us. It hung over JJ like a cloud."

"What frightened JJ so?" I asked. "He had everything and lost it all, his mind included. What drove him to madness? Don't get me wrong, Carol, you drive me crazy, could drive any man crazy, but I don't think you made JJ the way he was."

"I never knew where I was with him," she said. "His moods, his double life—me in one half, Miranda and two kids in the other." She frowned. "Except that it wasn't a double life, it was a triple life."

"What do you mean?" I asked.

"He didn't start out with the name Carlson. Carlstein was the name he was born with."

"Why did he change it, did he tell you?"

"He never talked about it. Someone else told me."

"Who, Carol?"

"It doesn't matter," she said, shifting uneasily. Whoever it was frightened her.

"Everything matters," I said.

"His brother," she said at last. "I thought he could be left out of the picture." Some of the dots edged toward each other. The old hippy with a ponytail, the one at the funeral. Perhaps he was the unspoken shadow, the one Raj couldn't name, the guard on the door for JJ, the higher authority Askari spoke of. "He was the devil on JJ's shoulder, laughing at him, mocking him," she continued. "Rebuking him for a cowardice that wouldn't allow JJ to live with the weight of history. But Conrad Carlstein really didn't care about being Jewish; to him everything was a joke, particularly religion. The world was a toy and JJ bankrolled his playroom. JJ paid for everything; his clothes, his house, his cars, everything. And all he could do was mock JJ by way of thanks."

Conrad Carlstein. My mother had said "Stein." Conrad Stein. The German Jew. She had never been good with names, they scrambled her head. But her naming of names had been good enough to identify another member of the Gemini Club. He was the shadow, the source of the fizz on Ernie's cigarette—the fear.

"What's the matter, Fin?" Carol asked.

"How well did you know Conrad Carlstein?"

"I don't think anyone really knows Conrad," Carol said. "On the rare occasions that JJ talked about him, he simply said that Conrad was old blood, blood he needed to wash out of his own veins. I don't think JJ ever managed it, though. Conrad was always a presence, somehow. He treated JJ like he was dirt, like it was him that underwrote everything, rather than the other way around. He acted like he owned JJ."

So, JJ couldn't wash his family out of him. Why did that feel familiar?

"Did JJ ever mention the word *Gemini?*" I asked.

"No," Carol said. "JJ didn't read horoscopes and he was a Virgo anyway. What are you getting at?"

"A club. At Oxford, with Askari and Mendip and one other."

One other. An American. On a Fulbright. McIntyre?

Jim McIntyre, for sure.

Carol said: "Conrad never mentioned anything about Gemini or a club. But I only met him three or four times. He didn't come out much, he said that everything these days could be done via e-mail: eating, business, thinking, sex, everything. I went to his house once—with JJ—a small place on Long Island. JJ owned it, of course."

"JJ didn't own anything when he died," I said. "Remember?"

Carol's hands rode over her face, a comfortless cosmetic-smearing massage. I wanted to hold her, clean her face with a washcloth, tell her she didn't need makeup.

"Who knows what JJ did or didn't own," she said wearily. "Who knows what was real about him. All I'm saying is that JJ hated going to Conrad's house. I remember: He told me not to say much, drink a lot and get drunk, do anything so I'd forget the place. He was scared of it, scared of Conrad too. The evening was weird, a dinner on the deck looking out over Oyster Bay, JJ quieter than I'd ever seen him, Conrad talking about philosophy, religion, sex. Not like he took it seriously, though; everything he said poured scorn on belief, passion, love. And he saved his cruelest words for JJ, said I should get rid of him, that he was a loser. Then JJ got stoned. Out of it. And Conrad moved in on me."

Carol's face creased in puzzlement. "He really thought he could, you know: with his own brother lying semiconscious nearby. It was like nothing was taboo for him. This was a man for whom sacrilege was the only sacred thing. But he was smart, observant, *sensitive* even; his conversation proved that much. He must have sensed I hated him, but still he put his face close to mine. I could feel his breath, smell the wine. He even took the band off that stupid ponytail and shook his hair loose, like a vamp limbering up for the clinch."

"So you fought him off," I said. She'd be good at that, tucking a man's tail between his legs and pulling hard.

"If you like, but maybe not in the way you think." The memory of that evening seemed to grip her, bewitch her, lash her to the end of her last statement. "I was smart enough to realize that he was a very dangerous man," she continued at last. "Outright rebuff carried too many risks. That was my judgment." She paused, waiting to see if I would challenge her assessment. I just nodded.

"Submission was out of the question too." A small echo of the determination she must have shown that night sounded in her voice.

"So I let him believe we were unfinished business," she added.

"Wasn't that even more dangerous?" I said.

She rounded on me, her hand sweeping away the copy of *Vogue* I'd forgotten still lay on my lap. "You weren't *there*," she hissed.

The coffee-slurping resident moved toward us and picked up the magazine and handed it to Carol. "Other folks may want to read this," he said quietly. "We should take care of the things we've got."

He turned away from me and leaned over Carol. "You coming to group? I don't think this guy is helping you any."

"Later, Harley." She patted his arm. "I'm okay. Really."

Harley grunted, thrust his hands into his dressing gown pockets, and wandered away from us.

"Unfinished business," I whispered to myself and then out loud: "And did Carlstein resurface to tie up loose ends? Dot the *i*'s, as it were."

Carol's gaze followed Harley, her lips relaxing into something approaching a smile. "Harley sells cars and thinks a customer drove off with his soul in the glove compartment. That's a metaphor for him, he doesn't believe that's what actually happened. We don't have Napoleon or Jesus Christ in here. But Harley's got problems that only the Wizard of Oz can fix, including the fact that he's in love with me."

Everyone was in love with Carol, it seemed.

She reached down to retrieve a flyer advertising a depilatory cream that had fallen from the magazine.

I gently pulled the flyer from Carol's hand. "You were saying about unfinished business. How did you finish it, how did you close?"

"That evening was the last time I saw Conrad before JJ's funeral. He called a few times; he must have found my number from somewhere—JJ wouldn't have told him and I'm not in the book. He got my e-mail address too. Anyway, he left voicemails and e-mails, continuations of what he'd said at the Oyster Bay house. He said he was patient, that he would have me in the end."

"So it isn't really unfinished business at all," I said.

Carol flipped through the pages of *Vogue*, shiny stylized perfection.

"I suppose not."

"JJ once said he couldn't cut free because there was a guard on the door," I said. "Mendip squeezes more and more on his little inhaler, his breath harder and harder to find. Even Askari suggested he owed allegiance to someone, some shadow—and it wasn't Ganesh. Everyone is frightened and has found a different way of expressing it. But maybe the source is the same bogeyman for all of them." Only McIntyre sought to falsify the theory. Smug, smart, unassailable. Fearless.

And yet the theory was attractive, deserved to be spoken out loud: "I think they fear Carlstein; he has some kind of hold over them that keeps the Gemini Club intact. Jesus, what did those creeps get up to in the Dreaming Spires?"

Carol didn't seem to be listening. "When my insurance is up and I have to leave here, I may go back to college, do something entirely different. Somewhere else—where they don't know me, can't associate me with what happened on the FDR Drive. That's the worst thing: the dead people, the names on the wall. It's not like I want to shout my innocence; I want to shout my guilt, even if it's guilt by association. I could put up with anything: losing my career . . ." She paused. "Losing you, even. But, Christ, those names, when I think of them my mind freezes and it's then I feel I've lost everything, including the will to live."

"But you know that you bear no responsibility for what happened on the FDR," I protested.

"Do I know that, Fin? Do I? I told JJ that I was seeing you and moments later he . . ." Her voiced trailed away.

"You know perfectly well that there were other things," I said.

She didn't reply.

We were silent for a while, the clack of the receptionist's switchboard vying with the stewing hiss of a near-empty pot of coffee on a hotplate.

"And you?" Carol asked at last. "What will you do?"

Let events take their course? Wait for Manelli to pounce? Watch the chart of plaintiffs and defendants breed like some amoebic creature whose only reason for living is to replicate, to beget an exponentially engulfing infestation? Feel Carol slip from my grasp?

No.

"Assert my rights," I said. "The right not to be hurt. The right not to be regarded as a lead in *Slaughter on the FDR*. My work, my clients. You. Everything. I want it all back."

Carol touched my hand. "I think those rights are in abeyance for a while," she said gently.

I felt anger well in me. "I don't have a therapist, Carol." Fear sparked, fear that Carol might get up and leave me right then and there.

But the old face was back, the one on the couch in the Tribeca apartment, the one that could grab every floating particle of data and understand it at every level.

"Proof of my innocence is out there," I continued. "In time it will emerge: the careless signature, the crony that talks too loud, a paper trail that leads back to JJ and the Gemini Club. It has to, a lie that big has to reveal itself in the end. But by then I will be ruined, in jail, or dead. I need a short cut, a way to get my would-be destroyers to turn on themselves or reason that I'm more use alive and rehabilitated than dead or ruined."

"That's like saying you'd be rich if only you had a pile of money," Carol said dryly.

I ignored her.

Stashed in a drawer, stored on a computer disk, under a mattress. Somewhere, the Gemini Club had left its stain, its imprint, the must and rumple of a slept-in bed. The NRI scam was too large not to cast its shadow, make its presence felt. Its size implied *infrastructure* and a frame occupied space; it had bulk, mass. There was the order-routing agreement, the sale and purchase agreement, the whole fucking Badla deal. Big stains.

But all of that was inaccessible to me right then. All I had was a stupid Victorian book by Rudyard Kipling and Ernie's letter to Terry Wardman—I didn't have that even, I had to get it off Terry first.

I needed to tap a new seam. In the Netherland Antilles, maybe? No—just more whispers and smoke. Casually sneaking into Schuster Mannheim or Mendip's room at the Regent for a rummage was a fantasy. At Clay & Westminster, perhaps: in Keenes's office, or on the computer system someplace. Maybe.

Or in Carlstein's lair, the black hole at the center of Gemini. In terms of astronomy and astrology, the analogy was off the mark, maybe—I didn't know what or where Gemini was in the night sky—but still it felt right, an authentic sense of the pull of a spinning vortex.

What had Carol just said? Carlstein didn't get out much. Everything via e-mail. *Everything*. Damindra Ketan's observation about Sunil Askari came back to me: *the modern scourge of e-mail*. One of Askari's two overriding obsessions, the other being my father. Maybe Askari hated e-mails so much because they were instruments of control wielded by Carlstein.

Then there was the Huxtable file at Askari's office, the one with which I'd failed to exinguish Raj. Full of e-mails. With numbers on them.

"Carlstein's house," I said. "His computer, his e-mails." I thought momentarily of the portcullis of passwords ready to slice down on trespassers. So what—if necessary, I'd take the bloody thing back with me to Terry's place and work on it there.

"Don't even think about it," Carol said. "He'll be there; he only seemed to come out to torment JJ, like some night animal. Now JJ's gone, he has no reason to go on the prowl."

Then another carrot was needed to get him out.

"I can't go while he's in the house," I said.

"At least you're smart enough to grasp that much," she said.

An orderly strolled over to us.

"Sorry to break in on you folks," he said cheerfully. "Dr. Trent wants a word with you, Carol."

I was glad to see her face darken with disappointment. She turned to me. "The guy's in charge of my brain. I gotta go." She kissed me on the lips, her eyes shut, like she was savoring her last ever moment of intimacy.

I was about to say that she didn't have to go anywhere unless she wanted to. No. Some progress had been made, I reasoned. Give it time.

She backed up. "I guess you won't be staying in your apartment if it looks anything like mine. Where will you be?"

"I'm staying with Terry Wardman, an associate at Clay & Westminster."

"Give me his number," she said.

I wrote it on the flyer for the depilatory cream, adding the number for Terry's cell phone, the one I'd picked up from his hall table a couple of hours earlier.

"How long are you going to be here, Carol?" I asked.

She thought for a moment. "I don't know. I'll call you."

I watched her graceful body disappear into the shadows of a hallway at the other end of the room.

"You're Fin Border."

I turned around to find that Harley had sat down next to me. He stroked an envelope against the grain of an incipient beard on his blotchy middle-aged face. His other hand was dug deep into the pocket of a red pinstriped bathrobe.

"Yes," I said cautiously. "What do you want?"

He opened the envelope and pulled out a letter. "You should leave Carol alone."

"And why is that any of your goddamned business?"

"You are the source of everything bad in her life," Harley continued.

"Dr. Trent has confirmed that, has he?"

"You're the signature on her death warrant." Harley handed over the letter. "Read this," he said.

I had learned to fear pieces of paper handed over by strangers.

A short letter. No header or footer, just one paragraph of italic type.

> *Kill yourself, Carol Amen. Kill yourself. I don't care how you do it, violently or silently, quick or slow. Just please do it, I implore you. You're trash, surely you must see that. You've read the rollcall of dead on the wall of your apartment. Now look in the mirror and kill yourself.*

Harley snatched the letter from me and stuffed it deep into his pocket.

My hand shot out and grabbed the cord of the bathrobe, pulling his bulk toward me. "Where did you get that?" I hissed. "Has she seen it?"

Harley sagged against me and let out a groan. An orderly across the room turned and eyed us suspiciously before starting to move toward us.

"I have her best interests at heart," Harley said. "You wouldn't want her to do something stupid, would you?"

"Why should that letter make any difference?" I said hotly. "She has already seen her apartment ransacked, dead names on her wall. Her response hasn't been to make an attempt on her own life."

"But she's thought of it," Harley said.

"How the fuck do you know? Or have you been steaming open her brain as well?"

"I don't have to, Fin Border. She does that for me in group therapy. We all open our brains in there."

The orderly was on us now.

"Everything okay, Harley?" he asked.

Harley jabbed a finger into my chest. "This guy's been opening my mail. He's got a listening device, he's wired. You said I'd be safe in here."

The orderly sighed and gave Harley a compassionate smile. "Don't worry, Harley, he's going now." The orderly glared at me. "Aren't you, sir?"

"But . . ." I started. But what? This wasn't the place for a rational argument.

"Yes, I'm going now," I said.

# FORTY-THREE

**G**et out of there."

I heard the voice before I realized I'd picked up the phone and put it next to my ear. It felt like only a couple of minutes since I'd gotten back from St. Cecilia's and found the door to Terry's apartment wide open. Oh Christ, I'd thought, expecting to find the place turned over, red names splashed on the wall. But no, two surly moving men heaving furniture informed me that they were clearing out the place, shipping the contents to storage, they'd be back later for the futon, pillow, and telephone, which Mr. Wardman wanted them to leave there. I had nodded vacantly, lurched into the spare room, and collapsed onto the futon, not even bothering to wonder if these guys were for real or just cool-headed thieves.

"Who is this?" I mumbled.

"Terry." The voice was clipped, like a computer voice.

"What's happening? Why are you moving out?"

"Shut up. The police will be around very soon to arrest you. You've been placed inside the Plaza on the night of Ernie's death. The

Indians are up in arms too; they've found a pile of corpses and a burnt-out law firm. They want you back."

I tried to sit up and my body reacted with fury, behaving like a network of irritable tectonic plates. I was now awake, though.

"How do you know the police are coming?" I asked.

"Hey, no questions. Keep my cell phone and look under the pillow."

My hand swept the cool underside of the pillow, stopping at what felt like an envelope. Jesus, another envelope.

"Open it later," Terry snapped. "Just get out."

"Wait a minute. What's going on? I can understand why I should clear out, but why you?"

"I'm the paradigm of knowing something but not enough to be of any use to anybody."

"Riddles, Terry."

"The contents of the envelope might help. Ernie's letter. Although, I expect it will merely add to the riddle."

"What's it say?"

"I have no idea," Terry said. "I don't know the code, nor want to."

"What *do* you know?"

Terry paused. "That Ernie was broken on the workbench of McIntyre and Mendip."

"They killed him?"

"They didn't have to. Look, you must leave. I must leave; I've reached a watershed and it's time for an unqualified attorney to start waiting tables on a beach somewhere."

"What about Pablo Tochera? Where does he stand?"

Terry sighed. "He's at a watershed of sorts himself. He has to choose between being the Puerto Rican figleaf on McIntyre's letter-head and live with being the little shit in the big shit's shadow. Or—he can keep his self-respect. Pablo's big on integrity, Fin; so's Julia, his wife. But it's a life decision what with the payments he has to make on a fancy house on the Upper East Side."

"When will I see you—to give back the cell phone."

"Just get out, the cell phone's yours until they cut it off."

"Where shall I go?" I asked.

"Over to you, Fin. Think while you move."

Move. That was a fucking joke. And think? Ha, bloody, ha.

"Do you know someone called Conrad Carlstein, JJ's brother?" I wanted to know if Carlstein had touched Terry with the fear.

Terry caught his breath. "Just stay away from him," he said and hung up.

It was hot and, even though a weekday, Central Park was teeming. I lay facedown, peering into the roots of the grass.

Nobody could see who I was. My hands shrouded my irregular scalp. I had slung my jacket over my suitcase and the garment bag was stuffed under it.

I was invisible.

Except to Paula, I hoped.

I'd told her I would be less than fifty yards from the Tavern on the Green. She'd be able to pull up and park. And find me. Assuming the police hadn't found me first.

I hoped she'd gotten the wig. She hadn't laughed when I'd asked her to get me one. She just asked what size and did I need anything else? No, just you, I'd said.

The envelope nestled in my pocket, next to the cell phone. I'd taken a brief peek: the same letter that Terry and I had studied in his office. The original. I wondered if Terry had taken a copy to carry with him into his new life. It depended upon what it said, I supposed, and Terry professed to be unaware of its meaning.

The sun felt good on my back, a healing influence. It had been too long since I'd allowed it direct access to me without the interruption of an office window. I thought about Carol. I didn't believe for a moment that she was capable of doing anything to hurt herself. If there was a grain of truth in what Harley had said, then it was merely Carol experimenting out loud with a palette of possible feelings, not actual ones.

"Wake ya?"

I smiled into the grass.

"Hallelujah," I said.

"You said it, counselor; with the wig I got you, there's a front row seat in a seventies gospel choir with your name on it."

I turned my head. Paula's face was a silhouette, a partial eclipse of the sun.

"Is the car nearby?" I asked, shading my eyes, but liking the view too much to shield myself entirely from it.

The silhouette nodded. "Can you get up okay?"

I started to raise myself. My skin felt taut, like tight scuba gear about to split. "I'll be fine once I get moving. It's just a bitch to get mobile."

"You're talking to the prototype bitch on that score." She handed me my jacket.

I started to pick up the suitcase and garment bag.

"Hold it, Mr. Schwarzenegger." Paula's hand beat me to it. "The garment bag is for me. You take the suitcase. Wouldn't look natural if you weren't carrying something. And keep your face to the floor. You've got top billing this morning."

I studied Paula for a moment. The sleek brown face, the placid almond eyes. She was smiling, trying to look carefree, happy with her rendezvous in the park. But I could see her anxiety.

I then bowed my head and focused on Paula's sneakers.

It was only fifty yards. Only fifty yards, I kept repeating to myself. But the eyes of the park were on us, plainclothed cops all around us, laughing at us. They would let us get near the car, let us think we'd made it. And then move in. "You didn't think we'd miss you, did you?" they'd say as they clapped on the cuffs.

A soccer ball rolled into the sight line between my shoes and Paula's sneakers.

I didn't look up.

"Hey." A teenage voice. A gimme-my-ball-back-mister voice.

Fuck off, I'm busy being a fugitive.

"Dude. How about it?" The voice was nearer.

I still didn't look up.

"Jerk."

I started to move my leg to get a foot around the ball, but before contact could be made, I saw Paula's sneaker scoop it up and send it out of sight.

"Arrright." A teenager's whoop of forgiveness.

Paula kept walking and I kept following. In a moment we'd reached her car.

It was a Ford, basic but new. I tried to act casual getting in the front passenger seat, but it hurt like hell.

Paula pointed to the radio. "You want to hear the news?"

"No."

She drove out of the Tavern on the Green parking lot and past two police cars. I ducked my head.

Paula jabbed the "on" button. "You better hear it once," she said. "Then forget it."

It didn't take long for me to recognize my name. At first it didn't seem like the name belonged to me, it was in the possession of an intense, ten-words-a-second reporter who confirmed I was a fugitive, that I might be dangerous, that I was implicated in the suspicious death of a senior UK attorney at the Plaza, that I was wanted in connection with the murders of two men in India. And there was more: a fire in India and another body. And, most infamously, I was the star of Slaughter on the FDR. With my leading lady, Carol Amen.

Paula jerked her head toward the backseat. "There's a selection of newspapers under the blanket."

I punched at the radio to clear my name from the airwaves.

"They can stay there," I said tersely.

"Thanks, buddy. They cost me three bucks."

I smiled. "Put it on the account."

Looking out of the window, I could see that we were headed east. "Where are we going?"

"East Rockaway."

I'd heard of it, but even after five years in New York, it was still just a blob on a railroad map.

"I thought you lived in Brooklyn," I said. Paula was always going on about the commute: Every day almost, there'd be a new episode with which to hound me before we could get to the mail.

"That's what I wanted people to think." We made our way down Fifth. Past Saks, past Rockefeller Center. I wondered when, if ever, I'd be free to roam down here again. And, even if I could, whether I would have any dollars in my pocketbook to spend.

"Why did you want them to think that?" I asked.

Paula's face hardened. "Jim McIntyre, that's why. The more you keep secret, the less you can be violated. At least that's the way I've figured it for the last seven years."

"I'm sorry," I said. "I should have guessed."

"The house in Rockaway is all mine, no loan," she continued. "I paid for it out of the seventy thousand from Schuster and with a life policy of Doug's. I rent a small place in Brooklyn. For appearances. I just go there to pick up mail. My calls are rerouted to Rockaway."

Very elaborate. McIntyre must have scared the shit out of her.

"Christ, the wig." I'd forgotten all about it, listening to her talk.

"Under the blanket with the newspapers," Paula said.

I fished around in a plastic bag and withdrew a brown clump of hair. It felt weird. Smelled too.

It took me a while to figure out the front of the thing, and when I did, I flicked it forward and, starting from its fringe, teased it onto my head.

"What do you think?" I asked, turning to Paula.

She stared at the road, said nothing.

Darker and longer than my original hair, but somehow in keeping with my face, I thought it looked okay.

"At least you don't look like a guy who's just been napalmed," Paula said.

We were silent until we got through the Midtown Tunnel and started into Queens.

"You got a plan?" Paula asked.

"I found Carol," I said. "Now I want to visit Conrad Carlstein." It sounded good, decisive.

"Who's he?"

Who indeed. The bravura ebbed quickly.

We came off 495 and headed east on the Grand Central Parkway. Sign after sign pointed to JFK. Getting a flight to anywhere would be impossible now, but my eyes still rested on each and every green invitation we passed.

"Don't think about it, honey," Paula said. "You wouldn't make it out of the parking lot."

"I know."

"And what about all these Indian folks I hear you've been shooting and burning? Jesus, Fin, what you get up to out there? Is a girl safe alone with you?"

I outlined some of what had happened in the last few days.

Then the broad brush summary: "We'll deal with the Stateside problems first," I said. "After that, I'll widen the net."

"That isn't a plan, it's a letter to Santa Claus."

She was quiet for a while. "You didn't kill anyone, did you?" she finally asked.

I could hear Ketan's head slamming against the flagstones. No, it was the heroin.

"Of course I didn't," I said.

"If they killed your mom, I wouldn't blame you," she added.

I keyed in Pablo's number on the cell phone.

Hesitating a moment, I told the secretary who I was. I sensed the wince down the phone as she informed me that Mr. Tochera was at a meeting, but she'd check to see if he was back. My name was in the domain.

"Hi." It was the lowest *hi* I'd ever heard.

"I'm not calling to screw up your partnership chances," I said.

"You missed your appointment with Manelli this morning." The thread of anger was there, but something else too, maybe the compassion Terry spoke of.

"Terry's leaving, did you know that?" I said.

"Huh. He has plenty of reasons to vamoose, I guess. He doesn't have a wife and big house to maintain and so can holler 'wagons roll' anytime."

"There's a club, Pablo, the Gemini Club. McIntyre, Mendip, Askari—that's the Indian lawyer—and JJ's brother, someone called Conrad Carlstein. They're responsible for the deaths of my parents and an Indian lawyer. They're laundering money for expatriate Indians on a huge scale. And, and, and."

"Proof?"

Agreements I had no access to. What *did* I have? A dog-eared book, an as yet meaningless letter, and corpses, two of which were being laid at my door.

"Not much," I admitted. "Yet."

"Listen, Fin, here's something for which there's already plenty of proof. Detective Manelli is squaring up to throw the book at you—not showing this morning put a hair up his ass and placing you at the Plaza has got his juices going even more. And then there's McIntyre—my boss, in case you forgot—he wanted to chew the fat with me a little."

"And?"

"He says that JJ Carlson had nothing when he died, hadn't had anything for a while, he didn't even own a suit. So how the fuck did he buy a car for a million dollars?"

"You know perfectly well that access to funds is as good as ownership and he was a zillion times better placed to secure funds than me. I don't see your point."

Pablo exhaled what sounded like a dying breath. "Jesus, Fin," he said finally. "Tomorrow night at around five, the big guys convene for a short meeting to put the wraps on the merger and sanction the press release. In that release the new partners will be announced and, in spite of everything, there's a good chance my name will be included."

"Congratulations, that makes everything worthwhile."

"Fuck you."

"Terry said you were big on ethics," I said. "Julia too. How do you think she'd feel if she knew what your comfortable existence was built on?"

"Keep Julia out of this."

"Let me ask you a simple question: Do you really believe that the car was mine?"

Pablo groaned a little. "No," he muttered.

"Are you convinced that the car was not mine? This is a different question, I think you'll appreciate."

"I'm not a fucking idiot, I can see the difference."

"Well?" I pressed. "What's your position, Pablo: convinced or merely agnostic on the subject?"

"The car wasn't yours," Pablo said without hesitation. "I know that, but that's not the point. McIntyre wants you fucked to Jupiter and back. The only advice I can sensibly give you is to find another attorney, outside Schuster, one who can do his best for you without his own organization pitching obstacles in his path. And before we go any further, let me say how sorry I am about your parents. I really am."

This wasn't the time for condolences. "You've already suggested that nobody worth their salt will act for me. And you said that before I was officially a fugitive. What hope have I now?"

"Hell. I don't know what to tell you; except that if you want someone at Schuster to act for you then it will be a new attorney and one selected by McIntyre."

Pablo was hurting; I could feel the pain. But I had to press his principles into action.

"I don't think that McIntyre pulled you off my case," I said. "I think you pulled yourself off."

"I can't stop you thinking what you think," Pablo said.

"And I also think that Terry pricked your conscience, told you some home truths about yourself, held up a mirror to you, the one with pro-bono Pablo on it, the one with the witty, self-effacing, basically decent Pablo etched into it. And you came to Kennedy Airport to bail me out. But now Terry's gone, leaving nobody to prick your conscience again. I'll be squashed and you'll be on the letterhead. *Que sera*. But let me tell you something, Pablo. Are you listening hard?"

"I'm about to hang up."

"Give me a minute and then you can do what you want. The only people who can clear me quickly, who don't need depositions and forensics and whatnot, are an anonymous coterie of Non-Resident Indians and the members of the Gemini Club. I'm in no position to square up to any NRIs; I wouldn't know one if he came up to me and screamed 'Badla' in my ear. So that leaves the Club. At the risk of straying into the realms of melodrama, Pablo, I'm telling you that I'm gunning for them, McIntyre included. Directly or indirectly, Gemini was the instrument of my parents' deaths and now they want to kill me and bury my reputation with the body."

There was a rustle on the line. Static? Or the click you're . . .

"You still there?"

"By a thread, guy."

"So, I intend to find something that will persuade them to exonerate me, to short-circuit the process, before Manelli catches up with me or the demented relative of one of the FDR victims does more than paint the walls red or send hate mail."

"You said that these people want to kill you," Pablo countered quickly. "So aren't your priorities a little screwy talking about exoneration? Exoneration isn't worth much if you're dead."

Exoneration was priceless. And yet Pablo was right, but for another reason.

"Exoneration isn't enough," I said. "A price must be exacted for what these people have done. And I want to be alive to see it paid." I flicked a glance at Paula. She was owed a big debt by McIntyre too. Her eyes stayed fixed on the road ahead, her face locked in a concentration disproportionate to the perils that the driving conditions represented.

"From where I'm sitting it looks like an ambitious agenda you've set yourself," Pablo said.

It didn't look like a pushover from the passenger seat of Paula's car either. "What option do I have: Turn myself in? I'll either be in jail or dead and, in a few years time, someone might scribble a corrigendum to my headstone saying—'Sorry, wrong guy.' "

Pablo tutted impatiently. "Time-out. What's all this to me? Is it some messianic bullshit: If you're not with me you're against me, as you fuck off into your conspiracy theory sunset? Or are you really threatening to bring me down with the others, is that the real point?"

People always said that, didn't they? *Are you threatening me, are you threatening me?* As if an answer in the affirmative always meant that all bets were off. I didn't want to threaten Pablo. I *liked* Pablo. Even so, there was some truth in what he was saying, the veil was thin. Nevertheless, I liked to think of it more as a dispassionate analysis of one prong on the fork of the future rather than a threat.

"If it is a threat," I said, "according to your own analysis, it's pretty impotent."

"What the hell do you want from me?"

"Just to be yourself, be ethical, be the Pablo as painted by Terry. And not to hoard anything that might help save me."

Pablo snorted. "McIntyre keeps his files and data locked up too tight for me to have anything to hoard."

I hoped that Conrad Carlstein wasn't quite so security conscious.

"Fine," I said. "I'm not asking you to break the lock on McIntyre's five-year diary or bug his phone."

"And what are you going to do?"

Decode a letter from a dead man and break into the house of a hippy in Oyster Bay.

"I wouldn't want to compromise your ethical position by telling you."

"Fuckin' Brit."

"I'll call you later," I said.

"Missing you already," Pablo said gloomily.

As I cut the phone, the car juddered as we crossed some railroad tracks.

"Long Island Railroad," Paula said, as if the end of my call with Pablo was a cue to start a commentary on the passing landmarks.

"So what do you think?" I said.

"About what?"

"About my conversation."

"Client-attorney privilege, I didn't listen in. Anyway, I could only hear one half of it."

I pressed hard against the headrest and shut my eyes. All I'd needed to achieve was a sporting chance that Pablo didn't turncoat and run to McIntyre. And I wasn't convinced I'd managed even that.

I keyed in the number of St. Cecilia's and asked to speak with Carol. Five minutes marooned on hold in their telephone system suggested that calls to Carol weren't going to get through.


Deacon Avenue was a respectable road of pleasant white clapboard houses. Not rich but solvent: Ford Galaxys in the driveways, the odd Corvette, a boat or two on trailers. The front lawns were small but manicured.

Paula eased the car to a halt at the end of the short street.

"We've passed my house," Paula said. "I wanted to check there were no visitors parked outside. Nobody's supposed to know about this place, but you never know. Stay here while I make sure the inside's clear and I'll come back to get you. If I'm running like an idiot, get in the driver's seat and have the engine running."

"Be careful," I said as she got out of the car.

She leaned through the open window and smiled. "If I were careful I wouldn't be with you, honey."

I watched her walk to around the halfway point of Deacon Avenue, before swinging into a driveway marked by a neat blue mailbox topped by a little plastic man set to crank the handle of a weathervane.

I tried to think about my next move, but was distracted by the throb in my hip and the raw pain of the burn on my back against a cotton shirt sopped with sweat.

The image that sporadically and indistinctly surfaced was that of Carlstein as a kind of hub, the unmoving center of the wheel that was the Gemini Club. While the others flitted around the world in their capacity as international movers and shakers, Carlstein stayed home, tending the fire, generating e-mail directives. Had that been his role at Oxford? No e-mail then, of course. As they sipped sherry and dangled muffins over the fire, had he said to them in turn: "When you grow up you'll do such and such and when my little brother gets out of diapers I'll arrange for him to be a Harvard MBA and have him appointed top banker and he will be our stooge. Then they'll invent e-mail—so don't expect me to travel, I'll work from home."

I had to get into his world; he would never come to mine except to destroy it.

I looked at my watch. Twenty minutes had passed. Strange; it had felt like time was as still as the man on the mailbox. I shook myself out of my stupor. Paula should have been back. Give it another minute?

No. She should have been back by now.

Boy Scout stealthcraft told me to go around the back of the house first: down the driveway and into a backyard of immaculate flower beds bordering a small patch of grass, as smooth as AstroTurf and with a pond at its center, fed by a concrete toddler endlessly pouring water from a small barrel. A paperback, bookmarked halfway through, lay in a deck chair facing the pond. I imagined Paula sitting there, reading, dozing, lifting her head from time to time to admire her nibble of paradise.

Edging along the back of the house I stopped to peer through a window. A patchwork of light and shadow, a display made uneven by the partial blocking effect of sparse trees on the rear boundary of the yard and the now descending sun. A kitchen counter, a table half in murk, a terracotta clock on the wall, and deeper into the house, light showing through from a front room. But no people, no noise.

I moved to the concrete stoop leading up to the back door, which I guessed led straight into the kitchen. The concrete was stained wet, the grass around its base soggy. It hadn't been raining and, while I imagined Paula as house-proud, even I didn't suppose that she would have swabbed the kitchen floor and thrown the slops out back before she would let me into the house.

I tried the door handle. It squeaked maddeningly but the door opened easily enough and I found myself in a kitchen, paneled in light American oak, homey and efficient. There was a wickerwork bowl on the counter next to the door brimming with keys and surplus fridge magnets, a tin of lubricating oil—presumably to fix the squeaky door hinge next to it, and a bowl of fruit on the shadowed section of the kitchen table; otherwise little else cluttering the surfaces, everything apparently tucked neatly into drawers and cupboards.

The terracotta clock ticked; there was no other sound.

But there was something in the air, a tang.

There was also something on the floor, a slick of water. The source of the smell?

The veneer of outward calm began to peel away.

Between the kitchen and the front room was a dividing wall about waist height and on it I could see shards of glass point viciously upward like some cruel and redundant security measure. Over some of the shards hung strips of glossy green. Seaweed?

I moved over to the dividing wall and looked into the room beyond.

And there she was. Paula kneeling, a sodden pile of multicolored offal-like material in front of her. But it wasn't offal; in the moment that it took for me to recognize Paula, I'd also divined much else about the scenario.

It was a pile of small fish, the tropical kind, a mound of golds, blues, and greens flecked through with silver. The dividing wall was three feet wide and along its length lay grit, weed, fishy toys, a rock pool or two sporting lifeless rainbows on their surface.

It had been the superstructure for what must have been a spectacular floor-to-ceiling aquarium. But now its residents formed a gelatinous pyramid on Paula's swampy carpet.

A shudder passed down Paula's back like a wave.

"I thought I was safe here," she murmured.

I walked out of the kitchen, down the hall, and entered the front room through the door. Crossing the carpet toward Paula, an unpleasant squelch accompanied each step. Kneeling beside her I placed an arm over her shoulder.

"I should never have got you embroiled in this," I said.

She held one of the fish in her outstretched palm. "Who did this?" An inch of faded blue, a streak of yellow, a dull dead fishy eye. "Was it McIntyre? Did he find out somehow, have us followed?"

Didn't Ernie once say that McIntyre was like a haddock with a beard? Did haddock prey on little fish?

I looked up and saw a parade of fish corpses tacked to the wall below an Ansel Adams print of Yosemite. Three rows of five, like the "kill" decals on a fighter plane.

Fifteen fish. Fifteen dead names on my apartment wall, on Carol's wall.

"No," I said. "It wasn't McIntyre. It was someone who is very angry about what happened on the FDR and wants to hurt me and anyone connected with me." It was also someone who seemed well able to trace people and get into their homes.

Paula got up and started to pull at one of the tacks on the wall to release a harpooned fish. When it was free she held it out to me.

"Colisa Sota," she said quietly. "Turquoise stripes on an orange background, like a kooky thumbprint. Pretty, so pretty. An underwater painting." She laid it gently on top of the mound, the fish pyre. "Now look."

"I knew every fish in the tank: the Poecilla, the Xiphophorus, the

Botia. With my eyes shut I can still see their colors, their shapes, the little telltale movements and flicks that singled them out, differentiated them. I knew what and how they ate, their reproductive cycles, their little personalities. Some might think me crazy, but I knew them as individuals, creatures each with their own special way of doing things."

I didn't think her crazy. The fishermen of Versova had their dignity; why not the fish woman of Deacon Avenue?

For five years I hadn't been aware of where she lived or that she was mother to a teeming subaqueous family. The only inkling I'd had, was one time when Paula expressed satisfaction with a plate of mahi-mahi at a fish restaurant down in South Street Seaport.

"I never knew," I said. "They must have been beautiful."

She shrugged. "I can get some more. You can order them off the Internet these days."

Poking me in the ribs, she added: "And I don't care how hurt you are, you can still help clear up this mess."

Despite the defiant pose, I knew that a part of her had been hooked, clubbed, and gutted along with her family. An irreplaceable part of her.

# FORTY-FOUR

Paula hadn't been kidding. An hour later, I was just starting to peel away a dozen or so towels from the front room carpet, a fresh plump pile ready to take their place. The vengeful victims of the FDR weren't going to get between Paula and a dry floor.

The broken glass was gone, the weed and grit and other aquarium paraphernalia in black trash bags. The fish disposed of—Paula wouldn't say how or where.

Only the open space between the kitchen and the front room testified to a more profound crevasse that had opened up in Paula's life.

I knew we probably shouldn't be hanging around like this. There was someone out there with a map and a pin stuck through the middle of Paula's house. They might want to make a return visit. But the cleanup was important, symbolically so. It had to be done. Just like sending my mother into the Arabian Sea. Everything else would have to wait.

"Fin." It was Paula. I hadn't heard her come into the room.

"That's enough housework," she said. "We should get out of here now. What do you plan on doing?"

"JJ Carlson's brother, Conrad Carlstein. I'm going to his house, see what I can find."

"What if he's home?" Paula asked.

As always, Paula had asked the key question.

"Get him out. Somehow."

"Maybe I can help, get him out, that is. Where's he live?"

"Oyster Bay, some small beach house owned by JJ. Except, of course, JJ didn't own anything. And, no, Paula. You're not coming—we have to put plenty of fresh air between you and this situation. That means we must go our separate ways. You've done more than enough."

"A beach house in the shadow of its big daddy on the hill," Paula said, almost a chant, her eyes shut, her lips pursed in an angry pain, her body swaying, swaying to the memory of something rotten.

Carol had said nothing of a large house nearby; only that it lay beyond a yacht club on Center Island, an isthmus crooking its coastline like a scooping hand to form Oyster Bay.

But I knew that someone else had just broken into Paula's life, someone who had sidestepped Paula's real estate, her chattels, left her fish alone. He had gone straight for Paula's body and soul.

"The big house," I said. "Is that where McIntyre attacked you?"

"I'm coming with you," she said.

"Surely . . ."

"What were you intending to use as wheels?" Paula cut in waspishly. "Who was going to direct you? Or were you set on the idea of discovering just how little public transportation there is on this island?"


Paula and I didn't look like the kind of couple who would be toting a hammer, flashlight, newspaper, and jar of honey, but when we set out, the Wal-Mart bag on the backseat of the Ford contained all four.

I'd had little choice but to let Paula come. It was her car. And it was as much her past as my present we were visiting. But I'd insisted she should stay in the car, in the background. She'd merely snorted and observed that I was no John Wayne and she was no blond bimbo, two statements with which it was impossible to disagree.

She wanted me to drive, she said; she would sit with the map on her lap and listen to soul on the radio. She would think.

And so it was, for the first ten or so miles of the journey north on short bland stretches of highway: Southern Parkway, Grand Central, 495. I lost track of them, but Paula would open her eyes at just the right moment, lift her hand languidly, and murmur, "This exit." Then back to the meditation.

When we left the roaring gray of parkways and expressways and became immersed in the lush, laid-back greenery unfolding on the North Shore, my cell phone rang.

"Harley showed me the letter." Carol's voice was firm. "He breached the rather lax security and intercepted my mail. For my own good, he said."

"You okay?" I asked cautiously.

"I think Harley hoped that I'd be on life support by now. If he couldn't have me, then no one could. Something like that."

I wondered, momentarily, how Harley was feeling, what he was doing to himself.

"I didn't think for a moment that you'd—"

"Sure," Carol cut in. "We all say all kinds of stuff in group. It helps to hear yourself say things out loud sometimes, then you realize just how crazy those thoughts are and you can banish them instantly."

"What are you going to do?" I asked.

"Keep busy. I've already been busy, made a phone call—besides this one."

"Who to?"

"Conrad Carlstein."

What? I was on the way to his place for possibly the most crucial unscheduled appointment of my life and she . . . and she . . . What the fuck did she think she was playing at?

"There was the small matter of some unfinished business," she quickly said, perhaps sensing the imminent flurry of incredulous "what-the's" on my part. "Maybe now it's time to get some closure on the issue." She was starting the slope down the other side of her high, the voice quavering slightly as if she was only now coming to realize the enormity of what she was saying.

"You want to get into Carlstein's house," she said.

I did, she knew that. It was the Plan.

"If you can wait until around midnight, then the house should be empty. I told you he was a night owl."

"What have you done?" But I knew.

"He thinks he's going to meet me at a hotel in Syosset."

"*Thinks* being the operative word, I hope. Where will you be?"

"At my mom's house in Scarsdale. She's in Florida right now." She paused. "Carlstein sounded like he was expecting my call, like I was only surrendering to an irresistible summons he'd started to transmit on the deck at his house. The man believes he sweats an unchallengeable phenome or pherome or whatever it's called."

"Are you sure he doesn't know where you are or where you will be?" If he could transmit, maybe he could receive as well.

"I don't see how."

The letter writer, the wall painter, the fish killer—they knew how. It obviously wasn't rocket science.

"You don't have to do this," I said.

"It's done already. If there's no car at the house, then it's on the way to me with him behind the wheel. If it's there, then I failed. And it's over to your Plan B."

I didn't have a Plan B.

"Thank you," I said.

"I'm not just doing it for you. Find something good, Fin. Carlstein's not going to like being stood up. Make it count. I don't know how fast he drives, but allow yourself no more than an hour in that house before you get the hell out. I can't give you a floor plan, so I can't tell you where he keeps the computer; I only remember the deck and some big open living area overlooking the water. That and the fact that I never want to go back there."

"I'll call you when I'm through."

"Sure. But if you get voicemail, it means I'm sleeping." She gave me her number in Scarsdale and then seemed to prime the defenses against any further meaningful dialogue.

Paula clicked her tongue. "Looks like I can sit in the car and be Jane to your Tarzan, after all," she said when I finally and reluctantly pressed the cancel key on the cell phone.

"Looks that way."

We slept in the car. I'd driven until we reached a park about ten miles from Oyster Bay and pulled up in the shaded corner of a lot that ran alongside. I'd gotten out Ernie's letter and the battered copy of Rudyard Kipling's *In Black and White*, determined to decode the language of the Geminis, but pain and fatigue corroded crossword puzzle reasoning: numbers on a sheet of paper, words in a book. How and where did they meet? ABC, one-two-three. Discrete worlds. It should be straightforward enough, I thought. Find the pattern and substitute. The sun was low, it was warm, a gentle breeze zephered through the open window, I could hear the birdsong syncopate with the little snicks of Paula's breathing.

Paula awoke when I returned to the car after taking my legs for a short postsleep stretch.

It was dark, the lot was empty, and we had just under an hour to cover the final tranche to Center Island, more than enough time.

"You want to get out and unbend yourself?" I asked the yawning Paula. "We've got plenty of time."

She shook her head. "Let's get this over with."

We drove.

"You know what—at first McIntyre was charming," Paula said suddenly. "He showed me around the place, talked me through the paintings on the walls, the landscapes, the portraits—not his own family, I wasn't sure it was even his own house. Anyway, he said the place had been built by the son of a bootlegger who'd gotten respectable. He told me that most money cast a shadow, that the French were maybe right when they said money had no smell, but they ignored the shadow, always a shadow. I remember laughing and asking what lay in the shadow of his millions. He seemed to take my question seriously and thought hard. History will have to be the judge of that, he said."

Paula took some gum out of her bag and handed me a strip before folding a piece against her teeth and closing her lips around it. She seemed to suck hard on it, as if its spearmint sap would strengthen her against the fury of her memory.

"I was at the house to help prepare for a symposium of bigshot lawyers who were flying in for a powwow on international regulatory cooperation. Naïvely, I suggested that cooperation sounded like a good idea. He was polite but dismissed my childish outlook."

I could imagine it. The highbrow lawyer talking down to his secretary, his condescension at the idea that cooperation was good in and of itself. For him, cooperation would be bullshit, bad for business, had to be scattered, sabotaged. Division, diversity, plurality spawned uncertainty, a quicksand of uncertainty from which only the lawyers could pull the poor bewildered businessman and for which they could charge egregiously.

"He asked me if I was shocked by his cynicism," Paula continued. "He was oily and unsteady with drink, kind of scared and careless all at once. I decided to play cool, I was used to his dark view on things anyway and so made out I didn't understand him, that I was the airhead he always supposed me to be. But cool wasn't going to work this time, he seemed to have his moves all mapped out regardless, all the angles covered like one of those kung-fu guys who know what you're going to do before you do. Everything moved quickly, kind of blurry, like being wheeled on a trolley from the ward to the operating room, looking up—the ceiling lights, faces with masks, muffled talk. Then I was sitting in a chair in a room with one light on. No portraits on the wall, just lewd stuff, Indian—kama sutra, real dirty, people in knots; except the wall in front of me didn't have pictures, only a mirror. And McIntyre was standing over me, a knife at my neck, a hunting knife, I think, the sort of blade that Rambo would use."

I mentally felt the weight of the knife, its carefully engineered ridges and serrations—precision intimidation.

Paula removed the gum from her mouth and carefully folded the tinfoil wrapper around it and dropped it in the ashtray. The muscles in her face tightened.

"He made me do things to myself. Things that I couldn't imagine, things that God has been kind enough to smudge in my head. But the stain's still there. And all the while he threatened me, my family, Doug. Told me what would happen to them if I didn't play ball, if I didn't do the kind of things that a black bitch does, if I didn't keep my silence. He didn't touch me with his hands. Talk and the knife—stroking me, turning circles on my skin, playing with pressure, seeing how far it could go without cutting. And his hand was a piston, down . . . down there. On himself."

She looked out of the window for a while. "And I was thinking. If I had stood up to him later, taken it all the way, ruined him, then none of this would be happening and we wouldn't have to take this drive. As it was, I agreed to the price that I thought was at the high end of what people like me could get: seventy thousand dollars and a ticket back to the pigsty."

"I doubt whether much would have been different," I said. "Except that you might have gotten killed." Then I asked, "Did you ever tell Doug what happened?"

"Not the detail," she said. "Just that McIntyre made a pass, acted improperly. Doug had a theory about McIntyre and his kind. It was a Wall Street thing, he'd say. How anyone who was anyone only wanted compliant shadows around them. They want you to be faded—the color of the wall. Then they'd need something from you. And if you didn't give it to them they'd get mad. They'd smash up the things you love, just so you knew who controlled the place. When Doug knew his condition was terminal, he'd read me newspaper articles about rich or famous people who'd died of cancer. He was straight about it, he said it cheered him up to know that these guys couldn't take out a contract on cancer and have it rubbed out. It was a great leveler, he said."

"He was right," I said.

"He was right about a lot of things, I guess," she said. "I doubt if his view would have been different if I'd told him the full story. It would just reinforce his theory, wouldn't it?"

"Yes."

"He wasn't religious or anything, but he always said that what Jesus preached about the meek inheriting the earth made him feel real good." Her voice cracked. "I just told him that was his excuse for being weak." She turned away from me; her shoulders shook a little. "I shouldn't have said that to him," she murmured.

"We all say things we shouldn't." But maybe that wasn't as bad as saying nothing at all.

# FORTY-FIVE

I turned to Paula. "How far?" I asked.

Her slender finger snaked along the map, dimly lit by the courtesy light. If her finger stopped, maybe we'd stop too.

"A town, then the causeway to Center Island," she said.

"Which town?"

"Bayville," she said without looking at the map. She was only giving me information I needed.

Bayville. That was the post office box address for Preeti. I could see Raj's flame-wreathed face in the windshield, telling me the box number: 9735.

We were driving through a leafy residential area, no sign of the water that I assumed lapped against the borders of the seaside-sounding town. "How soon? Bayville, I mean."

"Soon," Paula said. A sign welcoming us to Bayville immediately came into view and, turning a sharp right, we found ourselves on a waterfront, a beach stretching into darkness to one side and a modest, but amiable, row of shops and restaurants on the other.

My stomach contracted as we passed a small carnival, unlit, its little bumper cars draped in canvas, reminiscent of the wretched carnival on Chowpatty Beach on the way to the Towers of Silence. I sensed my foot press harder on the accelerator.

We were soon out of the town and the gray-black scenery spread around us, flat as a page. It was all beach, empty but for the skeletons of lifeguard towers and the odd, abandoned inflatable kiddy-boat or spade sticking out of the sand, as if some midget gravedigger had been disturbed and skadaddled. Even the late-night barbecuers had crawled home, leaving their scorched signatures and empty bottles.

A convoy of three limos came toward us.

Windows and sunroofs open. Drunk, tired, and happy revelers hanging out or standing up saluting or waving. A topless girl swirling her bra like a lasso above her head.

As they passed us, they hung farther out from the car, whistling and shouting. The causeway narrowed, and the beach all but disappeared. A dark shadow loomed ahead, a few lights winking above sea level indicating that the shadow was land. Center Island.

Another two limos passed. Clones of the first three.

There were lights at sea level too, on the road in front of me, not a car though. A light from a window. I slowed down.

There was a booth and a barrier. Fancy houses meant fancy security.

And next to the booth was a police car.

I picked up the map to see if there were any other points of entry. Stupid. It was a fucking island.

Carol had mentioned a yacht club. A summer party maybe. I glanced at the map.

I was now almost alongside the booth. Inside, a fat cop started to heave himself out of an easy chair in front of a little television.

I let my window open. The cop slid back the glass and poked his head out.

I smiled. "Cleaners for the Seawanaka Yacht Club."

The cop nodded and laughed. "It must be some party they're having up there."

"You bet," I said, slapping my hand against the steering wheel and returning the laugh. "I got a trunk full of clean-o-crap and ten extra pairs of rubber gloves."

The cop moved away from the glass divider and opened the door to the booth.

"You won't mind if I take a quick look inside. Just routine. I hope you folks don't take offense."

"Sure." I nodded, easing the gear shift into reverse, but keeping my foot on the brake.

As the cop swept his flashlight across the backseat, I could see headlights weaving toward us. A horn sounded.

The cop stood back. "Sweet Jesus." He sighed.

He moved back toward the booth as a pickup loaded up with about six teenagers in tuxedos and evening dresses came to an uneasy stop, inches away from the barrier.

"Say, Miller," shouted one of the teenagers, waving a bottle of champagne like it was a flag. "Open up. How about it?"

The cop turned to me. "See what I mean?" he said under his breath. "I wouldn't want to clean up after these assholes." He waddled into the booth and the barrier rose.

"Josh," the cop shouted as the pickup tore past, "there's a patrol not far up ahead, so I better not hear you been stopped and found DWI."

Through the exhaust and teenage laughter I could just make out: "You got it, Officer Miller-not-so-Lite."

I pointed at my watch. "I don't want to be rude, but—" The barrier was still up, but I didn't want to rush it unless I had to. If I ever wanted to get off the island, I'd have to come back this way.

"Heck, sure." Miller waved us through with a broad grin. "You be sure and drop off some of the half-empties on your way out of here."

Paula leaned across me. "You got it, Officer Miller," she said huskily.

The island's hinterland closed in around us. We were on a narrow road lined with high shrubs and big gates blocking long driveways to big houses.

"What kind of American accent do you call that?" Paula asked.

"The kind employed by a Brit who wants to sound like a contract cleaner who hasn't just shit his pants."

"We were lucky that Miller was a Grade A klutz. Next time you want to go native, warn me so I can bale out."

"That was a pretty neat idea about the Seawanaka Yacht Club, though?"

"You got lucky." Getting a compliment out of Paula was harder than making a claim for a stolen camera on a vacation insurance policy.

We heard the Seawanaka Yacht Club before we saw it. Or rather, we felt it. A seismic bass from a music system pumped through the car.

As we passed the white floodlit frontage of the club, we could see gaggles of partygoers goofing around on the front lawn, necking, throwing-up, tossing bottles and cans at each other, passing joints, usual party behavior. In the background, yacht masts swung in unison, kindly sentinels to carousing youth.

I drove carefully through a confusion of turning cars and exhausted bodies. The light faded and the music died back to a gentle vibration as we turned a corner and found ourselves looking out over an oily black slice of bay.

The road meandered toward a hill, and two houses gradually took shape out of the shadows. As I headed for the nearer, smaller one, I became aware that Paula, her face drained, had her eyes locked on the mansion at the top of the hill.

"You okay?" I asked.

"Just drive."

We coasted a little farther and stopped about twenty yards away from Carlstein's front door. A swathe of light spilled from an uncurtained picture window.

I heaved the Wal-Mart bag off the backseat and got out of the car. Almost immediately, I felt a sting on my hand, my burnt hand. Then I heard the whine of mosquitoes. To my left, a cloud of the little bastards circled above the lagoon, ready to scramble.

Ankle-high garden lights lit the uneven steps leading up to the front entrance. The door was the only piece of wood I could see; the rest of the one-story house seemed to be sheet glass. It didn't bode well for the means of entry I had I mind.

I skirted the garage—door open, thankfully empty—and went around the back, finding myself on a deck that projected out over the bay.

The tide was coming in. Beneath me, I could just about make out a pile of rocks and a few hunks of steel-sprouting concrete, fringed by water.

A loud crackle and fizz broke the silence. I wheeled around.

A mosquito zapper smoldered in an alcove at the back of the house. I tried hard to regain a normal breathing rate before peering into the shadows around it. There was a conventional window, to a bedroom, I guessed, in the wall to my right.

I took out my honey, newspaper, and hammer and laid them on the ground beneath it, but before going any farther, I checked the sliding glass doors that ran down one side of the deck. I didn't want the humiliation of finding one was open after I'd smashed my way in.

It was locked.

I checked the time. Fifty minutes to go.

The lid on the honey jar didn't want to budge and I was contemplating using the hammer when it suddenly gave and spun open.

Using one of the sheets of paper, I smeared a thick layer of honey over the window and then stuck another sheet flat across it, like a giant stamp on an envelope. I looked at the newsprint. Classified ads. I'd been careful to choose a section that didn't have anything featuring me.

Picking up the hammer, I gave the window a smart tap. There was a satisfyingly muffled crack and I saw the paper start to sag and split. I gathered up the broken glass before it fell to the ground.

I listened for an alarm, then reached through the hole and undid the catch.

Although the bottom of the frame was less than three feet off the ground, climbing into the darkened room reopened my wounds, and they hurt like hell.

I eased the curtain back and stood at the threshold. I felt my heart pounding. The wounds throbbed in unison. I breathed in, as slowly and deeply as I could; a blend of eau de toilette, stale sweat, incense, and maybe dope.

The room was silent, but it didn't feel empty. There was a low groan from somewhere to my left, followed by a series of juddering breaths. The hairs prickled on the back of my neck. I'd never felt them do that before.

The light wasn't good enough to see the bed immediately. There was a door ajar, a glimmer of tile beyond. The bathroom. Gradually, the outline of a dressing table started to coalesce, the reflection of the window I'd just climbed through bouncing back at me from a large, oval mirror.

I started to edge carefully to what I hoped would be the door out of the room.

Suddenly I felt something soft underfoot. A cushion? I stood still, let my heart slow down a little, and then moved one foot gently forward, testing the terrain. It was like walking across a minefield.

It wasn't a cushion, too big.

As my instep hit a solid obstacle, I heard a moan rise from the floor. I raised my hammer, then realized, in a flash of panic, what I was treading over. A futon. Of course. Carlstein wasn't the sort to have a four-poster and a Posturepedic mattress.

I froze, expecting the moan to mature into something more substantial. But it faded and I felt the body beneath me squirm and stretch, then settle once more. I let the hammer hang loosely by my side. I wasn't quite sure why I'd brought it with me.

My heart machine-gunned, like the clock that was ticking against me. But my body remained motionless.

At length, I knelt down. I could now hear short, rasping breaths, hardly audible above the sound of the ocean. Something didn't add up. I listened harder. There were too many breaths. Some were squeaky, others clicked.

I reached out my hand and touched skin, a face, soft, hairless, but cold and clammy. I could feel the warmth of more than one body waft up from under the comforter.

I eased myself upright. Biting my lip as I felt the wound on my hip split and start to suppurate.

Backing away, I tried to get my bearings again before moving to the other side of the room. I tested each inch of the floor in front of me with the toe of my shoe. No more bodies. I raised my watch, but couldn't see the dial. I felt as if I'd been in this room for the whole of my life.

I found the door and moved through into a hallway, only a little lighter than the bedroom but light enough for me to read the time. I'd been in the bedroom for fifteen minutes.

There was an archway to my left, beyond which I could make out a large open space, possibly the living room. To my right, three more doors.

First door, another bathroom.

Second, another bedroom, curtains tied back and light enough to see a single bed—made up and empty.

Third door. This room was dark, the curtains drawn. Again the smell of incense and dope, but no bedroom aroma, emptier and somehow more businesslike. I hesitated and then turned on the light.

A study.

If the pictures on the wall at Baba Mama's were colorful, then the gallery around this wall was a riot. Unsmiling faces stared out from knotted bodies in every conceivable convolution of union. Rapture was expressed through color rather than expression; golds, blues, reds danced in ecstasy around the actors and actresses in this finely drawn sex show and clothing dissolved into the background while key genital features were thrust, literally, to the fore: pink, pert, wanton.

My eyes were finally drawn away from the wall to a neat drawerless desk, modern and out of place. A computer monitor and keyboard sat at its center, the disk drive on the floor beneath, alongside a laser printer. There was nothing else. No books, no papers, no filing, no nest of goodies for the curious intruder. Only an old shoebox next to the printer, its lid askew. I laid the hammer down beside it.

One tap of the space bar on the keyboard and a screensaver culled from the wall gallery burst into life.

Twenty-five minutes. Thirty-five remaining.

I took a look in the computer document folder. There was plenty there, and all of it password protected. There was only one word that wouldn't be a wild guess.

I typed in *Gemini*.

Invalid password. I looked at the wall for inspiration. Unless the password was cock in every orifice, then I was out of luck.

There was no point hanging around hoping that it would pop spontaneously into my mind.

Maybe *Gemini was* the password, but not for the document folder.

I switched back to Carlstein's Internet page, but didn't attempt to go on line. I clicked on his mailbox and let the sent/saved e-mail menu drop like a flag. I tried to open the "saved" e-mail file.

Password protected. I typed in *Gemini.*

Invalid password.

Lateral thinking, crossword thinking.

*Havala.*

Invalid password.

*Badla.*

Fuck, fuck, fuck.

I needed time, oceans of it; that and an armchair and a gin and tonic, maybe an ambient CD on in the background.

*Huxtable.*

*You'll never get it, dimwit head.*

What about Towers of Silence? No: it would be one word, short, pithy.

Something connected with the Towers?

The name signaled from the Netherlands Antilles by Paula. The name that was a place.

*Dakma.*

Invalid password.

*Give up.*

Fuck you. There's an *h* in Dakma; Paula spelled it out, remember?
*Dakhma.*

Ten e-mails. He didn't keep much on the system; they were only a day or two old.

A glance at my watch, the leaking hourglass.

I opened e-mail number one. A header from someone called Ram Narian, aimed at a Durga Dass. The e-mail consisted almost entirely of numbers, a couple of pages of them. Just like the e-mails in the Huxtable file at Askari's office.

I printed it out.

On to e-mail two. This time to a Jowar Singh. More numbers. More paper spewed from the laser printer.

Three was to a high-class purveyor of oriental erotica based in Munich. All words—some distinctly colorful—but no numbers.

The cursor seemed sluggish, scrolling in slow motion. The printer didn't move at the speed of light, not even the speed of sound. Time flew, everything else just fucking dawdled.

I was opening e-mail eight when the door swung open and slammed against the wall.

Miranda Carlson stood there. She was even smaller than I'd remembered her from JJ's funeral, her face now somehow dehumanized and unhealthy, staring at me as a sick or wounded animal might at something threatening. A tatty feral thing in a stained blue nightdress.

Then she ran at me, her nails clawing for my face.

She was shrieking.

It didn't take much to get her to the ground; it was like pacifying a rag-doll. But she had drawn blood; I could feel a trickle of it down my cheek.

And she was still screaming.

I clamped my hand over her mouth until noise and movement subsided. I released my hand and her eyes shut and she started to sag.

Tucking her under my arm, I half-carried, half-dragged her down the hallway and into the living room. It was still dark outside, the panoramic window a mirror on a man struggling with a life-size doll.

I grappled with the locks on the front door and wrenched it toward me. My hand jarred badly as the door froze after an inch of movement.

I released the chain and stepped onto the stone veranda.

Paula was waiting for me.

"Take her to the car," I said. "She's sick."

Paula ran up the steps and gently took Miranda from me.

Time was just about up.

I ran back into the house.

Grabbing the e-mails from the printer with one hand, I flung the mouse around with the other and returned the screen to the start-up mode. In a few minutes it would revert to the saver and then dive into standby sometime after that. It didn't really matter, though. Carlstein would see soon enough that he was one window short and he was unlikely to blame it on the mosquitoes.

I turned around to find myself staring at a small child, a girl in a filthy pair of bunny rabbit pajamas.

"Mummy," she whimpered.

"I'll take you to her," I said, with a gentleness that surprised me.

I picked her up and ran to the front door.

She started screaming. "Way, way, way." Over and over.

"Yes, honey, we're going away," I soothed. "Right now. Away from this nasty place."

As Paula ran up the steps to take the girl, I saw headlights scythe across the horizon.

"Want way," the girl yelled as she struggled in Paula's arms.

"I told you, honey, we're going away."

"For Christ's sake, Fin," Paula snapped. "Miranda has two kids, doesn't she? There's a boy as well. Is she saying the boy's called Ray?"

"Shit. Ray, hon? Ray? You want Ray?"

She nodded sullenly.

As I ran back into the house, I could hear the car getting closer.

I crashed into the bedroom and flicked on the light and surveyed the clutter of clothes, bed linen, and a lot more besides. But no people, not even little people.

I heard a giggle and ran into the hallway.

A child's giggle coming from Carlstein's study.

Under the desk and with both hands in the shoebox was Ray.

I started to pull him away from the box.

"Cars, want cars," he screamed.

Inside the box was a jumble of die-cast model automobiles and what looked like miniature houses and walls.

"Okay, okay," I snapped and picked a car out for him. A red Ferrari, he'd like that.

The little boy struggled. "All of them, want all of them."

I grabbed the side of the box and caught the boy in the crook of my elbow, jerking him off the ground and against my flaming hip.

"We go," I said firmly, then reached down and picked up the hammer with my free hand.

I ran out of the house to see the grizzled figure of Carlstein at the rear door of the Ford with Paula shrinking back into the car, covering Miranda and the little girl.

Carlstein turned to me, his features buried by rough hair, his eyes burning under lush brows. "You've returned the black one to me. The last time I saw her was from behind a mirror. Before the night is out, shards from that mirror will carve epitaphs deep into every one of you." The voice was without contour, only the merest trace of a German accent.

I saw Paula's hand dart out from inside the car and slice across his face. Carlstein didn't seem to notice and no blood appeared.

"Leave them alone," I yelled. I made it to the car faster than I could have believed and with one arm around my grumbling bundle, I swung the hammer with my free hand and delivered a creditable blow to Carlstein's shoulder.

He fell back, his face now contorted in surprise and pain.

Momentarily I didn't know what to do next. Deliver another blow, or get out of there?

Paula's hand reached out of the car. "Give the boy to me."

I handed over the boy and the box to Paula and jerked the driver's door open.

Carlstein had recovered a little and his hand was curled around the edge of the door as I started to close it. I looked into his face, the hairy weather-beaten terrain contradicting a row of unrealistically white teeth, now slightly bared. For a moment I expected him to say something, *explain* himself. But he just stared at me.

I gave the handle a vicious jerk and felt it crunch Carlstein's hand against the frame.

He screamed and fell back.

I started the engine and accelerated hard, feeling the back wheels slither and spin.

The track curved away from Carlstein's house, ran along the end of mosquito lagoon, then seemed to loop up toward the big house. Where was the turnoff to the blacktop?

I looked behind me. Carlstein was back in the silver Toyota, a four-wheel drive, huge—lumbering but lithe, a motor home with warp power—and I could see it yaw as he floored the accelerator and started to close the gap.

I nearly missed it. A hairpin right onto another track leading around the lagoon and back to the main road.

Swinging the wheel, I hit a rut. As the car lurched, a productive retch sounded from the backseat.

"Bad news, counselor . . ." Paula sounded surprisingly calm.

"It's okay, I can smell it," I said.

Ahead I could see the blacktop. I speeded up.

I was able to snatch glimpses of the Toyota, across the lagoon, bouncing along the track, raising a cloud of cinder and stones. That monster could eat stones and shit them out the back.

The junction between track and blacktop was marked by an uneven ridge of asphalt that we hit at thirty. It wasn't fast but we all felt it. The front wheels ground against their arches as we landed and I fought to keep the car on the road. The shingle beach lay four feet below the embankment on the far side.

The relief at finding myself facing forward and in possession of four still-inflated tires was soon overshadowed by the flash of silver in my rearview mirror.

Ahead of us, on our left, was the Seawanaka. The party was over. Guests clustered around the entrance as people and limos spilled lazily onto the road. I sounded my horn and flashed my lights and swept past them.

I took another look in the mirror. No bodies in the road, no overturned cars. Only the headlights of a silver Toyota, fifty feet behind me.

The ride through the winding lane between the Yacht Club and the causeway was a blur of swerves, as I fought my way around two or three slow-moving limos filled with drunken teenagers. In this environment Carlstein and I were pretty evenly matched, but sooner or later, the relative pedigrees of our automobiles would decide the matter.

Headlights filled the rearview mirror; they could only be a few feet away. They flashed: from full beam, to dipped. On off, on off. Meaningless, threatening Morse Code.

Suddenly our car shuddered violently as the Toyota accelerated and rammed us. My head hit the steering wheel, and I heard the cell phone fly from the passenger seat and fall heavily against the bulkhead of the floor. Pitiful cries came from the backseat.

We emerged from the cover of trees and onto the causeway toward the sentry post.

I'd forgotten Officer Miller-not-so-Lite. I really had. I almost laughed out loud. Then again, what would I have done differently, if I *had* remembered him? Would I have given more thought as to whether it would be better to give myself up to him or have him rescue us from the bouncing headlights?

Maybe I would have thought about it more, but the answer would have remained a resolute "no."

I slowed up as we approached the booth, figuring that Carlstein wouldn't pull anything in the vicinity of Bayville's finest. In the rearview mirror, the glare was less intense, hanging back a little, not hugging what was left of my rear fender, and he had dipped his headlights, now a thoughtful late-night motorist rather than the silver angel of death.

The barrier was open and Miller was chatting to the driver of a small truck. *Courtly Catering Corp.* was emblazoned in gold paint on its side.

As I crawled through the narrow gap between the truck and the railing, Miller waved at me.

I took a swift look at my backseat: Paula with one arm around a slumped Miranda, the other slung over a lumpy coat—presumably the children underneath. Paula had tried to account for everything, only Miranda's blue nightdress seemed incongruous. But there was no time to improvise further.

I waved back at Miller, fixed a grin on my face, and wound down the window.

"You got anything for me?" Miller asked cheerily.

"Sorry, officer. The empties were empty. Not a drop."

He pointed at the backseat. "Looks like you picked up some stragglers, though."

Miller laughed and said something I couldn't hear to the man in the truck. Then he waved me through. "You drive safely, y'hear."

The Toyota edged forward but couldn't get through the gap and had to wait for Courtly Catering Corp. to finish its conference with Miller. But I knew it wouldn't be long before I'd have silver on my tail again.

I accelerated. The plan was to get through Bayville and, assuming the Toyota wasn't right behind me as we hit the sharp left at the end of the shorefront, to peel off immediately into a side road, or even a driveway, and let Carlstein roar by. At least, that was how they did it in the movies.

"He still with us?" Paula had raised herself and turned to look out of the rear window. "Shit," she said, answering her own question. "A way off and a small truck between him and us. But he's still there."

The road was clear. The beach was deserted. In a few short hours the place would be packed with vacationers.

My father had said that when he retired, he was going to live near a beach, the one in Corfu. The one in the photo.

My plans didn't stretch much beyond the turn at the end of Bayville.

The hands around my neck were killer hands.

Nails dug into the skin around my Adam's apple, the bony fingers pressed deep. Even before I realized I was struggling for oxygen, I could feel my eyes bulge.

And she swung me from side to side. My wig started to come loose, obscuring my view of the road.

"You bastard. You lousy shit." Miranda's words were carried on hot, vomit-stained breath; burning spittle rained on my cheek.

As she swung me, I gripped the steering wheel with my burnt right hand and tried to release myself from Miranda's grip with my left. The car zigzagged crazily, slicing into the shoulder and throwing up a shower of pebbles before tearing across the road to perform the same trick on the other side.

"*You bastard,*" Miranda screamed.

I was going to lose control completely in a matter of seconds. If I hit the beach, the car would roll or stop dead.

Paula had started to get hold of Miranda and the grip loosened for a second, long enough for me to grab a breath, clear wig hair out of my eyes, before the vice was reapplied.

To my left was a wide gap in the shingle leading into an empty parking lot, an acre or three of level asphalt.

I turned the wheel and braked, feeling the car list dangerously. I accelerated into the parking lot.

In the rearview mirror, I saw the flash of gold as Courtly Catering Corp. carried on into Bayville. Then the silver of the Toyota appeared and swerved into the parking lot behind me.

"Let go of him, you fool," Paula screamed. "We want to help you."

"You crazy fucks have killed me."

I heard the sound of knuckle meeting jaw at high velocity and the grip around my throat loosened and fell away.

There were several options. Stop; then meet and greet with Carlstein. The several acres of parking lot were deserted. Officer Miller was a mile away, hanging on to the shirttails of the Seawanaka hoedown.

I could leave the parking lot and continue with the chase. Brother. I wasn't cut out for this.

Or . . .

On one side of the lot there was a pedestrian tunnel that ran under the road and led to the beach. It was low, but wide, though drifts of sand had clogged its edges.

I played out a few circuits with the Toyota glued to my rear fender, reaching eighty on the straight, swerving around the occasional parked car.

On the third lap, I put the tunnel in my sights and aimed.

I was doing sixty when I hit the lip of the ramp leading down to the tunnel. Too fast and I would fly into the roof of the underpass, too slow and I would clog up in the sand drifts.

"*What the f . . . ,*" I heard Paula scream in disbelief.

The futility of ducking was obvious to me, but that didn't stop the reflex action. The steering wheel pressed harshly into my forehead as the car turned dark. But the roof was still on.

I braked.

I heard a thunderous smash and thought for a moment that the road was going to collapse on top of us.

Raising my head, I turned to look behind us. Paula was doing the same. Even Miranda, spaced-out and sporting a livid red bruise on her left cheek, seemed mesmerized by the sight. A giant Toyota snout poked into the entrance of the tunnel, headlights still on, engine roaring. Carlstein's car was juddering like a harpooned whale, caught by the pillars halfway along the car, pinioned against the ceiling of the underpass.

The heads of the two kids poked out, wide-eyed, from under the coat.

I got out of the car and walked back down the tunnel. I didn't know quite what to expect, quite what I wanted.

The noise. I wanted the hideous noise to stop.

The windshield frame was ripped away, exposing the interior, like it was a 3D graphic design, cut away to maximize the impact of the interior layout.

Carlstein was slumped against the wheel, smothered by the airbag.

I went around to the side of the vehicle and reached in to find the ignition key. I fumbled around the steering column, but his arm was in the way. I didn't want to touch bare flesh, so I withdrew and pushed gently at the white cotton shirt to try and separate the body from the steering column.

Staggering back, I clamped my hand against my mouth.

Blood spurted over Carlstein's shoulders and down his shirt front.

He no longer had a head.

Edging along the side of the car, I looked on the rear seat. I could see his face in a tangle of metal, staring at me in surprise, his ponytail as pert as a palm tree.

For an instant, I embraced a vision of Carlstein, a Zen-like sense that I was a collection of molecules in a universe of molecules, that Carlstein was still a collection of molecules, just that some of them were occupying a different position in space from a few moments earlier. And that if space and time were illusory, then nothing really had changed: Carlstein was still Carlstein. He was behind the windshield of a Toyota or a two-way mirror watching McIntyre forcing Paula to violate herself. Still exerting, controlling, manipulating, potent as ever to violate and invade.

A less metaphysical thought struck me: All this wasn't just about Non-Resident Indians and money laundering. It couldn't be. The Gemini Club wasn't a League of Gentlemen looking to subsidize the wine tab. There had to be a monstrous baseness at its heart.

With that thought I turned to more practical and immediate issues.

When I moved to switch off the Toyota's engine, it occurred to me that getting the Ford out of the tunnel wasn't a simple matter of driving forward. Within yards we'd be on the beach in three feet of sand, immovable.

That meant reversing the Toyota, dealing with Carlstein's torso.

I ripped the airbag from its mooring and reached across to unlock the seat belt still slung over his shoulder and across his chest. I felt the blood soak into my own clothes. The belt itself was saturated. I glanced at his neck. Apart from the blood, it looked like a piece of complex electrical equipment undergoing a major overhaul on a workbench.

I pushed the body so it lay awkwardly over the armrest and onto the passenger seat, and then perched myself on the edge of the driver's seat. Squeezing my leg into the cavity under the steering column, I slid the transmission into reverse and pressed the accelerator. The engine screamed and there was the abrasive shriek of metal on stone before the Toyota sprang from the tunnel's clutches. I straightened the wheel and the car started to drift up the ramp.

Could we be seen from the road?

It was academic; we just had to get out of there.

I allowed the car to go twenty feet or so before braking and turning off the engine.

Paula and Miranda stood in front of the Ford. Miranda was shaking violently, knuckles white in the headlights as she clutched at the coat that was draped around her shoulders.

The bridge rumbled as a car went over it. Paula and I held our breath, and Miranda started to groan.

The car carried on toward Bayville.

# FORTY-SIX

**W**e needed a haven, a refuge. To regroup and consolidate. Do things real humans do: eat, pee, rest. And then?

Go to Paula's? No way. I didn't want to sleep with the fishes.

I looked in the mirror; nothing more threatening than a UPS truck.

Nobody said anything, not even to curse the stink in the car.

I was worried about Miranda, she looked pretty sick.

Pablo's wife. Julia. A nurse, Pablo had said.

He'd be asleep.

I tried the cell phone. Dead. The fall to the floor had crippled it, ruined the battery maybe.

It was a risk, but I pulled up at a gas station to use a pay phone.

I dialed Pablo's number.

"*Si.*" He obviously dreamed in Spanish.

"Carlstein's dead," I said.

"Sheesh. You kill him?" There was a loud crack, the phone falling to floor maybe. "Don't answer that." He sounded wide awake now.

"No, Pablo, I didn't kill him." It was a bridge that had killed him.

"But I've got some sick people here. I need to come to your place. Perhaps Julia can take a look and see whether we need to go to the emergency room."

"There's a limit to what I can do, Fin," Pablo moaned.

"Nothing unethical, Pablo. I'll only pressure you within the envelope of what's okay and it's hardly unethical to take in Miranda Carlson and her kids, is it? Just for a few hours . . ."

"Fuck. You didn't say it was her."

"Well, it is. Now just give me your address."

He moaned some more and then told me.

I then called Carol's number in Scarsdale. Voicemail. Maybe she wasn't there yet, perhaps she was but was sleeping—she'd said that was a possibility. At least Carlstein couldn't get to her.

But, with the cell phone out of commission, she couldn't call me.

I left a short message: We're okay, will call later, love you.

"We're going to Tochera's house," I said to Paula on returning to the car. "I tried Carol. No answer."

"Another JJ victim," Miranda murmured.

"I thought I was the villain of the piece," I said.

"Why did you pick me up? The kids were asleep and I was . . ." Her voiced trailed into nothing.

"We didn't come to find you, but we found you," I said. "You were sick, needed help. I knew we couldn't just leave you there."

She leaned forward, the warm cloud of her acid breath on my neck. "Maybe you knew more than you knew."

I sensed her press back into her seat.

She continued, as if we didn't exist. "For eight years JJ kept me in a doll's house," she said. "The world wasn't supposed to crash into our lives. Not the real world. Everything was supposed to be perfect on Park Avenue."

Park Avenue? What about the aerie on Central Park West—it must have been the bachelor pad, for nights when he wasn't married. I wondered if Miranda even knew of its existence. The wife is always the last to know.

In the rearview mirror, I could see her pull the kids toward her. They were quiet now, subdued.

"And then you and that car," she said.

"You don't seriously think I owned that car?" I tried to submerge the anger I felt, tried to occupy her place for a moment: a mother, a widow, something—Christ knew what—in Carlstein's life. A body self-evidently wracked by bone-rotting weariness.

"We were like something out of a magazine," she said. "I didn't really understand what he did, except that he was the best. You know, the dumb trophy wife thing. And I sure as hell didn't know about the drugs." She laughed. "Or about Carol Amen. There were others; I always knew. You can just tell. But he kept them out of our lives; he even used to get mad if he heard someone had split up because of another woman. He used to shout about it and say they must be crazy." She paused. "But Carol Amen. Conrad said she was different, not one of JJ's casual fucks."

I felt a vicious stab at the back of my head, a finger. "You were the only one who managed it."

"Managed what?" I asked cautiously.

"To take something from him that he really wanted."

Except that I hadn't. I'd been Carol's ruse, her tunnel out of Camp JJ. I'd only taken her after JJ was dead.

Miranda was quiet for a while. I could see her stroking the children's hair as her eyes flickered blankly across the passing scenery.

"And despite everything he was supposed to have, he left us nothing," she said suddenly.

"What happened to it?" I asked. "He was rich, super rich."

"It's off the map," Miranda said. "In a trust. Everything he had is in the trust. And I'm not a beneficiary. Nor are the kids. Some bastard attorney in the Antilles told me I wasn't an object of the trust." She gulped hard. For a moment I thought she was going to throw up again.

"Object," she managed. "What kind of word is that for his family? *Object?* Jesus."

"Is the trust called Huxtable?" I asked.

Miranda groaned like I'd hit her. "Yes."

JJ had wrapped his life up and pushed it out to sea. Or someone had done it for him. Carlstein? The Geminis?

"They wanted me out of the house," Miranda said. "They told me I could stay a couple weeks. Big of them. But Conrad showed up. I didn't know that JJ even had a brother until the day before the funeral. That's when I learned the real family name. Anyway, he said he was going to take us in."

I wondered if she knew that Carlstein's house had been JJ's or, rather, Huxtable's. I wondered if she knew that Carol had been privy to the existence of a brother, to the existence of a prior name, that she'd known about all that long before Miranda.

Miranda let her window down and turned her face into the wind.

After a while, she pulled back her head and closed the window. "Conrad was good to us. For a while I thought he was just a harmless old hippy, nothing like JJ. But I soon learned that he was all about manipulation: first JJ, then me. And then I found him in the study with the kids, pointing at the pictures, explaining them. He laughed at my anger, my fear. He seemed so confident that he could control me with that brain of his, and if not that, those pills he made me take."

Her voice merged into a moan.

Then I felt her breath again on my neck.

"But you still occupy a piece of my hell," Miranda's whispered. "Don't think I don't think that. But maybe the car wasn't yours. Maybe." She paused and then added: "But you got me out of *that* place."

In the mirror, I saw her turn her attention away from me and snuggle up to the kids.

I glanced at the clump of e-mails on the passenger seat.

Numbers. What was in there? A weapon? Something with which to save myself and extract a price? And I owed so many people, more people than I was able to think about. I owed it to them to breathe life into these dead numbers.

# FORTY-SEVEN

**P**ablo Tochera lived in an ivy-clad four-story brownstone on Sixty-second between Madison and Lexington Avenue. Whatever McIntyre felt about tokenism, he had obviously been prepared to pay well for it.

Julia, Pablo's wife, opened the front door, smiling more out of duty than pleasure, I sensed, and after strained introductions, led us through a hallway hung with classical prints of billowy birds of paradise, into a white and canary yellow painted oak kitchen where she asked us to sit at a large stripped pine table.

Miranda sat with both children on her lap, one on each leg. Her eyes were closed and she rocked gently.

Julia studied the kids for a moment, asked them their names, and then sat down herself. She looked like she had gotten used to sitting at the head of the household table, this statuesque Puerto Rican with black hair that could have made it to the floor without a split end if she'd let it grow that far. As it was, the hair maintained its lustrous shape to just below her shoulder blades.

"Hey, guys, how you doing?" Pablo shot a nervous glance at Julia and came and sat next to me.

Julia got up. "I'm going to take this lady and her children upstairs." Her voice was softer than I'd expected. Professional but compassionate. It would be easy to be scared of her, but easy to respect and like her too.

Pablo nodded. "Sure, hon."

Julia gently pried the little girl from Miranda's arm. "Come on, Sarah. You, me, Mommy, and Ray are going someplace nice. We're going to have some fun and let these deadbeats do their thing down here." She kissed the girl on the nose. "Okay, sweetie?"

Sarah clung onto her and looked at her mother for confirmation. Miranda nodded weakly.

"Sure," Sarah said and clung even tighter.

Miranda, with Ray sitting upright in her arm, obediently followed Julia out of the room.

"Cars," wailed Ray.

Pablo picked up the shoebox. "This?"

Ray nodded firmly.

"I'd like to freshen up," Paula said.

"Sure," Pablo said. "Up the stairs, second left. Julia will be in there. Ask her to get you towels and stuff. Find you a bed maybe, if you want one."

"Paula," I said. "You reckon you can stay awake a while? Pablo's going to need your help."

She smiled. "It's office hours; why not? Just so long as nobody messes with my lunch break."

"Thanks." I hoped that my face conveyed a prayer just answered.

I turned to Pablo. "You got a computer here? One with a modem?"

"Wiseguy. Being home doesn't mean I stop working. I've got a modem wire stuck up my ass when I sleep."

"I want you to set up two Websites for me," I said. "Give the first any domain name you want. Something boring like . . ." I tried to think of something that wouldn't attract attention or looked as if it led into a pornographic site.

I'd been thinking about where to take this. Thinking, too much thinking . . .

"Numberland," I decided.

"What's all this for?" Pablo asked. "I don't know how to set up a Website."

"Paula does."

Pablo looked worried.

"It's not unethical. I promise," I said, putting my arm around his shoulder.

"Thanks, Fin. I feel better already. And the second site?"

"Kipgem." It was unlikely that the name was already taken. "All I want on it is a header saying: *In Black and White* by Rudyard Kipling. Then underneath, in block capitals, put an instruction to read the "Gemini" story to figure out the numbers."

"You're a fucking piece of work, you know that?"

I took a scrunched-up wad of paper out of my pocket. "I'll need copies, Pablo." The e-mails. I hung on to Ernie's letter and handed the rest to Pablo.

"These are for the Numberland Website," I said. "List out the numbers exactly as they appear in the e-mails. Watch it, there are some letters of the alphabet and some dots. Make sure you transcribe them exactly."

"What do they mean?"

"I don't know yet," I said. "But I will." I needed a quiet space to do my crossword puzzle. There was a big prize for this one.


I sat at a small desk in a guest room. The bed looked tempting, but I had work to do.

The walls were covered with pictures of sailboats. They traced Pablo's ascent up the corporate ladder. A few dinghies. Pablo, younger, thinner, in orange with a dumb hat at a rakish angle. Julia smiling grimly, like she felt seasick.

Then a small cruiser. Pablo more serious, attired in a more afflu-ent outfit. Not so happy, perhaps, not so carefree.

Then a mother of a motor launch, the name *Julia I* in swirly italics on its prow. First of many more? No people in this picture. All boat.

The spare room had gone the way of most spare rooms—it was a dumping ground for stuff that the Tocheras couldn't quite bring themselves to discard or that they felt guilty about not using. Instead of idle exercise bikes and painting easels, this room contained flotsam from Pablo's sailing era. He'd graduated from sail to steam, but nostalgia still gripped him in the shape of old ropes, cleats, foul weather gear, tarps, a precomputer age compass, and what looked like some distress flares. I was prepared to bet that Julia gave him grief about the mess.

But it was a good room to work in.

I fanned out the e-mails in front of me to get an impressionistic feel of their visual texture. I laid my hard-won copy of *In Black and White* next to them, opened at the "Gemini" story. I had a sharp pencil and a sheaf of unlined paper.

Then I took Ernie's letter. There was an orderliness to the e-mails, the discipline of typeface. But Ernie's letter . . . scratchy, angry, inscrutable, yet possibly the most important.

I'd start with Ernie's scrawl.

The trick, I reckoned, was to make a few general assumptions and then apply them. First off, the code had to be readily applicable; in other words, you wouldn't need anything other than the "Gemini" story to crack a message, and that meant no rulebook; the players had to be able to commit the rules of the game to memory. And the players had to be able to play the game in most surroundings, however uncomfortable. There was no point in sending a message if the recipient needed a lab furnished with an Enigma machine to understand it. There was no point either, if the recipient would be dribbling in an old folks home by the time he'd figured it out.

Sensible assumptions, I reckoned. If I was wrong, then I was in trouble. The Oxford foursome might well have sat in a cozy college room, sipping sherry, deciding that they'd chuck all sensible assumptions out of the mullioned window.

The code had to be good enough to give an expert the runaround. Without a key text, codes were pretty much impossible to translate, but someone with time and a computer could perhaps do it: spot the repetitions, build a profile, the kind of shit statisticians like to go on about. If there was enough material to work with, a techie could do it.

*With* the key text, a techie could probably hack it in no time. But even then, some tricks could be built in to make life difficult.

Anyway, I was no expert, no techie. And I hadn't studied at Oxford.

My principal assumption was that the numbers related to letters in "Gemini." The words of "Gemini" would be sequenced and then maybe the first letter of the word would be a letter of the code. A cunning bastard might make it the second letter, or even make it the first letter for the first ten letters and then shift it to the second, or even the previous letter. That would reduce repetition and panic the unwary.

But that would fly in the face of my first assumption: Keep it simple.

Start at the beginning? The first letter of the first word in "Gemini" is *A?* No, I reckoned. Too simple. The start point would be somewhere else. Maybe predetermined or embedded in the code itself.

I began to work, looking for patterns, matching, rematching, comparing. Guessing, mostly guessing.

An hour later and I was nowhere. This was a crossword that didn't want to get filled in.

I pulled Carlstein's e-mails in front of me, scared now that these too would defeat me, but I drew comfort from their neatness, a spur to neat thought.

More assumptions were needed.

There were letters mixed up in the numbers.

If numbers were letters, then why not the other way around? Letters were numbers.

I scanned the e-mails, looking for patterns. A few showed. There were breaks, which maybe mirrored normal paragraph breaks.

Most of the numbers seemed to have one or two digits, a few with three. But there were some that had dots above or below them or, in a few cases, below *and* above.

Why the dots? Fucking dots again. I remembered Ernie's remark: Dots can place you in the frame, give you bearings. Every e-mail started with a number that was followed by a single dot. Dots as bearings, as coordinates. Maybe the first number showed the location within "Gemini" from where the translation should start. It could point to a word or a line or a paragraph. Or something else. Hell's teeth. Just keep calm.

I needed to try out a few permutations to see where I got.

I'd try the line approach first.

I picked an e-mail at random. The first number was sixteen. I counted sixteen lines into the text of "Gemini" and tried to apply the code.

It didn't work. There was no meaning; only random letters emerged.

I put the e-mail aside. It was jinxed, like Ernie's letter.

Now for the paragraph approach.

I took the shortest e-mail.

22 . 36 ¨ 28 8 16 31 4 18 3 10 29 44 23 19 19 37 36 173 19 5 50 44 106 41 31 ¨ 19 18 3 36 . 9 2 76

First number: 22. I counted to paragraph twenty-two of "Gemini." It started:

*Then Ram Narian who has his carpet spread under the jujube-tree by the well, and writes all letters for the men of the town . . .*

Nice. I tried to imagine what a jujube-tree looked like. It sounded pretty. And the name Ram Narian, the addressee of the e-mail. There was an internal logic at work here.

But was a jujube-tree one word or two words for the purposes of the code? I'd have to try both.

I assumed *jujube-tree* was one word. I wrote a number against each word. All the way up to 173, the highest number featured in the e-mail. The page looked like an unholy mess.

The result was even worse. D, something—this number had dots on it—S, W, T, W, W, N . . .

There was no point in continuing. If this was right, then it meant there was a code within a code, and I wasn't sure I had the stamina or the gray cells to tackle *that*.

I then assumed that *jujube-tree* was two words. D, something, SAIWANTSDOLLSDALHIDGSI, something, LAND, something, URCH.

It didn't look great, but words were starting to form. A beginning of sense, a shade of meaning.

WANTS, DOLLS, LAND. Statistically, it was bordering on the impossible that these words could appear by coincidence. I'd found the starting point, but I still didn't have any real sense of what the e-mail was going on about.

I looked at: "D, something, SAI." How about DESAI? An Indian name. An Indian guy WANTS something. DOLLS? Surely not. LAND, maybe. And maybe DOLLS was simply short for DOLLARS.

An Indian wants dollars for land.

URCH, what was *that*? Church, lurch.

Purch. Short for *purchase*. A land purchase.

An Indian called Desai wants dollars for a land purchase.

I tipped back in the chair and stared at the picture of *Julia I*. I was sweating with excitement, almost euphoric.

Hold on. I hit the brakes. There were seven e-mails here, this one was the shortest, and I'd covered just one sentence. It would be Christmas before I put the pencil down. I could finish the job in jail or whichever quarter of the afterlife I wound up in.

I needed rules, not guesswork. Guesswork would take too long. I looked at my watch. Twelve-thirty P.M. Yeah, far too fucking long.

An hour later, I had my rules. I knew that the letter E was statistically one of the commonest letters. I also went back through the passage in "Gemini" carefully and noted that there were no words beginning with E. That explained the nonstandard cipher for the E in DESAI. But it didn't repeat anywhere else. For good reason: If E was the commonest letter, then it would show up like a beacon if the same cipher were employed throughout. It would give too much away. But the code writer also wouldn't want E to be too difficult for the informed reader to find.

Where was E, then?

The three-digit numbers, that's where. These were random red herrings. No matter what the number, they always meant E. Of course, in another e-mail, the paragraph chosen for the code breaking might contain words starting with E. In that case, the three-digit ploy wouldn't be necessary, unless there were only one or two words starting with E and the beacon problem would arise again.

I checked the other e-mails. Some had three-digit numbers and some didn't. That made sense.

Something else I realized. There were no numbers between fifty and one hundred. If the letter E was designated by any number over one hundred, that meant everything else was covered by one through fifty.

I decided that the numbering was done in blocks of fifty. It made things more manageable. I liked it.

What about the dots? These I figured out to be variants on the E problem. Some letters didn't feature as first letters of words in the chosen "Gemini" passage. K, G, and V were examples. So the code writer finds a word with the letter in it and the dots signify how many letters the reader has to count into the word before he finds the right letter. So when faced with ". . . 43," I counted to the forty-third word—"six"; three dots, so third letter in.

X.

Piece of cake. Bearings, coordinates. Thanks, Ernie.

But there were dots above some of the numbers too. This took a while, but the fact that the code was built in blocks of fifty gave me the clue. The top-line dots told you which block to look in. Another bearing.

So with ". . . 9," I knew I was looking for the third letter of the ninth word in the second block of fifty.

V. Too right. V for Victory.

I allowed myself one minute to reflect on my progress. I looked at my watch: 2:00 P.M. I realized that I still had seven e-mails to translate in just under two hours, assuming I was to follow the new timetable that had half-formed in my mind, among the swirl of numbers, letters, and dots.

And I could feel my hip throb. Fingering my pants, I groaned as I found a sticky damp patch around the pocket. I sensed that the wound was infected. My sweating wasn't just euphoria; it was fever.

Before attacking the remaining e-mails, there was one more thing I had to do.

I picked up the phone on the desk, a shiny blue model motor cruiser with an earpiece, mouthpiece, and keypad.

I tried to get Carol. Voicemail again, but a different message. She was tired, she said, drained from what she'd done. She was sick of everyone, me included. She wanted to be left alone for a while, would call later. Maybe.

I tried to analyze the voice, as if it were another version of the "Gemini" code, susceptible to a single interpretation, that it could yield unmistakable meaning. I listened to the message twice more. But I got more confused on each hearing. Perhaps she simply meant what she said. She was tired, needed sleep. Perhaps that was all it meant. But *sick of everyone. You included.*

Time didn't allow a St. Cecelia–style analysis.

I called Mendip's direct line, the one that would sound in the cubicle near reception. A secretary picked up. I didn't recognize her voice.

"He's out," she told me curtly. A polite inquiry as to when he'd be back was met with a similarly brusque response.

"Who are you?" she asked.

I am the guy who has had his life trashed by that respectable, slightly ruffled old gentleman whose name appears at the top of the letterhead. That's who. "It doesn't matter," I said and hung up.

To say that I had been relying on Mendip to pick up the phone was an understatement. However difficult the conversation would have been with him, there were the tracks history had laid down for us. Talk had familiar rails to follow; we both knew where the curves were, where the points played tricks.

There was no history with Jim McIntyre. He was right off the rails.

"He's in a meeting," McIntyre's secretary announced smoothly. Lovely voice. A bit like Paula's. Old habits died hard with McIntyre, it seemed.

"Could you tell him it's urgent?"

"Who shall I say is calling?" There was a touch of skepticism in her voice, like the name I would give her couldn't possibly pull

McIntyre out of whatever he was doing, even if he was just filing his nails.

"Bill Gemini."

"Sir?" Maybe she wasn't such a good secretary after all. My father always said that no secretary should ever sound fazed at the name of a caller. His favorite example was a client called Jerkov.

"Gemini. G-E-M . . ."

"I got it, thanks." There was a click on the line as she put me on hold.

"Who is this?" A voice, bursting with impatience and confidence. Unquestionable authority expressed in three words. Quite an achievement.

I hadn't settled on a first line. So I started with the facts. "I understand that the merger is wrapping up at five," I said. I could hear the slightly shrill timbre of my voice.

"Who is this?" It looked like we were still at square one.

"I thought your secretary gave you my name." This time I managed a slightly lower register.

There was a pause. "Border," he said. My name came out as a disgusted whisper, something found rotting between two teeth to be pulled out.

"I know about the NRIs," I said. "I know about your little club at Oxford, I know about "Gemini," and I have plenty of hard copy material."

"You don't know anything, you piece of shit." The man had studied the wavelengths of the human voice and isolated the frequency that transmitted pure nightmare into the mind of the listener.

I didn't answer. Let him speak, see what comes out. Basic interview technique. He'd know that, though.

"And what's this garbage about Gemini?" It had been worth waiting; same nightmare coming over the line, but one now tinged with caution, perhaps. "I don't know what the hell you're talking about."

"Then why did the name get you out of an important meeting?"

McIntyre laughed. "Cap Gemini is a longstanding client of this firm. So if I hear the name of an important client then I attend to it. Perhaps if you had paid more attention to such basic rules-of-thumb, you wouldn't have wound up in this mess. You're finished, Border. Not that I give a fuck."

He was a quick-thinking bastard, I'd give him that.

"That's interesting," I said. "I was one of the foot soldiers serving on the Conflicts Committee for the merger. I went through every client you have with"—I couldn't resist it—"that fucker Ellis Walsh. And Cap Gemini didn't show up anywhere. It's a big company, it would register on the radar screen if it was a client."

McIntyre started to say something, but I hadn't finished. "Perhaps it's also worth mentioning, at this point, your client Reno Holdings and its interest in a rather dubious Turkish company called Saracen Securities. Drill down some more and you find Huxtable BV. And its illegitimate brother, Huxtable Trust Company. Are these clients of yours as well? You should get a better client list. But I don't think I'm telling you anything you don't already know."

The pause lasted so long I wondered if he might be up to something on another line. But I'd gone this far and wasn't going to hang up now.

"What do you want?" he asked finally.

"To talk. Face-to-face."

"Why the fuck should I be prepared to do that?"

"Because if you don't, there won't be a merger at five o'clock."

Again the mocking laughter. "You're nothing. You're less than nothing. You can't threaten me."

I tried to picture him. He was small, a brittle plaster Napoleon with beard and mustache. The image gave me strength. "Of course I can threaten you, I *am* threatening you. I can beset you, you weasel. I've had people fall about me like bowling pins, and a few attempts made on my own life. Don't make the mistake of thinking that it has weakened me. It hasn't."

"So you're a big guy now. So why, Mr. Big Guy, don't you simply go to the authorities with this truckload of shit you've stepped in?"

There were plenty of answers to choose from. "Apart from the fact that I'd be likely to spend some time in jail, I want certain things from you, and it doesn't suit me to have the leadership of Clay & Westminster, Schuster Mannheim, and Askari & Co. rounded up and ruined."

"Blackmail," McIntyre said smoothly. "And for some reason I thought you might be a man of principle. That makes things easier." He paused. "So let's say we meet; how are you going to arrange things so that you don't get pulled in after five seconds? I don't fancy a rendezvous in Central Park either. It's too hot and, anyway, I've got a merger in a few hours."

"Your office," I said. "In two hours. Have a security pass waiting for me, in the name of Colin Brown. Nice easy name, you should be able to remember it. I expect you have your own special arrangements for elevators, don't you? Use them."

"Go to Rockefeller Center, enter the GE Building from the Plaza side, and head for the elevator banks . . ."

"I know where to go," I snapped.

"Suit yourself, Jesse will see to you." I heard a sigh. "Border, you're crazy. I'm going to blast you into outer fucking space."

He hung up.

There was no time to reflect on the call; it had taken up too much time already. I needed translations of the e-mails if I had any chance of remaining earthbound.

Jesus, the hip hurt badly. I could feel it pulsate, a power drill burrowing its way through from the inside. And my back, ridged by what felt like molten lava. I was sweating like a burst pipe.

# FORTY-EIGHT

My pockets were crammed. Inside my jacket: e-mails and their translations—six out of seven, at any rate. Ganesh lurked heavily in my right pocket—I wanted to present Ganesh to McIntyre, as if it was evidence of something, see what response it elicited.

As I marched down the boutique-lined Promenade of Rockefeller Center, I toyed with Pablo's cell phone in my sweaty hand. He reluctantly accepted that borrowing it didn't entail too much of an ethical breach, even though it was Schuster Mannheim property.

I gazed onto its screen. A globule of sweat obscured it for a moment. I could see a shadow in front of my eyes as another blob aimed for critical mass on the rim of my glasses.

The glasses had been Paula's idea. A pair of black-rimmed, half-frame reading spectacles borrowed from Pablo. Geeky, but I supposed they might add another layer to my now rather tired disguise. They were certainly an efficient conduit for sweat.

I wiped the screen clean. Plenty of signal. It was time to ring Pablo. Skirting the sunken section at the end of the Promenade, I was almost blinded by the giant golden figure of Prometheus as he hovered majestically against his waterfall backdrop. A Rockefeller security man was watchful above him while a uniformed maitre d' to the diners in the restaurant laid out over the mothballed ice rink strutted about below. Was Ganesh a match for him?

Before I'd left Pablo's, he and Paula were experiencing problems. The domain name Numberland had been taken; either that, or the site wouldn't take with that name. And it appeared that Paula and Pablo couldn't see eye-to-eye about anything. Maybe Paula was projecting some of her hatred for McIntyre onto Pablo. And maybe Pablo was . . . I didn't know what Pablo was doing.

I had left them squabbling, each maintaining that, if they hadn't been saddled with the other, they could figure it out.

Pablo took my call.

"How's it going?" I asked.

"Fine." It sounded as if Pablo was speaking through clenched teeth.

"Is it done?"

"Nearly, nearly. I hit a few dead ends on the way, but I think I got it licked." He paused. "Paula's smart, I'll give her that. She helped. A little."

"You've got a substitute domain for Numberland?" I asked.

"Sure."

I waited.

"Well, what is it, Pablo? The new name."

"Yeah, right. The new name. Cacacoo."

"*What?*" I was beginning to appreciate what Paula was up against.

"There's not a lot left that isn't taken, you know." He sounded professorial, like he was lecturing a newcomer to the game. "*Caca* is 'shit' in Spanish, you know."

"I know. And 'coo.' What's that?

Pablo hesitated. "Well, coo is, well. Just coo. It isn't anything, I guess. Sounds nice, though: cacacoo, cacacoo. It has a rhythm."

"Like Salsa."

"Right."

"Okay, whatever," I said, "listen to me. If you don't get a call from me by seven tonight, then I want you to arrange for an e-mail to be sent to every employee in Clay & Westminster and Schuster Mannheim, or whatever the name of the merged firms might be by then."

"It will take weeks to send them to every employee." Pablo's voice was starting to rise.

"There will be a global distribution icon," I explained. "It'll take no longer than if you'd sent it to one person. Paula will show you how."

"And what's in this e-mail?"

"The two Website addresses: Kipgem and"—I could hardly bring myself to say it—"Cacacoo. Along with an instruction to open the sites. Then you outline an offer to the first five employees who manage to decipher the code. They get two hundred thousand dollars each. Say that the competition is in honor of the merger. Say that it's the personal offer of Jim McIntyre. Out of his own pocket."

"I can't do that, Fin." I'd pitched him an unethical ball.

"I hope it won't be necessary," I said. "But if it is, then remember this. I'll most likely be dead and it will have been McIntyre or someone connected to him that did it."

"That's a little extreme, Fin."

"They tried to kill me in Bombay. . . . Shit, Pablo, we've been through all of this."

"Perhaps Paula can press the button," he said. "I can show her how."

Pablo was a resourceful lawyer. If it worked for him, then it worked for me.

"Seven o'clock, Pablo. Not a second after."

"I think you're about to do something dumb. It's not too late to change your mind and deal with the matter through more conventional channels."

"I don't know what conventional means anymore." I hung up.

Nearby were two cops, standing next to a nest of newspaper racks. They seemed edgy, expectant—of me perhaps. I sidled toward the revolving doors and dissolved into the lobby.

Inside this cathedral to capital, solemn murals sought to persuade that man could vie with the gods: Abraham Lincoln, Ralph Waldo Emerson. As I trotted down the North Corridor, the murals got bolder, seeming to suggest that man had conquered the entire cosmos. Then it suddenly struck me that the money used to erect this place was from the same source that had built the Cloisters. Old man Rockefeller was obviously a shrewd hedger of bets.

I'd reached the fifth elevator bank and found a badge saying "Jesse" level with my eyes, Jesus, how tall was this man in his crisp blue uniform, curly wire running from behind his ear down the back of his shirt, a bald head that shone like polished mahogany?

"You have a pass for me," I said.

"Name, sir." Jesse smiled.

For a moment, I forgot the name I'd given myself. Codes, false names, false hair, wacky spectacles. This was getting crazy. I took a deep breath.

"Brown," I said. "Colin Brown." Like it was Bond, James Bond. Shit, I needed a dose of reality before I became eternally locked in this twilight world.

Jesse led me to an elevator and jabbed the call button.

The elevator arrived almost immediately and, as he held the door open for me, Jesse turned a key sticking out of a discreet hole near the floor. He then pressed the button. "Sixtieth-floor express. No stops." His smiling face disappeared behind the closing doors.

The doors opened onto a hallway paneled in some grotesquely expensive wood veneer. A smiling woman stood in front of me. Schuster Mannheim plainly didn't like people to suffer withdrawal symptoms from lack of smiles. The hallway could have been a catwalk; that's where the woman looked like she belonged.

McIntyre's secretary. She was the image of Paula, fewer worry lines, but they could have been sisters. She didn't look like she'd been invited yet to the house on the hill.

"Hi." That one syllable could sound so good. "Mr. McIntyre is going to be held up a while," she said with a small pout of disappointment. "He said you were sure to understand, and told you not to worry." Her face wrinkled in bewilderment. "He said you weren't to read anything into it. Whatever that means." She laughed. "I think this merger has made us all a little screwy."

I nodded. She was right, and then some. "Not to worry," I said.

She started walking down the hall. It was empty, like they had cleared the way in honor of my arrival. They didn't want me frightening the horses.

"We've got a great room for you, with a great view. Coffee? Tea?" She gave me a mischievous version of her smile. "Some cookies, maybe?"

It was hard to believe that I was talking about cookies when so much was at stake. I was being offered refreshments before I became the main course in the lion's den.

"Cookies would be nice," I said. "And some aspirin, something strong if you have it."

She frowned. "Ibuprofen or acetaminophen or what? We have to be careful. You may have a reaction to some formulations." Again the laugh. It trilled more than Paula's and would have bugged me after a while. "Heck, we're a firm of attorneys," she prattled. "We have to think about that kind of thing."

"Ibuprofin will be fine." I smiled weakly. "I'll sign a disclaimer."

She opened a door onto an empty meeting room.

"You make yourself cozy and I'll bring your order. Then I'll call when Mr. McIntyre's ready for you."

It was hard to make myself cozy in the wood-paneled anteroom of the gods, with its view over the Promenade leading to Fifth Avenue: Saks dead ahead and St. Patrick's Cathedral a block to the left. More gods . . .

Turning away, I looked at my watch. It seemed that the merger could wait too. It was already past four and I didn't anticipate finishing with McIntyre—or he with me—in less than an hour. Still, it was his firm, his timetable. I had my own and it said seven o'clock on it, in big letters.

Sitting down at a table as long as a runway, I pulled out Ernie's letter and a photocopy of the "Gemini" story that I'd had Pablo make—I wasn't going to carry Mr. Muckerjee's original around with me.

So, Ernie knew the code. He wasn't a founding member of the Gemini Club, but he had clearly been near the center. And what of my father? Had he paid his subscription and been handed the Club manual?

I shook the thought from my head and focused on the paperwork.

Time for another run at Ernie's letter. Now I had rules, signposts, now the handwriting didn't seem so intimidating, less angry, more that of someone in a desperate hurry to do something right before he died.

After finding the relevant paragraphs and carefully numbering the words in blocks of fifty, I expected meaning to emerge.

But it didn't. Gibberish. What the hell was Ernie playing at?

I took a sample section from the middle of the piece. Garble.

I was missing something.

Ernie had already helped me find the key to the other e-mails, but the cloak over his own had a double lining.

There was a knock on the door. A maid came in with a tray stacked more densely than the Rockefeller development around me.

Sandwiches, cake, cookies. Shrimps, bigger and pinker than thumbs. Little puff-pastry canapés with poppy seeds on top. Strips of cold teriyaki beef, for Christ's sake. Bud, Coke, Pellegrino water. Tea, coffee. And ibuprofen.

I stared at the crisp white napkin sitting on the fine bone china plate.

At one corner there was a large blue logo, picked out in intricate cotton. Two hands, locked in a handshake. I wanted to vomit. On one, a florid S. On the other, a W. Over the top of the fingers, an ampersand. I could figure out this code. Schuster & Westminster. So, this was what the PR suits had come up with for their six-figure fee.

I turned to the food. A trick? Poison the upstart Border. Or maybe get him to stuff himself to death.

I tipped the napkin off the plate. There was the logo again, a neat monogram on the china. They were determined for this merger to go ahead, and believed it would. They'd already paid for the wedding gifts. I picked up the knife and fork. Again, perfect little handshakes.

The food was a diversion, a distraction.

Put distance between yourself and a problem. Step back and see it for what it is. Dad used to say that.

Ernie too.

No. Not quite.

Ernie said that the original thinker was the one who stepped sideways. Take two steps to one side, he'd said. Then you'll see the thing from an angle that everyone else has missed.

Two steps sideways.

To the left or right? Backward or forward?

Intuition told me forward.

For the counterintuitive Ernie that meant backward.

Two steps sideways—to the left. Backward.

I started counting words in the Gemini text and then applying them to the numbers in Ernie's letter. But instead of taking the first letter of the relevant word, I took the penultimate letter of the preceding word.

Fragile shoots of meaning began to materialize from the dead paper.

"August is the cruellest month."

A misquote from T. S. Eliot. An echo of Ernie. A section from *The Waste Land*. He recited it often. In the original poem it was April, wasn't it? How April bred lilacs out of the dead land, something like that.

And August was the month—this month—when Ernie had checked into the Plaza and had been strangled on one of their faucets.

And the quote came from the first section of *The Waste Land*. The section headed: *The burial of the dead.*

This was Ernie's epitaph. He'd always want the last word.

There was no time to reflect, only to translate.

He was guilty of much, he said. *But the darkest crime still lies in my head, my heart, as yet uncommitted.* The body would hold out no longer, though. He couldn't control it; the demons held sway. He had to stop the demons before he was damned by his body.

*Carlstein wants me to commit the crime. More than anything he wants to put me beyond redemption.*

Ernie spoke of a journey. Or rather two journeys. One his, the other . . . He wasn't clear. The code failed at certain points. Maybe Ernie had been in no fit state to write fluent code.

*My journey lies beyond the bolted door where stirs hope born of mutilation*. The bolted door—up the stairs at Baba Mama's, turn left for her sanctum and, to the right, the bolted door, the one Raj had giggled at, the one he said was not for us. Ernie must have known that I would take that journey.

*The hope is real and so is the pain. The pain is perhaps too high a price to pay. Pain is the ransom. Hope is released upon payment. The hope is the promise of a state of grace. As a Hijra.*

*Hijra?*

The *other* journey was across an ocean, a one-way ocean, he said.

And who were these one-way sailors? PI, something, IES. An Ernie word, maybe, something typically Ernie.

*Pixies*. He liked that word. He used it to refer to people he considered pretty, rascals perhaps, but vulnerable with it. Little people that needed protection.

So, the Pixies went across the ocean and couldn't come back. The next few words meant nothing. Then he spoke of a ship's masts waving in the wind and a stoney Vig Dolorosg—no, Via Dolorosa. Of course. The route of Jesus to the crucifixion. Who had used that term to describe my wanderings in Bombay? Along my father's Via Dolorosa. Mendip. It had been Mendip.

The imagery shifted. It said Ellis Island, I was sure. I checked again. I was right. He was talking about the staging post for immigrants into the USA, the forbidding blob to the right of the Statue of Liberty.

*I am the landlord of the halfway house to hell, the receiving station at the other side of the Styx. I am the stevedore unloading the cargo of the damned.*

He wasn't the only landlord, he said. A collective held the deeds to the estates. There was a black synod, of which he was only a minor cleric.

And the bishops, who were they? A grim quartet of Askari, McIntyre, Mendip, and Carlstein.

But not my father.

Then more garble.

I glanced at the time. Five-thirty. What the fuck was McIntyre doing?

What the hell.

The next word I could read was *Protector*. *Of the pixies* followed easily enough.

He had failed, Ernie said, to protect them. He had wanted to. But he loved them too much. He wanted to dance with them. A dance with purity, a defiling dance.

*The tusks of Ganesh are blunted, his four arms folded. Lazy God? Leaving the fate of the Pixies to me. Without the hope that lies in mutilation, the Pixies will feel the ugliness of my skin. With the hope, I am the smiling eunuch, their smiling Hijra protector.*

Ernie was never to the point. His journey to a message was always via a roundabout route.

There was a quiet tap on the door and McIntyre's secretary poked her head around.

"Mr. McIntyre will see you now," she said. She looked at the tray of food and frowned. "Not hungry?"

No thanks. I wondered if I'd ever be hungry again. Ernie's letter spelled death to hunger.


McIntyre sat in an armchair. He looked relaxed, hands folded on his lap, the dead lights of his eyes guttering but ready to flare. A gentle smile rippled through his dark, close-cropped mustache and beard.

Mendip stood near the window. Fidgeting. I could hear his breath wheeze from where I stood, a hand flicking over his five o'clock shadow compulsively, his gaze alternating between me and the endless view outside.

McIntrye motioned me to sit at a large round drum table, two hundred years old or more, exquisitely inlaid. A hundred thousand, on a bad day at auction.

The place was full of antiques. I scanned the huge room.

Then I saw him. The snail in the corner. Askari, merged with the dimpled brown leather of his armchair, set near a large bookcase. Camouflaged.

McIntyre cast a swift glance at Mendip and Askari. Then me. "There have been enough misunderstandings, I think." The snap in the voice had gone; it was all massage oil.

"If you call killing my father and mother and a few others misunderstandings, then I entirely agree."

"We didn't kill your father, Fin." Mendip could hardly speak; he fought for oxygen like he was under water.

"Okay," I said. "It was Damindra Ketan. It comes to the same thing. You were the puppet masters."

Mendip didn't react.

"It isn't the same thing," McIntyre said. He leaned forward and lifted a small teapot that stood on a delicate stem table. He slowly poured himself a cup of tea, indicating with one hand that I was free to do the same with the china on my drum table.

"Your father cut himself adrift," McIntyre continued. "He put himself beyond our help. Sunil tried to bring him back." Askari nodded solemnly, his sour-milk eyes brimming. "But he was out of his depth. He simply didn't understand what he was dealing with, and when we tried to throw him a lifeline, he swam out farther. I have no idea if Damindra administered a coup de grace, perhaps he did. In any event, he would only be killing a man who was already dead."

The bastard was trying to tell me it was a mercy killing. It was breathtaking.

But it wasn't merely the fact of my father's death that required explanation; there was the "where" too.

"Why the Towers of Silence, then? Why there?" I kept my voice even. Maybe I was expected to shout, lose it. But I didn't shout.

Askari stirred like a waking ox. "Who knows? It was a place of your father's choosing. Perhaps he wanted to upset my best clients. Perhaps he became lost. It is without meaning, without consequence."

*Without consequence.* Everything in India had consequence.

"What about Raj, was that a mercy killing too?" It had taken less than a minute to break my own rule on shouting.

Askari lumbered over to me and peered into my face. He then spat at me. Thick, hot spittle snaked across my cheek and stained one lens of my ridiculous spectacles. I met his stare and didn't even raise a hand to wipe away the spittle.

"All I know,"—Askari's voice was curare-soaked velvet—"is that because of you, a business started by my grandfather and one which has become, under my stewardship, one of India's treasures, has been turned to ashes. This is all I know. Do you think I am concerned one iota that a clerk was turned to ashes in the process? My only regret is that you did not burn with the building."

"Time-out. Take a seat, Sunil," McIntyre said, smiling like an understanding uncle. "Don't let this kid wind you up. We can do business and then he's out of here."

I turned to Mendip. "Why, Charles? What are you doing with these people? My father worshiped you; fifteen hundred people worship you. What brought you to this? You didn't want me to go to Bombay, did you? You had half a conscience, what happened to the other half?"

He just stared at me.

"You see, Fin," McIntyre said, "when you spend time together, cooped up, if you like, you either get to hate each other, or you come to tolerate different points of view. We"—he spread his arms to include Mendip and Askari—"learned to tolerate each other. We're different, of course, but we complement each other, and we have similar worldviews."

"I'm surprised you've managed to restrain yourselves from going out together and invading Poland."

McIntyre's face momentarily tensed. Then he forced himself to relax. "So, Fin. In your short but busy visit to Bombay, what did your researches uncover? Enlighten us."

My mouth was dry. Tea would be good, but I didn't want hospitality of any kind from this man.

"You run a comprehensive laundering service for Non-Resident Indians." It sounded like I was reading from a cue card. "It may have started with gold from the Gulf into India, but now you'll deal in anything; shares, land, equipment, anything. Ketan Securities is the conduit, and massive sums of money pump through it. The tie with the NRIs is Huxtable BV, which in turn is owned by Saracen Securities, a Turkish company. You are consolidating the structure by bringing Ketan Securities into Jefferson Trust via acquisition. Saracen, a client of Clay & Westminster, is to be acquired by Reno Holdings, a client of Schuster Mannheim. When the consolidation is complete everything will revolve in one harmonious and unshakable orbit. Where the merger of Schuster and Clay fits in, I can only hazard a guess, but I expect it has a role."

I'd already exhausted the contents of the cue card. I was still trying to make sense of Ernie's epitaph.

McIntyre nodded. "Nice executive summary. Neat, concise. Rounded off with a little lyricism. 'Orbit.' Cute." He turned to Mendip. "Pity we can't keep him, Charles. In other circumstances, he'd be partner material."

He waved his hand at Askari. "Anything you'd like to add, Sunil?"

Askari scowled.

"Okay," McIntyre continued. "And what documents do you have that show the connection between Huxtable and Ketan, between Saracen and Huxtable? Where is the link between Huxtable and these NRIs? What do you have, to show that Reno wants Saracen? Show us. *Show us* the agreements, the contract notes. Show us the thread leading out of India, and leading into the States. And show how this has anything to do with Clay & Westminster or Schuster Mannheim. Or rather, Schuster & Westminster. Show us. I don't see a document case with you, Fin. I know you'd keep originals elsewhere, but surely you'd have copies for us. If you're going to blackmail us, Fin, you need the paperwork. We're attorneys. We need paper."

I pulled the e-mails out. I began to doubt myself. Proof? Maybe proof was measured by the weight of paper, not the content. Law courts were always filled with dozens of ring-bound files. Mountains of papers, tabbed, cross-referenced, capable of withstanding forensic cross-examination. A good advocate could turn a birth certificate into a death certificate. But he'd need a ton of paper to perform the alchemy. Maybe, in my frenzied tour of Long Island, I'd forgotten the meaning of evidence: cogency, directness, provenance, corroboration. I'd put evidence at the top of my timetable, and then grabbed at circumstance and hearsay. I'd ignored its true meaning.

And as to my darker suspicions about what lay behind Gemini, I had only one piece of paper. The fractured monologue of a demented man at the point of death.

I handed the e-mails to McIntyre. He took out a pair of tiny reading glasses, nicer than mine, and peered at the sheets, riffling through them all in less than a minute. He put his reading glasses back in a leather pouch.

"Numbers, Fin," he said. "All I see is numbers." He held the sheaf up in the air. "Sunil, Charles. You can look at them for yourself, but I suggest you don't bother. Like I said, just numbers."

"It's not all numbers," I said. "Look at the headers, the names."

McIntyre clicked his tongue in irritation and took up his reading glasses again.

"Kirpa Ram, Jowar Singh, Durga Dass." McIntyre looked at Askari. "I'm sorry if my pronunciation is less than perfect, Sunil." He turned over a few more pages. "Ram Narain, Ram Dass. More Indian names. I've never heard of them."

He carefully placed the e-mails on the little pedestal table, putting a milk pitcher over them to keep them in place.

"Who are these people?" he asked.

"You know who they are. They're characters out of a short story by Rudyard Kipling. A story called 'Gemini.' "

McIntyre laughed. "So these guys are our money launderers. Guys out of a work of century-old fiction. You must've bumped your head quite badly on the way here, Fin."

"I know what these e-mails say, McIntyre. It's not as difficult as you think. They're about deliveries of money. More money than most people can dream of. Arrangements for share deals. Bribes to officials. Account details. There are names in there, big and small. And they aren't fictional."

McIntyre still looked relaxed. "But not our names, Fin. Our names won't be in there."

He was right. In theory. Clearly, the names of the black synod must never be set down in writing. But Carlstein had been careless.

"Only once, McIntyre. But once is enough."

Once was evidence.

McIntyre's ice melted a little, enough to let me know that inside, lava bubbled. He pulled at the e-mails, knocking the milk pitcher to the floor, the white liquid disappearing almost immediately into several inches of carpet pile. "Whose name? Where?"

"I'll let you find it for yourself," I said, as calmly as I could manage. "But it's your name, McIntyre."

I could see that he wanted to claim that I was bluffing. But then maybe he realized that I would never risk coming into the lion's den without something moderately ballistic in my back pocket.

He settled back into his chair. Both Askari and Mendip came forward and started looking at the e-mails. The threesome looked as if they were ready for the Gemini Club photograph. McIntyre in his seat, Mendip and Askari flanking him. Only Carlstein was missing.

"You told me that you wanted to meet face-to-face," McIntyre said. "So what do you want? If you don't go wild, I imagine we might try and accommodate you." He paused. "But if you step over the line, then I won't be able to stop Sunil from tearing out your fucking throat."

"The victims of JJ's suicide may never get anything," I said. "JJ created a cloud of confusion. He caught you off guard, I think. His brother had driven him too far, hurt him too much. Whatever. It was one hell of a problem for you, until you realized that he'd also served up my head on a plate. And in the confusion, you know that you'll be able to help things drag on for years, and most likely end with a settlement hatched between the insurers, way below the mark. You'll exhaust them.

"So," I continued. "I want fifty million dollars paid over immediately to Marshall, Forrester, Kellerman, and Hirsch on behalf of the Huxtable Trust Company. It's a settlement. They may or may not take it. But you must pay it. I don't care if the money comes from Huxtable, or some of your NRI friends, or out of your own pockets."

Askari looked like he was going to make a run at me, but McIntyre raised his hand to hold him back, confining himself to the observation that Marshall, Forrester were schmucks and ambulance chasers. They gave the profession a bad name, he said.

"That may be so," I said, "but my demand still stands. Next, I want you to pay Miranda Carlson five million dollars. I want you to honor Huxtable's obligation to Delaware Loan of nine hundred and fifty thousand plus interest. I also want my fifty thousand plus interest returned to my Chase account. Finally I want you to pay one million dollars to Paula. This has to come from your own bank account, McIntyre. It doesn't go near to repairing the damage you've done her, but we're attorneys and everything has a price tag, doesn't it?"

I paused. "That's the money side of things. Now for the people. First me: exoneration, rehabilitation, nothing less than total, Manelli off my back, extradition proceedings dropped, litigation cleared up. You have the power to do this."

McIntyre laughed. "You think we know what JJ did? Part of a grand strategy of ours? You were right, he caught us off guard, the crazy fuck. Maybe you *did* own the car, maybe it was part of your own screwy strategy. Beats the hell out of me, confused Carlstein too; shearing off his head reduced his stress levels on that score." So, even the death of a club member didn't bother him.

"I don't care if you fabricate the evidence, just do it, clear me." I paused. "I understand that you will be announcing new partners on the merger."

McIntyre nodded almost imperceptibly.

"Is Pablo Tochera still on that list?"

McIntyre laughed. "Fuck no. I found out that he went to JFK and bailed you out. I only put him on your case because I thought he was a lousy lawyer. Well, he was better than he was supposed to be. He has no future with this firm. You've made sure of that."

"Put him back on the list."

McIntyre snorted.

"Someone else too," I said, ignoring the interjection. "Terry Wardman. I don't know where he is, but tomorrow I want him to wake up as a partner."

"We can't do that," Mendip wheezed. "He's not a qualified lawyer. Only lawyers can be partners, you know that."

I studied Mendip. There was so little of him left, he was like a blood donor that had gone all the way. Drained dry.

"I'm aware of that," I said. "But when the mistake is realized, the compensation you'll have to pay should be enough to settle his score. Maybe he can finance a sabbatical to qualify and *then* you announce his partnership the second time around. I don't care. Just do it."

I looked at my watch. It was just after six.

"Are we keeping you from another appointment?" McIntyre sneered.

They were keeping me from another life. A life I hoped to be a bit better at, next time around.

McIntyre stood up, took out a handkerchief, and laid it over the shadow of milk on the carpet.

"No use crying over it," he said casually. "You're a loser, Border," he continued. "Like your father. Like JJ Carlson, like Ernie fucking Monks. No sense of the big picture. A force with one hundred and twenty billion dollars behind it. Think of it. An aimless, fragmented block of money, frustrated ambition, hidebound by red tape and interference. Whatever else he might have been, Carlstein was a visionary, we were just the lawyers, the servants, as lawyers should be. But no doubt you find that distasteful."

"I do," I said. "But I like it a whole lot better than shipping children and women out of Bombay as prostitutes and sex slaves."

I pulled the Ganesh figurine from my pocket.

"You have perverted this to your own use," I said. "Just like you've perverted everything else."

Ganesh on the school uniform of a Pixie, Ganesh on a novice whore's schoolbook in Baba Mama's. A school endowed by the Gemini Club. And my father. And JJ.

McIntyre didn't blink.

"You better have a lot more than numbers and a silly statue to show us on this one, Border."

I did. I had the epitaph of a man who could no longer look himself in the face. A man who could see waving masts on the way down the Via Dolorosa. The waving masts of the Seawanaka Yacht Club. The big house on the hill. A halfway house to hell.

"There's a school," I said. "Endowed by the Gemini Club and others of your inner circle. There's a whorehouse in Bombay, a staging post, a training ground. And then there's a big house on Centre Island." The baronial version of Ellis Island, death row for Pixies. "The place where you paraded Paula for Carlstein's pleasure and took a jerk-off as tip."

Mendip grimaced.

"Lies and speculation," McIntyre said, coming over to me, picking up Ganesh. He studied it, stroked it, and then, without warning, slammed it down into my lap. All other pain stepped aside for the crushing agony delivered to my testicles.

"I don't think JJ was the victim of speculation when he killed himself," I stammered when I'd recovered a little, the shooting pains beginning to give way to a dull ache. "I think he realized he'd become nothing more than a gargoyle pinned to the facade of your satanic cathedral. You and Carlstein had taken nearly everything from him, and were about to take the rest. Maybe he threatened you back, said he'd blow the lid off the whole thing. And you told him—go ahead, make your confession, see what happens when a penniless coked-up paranoid goes head-to-head with a brilliant lawyer and a few billion in vested interests. So he decided to make a wave so big that there was a good chance you'd drown too."

"Psycho-crap, Border. Carlson's brain was Sloppy-Joe by the end, and no more capable of thought than that milk on my carpet."

I ignored him. "And Ernie Monks," I said. "You must have dangled dirty carrots in front of him for years. You drove him mad."

"He ate a few of the carrots."

"I don't think so." There would be no point in varnishing the truth in a deathbed confession. *But the darkest crime still lies in my head, my heart, as yet uncommitted.*

I then turned to Askari. "What's a *Hijra?*"

His face curdled. "Disgusting creatures. Men who aren't men. Men who cut off their seed. They are vermin."

The men behind the bead curtain at Baba Mama's. Transvestites? Transsexuals? It sounded more profound than that.

The twine around Ernie's penis, the hairless body, the wig. Only through pain could he become a Hijra, he'd said. But in the end, his pain was too great, and he'd killed himself. He hadn't been able to protect the Pixies, because he couldn't stop wanting them for himself.

"The Hijra dance at the birth of a child," Askari went on. "At weddings, at anything auspicious. They demand money for their lascivious dances. But they are whores, worse than whores. You know that when they cut off their manhood, they insert a twig in the hole, to keep it open. So that they may urinate. They are an abomination."

Askari marched across the room and leaned over me. He smelled of lavender, violets. Sweet, sick. "They claim authority from the gods. Shiva. The mother gods. The gods disown such foul disciples. It brings shame on them and on India. They must be kept behind closed doors."

The bolted door again. *Behind that door is not for us.*

"And how did Carlstein keep you behind the door of the Gemini Club? What predilection did he appeal to?"

Askari growled.

McIntyre moved behind him, coaxing him back to the armchair. "It's okay, Sunil. It won't be long now. Then you can go back home."

McIntyre turned to me. "And what about your father?" he said. "You think he didn't like the carrots?"

The blur of wood nymph flitting across the bedroom of a house in Hampton Court.

At this, Mendip raised his head and struggled for breath. "That's enough, Jim," he managed.

"What's the matter?" McIntyre seemed angry at Mendip's interjection. After all, McIntyre was chairman of the Gemini Club now that Carlstein had been ousted. McIntyre held the gavel, and points from the floor had to follow the Chairman's agenda.

"I'm sorry, Jim." Mendip rested his hands on the desk. "Sinclair Border was a friend." Mendip looked up at me. "He never touched the girl at the house, Fin." He was struggling for air. "He wanted to tell you, explain. The truth is, he was trying to save her."

McIntyre was furious. "That was fucking gratuitous, Charles."

"Perhaps," Mendip conceded. He slumped into the desk chair, exhausted. "But it's the truth."

"*For Christ's sake, Charles . . .*" It was the first time I'd seen McIntyre begin to lose it.

He took a small sip of tea, in an attempt to finalize the exchange. "Just take a few pulls on that little machine of yours and shut the fuck up," he said viciously. "Anyway. Carlstein's dead. In some ways I guess we have Billy the Kid here to thank for freeing us."

He then turned to me.

"Back to business," he said. "That's quite a list of demands you've given us. Now why do you think we would be prepared to pay more than ten dollars into the lawyers' benevolent fund and leave it at that?"

"There's a computer on your desk," I said. "Log onto the Internet. If you know how."

"You're an asshole," he muttered, but got up and went around to the back of his desk, shooing Mendip out of his chair.

"Search for Kipgem," I said.

I went around to the screen. McIntyre was online. The system was searching. The hourglass cursor, a spinning globe. Antennae reaching out into the eternity of the Web. But nothing to show for it except a message saying that the page could not be found.

"Try Cacacoo."

McIntyre winced. "You're kidding, right?"

Thanks, Pablo.

"Just do it," I hissed, sure that McIntyre could smell my rising panic.

"You're the guy with the gun."

I wished I was, but my holster was empty. I was empty, like the screen.

Cacacoo was a no-show.

I saw McIntyre relax. "So what now, Fin Border?"

Had Pablo failed to get the sites up and running? He'd sounded so confident. If he had gotten them up, then where were they? Why didn't they show on a search?

That was it. The search engines might not pick them up. They needed to be registered, didn't they? With Yahoo or something.

A Web search for the single word was no good; you had to type in the exact Web address to get there.

"Type in a full site address: www and all that shit."

"You do it," McIntyre said.

I did. Kipgem came up within five seconds. It told the reader to get their hands on *In Black and White* and flip to "Gemini."

McIntyre sat back slowly and stroked his beard. If the tape had stopped right there, I would have been happy. He looked as if someone had just thrown up on his three-thousand-dollar suit.

Mendip and Askari huddled behind McIntyre and peered at the screen.

"Cacacoo next," I said. "Doesn't sound so funny now, does it?"

This took a little longer, the globe did a few extra orbits, but there they were. Reams of numbers. It was beautiful.

I went back to the drum table and poured myself some tea.

"Two Websites," I said. "Unconnected. No hyperlink between them. The deal is this: If I don't send a message saying I'm safe before seven tonight, then an e-mail will be sent to a few thousand interested parties, giving them both Website addresses and telling them to take a peek. The e-mail will contain an irresistible incentive to do this."

I paused, waiting for some reaction. There was none. I had their attention.

"That's round one," I continued. "Assuming I give the safety signal by seven tonight, then the Websites stay unhooked. For a while. Then there's another deadline. Close of business tomorrow; call it 6:00 P.M., to give a little leeway. By that time you will have completed my shopping list. Or else the e-mail goes down the wire."

The trio had taken up their original positions.

"Very elegant," McIntyre said, "but—"

"I know what you're thinking," I said. "The blackmailer always comes back for more. But this isn't about me."

"Zip it," McIntyre snapped. "You've missed the point. You need to stop talking and start listening, because I'm about to tell you where we really are."

He raised one hand. "This hand is your position. A few dumbfuck e-mails and a mechanism for disseminating them independent of your being alive. My guess is Pablo Tochera is your button pusher, and I can't be sure that you don't have others. But that's all you have, Border."

He raised his other hand. "And this is our position. We have Carol Amen. Before he lost his head, Conrad was a sight smarter than you gave him credit for. Miss Amen was in no condition to sound convincing, so Conrad took a rain check on her tempting offer of a rendezvous, and arranged to have one of our friends pay her a visit."

My blood turned to ice. I should have known that Carol's voicemail message was screwy, that she was under threat when she made it. I felt in need of Charles's inhaler. "What have you done to her?"

"Nothing. Yet. As for the future, her life can take one of two courses. If the e-mails remain locked in their box, then she will find that India fulfills her basic needs: food, shelter, television, and maybe some out-of-date *New Yorker* magazines. Her body will be respected. She will be unharmed. Unmolested. Unemployed. Not a bad life really."

"And if the e-mails go out?"

"That really doesn't bear thinking about, Fin. The traffic you speculate about between Bombay and the States can work as well the other way. She will be subjected to every indignity you can imagine, and plenty you can't. She won't die. She'll want to, but we won't let her. We'll keep the respirator switched on. At some point she may succeed in killing herself. But not before we've made her worst nightmare look like a walk in the park."

It was the calmness with which McIntyre presented his position that was so shocking. It was as if he were goofing around with some minor boilerplate provisions in a sale and purchase agreement.

He mimed trying to force his hands together. "So you see, on the basis of what you've suggested, the two hands can never join in a handshake. It's a standoff. The most important thing to you is Carol Amen, even more than the exoneration you crave. We let her go and there is nothing to stop those e-mails from flying out of their box. But if those e-mails fly, then the Amen girl gets fucked to pieces by the lowest life forms rising from the sewer. If the e-mails don't fly, you can keep her in comfortable spinsterhood, somewhere in India."

I wanted to kill him. "No," I said. "Carol stays here, in the US. Then the e-mails will be neutralized."

McIntyre shook his head. "Wouldn't work. You would always be a threat, dead or alive." He shrugged helplessly. "You created this situation, Border. I'm just trying to be practical. I'm trying to help."

I was in a vice.

"How would I know that she was safe?" I asked.

McIntyre smiled at the desperation in my voice.

"And the money? My name?" I added.

McIntyre stroked his chin. "We'd have to work out how to let you know that Miss Amen was having a swell time. As for the money, you can go fuck yourself. We won't pay a dime. And who gives a shit about your good name, that got sunk with your father, God rot him."

There was a knock at the door.

McIntyre's secretary appeared.

"Jim. I know you didn't want to be disturbed, but there's a Detective Manelli waiting to see you."

"Ah, your friend," he said turning back to me. "I'll see him in my meeting room." I couldn't fail to be impressed by his reaction. There was none. For a moment he didn't even move. Mendip and Askari, on the other hand, acted like two kids who had been caught smoking behind the bicycle shed.

There was a door in the corner of McIntyre's office and he made his way to it. "Send Manelli round," he said. "Not through here."

His secretary nodded and left the room.

As McIntyre opened the door, he turned to me. "You don't want Manelli's cuffs on you. Nor do I. So I reckon we'll keep you safe for a while. Jesse will be up in a moment to help."

"I've got to make a call by seven," I said. "Otherwise the e-mails go out."

McIntyre rolled his eyes. "So make your call. I've just told you that you're safe."

"You don't seriously expect me to take your word for it."

He held his hands out again. "Standoff, Fin. Think about it."

He then left the room.

Askari grunted and picked his teeth.

Mendip toyed with the e-mails and wheezed over them.

"And what did Carlstein give to you?" I said to him. "What could possibly bind you to him?"

Mendip didn't look up. "These people love India. Most of them merely want to invest inside and get a proper return for their money."

"Who gives a fuck about NRIs?" I replied. "The other thing, Charles. The other thing."

Mendip came over to me. His face wore a bluish tinge, his whole body drooped. He looked like he was dying and knew it.

He lifted Ganesh from my hands and studied the inscription. My testicles tightened defensively as he gently replaced the statue on my palm.

"I didn't have many friends at Oxford," he said. "A provincial schoolboy from the north, you know. Unsophisticated. Respectable and poor. And here was this giant man—Carlstein—with a giant brain and funny accent who knew no boundaries, would try anything, to whom nothing was sacred. During the mid-sixties in a small north-country seaside town, everything was sacred. Carlstein was a jewel in the mud for us, wasn't he, Sunil?"

"You have little breath, Charles," Askari muttered. "Why waste it?"

Mendip kept his gaze on me. "You probably think of Gemini as dinner-suited students supping fine wine, eating the obscurer parts of animals cooked according to classic French principles, and all the while reciting Proust or Seneca in the original. There was some of that, I'll grant you. But for the most part it was about ideas: about class, about statehood, about eroticism, about law and morality. We loved law, all of us—my God, we all got firsts. But a diet increasingly weighted to the darker side of the Greeks, to Wilde, to Huysmans, de Sade, Genet, Huxley and his mescalin—you can guess the others—well, a diet like this in such a rarified environment, is bound to have an effect."

He laughed. "Bill Clinton and his uninhaled joint. My God, I wish . . ."

"But why didn't you leave it behind at Oxford?" I asked. "Why was anything that followed remotely necessary?"

"Ah." There were decades of regret bundled in Mendip's exhalation, it was the musty puff at lifting the lid on a long unopened suitcase. "The belief, at every stage, that one had gone too far. And the discovery with the next step that the previous one wasn't so serious after all, that it could have been retraced—but that now it was too late. And always the figure of Carlstein over us. He lived in a vacuum to ideas alone—reality didn't seem to impinge on him and bring him to heel."

"But a slave trade, Charles," I said. "Why not flee, start afresh on the other side of the world? Change your name, get plastic surgery, kill yourself. *Anything* but get mixed up in that."

"At some indefinable point, sins of omission become ones of commission," he said. "It wasn't a slave trade at all in the beginning. An immigration service, there was even a quasipolitical philosophical theory that went with it, one of Carlstein's. Anyway, just as money wanted to find a haven, so did people. Carlstein came into contact with more and more facilitators, middlemen, wealthy benefactors with special needs, if you will. A shift of emphasis here, an exception there. The school in Bombay was real, you know. Genuine for Sunil, me, JJ, your father. For a while we pretended to ourselves that the prostitution was an intermittent and unintended sideline from what we could rationalize in more favorable terms. We were busy building empires, after all—legal and legitimate empires—and we allowed ourselves to build the palaces before the revolution was complete."

"And my father?" I whispered.

"Carlstein always looked for weaknesses in people: his brother, Ernie, me." Mendip sighed. "He couldn't find the weakness in your father. It infuriated Carlstein, possessed him. To him it was a fundamental breach of metaphysical laws. Your father became a project for him. And then Ernie's file came along."

The half-eaten file, Bombay breakfast of scam and eggs.

"The drink did the rest, Fin. But he would never have touched that girl. He turned the torment onto himself, tortured himself, destroyed himself."

"And you killed him," I said.

Mendip shook his head. "It wasn't like that. It wasn't a simple case of saying: Border's a threat, kill him." He turned to Askari. "Tell him, Sunil."

"I do not want to talk."

"And why are you prepared to talk, Charles?" I asked. "Is it because, with Carlstein dead, you're able to restore the obligations you owe to me as godfather?"

Mendip shrugged.

Jesse came into the room. Ear-to-ear grin. "Sorry to keep you waiting gentlemen. Okay, Mr. Brown, sir. Mr. M wants you with me." He crooked his arm in mine and led me out of the office and into the secretarial area.

"Patti?" He nodded in the direction of McIntyre's secretary. "Mr. Brown isn't feeling so good. I'm taking him to the restroom to freshen up."

Patti shook her head. "All that food and you didn't eat a thing. You should take better care of yourself."

"I intend to," I said.

In the hallway Jesse placed a thumb and forefinger on the spiral wire sprouting from behind his ear. "See this, Mr. Brown? Any fooling around and a dozen quarterbacks will flatten you." He paused. "You're a Brit, ain't you? Know what a quarterback is?"

I did. JJ had taken me to a few football games.

We headed around the corner in the direction of the elevator banks, and nearly collided with a scurrying figure loaded down with a pile of documents.

It was Chuck Krantz.

"You're in the wrong building, Chuck," I said. A couple of documents had fallen to the floor. I could see "DRAFT PRESS RELEASE" stamped in red at the top of the front page. And underneath, the clasped hands insignia.

Krantz eyed Jesse. "Where you taking him?"

Jesse winked. "Just to the bathroom, Mr. Krantz. He don't feel too well."

Krantz smiled. "Good."

"Don't wait around on my account," I said, as he picked up the rogue press releases. "I'll let you finish being McIntyre's paperboy."

"Fuck you," Krantz said and continued at a trot down the corridor.

We passed the men's room. "It's here, Jesse."

Jesse laughed. "Very good, sir. But this one's for executives only."

We got to the elevator. The doors slid open as soon as Jesse pressed the call button. Once inside, he leaned down and reached for the security key.

My hand was already in my pocket as my head told me there might not be another opportunity. Since I had been with him, his head had towered above me, now it was below, within easy reach.

I'd expected a crack, like the sound of a spoon against the shell of a boiled egg. But as Ganesh connected with the back of Jesse's head, all I heard was a dull thud and a surprised grunt.

Jesse crashed to the floor and for a moment I stood transfixed. I heard Damindra Ketan's skull *crack, crack, crack* on the flagstones at the Towers of Silence, in time with my heartbeat. But if Jesse were dead, I'd have no excuses.

But there had been no crack, and there was no blood either.

He gave a moan as I tore the wire from his ear and ripped it out of the radio.

I turned the security key, punched Floor 53.

Refurbishment, Ellis Walsh had said, as we'd ploughed slowly through the client lists for the Conflict Committee. Extra space for Clay employees who'd made it to the lifeboats.

It was less than five seconds before the door opened at Floor 53. It was a steel-floored wasteland, interrupted only by a few trestle tables laden with a workman's kit, bordered by a horizon of windows. A tangle of wires hung like creepers from the ceiling cavity.

The air smelled of dust and laborers. But there was no one around. This wasn't a twenty-four-hour project; the refugees from Clay & Westminster could kick their heels in their old lodgings while a new home was built during normal business hours.

Jesse was starting to move.

I lifted him from under the armpits, a dead weight and havoc on my suppurating hip that now felt like an overripe melon about to explode.

Tie him up? I looked around me. Short of ripping some wires out of the ceiling, there didn't seem to be anything with which to improvise. The wire from his radio? Too short. Anyway, I didn't want him stuck here all night if he had a fractured skull. Let nature takes its course, I decided.

I got back into the elevator, turned the key, and aimed my finger at the lobby button.

When the door opened again, I limped slowly toward the exit.

Beyond the barrier, I saw more police uniforms. Three.

Manelli had backup.

I went through the turnstile. It clicked easily; it didn't mind my passing through.

A few feet away from the bank of revolving doors, I heard, not a

"Stop that man" or "Hey you," but the unmistakable hiatus of recognition, of impending pursuit.

I broke into an ungainly run and crashed through a half-open segment of the nearest revolving door. It already contained a man who, somewhat imprudently, was reading a newspaper. I passed my hand over his shoulder and gave the glass a decent shove.

"You see that? The fuck . . ." he screamed.

Outside the building, the crowds had thinned. I needed cover, camouflage. Looking down into the ice-rink area, I could see that the restaurant was still busy, roving waiters cruising a sea of clamoring tourists.

I galloped down the stairwell into the throng. Glancing up, I saw two cops leaning over the balustrade. It occurred to me that Detective Manelli could not have been expecting to find me with McIntyre, otherwise I would have been surrounded by flashing lights, megaphones, and darting SWAT teams. Therefore I should be using open ground while I had it, before the dragnet was mobilized and I could be cornered.

One of the cops pointed. He'd seen me. The other held a radio close to his face before following his colleague who was now headed for the stairs.

I was near a stupid glass bubble of an elevator that took tourists the fifteen feet from street level to the rink. Charging through a small group of people, necks craned, compact cameras focused on the GE Building, I rammed my arm into the narrow gap of the closing elevator doors and pried them open. The startled occupants continued to lick their ice creams and fiddle with Saks shopping bags while they wondered whether to scream, whether I was going to pull a gun.

"It's okay," I said breathlessly. "Late for a date."

They didn't look like they believed me, but the journey was too short to matter much one way or the other.

Fifth, get to Fifth, I screamed to myself as I placed Saks in my sights and ran for it; but I wouldn't be aiming to take sanctuary there; or even in St. Patrick's Cathedral to its left. A yellow cab would provide a more mobile and practical haven.

The traffic on Fifth was moving fast and even though there were "free" lights aplenty on passing cabs, I knew the operation of hailing and entering would cost more time than I could afford, particularly as I could see that I wasn't the only one on the sidewalk with the same idea.

"FUCKIN' DYKE FASCIST VERMIN."

I wheeled round to find a scabrous bum frothing at some poor tourist who'd got in the path of his three-coach train of shopping carts filled with empty soda cans.

Without stopping to think of the consequences, I wrenched the pushbar of the rear cart from the bum's hand and swung his wretched convoy into the oncoming traffic.

It was hardly an F1 McLaren onto the FDR, but my version served well enough. In the shower of cans that rained down after the impact of carts and postal van, traffic on Fifth came to an abrupt halt to a modest accompaniment of crunches and splintering glass.

I ran into the traffic and yanked open the rear door of a cab that had slowed to a near stop in front of Saks.

"What's happening, man?" asked the driver, jerking his head toward the west side of the street. He didn't sound that interested.

"A derelict hurling soda cans at cops," I replied as calmly as possible.

He sniggered. "Good," he said before accelerating hard. "Where to?" he added as an afterthought.

I was only a few blocks from Pablo's house, but I figured it might be better to take a roundabout route to ensure I wasn't being pursued. Pablo and company had enough to contend with already.

"Er, corner of 42nd and Fifth, then somewhere else," I said.

I looked at my watch. Two minutes to seven. Hell's teeth.

I called Pablo.

"Fuck you," he blurted. "I was—I mean Paula was—about to hit the red button."

"There's two minutes left," I said indignantly.

"Not according to CNN, there isn't. It was seven about five seconds ago, you crazy fuck. I nearly had heart failure. Sheesh, the world goes kawoosh because a fucked-up Brit can't tell the time."

"Fin the Quartz" belonged to another era.

Pablo allowed himself a couple more expletives before seeming to calm down. "You okay?" he finally asked.

"Everything hurts," I said. "Even my wig."

"Where are you?"

I looked up at the driver. He had the radio on, and the Lucite window that separated us was open only a couple of inches. I reckoned he wouldn't hear much if I kept my voice down and my mouth close to the phone.

"Fifth Avenue, and I'm in trouble."

"You've been in trouble since I've known you."

"You are too. Get the women and kids out of the house, wipe as much as you can off the computer, and wait for me at the corner of your street and Lexington."

"Fin, what the fuck am I supposed to tell Julia?"

I lowered my voice still further.

"Tell her your boss is running schoolkids out of Bombay and into the States. Prostitutes. Slaves, Pablo."

"I can't hear you."

"Just get them out and be at the corner of Lexington. I won't be long." I snapped the phone shut. Suddenly I felt sorry for the bum and his soda cans. But he was shouting at a tourist, wasn't he? That wasn't neighborly. And yet it didn't warrant having his business empire obliterated by the traffic.

# FORTY-NINE

**P**ablo wasn't standing on the corner.

I got out of the taxi. For a moment I stood there and swore under my breath. Passersby gave me sideways glances.

I didn't care. Without Pablo, I was nowhere.

"Ain't you got eyes in your fucking head?"

I could have hugged him.

"Where were you?" I asked.

He pointed to a parking garage over the street. "I was waving my arms like a fucking windmill, you jerk. *Sheesh*. And you stand here looking like a street sign."

"Where are the others?"

"On their way to Vermont. We got a lodge on Lake Champlain. They'll take a flight from La Guardia to Burlington."

A hell of a way, but the farther the better.

"Where's the car?"

Pablo aimed a mock slap at my face. "In the fucking garage, where'd you think? I'm going to leave a silver Jaguar out in the open for some asshole to take apart after they're through with my house?"

"I'm sorry, Pablo."

"Don't be, Fin." He sighed. "I should have known better than to think I could join the big guys."

"You're better than them."

He smiled. "I know."

"We need to go back into the house," I said. "I need to fetch a couple of things." I touched the wig. "And I want to get rid of this."

Pablo pulled a huge bunch of keys from his pocket. "Then where?"

"Centre Island."

He whacked the keys against the palm of his hand. They must have weighed a pound. Jesus, that would hurt. "You fucked-up Brit. You're not suggesting we go to the house that McIntyre uses up there?"

"Just give me the keys, Pablo. I'll let myself in. I won't be a moment."

He dangled them in front of me and then jerked them aside as I tried to take them. "The guy who can get into my house when it's locked up hasn't been born. Let's go."


It was getting dark when we pulled up at Officer Miller's checkpoint. Two or three coats and a random selection of knitwear covered me in my hiding place on the floor at the back of the car. It was hot as hell.

I heard Miller's voice. Genial but curious.

The Yacht Club, Pablo explained. They were collecting old clothes for charity. For children, added Pablo.

I hoped Miller wouldn't notice that the clothes piled up in the back were for rather oversized children.

Miller and Pablo then swapped stories about the weather, goings-on at the Yacht Club, kids running wild, headless torsos in the back of Toyotas, Miller's regret that the wreck had happened outside his jurisdiction, which, in actuality, ran to only a few feet either side of the booth. It was turning out to be one hell of a summer. He'd be glad when Labor Day arrived and things would wind down.

Pablo talked about his boat.

I heard the door of the booth open, then footsteps.

Shit, no.

"Yeah, here it is," I heard Pablo say, obviously passing across a photograph.

"She's a beauty," Miller said. "I wouldn't want to make landfall, if I had me a boat like that."

More footsteps and the exchange of farewells. Then I felt the car move forward.

"You like your boat," I said, burrowing out of hibernation, swathed in sweat.

"I love her," he said, adding quickly, "nearly as much as Julia." He tapped the photo on the wheel. *Julia I*. There was passion in Pablo's eyes. "You know," he said, "when McIntyre got to hear I had a boat, he said that I wouldn't get a chance to use it. I'd be working too hard. He said he hated boats, anyway. Why the fuck does he have a place out here if he doesn't like boats, for Christ's sake?" He placed the photo back inside his wallet. "Asshole."

"Can I ask you something, Pablo?"

"Shoot," he said amiably.

"When McIntyre made you take on my case, what exactly was going through your head?"

To my surprise, he didn't hesitate; no "sheesh," no expletive. "Partnership, Fin. Pure and simple. The first person in my family to be something. Not just have money, but really be *something*."

He took his hands off the steering wheel for a second and rubbed his face. "It clouded my judgment a little."

We passed the Seawanaka Yacht Club. Pablo allowed his neck to swivel with the view. "That would be neat," he whispered.

"Why don't you join?" I asked.

He stared ahead. "Not their type. And too far from home." He slowed down. "That the house?"

We had rounded the corner and, ahead, the land dipped into the valley of mosquito lagoon; Carlstein's house lay beyond, a shadow in the twilight. To our left, the road hugged the hillside, dropping a little, before disintegrating into dirt track for the climb onto the ridge. The big house was silhouetted against the darkening sky.

I half-expected to see lightning fork around its gables, for thunder to rumble among the turrets. The House of Usher, the Bates Motel.

But everything seemed quiet.

And inside? Wood paneling and echoes. Servants' quarters, dumb-waiters, light switches from a different era. Big, open fireplaces. Forbidding portraits of men with facial hair and women with dresses as big as tents.

The skitter of rats. Dust in the corners. Two-way mirrors on the wall. What else in the corners, in the dark crevices, the cellars? People. Little people. Petrified Pixies in the staging post to hell. And Carol?

"How far do you want me to go?" Pablo asked.

I didn't want to get too close. "Anywhere here."

Pablo edged the car off the road and onto the grass shoulder. The plastic cylinders protecting a row of small saplings against gnawing wildlife were no match for the Jaguar. Pablo parked over three of them.

He grinned at me. "A while back, I planted four trees in Central Park," he said. "So I figure I'm still in credit."

"We can be seen here," I said. "Does McIntyre know what car you drive?"

"Apart from my boat, McIntyre knows jack shit about me. He even calls Julia 'Connie.' " He rubbed his chin again. "So now we watch?"

I'd promised that was to be the full extent our activities for the evening. Watch the house, look for movement. Make deductions. Draft a new deal.

I reached for a pair of small rubberized binoculars, German and good quality.

"I borrowed these," I said. I'd borrowed a few things from Pablo's marine kitbag in the guest room.

Light showed in a couple of the curtained windows. I could make out the shape of a car near the inky arch that I took to be the front door.

I rested the binoculars on my lap. "Maybe they've pulled out already," I said. "Just forgotten to switch off the lights."

"You think they did stuff in the house itself?" Pablo asked.

Carlstein had, McIntyre had.

But that wasn't its primary function. It was a staging post. A halfway house, Ernie had said.

"Perhaps we're too late," I muttered.

Perhaps not, though. "If they had people and stuff to move," I said, "they'd have to get past Officer Miller, wouldn't they?"

"He's useless." Pablo turned away from the house and scanned the bay with the binoculars. "He liked my boat, though. So I got to make allowances."

I jabbed Pablo in the arm. "Boats," I said. "Of course. They'd move everything out by boat."

"And they'd have to move out at night."

A silent retreat from the beachhead, a cruise down Long Island Sound to another hideaway.

"I want to look," I said.

"There's nothing to see," Pablo said, after another sweep with the binoculars.

"Not from here," I said. "Around the back of the house. There'll be a slipway or jetty or something."

"I thought you said we'd just watch from the car."

"I said we'd just watch. I didn't say it would be from the car."

He was silent for a moment. "You want me with you?"

"No, stay here." I wasn't going to restrict myself to watching. "I'll have the cell phone."

"Yeah, my cell phone," Pablo said. "What am I supposed to use, a fucking tin can?"

"Oh," I said forlornly.

"It's okay, guy. I took Julia's."

I took the bag off the backseat and got out of the car.

"What else you got in there?" Pablo tried to catch the edge of the bag as I walked by his open window.

"You can keep the opera glasses," I said and set off.

At the point where the road forked, I carried on toward Carlstein's house, keeping half an eye on the top of the hill. The angle was bad and my view of the house started at around its second story, the rest obscured by the ridge.

Now that I knew my way around, distances seemed less than before and it didn't take long to find myself edging along the shrubs that ran alongside the dirt track.

I ignored the mosquitoes, but my hip was hurting badly, slowing me up. It was difficult to ignore. Antiseptic hadn't been enough, Julia had said; what I needed were antibiotics.

Carlstein's house looked empty, no car in the garage, no light. He was dead. And yet an aura hung over the place.

Again I went around the back and onto the deck. I glanced quickly at my handiwork on the rear window. A black mass of bugs and mosquitoes had gathered on the honey-drenched newspaper.

Out in Long Island Sound, the lights on a few late-returning sailboats rose and fell in the gentle swell.

I looked over the edge of the deck. There was only a small strip of concrete-strewn beach between the water's edge and a shore that rose in a tangle of brambles and loose boulders into the darkness beyond.

I suddenly realized that this wasn't just a dumping ground. All this shit was there for a reason. To discourage visitors.

I climbed down the rusty ladder onto the beach.

Picking my way along the shoreline, I stepped over the dinosaur-like remnants of long-dead saddle crabs, and felt the crunch of oyster shells where the gulls had lifted them from the mud and slammed them against the rocks.

Then there was the human debris: empty cans, beer bottles, toilet paper, sanitary napkins. And the concrete boulders. A grudging sliver of moon bathed their hard edges with light, throwing strands of steel like rusty corkscrews into sharp relief.

The beach widened into a sandbar that cut into the entrance of the bay.

I could hear noises. Voices? Maybe. And scraping, banging.

All I could see were points of light out over the water. Some moved and some stayed still. More sailboats? I couldn't tell.

I crouched and moved nearer.

Not boats. People holding lights. They seemed to float on the water. Then I realized they were on the sandbar.

I was a hundred feet away from the base of the small cliff beneath the house. I moved toward it. There seemed to be no trash here, just a few large rocks. McIntyre obviously didn't want his immediate surroundings looking like a building site.

The noise had stopped. The lights were no longer moving.

Keeping one eye on the motionless lights in the bay, I clung to the eaves of the cliff, feeling the sand turn to coarse reeds on a marshy base. The blades of grass swished against my thighs and a few birds rose into the sky with a clatter of wings and a chorus of indignant squawks.

I could hear shouts. I kept my head below the tops of the reeds. Even if I'd stood up and waved my arms, it was unlikely I'd be seen, but whoever was out on the sandbar had been spooked by the birds, and they'd be wondering what had spooked the birds first.

A boat engine growled and spluttered, followed by several more. A flotilla. The retreating armada on the move. I could see lights slide at speed out of the bay and into the Sound.

People, equipment. They'd gone.

Was Carol huddled in one of those boats? Did she know what McIntyre had planned for her?

I walked farther along the edge of the cliff. It was only twenty feet high, but there seemed no way up it.

There was another noise. I stopped.

It had been nearby. An animal, maybe? But there'd been no scurry in the undergrowth, no thrash of reeds.

I held my breath.

A whimper, a rustle. Just a few feet away.

I moved toward the sound. Whatever it was would be able to hear me. It could escape or attack if it wanted. But it stayed put.

I parted the reeds. A small, solid bundle lay trembling on the boggy reed bed, like an oversized hedgehog, curled up for safety. I could feel its fear rise up to meet me.

"It's okay," I whispered.

The ball stayed curled up. I prodded it gently. Somehow it was still an animal to me, although I could see it was human.

A face appeared; huge eyes catching the meager moonlight, blinking in its beam.

The face of someone little more than a child. The corner of her mouth drooped; in fact the whole of one side of her face sagged. If she'd been older, one might have thought she'd had a stroke. But kids didn't have strokes, did they? I looked closer; there was scar tissue across her cheek.

But she was still beautiful, still recognizable as the girl in Raj's photograph. My father's wood nymph.

I put down my bag and touched her shoulder. "Preeti?"

She unfurled a little.

"Who are you?" The voice was so feeble, a helpless murmur.

"I'm a friend of your brother. Raj asked me to find you."

And I had found her. I'd been looking for someone else, but I'd still found her. That was only part of the promise, though. Make sure she's all right, Raj had pleaded, as the flames consumed him.

She didn't look all right at all.

Preeti sat up a little. "I have not heard from my brother. You say he was a friend of yours. How is he?"

I hesitated, tempted to lie, but her open, damaged gaze made it impossible. "He's dead, Preeti," I said. I reached for her little hand and held it in mine. "I'm so sorry."

She sat stock still, her hand limp.

"I felt it," she said. "I felt his heart stop beating. A brother's heartbeat can be felt in a sister's breast."

She looked up at me. "How did he die?"

His boss had tied him up in red tape and torched him.

"There was a fire."

She removed her hand from my clasp and placed it on her cheek.

"Someone burned me once," she whispered. "Now I know why. It was so that I could feel some of Raj's pain."

"What happened here, Preeti?"

"They moved us out. They told us we would be taken to a safer place, where the immigration authorities couldn't find us. Then we would be put to work again."

"But they said that I was unlikely to find work." She stroked her face. "Because of this . . . I think they were going to kill me. So on the way to the boats, I slipped away."

"Was there a white girl?"

She shook her head. "Everyone was from India. About fifteen of us, boys and girls."

"Is the house empty?" I asked.

"I do not know. I saw no one, but we only passed through a little part of the house to get here."

She pointed along the cliff. "We came down some steps, onto the beach. They were very dangerous. One girl fell. That was when I ran."

She started to curl up again. "I hope she is all right," she whimpered. "This is a place of pain. I cannot believe Mr. Askari would have sent me here if he had known what it was like."

Elaboration on the true nature of Mr. Askari could be adjourned for the moment.

"I want you to wait here for a while," I said. "If I don't come back within an hour, then carry on down the beach until you get to a house. Go around the side of the house and walk along the track until you reach the road. There will be a silver car parked a little way along. There will be a man in the car. He is a friend; stay with him and you'll be safe."

Preeti rolled herself into an even tighter ball. "I will not go to a man in a silver car. I will only go with you. Or on my own, if you do not come back to me."

"I'll come back."

I almost passed the dark scar in the rock before I noticed it. A rusty ladder climbed vertically from the beach, narrow, unwelcoming, and treacherous. On the cliff face itself hung a thick rope. Following it upward, I could see that the rope was connected to something at the top.

A gantry, maybe.

A winch.

The rope just dangled; there was no hook, no nothing. Scanning the immediate area, I could tell that there had been a good deal of activity recently. The scree and sand was scuffed and pitted. By feet and heavy objects.

I placed my foot on the first rung of the ladder. My hip exploded with pain and I dropped my leg back onto the beach.

Twenty feet wasn't such a great height, but in my condition it was K2.

I removed a couple of things from the bag, then slung it into a clump of reeds and started back on the ladder. I was short of breath and my eyes were clouded with sweat.

"Don't move a fucking muscle."

A beam of light hit me at the same time as the voice. The top of the ladder was the brilliant white center of a powerful flashlight or, perhaps, a searchlight.

My limbs locked, my hand shielding my eyes, trying to peer into the sharp contrasts of black and white.

Someone broke the light beam by pitching his body over the edge of the ladder to start a descent. I couldn't see who it was. I was only aware of the confident movement of strong legs planting themselves firmly on each rung of the ladder.

"Bring him up here," someone shouted from above. McIntyre?

Then I caught a glimpse of white; a large, square dressing on the back of a shaven head.

Jesse jumped the last three steps, walked over to me, and, without a word, planted a massive punch in my stomach.

As I dropped to the sand, clutching my intestines, Jesse stood back and rubbed his knuckle. "Fucking attorneys," he hissed.

"Stop horsing around, Jesse." The voice from the top of the cliff. Angry, authoritative. It was definitely McIntyre. "Just get him up here."

Jesse grabbed my collar and jerked me upright. "Get up the ladder, motherfucker."

I leaned against the cold, rusty rungs and could feel the dribble running down my chin. My legs start to give way under me. In the distance I could hear more birds taking flight. They didn't sound like ducks. They sounded like vultures, circling, ready for their next meal.

"I can't move," I wheezed.

Jesse pulled his fist back as if to hit me again, then stopped and looked around him.

"Then we'll have to give you some help, won't we," he said.

Tugging at the end of the dangling rope, he formed it, in an instant, into a crude noose, which he looped over my neck and pulled tight.

He lifted his head. "Start that winch, Mr. M," he shouted.

He then patted me on the cheek. "Cheerio, old fellow. Express service to the top floor. This time, no stops."

As he bounded up the ladder, I pulled at the rope, jerking at it, tearing at it as it dug deep into my neck.

I tried to scream but only managed a rasp.

My head started to explode as I felt my feet leave the ground and kick frantically against the cliff wall. I clawed at the noose, driving my fingers between the coarse rope and my flesh, but it made no difference; there was a vice closing on my throat and inside my head was a fireworks display.

Thoughts cascaded and then I wasn't thinking anything at all.

The first thing I sensed was movement. The world was moving. Flying by. Then pain. My back was on fire.

I tried to swallow. The vice still gripped and I gagged. I wanted to bring my hands to my throat, feel it, comfort it. My skin on my skin. But my arms weren't responding, they were being held by something above my head. It was like I was on the rack.

And still the world was moving. Pictures passed me by. Tables; one with an old black telephone, like my grandfather's, another with a large Chinese vase, blooming with vivid yellow and white flowers.

Then I could see up a grand staircase, a huge picture window at the top where the flight hit a landing and split in two.

Thoughts started to return along with a blunted ability to analyze. I concluded that the world wasn't moving, after all. I was. Jesse was dragging me by the wrists. The pictures, the tables, the vase, the telephone, were landmarks on a floor-level tour through the halfway house to hell.

A phone rang somewhere: contemporary, electronic, out of kilter with the house.

I felt someone rummaging in my jacket pocket and removing my cell phone. The noise suddenly got shriller.

I looked up to see McIntyre peer at the screen and then press a button. He listened for a moment before switching it off, before placing it carefully beneath the heel of his shoe and grinding it into an inoperable mess.

He turned to Jesse and nodded.

Jesse tapped me in the ribs with his toecap. "You be good while I'm gone."

He marched across the hall and fought for a moment with a giant latch handle on the front door.

I heard the house echo as the huge door closed behind him.

"I thought we had a deal, Fin," McIntyre said.

I could only manage a croak.

McIntyre said, "You sure got Jesse pissed with that bump on his head."

Footsteps sounded from down the hall. I tried to move, but everything hurt too much.

"You should have stayed away, Fin." It was Mendip's voice, but I sensed he hadn't come alone. I swiveled my head and looked up.

Flanked by Mendip and Askari was Carol. Her face was as wretched as the tracksuit she wore, the same one she'd been wearing at St. Cecelia's.

"Fin," she whispered. Her voice barely covered the distance. She began to move toward me.

Askari gripped her hair and pulled her back into line.

I opened my mouth to scream at him. I squirmed, raging at my impotence.

McIntyre knelt at my side, keeping his eyes on Carol.

"Have you any idea what she'd be worth to the right customer?" he said. "I wish we'd got the mother: a pair. Like vases and candlesticks, more valuable as a pair." He poked me in the ribs. "A bit of makeup, around the eyes, redden up those lips. They could have danced together, undressed each other." Ernie had said he wanted to dance with the Pixies, *a defiling dance*. "Maybe bathed together. Oedipus becomes Shedipus. Jesus, it gives me a boner just thinking about it."

He seemed to retreat from the fantasy and straightened up. "Still, we got her."

I started to squirm again. McIntyre pulled me upright. "Here, let me help you. Get a better view of your loved one." He slid me along the floor and propped me against the wood-paneled wall. I could smell the polish; it tormented my throat and made me gag.

"You ever get Carol to fix up the threesome for you?" he asked. "Heck, I'd respect you for that."

"Stick to business, Jim," Mendip said. He drew heavily on his inhaler, as if his lungs couldn't cope with his own stench.

I moved my legs and arms a little. I didn't feel paralyzed anymore. The vice was still on my throat, but air could get past it now.

The front door opened and Pablo appeared, Jesse herding him from behind. From the outside, I could hear a distant rattle. It was familiar, but at that moment I couldn't place it.

"He was near the house, Mr. M," Jesse said. "Cut loose from that nice silver car of his."

Pablo glanced at Carol, winced, and then looked at me. "You okay?"

"No," I croaked.

The rattle had turned into a steady throb that was starting to vibrate through the house. I could feel it pulsing through my body.

McIntyre raised his eyes to the ceiling. "They're here." He turned to me. "Like I said, I thought we had a deal. I'm a lawyer, you're a lawyer, and we struck a bargain."

"A standoff isn't a deal," I said. I had to draw a nigh-impossible breath between each word.

McIntyre shrugged. "Well, this is the position now." He moved over to Pablo and clapped him on the back. "You're now keeper of the key, Pablo. You're a big guy now. As of this morning you're a partner. Something to celebrate with Connie." He turned to Mendip and Askari. "His wife. A good family man, the kind we like at the top table."

"I don't want a partnership." Pablo's words were barely audible above the now deafening noise from outside. "I don't want anything to do with you."

"Time-out, my Latino friend." McIntyre's face was pure threat now, the smile gone. "You'll take the cap, and you'll fucking wear it. If you don't, then this lady will be fucked until she splits open. And to reinforce the point, you and Connie will take delivery each day of a piece of one of the kids we just shipped out of here."

Pablo looked at me.

"Go on," McIntyre said, "ask his advice. He should understand the meaning of standoff by now."

"Do what he says, Pablo." I didn't know if he could hear me. The noise shook the house now. It was a helicopter, maybe two of them.

That explained the ugly expanse of asphalt in front of the house. McIntyre hated boats, didn't he? And a car meant running Officer Miller's puny gauntlet.

Carol shook herself free of Askari's grasp and ran over to me. She fell on my chest; her eyes scanned my face, her hands running gently over the bruised skin on my neck.

She turned to McIntyre. "Why?" she asked. "Don't you people have enough, what more could you want? So you take our lives, what's next? Where do you stop?"

She got up and started to move toward McIntyre, her arms semi-outstretched in a kind of bewildered supplication rather than aggression. Jesse stepped forward and delivered a sweeping kick, Carol's legs buckling under her. Jesse then stood over her like a proud matador.

"It's not about killing, Carol," I said. "It's about something much worse. For you. We have no choice. They'll kill me whatever happens."

Jesse went to the front door and opened it, allowing Carol to crawl back to me. The noise and clatter swept in like a storm. I could feel Carol's wet cheeks on mine, her hands in what was left of my hair. Her hair blew in the wind, and it was like the storm was pulling her away from me. But it was Jesse wrenching her from my grasp.

Through the swirl and mayhem, the tears and the despairing face, I could see her lips move. But I couldn't hear her.

I tried to stand up, levering myself up against the wall.

McIntyre was shouting instructions into Jesse's ear, pointing this way and that, directing everybody to their proper positions for the final clear-out.

Askari waylaid Jesse and helped himself to the handgun that poked out from his belt. He nodded and let Jesse move out through the front door, then stood over me, pointing the gun at my head. His face was expressionless.

He kicked me, and waved the gun upward, indicating that he wanted me to stand. Fuck him.

He kicked harder. I started the struggle to get upright. Suddenly I felt Mendip's hands under my armpits. His face was gray-blue, taut, wracked by the battle of his spongy lungs for air.

He helped me up and guided me to the door. His arms felt weak. Who was supporting whom?

There was a hurricane outside. Except no rain, just the blast of whipped hot night air and the shrill whine of two helicopters, parked near each other, their blades almost touching.

I looked up. Even the sad sliver of moon had gone. There were no stars either. How was that possible? It had been a beautiful day, not a cloud in sight.

Where were the stars, for Christ's sake?

Askari moved his gun in a series of downward jerks. He tapped his head with his other hand.

What was he—?

I felt the air whip around my head.

Why should he care if I lost my head in the rotor blades? Inconvenience, I guessed. They'd cleaned out the house. It was now a respectable Long Island retreat. My brains on the asphalt might tarnish the image if the police got to nose around the place.

How *were* they going to kill me?

Askari shoved me through the door of the helicopter. The interior was like the crowded rear section of a cheap flight. Carol was already in one seat, head lolling back on the rest, like she was unconscious, with Jesse leaning over her. He pulled up sharply and now I could see the syringe in his hand. In-flight refreshments had just been served.

A helmeted pilot sat in his seat like a statue. A trusty butler in a hard hat, who sees nothing, hears nothing.

Jesse shoved me into the empty backseat, took out a vial of liquid, and jabbed the syringe into it. Under my feet I could feel a solid lump and, glancing down, I recognized the shape of a sandbag.

So I was to be knocked out and dumped at sea.

Above the noise, I heard a shout.

It was Askari. He was gesticulating at Jesse, who handed the gun over to Mendip, and pointed to the other chopper. I watched as McIntyre and Pablo climbed into it.

Was Mendip coming with us? Four seats, but five people, including Jesse and the pilot. Would the whirlibird even take off with that load? Or had Mendip been deputed to be the last one aboard the escape chopper, the last guy on the roof of the US embassy in Saigon? His commission to see us off safely first.

My hand burrowed into my pocket.

In a moment I'd be out cold; would I even be aware of the instant of my death?

Lawyers like to use a Latinism when there isn't a fixed time for an event. *Sine die,* they say. Without day. It doesn't mean it won't happen, it's just that you don't know when. From the moment that the flashlight blinded me on the beach behind the house, I'd told myself there might be a better time to act. *Sine die,* I'd told myself.

Now, the time was fixed.

The time was now.

I curved my fingers around the short cylinder. I kept my eyes on Jesse as my fingers felt for the tab. He turned to me, syringe in hand, an echo of Damindra Ketan at the Towers of Silence. But this time I wasn't going to turn the syringe back on my assailant.

Jesse gave me a strange look, like he sensed something was wrong.

I pulled out the cylinder, ripped off the tab, and leaning forward, I dropped it between the pilot's legs. I heard it bounce against the foot pedals, spluttering on the floor.

When you shake up a can of Bud really hard, the geyser that erupts when you pull the tab can be spectacular.

But this wasn't a can of Bud, and instead of beer spewing out, it was flame.

And a distress flare isn't just supposed to behave like a top-of-the-range Roman Candle. It's supposed to send a little ball of phosphorous, or whatever, a thousand feet up into the air. You're supposed to see the resulting supernova from the fucking moon.

The pilot didn't need any explanation at all. He was already out of the chopper; a neat parachute roll on the tarmac and he was away.

Jesse was also trying to leave, but he was in an awkward position between the front and rear seats.

I had nowhere to go.

I leaned across the gangway and tried to spread myself over Carol.

In the confined space, the blast was ear-shattering. I could feel the wave of heat pass over my back. The whole chopper shook.

The cabin filled with thick smoke that corkscrewed out of the open doors. If those doors had been shut . . .

I twisted my body around and caught hold of Carol, tipping her over the front seat and giving her a shove.

I was choking badly now, and ready for the others to reappear and finish what they'd started. My body was seizing up, giving up. I was finished.

A pair of hands appeared on my shoulders. Old hands.

They pulled at me, a compassionate removal of my arms from their sockets.

I hit the asphalt.

The smoke was clearing and I could see Mendip's face staring into mine.

A bloodless face, an old, old face, engulfed by despair.

He coughed viciously, swayed a little, but then broke into a stumbling run, waving his arms at the other helicopter that was starting to rise from the ground, hovering uncertainly, a face pressed against the window behind the pilot. Whose face? Pablo's? McIntyre's or Askari's?

I managed to crawl over to Carol. She looked like a sleeping child that had fallen out of bed and not even woken. I swept the hair from her face.

Nearby, the belly of the chopper fizzed and spluttered, as if it had a terminal case of acid indigestion. I was in a trance. I had to move, move myself and Carol. But I couldn't.

In the distance, the other helicopter retreated over the Sound. Then the clatter of rotor blades was replaced by the wail of sirens. A whole orchestra of light and sound, appearing over the brow of the hill like a Wurlitzer from the pit of an old Broadway theater.

The cops could put out the flames in the chopper, I thought. That was their job.

# FIFTY

**D**etective Manelli said he was confused.

He had an unconscious Carol (or, rather, he didn't have her any-more, she was in an ambulance on the way to the hospital). He had a patch of slime and some scattered body parts spread in a wide radius around a burnt-out helicopter now covered in foam. I guessed these were the remains of Jesse; he must've ignored Askari's advice and leapt upward when he left the chopper, caught himself in the still-rotating blades. Strange what one misses; I hadn't noticed the mess until Manelli pointed it out.

He had an old guy who couldn't breathe, let alone talk.

He had an empty house, quiet as a fucking grave, he said.

"And I've got you."

He rested a foot on the ramp at the back of the ambulance, where I sat with a blanket wrapped around my shoulders.

"And I've just finished a call with your counsel."

Pablo? Where the hell was Pablo?

"Mr. Jim McIntyre," he said in mock awe. "Senior partner of

Schuster Mannheim." I didn't correct him; he wouldn't be interested in handshake logos.

"You've got the top man working for you," Manelli continued. "Meant to scare me, I guess. But I've met him before, checking he wasn't taking his attorney's duty to his client too far, like maybe harboring a fugitive. Not in the Rockefeller Center itself, of course—that one caught me out, I'll admit—he says you never made it to his office. I'm not sure I believe him. Cute trick with the cans, by the way: Interfacing with traffic seems to be your bag, doesn't it? Anyway, McIntyre seems a nice enough guy—for an attorney. He says that he has some very disturbing evidence about the old guy who can't breathe. He may seem like a nice old Brit, but it turns out he's the devil. Mr. McIntyre says that you're one of his victims. He says I better be nice to you because the weight of his firm will be behind you."

Manelli drew close to me. "I don't give a fuck about Schuster Mannheim or its senior partner; all I care about is understanding this mess. We get a call from a pay phone at La Guardia. A lady with a Spanish accent. She tells us nothing; just mentions your name and tells us to get up here."

So it was Julia Tochera who had called. The nurse had decided on intensive care. Manelli must have taken her seriously, the burnt-out helicopter had a neighbor with "Police" all over it. The guys in cars were presumably local, although I couldn't see Officer Miller anywhere.

Manelli seemed to scan the scene with me. "And I find this," he sighed.

But it was McIntyre's message that really interested me. The message was for me, not for Manelli; it was a cancerous olive branch, being held out from a clattering, panic-stricken bubble somewhere above New York.

McIntyre wanted my silence, and presumably Carol's too.

Was there enough to pay for it? To cover Gemini's debts?

There might be, just might be.

And what about Charles Mendip?

Did *omerta* feature somewhere deep in the Gemini code?

Was he to be the sin-eater for them all? Would he have the stomach for it? Would he be able to breathe at all with the extra weight?

A young uniformed cop ran up to Manelli and whispered in his ear.

Manelli turned to me. "The girl you said we'd find on the beach, she isn't there."

Where was Preeti? A fleeing shadow along the shoreline, perhaps. She could run fast; I remembered the speed with which she'd crossed my father's bedroom. But that was a long time ago.

Another policeman approached us; he was carrying an oxygen bottle with a tube that snaked up to a plastic mask strapped over Mendip's mouth. Mendip was leaning heavily against him.

He guided Mendip to the ramp where I was sitting, and set him down next to me, resting the oxygen bottle on his lap.

"Only two ambulances showed up," the cop said. "One has taken the woman. I've asked for another but they can't say when it will show."

"Jesus," Manelli moaned. "Anyone would think I was dealing with a low-grade mugging here."

I looked at Mendip. Each breath was a battle for him and his eyes slid drunkenly in their sockets, never settling on my face. I wondered what it would do for his asthma if I told him what his Gemini brothers might have in mind for him.

A man in a suit approached us.

I'd seen him before.

"Hi, Manelli," the man said. "What's up?"

Manelli looked surprised. "Cy, what you doing here? This isn't your territory."

Outside my apartment block, in the driving rain, the man leaning against his car, looking up at me. He must have been a cop after all.

The man frowned. "Yeah, I know. I'm supposed to stick behind the desk, play with my computer. That's all you think us college guys are good for."

Manelli seemed embarrassed. "Cy, you're in the wrong place."

"Sure, Manelli." The man fixed his gaze on me. His eyes burned with something, something more than the thrill of a techie cop getting a look in on the action. "Fin Border," he whispered. The voice was cultured, the suit well-tailored.

"Yes, it's Border," Manelli replied.

"You going to lock him up?"

"You better leave, Cy . . ." Manelli moved toward him. "Your boss will be none too happy when he hears about this."

"He can fuck himself," the man shouted. "He didn't have a daughter on the FDR that day. Border didn't kill one of his kids." His hand moved inside his jacket. "You like my makeover on your apartment, Border, you fuck? Did your whores understand the messages I left for them?" He pulled out a gun. "But you, Border, only a bullet will do for you."

The surrounding policemen hesitated momentarily, then grasped the situation and started to move.

Reaching out, I could have stuck my finger down the barrel.

I started to pull myself into the interior of the ambulance, effectively boxing myself in. I was the cornered animal.

A daughter, for Christ's sake.

I held up my arms in a futile appeal.

My need to live suddenly overwhelmed me. It was everything. Now there was a deal to be done.

I looked into the man's face. He was also overwhelmed—with the need to kill me.

It was everything to him.

"It wasn't me," I pleaded. "I'm sorry about—"

A blast filled the air. What was left of my eardrums, after the exploding distress flare, seemed to disintegrate in my head. Cordite tingled in my nostrils.

But how? I was dead.

There was a weight over my chest.

I peered down my body and met the empty stare of Mendip, his open mouth a cistern filling and then emptying blood into the oxygen mask that lay askew on the side of his face. When the blood had filled the mask, it overflowed onto me. I felt its warmth. I could smell it.

# EPILOGUE

## Spring 2002

We—that is, Carol and I—rescue kids. Try to, at any rate. We operate at the unfashionable end of the rescue spectrum where the kids are calloused and knowing beyond their age or otherwise damaged in ways unappealing to the section of the public that still watches documentaries. The kids come from countries that give most people goose bumps, assuming they've heard of them: Nepal, Bangladesh, and, of course, India; although Cambodia, the Philippines, and Thailand have now joined our repertoire. Travel isn't easy and so international expansion is going to be a slow process. Terry Wardman handles the more complex visa requirements, gets us into places that don't want us, would want us even less if they knew what we were really doing. Maybe they *do* know. Terry will have to turn the valve the other way to get us out if things burn too ugly.

McIntyre and Askari can't understand us. Why bother, they say. If we want to enter the do-good hall of fame, there are plenty of other routes. Nobody gives a shit, they say, it's so *marginal* and there's plenty else to worry about. Anyway, they say, the human traffic will dry up. But it hasn't dried up. The money's too good and the market's still there, flourishing, even; following different paths, to be sure, with different players, but still very much there. And that makes me angry, Carol too. We have found a niche where anger works, where it has energy *and* direction; not so much a motive as motive force.

But we need McIntyre and Askari. And we have a deal, a more symbiotic standoff: They help with making the contacts, establishing the conduits, maintaining the expense account. And we . . . well, it's more a case of what we don't do. We don't tell tales: to the authorities, to the Lords of the Pixies. We don't let e-mails fly. We let the old gents sit at their senior partners' desks and stay great and good.


Shamira is typical. It isn't her real name, not because she or I mind telling you, but because even her name was a casualty of the spiral of despair and decay that characterized her life from the age of nine. Nepali, fair-skinned, now thirteen. Sold by her stepmother to a man in Katmandu to "work" for him. Sold on. Shipped to Bombay, beaten and screwed in a Falkland Road hovel, handed over to truckers and millworkers as much as twenty-five times a day. A hundred rupees for a role in the destruction of a child, an active role. There are few waxwork extras in this Bollywood movie. Shamira is one of maybe seven thousand similar cases finding their way from Nepal to India each year. Down a sick pipeline.

Shamira's typical, but individual. All of them are. They share characteristics: All are victims, are bruised, are wrecked. Streetwise, yes, but all retain sad vestiges of the child: of innocence—love of films, a doll, a cuddle. Hideous faux adults, piteous children. Pixies. Each one with a story taken from the same ugly anthology, but each uniquely heartbreaking, each retaining the potential to grow into something different—if HIV will let them get that far.

Shamira won't ever reach the States. Damaged goods kept for the domestic market, nonexportable. But we can dress her in a uniform proudly bearing the badge of Ganesh. The school is run properly now, the curriculum befits a child. But still she dreams of the States.

And that's the irony. In some ways the ones who *are* shipped abroad have it better. Carlstein's philosophy had a sick kernel of reason. They avoid the mill of prostitution in the subcontinent, are kept clean for their discerning patrons abroad. But in the end, it's only a comparison between two hells on different rungs of the same ladder, where gods and demons vie for souls with equal vigor, it seems.

Askari once gave us a glimpse of the secret rituals for the Devadasi cult, where girls as young as ten are dedicated to Yellamma, the Mother of All. "Dedicated" being a euphemism for sale into prostitution. A thousand or more every year find their way into the industry in this fashion. There are other sects, cults, and superstitions that feed the machine, but, I suppose, mostly it's old-fashioned grinding poverty that provides the fuel.

Sometimes we work with the agencies, the nongovernmental organizations, NGO's: the National Network Group Against Trafficking, Sanlaap, and others with flourishing acronyms. But Askari gets jumpy when we near officialdom, even quasi and unpopular officialdom. The Lords of the Pixies might get to hear and, with his cover blown, Askari would be dead in five seconds, McIntyre too. Exposure is a far more potent threat than the e-mails could ever have been.

So, Askari doesn't want the authorities involved. Okay, we say, fair compromise. We'll stay freelance, guerrilla style, beyond the bounds. If it works—even a little—then we'll stick with the methodology. But only as long as it works. Sometimes, Carol and I argue about strategy, but mostly it's about how to pay the grocery bill. We don't want to ask for McIntyre's subsidy to keep us fed. We have a small law practice, strictly non pro bono, to keep the rent paid. Small stuff, in keeping with the slender reputation and status McIntyre has left us with.

McIntyre proved himself the master over the system, for himself, for me. I don't think it was easy for him, juggling a merger with one hand and whipping up a smokescreen around us with the other, and I can only assume he had a third with which to hold the hands of battered clients in the wake of the World Trade Center attack, Jefferson Trust no doubt included. Pablo helped, making sure the forensic people came out with the right answer: that the McLaren sale documents were forgeries, that the damn car wasn't mine. That was the easy part: After all, I *was* innocent. The hard part was tearing down the signposts that might point to McIntyre and Askari and erecting new ones directing official traffic exclusively to Charles Mendip. As Manelli and the District Attorney grasped at the evidence, they found out just how little they had: evaporated junior employees at Delaware Loan and the McLaren dealership—paid to disappear by McIntyre; Huxtable Trust now an empty shell surrounded by a wall of silence and shredded paper. The Indian authorities were no help; officialdom greased by Askari and further incentivized by the fact that the names of some very senior functionaries appeared in Carlstein's e-mails.

Every so often Brad Emerson of *America Daily* tries to fan the flames under the lies and conspiracy, but a few letters and visits to court normally neutralize the more extreme acids in his prose.

The fires of litigation still smolder, but they are underfed, desultory; effectively doused by fifty million paid over to the victims. My name appears on bundles of court papers, but with no assets and the police uninterested in me, I feel my presence is more for old times' sake than anything else. But the smell still hangs over us—Carol and me—it always will, I guess. It decays like radioactive material, in half-life steps, never quite dissipating altogether. So our little law practice doesn't get much quality work. An attorney gets the clients he deserves. And I have a different view of reputation now. Reputation: the world's opinion of you. It can evaporate in the rustle of a newspaper, or in a shower of soda cans over Fifth Avenue—the final bill for my daring stratagem was twenty thousand bucks—McIntyre paid.

Paula got her million. She's in Florida now; more exotic fish down there, perhaps. Miranda got her money too. Where is she? No idea. But I got a letter from her saying that she'd sacked her attorney and would no longer pursue me.

But Pablo remains part of our life, sentinel over McIntyre, partner with me over too many malt whiskeys too often. A wise counsel when we fuck up, which is frequently. He often refers to me and Carol as the lunatics who've taken over the asylum. Any keeper other than Carlstein must be better, we say. Sheesh, he says.

We often think that one day the ax will fall on us. Wielded by the Lords of the Pixies, by a pimp, by Askari or McIntyre. There'd be reason enough and it would be easy. So each day's a gift. And we try to return a day of life to a Pixie in thanks. I don't keep a tally. We're not talking billable hours here.

Preeti is married now. To an American. On and off we hear from her and she responds when we ask her for details that might help us in our work. We call on her knowledge less and less, we have moved on, built our own database and have no need to remind her of her old life.

I've been back to the Towers of Silence. It doesn't seem such a dark place now. I didn't see a single vulture—I'm told they've pretty much died out from disease. The cross my mother planted is still there, but it doesn't summon her up for me; it doesn't need to: Her blazing journey into the Arabian Sea remains as fitting in hindsight as it did when I let her slip. The image of it fills me with memories as powerfully as the flood tide.

The Towers don't seem so relevant to my father either. Maybe Askari was right: The location was a coincidence; destiny didn't dictate where my father should die, where his killers should kill him. My father had no reason to prostrate himself in front of Zoroaster, God of the Persians, the Parsis. It was where it happened, that's all.

So many gods. Gods divine: of the soul, of love, of eternity. Gods of the flesh, of money, of man's deeds. Gods handing down stone tablets of superstition or truth. Either way, the tablets are law. Imperatives to be followed. A world full of jostling, often contradictory, imperatives: *all* to be followed. Sometimes, I look up at the Credence Building, a brick in the wall of buildings that obscure the space that was once the World Trade Center, like a tarpaulin in front of a fatal car wreck. The Clay & Westminster attorneys have gone uptown to their new home, but I imagine the not so little army of remaining lawyers, drafting, reviewing, arguing, mooting, sifting through the imperatives looking for some way to turn the tablets on their head. Switching superstition into truth and vice versa. An ancient alchemy. All that brainpower, paper, money, time, and sweat devoted to liquidizing the tablets, molding tombstones of done deals and lawsuits won, offshore havens fortified, fee notes dispatched. Isn't there a better alchemy?

Then I kick the sanctimonious part of me. Most of them are honest enough; they just do what they do. Hell, I've got no answers. I have Carol and a career niched into the two oldest professions. Some people would say that I should just count myself lucky and leave off judging others. But I won't leave off. I won't stop being angry. I won't hang up until the phone call is truly finished, until there's nothing more to be said.

# ACKNOWLEDGMENTS

I owe so many people my heartfelt gratitude for their enthusiastic and unstinting help over the years leading to the publication of this book. Joanna Mackle, whose insights did so much to turn a dream into a plan into something typesettable. Mark Lucas, my agent—ever the mentor, friend, and consummate professional. His marvelous colleagues at the LAW Agency. George Lucas and the dedicated team at Atria Books steering the new guy round his new block. Vinita and others in Bombay who helped shed light on a place few, if any, should claim truly to understand. The multitalented Herb Sontz—sourcebook on everything from US securities law to the location of all the cemeteries in New York and New Jersey. Jeff and Kate Tollin, cherished friends and wholehearted givers of time and inspiration—and their house. And finally, my family, who have put up with night owl, grumbleguts Daddy and his bloody keyboard for longer than they care to remember.